DOLL³

THE HUNTING

DOLL³

THE HUNTING

MIRACLE AUSTIN

Wings & Fangs
PUBLISHING

DOLL³

THE HUNTING

Copyright © February 14, 2019

ISBN-13: 978-0-9986182-4-1

Editor: Rebecca Jaycox
Interior Design & Formatting: We Got You Covered Book Design
www.wegotyoucoveredbookdesign.com
Cover Design: Drop Dead Designs

Published by: Miracle Austin

Published in (United States of America)
10 9 8 7 6 5 4 3 2 1

To all of my current and new readers:

I'm extremely grateful to each of you for your wonderful support.

Thank you…

ACKNOWLEDGEMENTS

Thank you all for working with me to bring my book to life:

Rebecca Jaycox, my awesome editor, a.k.a, *The Sledgehammer*; DC Gomez & family for your Spanish translation expertise; *Drop Dead Designs* for the beautiful cover work; and Molly Phipps, owner of *We Got You Covered Book Design*, for the fantastic formatting. I'm very thankful—couldn't have done any of it without my *Creative Dream Team*.

Most of all, Mama, thank you again for planting the seed to inspire me to write the *Doll* series.

FOR MY
READERS

Wow!!!

If you're reading this, then I know you've been on this journey with me from the beginning with my debut novel, *Doll*.

I must confess I never imagined I would write a book, let alone a series. It's interesting how an idea can start with just a few words scribbled down on the back of a crinkled, stained receipt and transform into something much more. *Doll* was never supposed to be a book—only a short paranormal story with unexpected love elements, composed of ten thousand words. However, it kept growing.

Once I completed *Doll*, I figured it would be a stand-alone, but some readers asked if a sequel would happen. Initially, I dismissed the idea, until one day the characters spoke to me, and you know what happened after that.

When I was almost done writing *Doll 2: The Revealing*, ideas for *Doll 3: The Hunting* began to formulate in my mind. So, here we are. You're about to flip through the pages of the final installment of the *Doll* series.

Furthermore, I included **Mi Quinceañera Loca**, a short story (mini-series), and a short excerpt from my future book, **Misties**. Thank you for being on this journey with me again and for choosing to read my works. I hope that you enjoy.

Miracle Austin

Okay, ready, set, mark, and go!
Step into the world of

DOLL³
THE HUNTING

PROLOGUE

I F SOMEONE TOLD YOU THAT YOUR LIFE WOULD NEVER be the same again after one night, then would you have believed that person? In the beginning, I wouldn't have—now, absolutely. My entire life began to change during my junior year of high school and continues to as you're reading this.

Many people would honor a *help-me-to-forget pass*. Not me—I'm ready to face my enemies head on—at least, I hope so. I have an idea what awaits me.

You're aware of my current supernatural powers, and I hope to put them to good use when I need to. However, I'm still uncertain about which path, the *light* or *dark*, to walk. Darkness has been following me for a while now. It's only a matter of time when it finds someone I care for again. I must make a decision sooner rather than later, right?

School will be starting soon, and I'll be traveling back home to Frost, Texas. College acceptance letters, football games, homecoming, secrets, regrets, prom, graduation, and farewells define the senior year of most teens.

Yet, discovering the Dupuy Silver Slayer stalking me, unraveling Mr. Fox and Verlinda Dawn's twisted plans, and keeping the ones I care for the most as safe as I can, means more to me than all the high school fluff. I'm Tomie Dupuy—pronounced *Toh-me Due-pwee*—**Teen Warlock**.

Let's jump right back in.

CHAPTER
ONE

CURLED UP IN A LOOSE BALL, HER LIFELESS BODY LAY there so still.

"Sabra. Sabra!" I yelled. Tears floated in my eyes.

Just one breath, that's all I needed to see—nothing happened. I slid my entire body over the concrete floor, avoiding some shattered glass pieces, to scoop her up into my trembling hands.

Small shards of glass glistened from her paws like diamonds. Lisette stayed back with tears in her eyes and quivering lips. She snatched a towel from one of the drawers.

As I picked Sabra up, I stood and cradled her close to my chest. Warm blood from her mini paws saturated my white shirt. Sabra probably tried to protect the house by going after the hooded stranger's ankles, and the stranger either kicked the life out of her or worse. I placed her down on the countertop on top of the towel. She remained motionless. Lisette began to stroke her head and back with a shivering hand.

Pacing back and forth, I tried to think of a spell to revive her. *Wake up, wake up this night and be strong as you've always been, little one... Sleep no more and open your eyes to the light.* I repeated both spells several times in my mind and even combined them. Both were useless because everything I thought would work, didn't when I tried.

Lisette looked up at me, her tears falling down onto Sabra. She touched my arm and nodded for me to stop. There wasn't anything left for me to do. With her index finger, she tapped her paws twice, and the embedded glass floated out onto the table away from Sabra. The bleeding stopped.

"Tomie... please stop. She's gone. You shouldn't be toying around with returning spells anyhow." Lisette reached over and squeezed my shoulder, as I leaned in over Sabra.

"No, no, I gotta keep trying," I shouted, banging my fist against the counter. "If I would've stayed home tonight as I intended, then she would be alive right now."

"Don't know that for sure. Something awful may have happened to you, Tomie. I'll be back in a few minutes." She whimpered, avoiding eye contact.

Lisette climbed up the stairs one by one, never looking back at us. I figured she was going to find something to bury Sabra in. I weaved my hands in and out of my hair.

How could someone do this to something so innocent and weak? Then again, those were the characteristics evil craved most. Why couldn't Lisette or I restore Sabra's life? We had all the tools in front of us, and I had an entire spell book inside of me. I knew I needed to accept Sabra's fate, but I couldn't. She didn't deserve what had happened to her tonight.

Closing my eyes, I flipped through all the pages of the book inside of my mind until I came across something. After reading it a few times, I questioned if it would work. Lisette returned. When I turned around, I noticed she carried a metal shoebox under her arm. She had tissue balled up in her hand. Her eyes were red and puffy.

Before she approached, I said, "Lisette, I think I found a way to bring Sabra back."

"Tomie, I don't think we should pursue the dark resurrection spell you're referencing."

Cocking my head and shaking it, I said, "Hold on, how do you know what spell that I'm... Oh, you *glimmed* me again, right?"

Lisette didn't respond, twin tears leaking from her eyes.

"Why not?" I planted my legs wide and crossed my arms.

"She's gone, Tomie. I need to accept that, and you need to, as well."

"What? Why should we accept it when I know I may be able to do something about it?"

DOLL³

"It's not up to us to choose life again for something that's no longer here. When a *supra* commits that type of magic, then know you're opening yourself to unknown darkness and monsters."

"Lisette, I completed the awakening spell with my mom at the lake."

"That spell merely allowed you to communicate with her face-to-face for a short time until she needed to retreat back into her unseen world."

I stared down at my reflection on the counter. "My mom can never return, even by a resurrection spell?" I stuttered.

"So sorry, Tomie. She chose to end her own life with a forbidden spell, and her spirit will forever wander that area, as part of her eternal punishment." She lowered her head.

"If she hadn't committed the forbidden spell, then could a resurrection spell have brought her back?"

"Possibly, but those types of spells are used sparingly, and the *Upper Witch Council* should grant special permission before a witch or warlock partakes in such a spell."

"Well, I don't think Mr. Fox and Verlinda will be making an appointment anytime soon with them."

"You're right. They're pursuing the dark realm of magic, and the council steers away from it."

"Why?" I hugged myself tighter.

"The council is aware dark magic possesses way more consequences than light magic, some more unknown and permanent."

"I know we've talked about this before, and it seems to me that dark magic is the path I should consider to battle dark witches and the slayer."

"Once you start messing around with dark magic, it can swallow you up and never release you from its eternal grasp, especially if hate resides in you. I know that's not who you are."

"How do you know? Maybe it's who I need to be," I roared, tears streaming down my face. I started pacing back and forth.

"Tomie, listen to what you're saying… You don't want to fall into that dark world."

"Maybe I do, Lisette!"

"Hey, you guys, everything okay down there?" Caya and Sari asked in quivering voices from the top of the stairs.

"We're just talking about something," I replied, as I wiped my face with the end of my cape.

"Sure?" Sari asked.

"Yes. Be up in a bit," I said.

Caya asked, "What happened down there?"

"Will tell you both everything soon. Just give us some time," Lisette snapped, looking up the spiral staircase and bright lights above her.

The girls quieted, and their shadows retreated back from the basement opening.

"What do you know about dark magic?"

She paused for several minutes, and then she gazed into my eyes.

DOLL³

"Years ago, I delved into dark magic." A heavy sigh slipped off her lips.

"Wait, I remember you hinting something about that, but you never finished."

Staring down at Sabra as she brushed her head with an index finger, she glanced up at me. "I've never told anyone about this, not even Crow. I need to share what I did with you, so you can understand the power of *darkness*."

Before Lisette could begin, I noticed Sabra's right paw twitch. Then, it did it again. "Look," I gasped, pointing down at Sabra and rubbing my eyes with my hand. Lisette's attention shot straight down. Within a minute, Sabra's closed eyes opened up. She blinked a few times.

CHAPTER
TWO

"OH, TOMIE, SHE'S BACK! YOU DIDN'T DO THE reanimation spell?"

"Dang, I swear that I didn't do anything. By the way, what's that?"

"Never mind about that spell because it's extremely dark magic. Promise me you didn't cast that spell."

I placed my right hand over my heart and looked into her eyes. Her eyes shimmered with a golden haze. I felt a little weak in the knees.

"What did you just do to me?"

"Deep *glimmed* you."

"Come again?"

"Not only did I read your mind, but I also needed to listen

to your heartbeats, which provided me confirmation you're telling me the truth."

Narrowing my eyes at her, I said, "Why couldn't you just believe me when I told you the truth?"

"Tomie, I needed to make sure. I just want to protect you as much as I can from doing something that you'll regret."

Sabra stretched out her right leg.

Lisette pulled her hair back into a bun and placed two pencils inside to hold it. Then, she retrieved a mini medical kit in a drawer next to her. She cleaned up the dry blood from Sabra's paws with some water from a water bottle, dabbed some antiseptic on each paw, and bandaged them up. She rolled her up in the towel, picking her up in her arms.

"Think she's going to be okay, Lisette?"

"Yeah, I do. She's a fighter."

We made our way up the stairs; she waved her hand over the light switch, and all the lights turned off in the basement.

"I'm going to call my veterinarian in town." Lisette traveled to her bedroom with Sabra.

While she was on the phone, I updated Caya and Sari about all that had happened, regarding Sabra. I decided not to share everything at once. Sari and Caya both watched every word leaving my mouth.

Sari had been so shaken up during Pepper's funeral when Opal tried to throw her into ongoing traffic. I'd avoided telling her about Mr. Fox and Verlinda Dawn's plans with Pepper, though, at least for the time being; it would've overloaded her and sent her straight into super freak-out mode. I figured she needed to know about Opal being set free from her glass prison.

"Oh, Tomie, I'm glad to hear Sabra's okay, but Opal is out!" Sari shrieked and started pacing in the living room.

I grabbed her. "Hey, now, it's going to be okay. I'm not going to let her hurt you." I pulled her close, and she nestled her head against my chest, as I stroked her back with both of my hands, looking over at Caya on the couch with her head bowed down.

"Hey, I need to go. It's a little drive home." Caya stood up and grabbed her Harley Quinn mini backpack with a slight frown on her face.

"It's late, Caya. Sure Lisette won't mind if you spend the night."

Sari lifted her head and gave me the *look* with both eyebrows raised and resumed her position.

The couple life came with its pros and cons. Sari was my first committed relationship. I'd seen love triangles in plenty of movies and even witnessed a couple in the school cafeteria. The live action ones involving the jocks and cheerleaders were the best. I never imagined that I would be involved in a tangled one.

"No, I better go." Caya started towards the door.

"Let me at least walk you to your car. It's dark out there,"

DOLL³

I said.

Sari cleared her throat. "The outside lights are on."

"It's okay. I can take care of myself."

"Caya, I never said you couldn't. Anyhow, thanks for driving us back and saving us seats at the talent show earlier."

"Sure, it wasn't a big deal. See you around, Tomie. Bye, Sari."

Sari wiggled her hand up in the air.

Caya opened the front door and left.

CHAPTER
THREE

"HEY, SARI, DON'T YOU THINK THAT WAS A LITTLE rude?" I asked.

Sari scuffed her shoes across the floor without any eye contact and said, "What?"

"Not answering Caya when she was talking to you."

"No, what's the big deal anyhow, Tomie?"

"It's not. Just—never mind," I huffed.

"Say it," she shouted, lifting her head off my chest.

"This isn't that serious."

"It must be."

"Sari, what's wrong with you?"

"Nothing. I just wasn't in the mood to talk to her."

"Okay, fine. Let's drop it. You're acting really childish right now, which is unlike you."

"Whatever." She pulled away from me and sat down on the couch.

Lisette opened up her bedroom door and entered the living room. She had changed out of her costume into some navy blue leggings with canvas tennis shoes and a Captain Marvel T-shirt. Sabra rested inside her hot pink kennel wrapped up in the towel; she was squirming around and popped her nose out of the opening to sniff the air through the caged bars. Lisette sat it down on the floor.

"Where's Caya? Everything okay?" Lisette asked. Her eyes met mine, and she communicated with me telepathically.

Tomie, Sari seems to be upset about something.

Yes, it involves me confronting her about not telling Caya bye. No big deal. I just think she's really scared about the Opal breakout and also jealous of my friendship with Caya.

I agree. Want me to talk to her, Tomie?

Nah, she needs to rest and cool down.

Okay...

"Well, I'm going to teleport with Sabra into town for Dr. Babette to give her an X-ray and check her all out. You both will be okay?"

"Of course. I'll get Sari situated in the other bedroom."

"Lisette, I'm glad Sabra is going to be okay," Sari said with a semi-smile.

"Thank you. Dr. B is great with all animals. He'll take good care of my baby girl, in no time. When I return, I'll need your help with something."

"Sure, what do you need me to do?" I placed one of my hands in my pocket and bounced back and forth on my heels.

"Help me with a unique lock-out spell. This one will be a little different than my original one." Her eyes squinted towards me.

"How?"

"It will be triple secure." Lisette clapped her hands together in the air. "Should be home in a few hours."

"Need to get Sari back home later today."

Bending down to grab Sabra's kennel, she said, "Yes, after we all get some rest." They were gone in less than fifteen seconds.

I used the bathroom first and changed out of my costume into some black and blue plaid lounge pants and a Batman T-shirt. I strolled into my bedroom and grabbed a Frost baseball shirt for Sari.

She entered and sat down on my bed. I handed the clothing over to her. Before I left, she grabbed my hand and pulled me down to sit next to her.

Leaning in, she kissed me really slow.

"Wow, that was nice. What was that for?"

Sari stared deep into my eyes. "I don't want to sleep in the other room tonight." Her eyes scanned over my bed.

I took a few deep breaths, clearing my throat.

"Umm, what do you mean?"

"Now, Tomie Dupuy, what do you think I mean?" She winked.

My eyes grew wide, and my feet began to tap on the floor.

"Sari, are you saying that you wanna…?"

She scooted closer into me and rubbed my back with her soft and jittery hands.

"Yes, that's exactly what I'm saying."

"Wow!"

My hands began to shake, and my feet tapped louder. I could feel sweat running down my back.

"Tomie, I'm ready."

"What? You sure?"

"Aren't you? Don't you want to?" She winced.

"Yeah, I mean… Yes, but-but," I stammered.

Balling a section of the comforter in her hand, she blinked several times. "What?"

"Like right now? Here?"

"No silly, you could teleport us somewhere really special." She released my hand.

I took a few more deep breaths and wrapped my arms around her. "Sari, listen, I love you so much. I want to do this when I know you're truly ready. Honestly, I know exactly why you want to do this now."

"You do?" She glanced away from me for a few seconds, dropping her chin to her chest and fumbling her hands in her lap.

Elevating her chin up with my hand, I stared into her dancing eyes. "Yeah, I'm not going anywhere. My heart is yours, as long as you want it. There's no need for you to think you need to compete with Caya or anyone else."

"Really?"

I cupped my hands around her face and kissed her on her forehead and allowed my lips to skate down to her ruby ones.

Sari batted her beautiful, thick eyelashes.

Grabbing her hands, I placed them over my beating heart. She did the same with mine; we smiled.

"Tomie, thank you."

My eyes flickered. "For what, girl?"

"Everything you just shared. I was really, really nervous."

"Believe me, I know."

Her brown eyes captured mine.

"Did you *glim* me?"

"Yes."

"I kinda figured, and I'm not mad that you did."

My heart beat so fast. I just smiled and kept my cool as best as I could. I didn't want Sari to see me this way because I knew how she was already feeling. I took some deep breaths to slow my heart rate down. I needed a temporary distraction after this heavy conversation.

I glanced down at my watch; more than two hours had flown by.

"Aww man, we've been talking a while. Bet Lisette will be

returning soon. Go ahead and get a shower. We'll talk more later." I walked her to the bathroom and closed the door on my way out.

I needed to sit down on the couch for a moment and replay everything that just had happened between us. If I wouldn't have interceded, then things could've gotten heated up in no time. I wouldn't have minded an amazing make-out session, but I knew going to the next level wasn't the best decision for us, tonight.

Slipping on my tennis shoes, I opened the door and noticed Crow's truck pulling up. He waved and I did, too. He parked and Lisette jumped out.

"How's Sabra, Lisette?"

"Dr. B X-rayed her and found she had a simple fracture on her left leg. He placed a splint on it. She was given some pain medication and is on cage rest for a few days, to minimize movement in order for her to heal properly. I can only take her out to use her litter box. He's probably going to keep her for forty-eight hours to monitor her. Dr. B also shared he could release her early, pending how she does."

I released a huge breath.

"Going to head out, guys." Crow leaned over to kiss Lisette and hopped back into his truck. As he was driving off, he beeped his horn.

Lisette stood next to me.

"Did you and Sari have a good talk?" she asked with a large smile.

"We sure did."

"Hope I didn't interrupt, anything." She tapped me on my arm.

"Nah."

She giggled. "I had a feeling you may have been busy."

My face felt really warm.

Clearing my throat, I said, "Ready, Lisette?"

"Of course, let's do this."

I followed her to the back of the house.

"First, I need for you to find the lock-out spell from your internal book."

Once I flipped through several pages in my mind, I came across the one she wanted. The spell called for rope, four yellow candles, thirteen dried and crushed scorpion tails, and a strand of hair from the person wanting the protection.

"Lisette, you're going to need some strange ingredients."

"Yes, what are they?"

I shared the list with her.

Closing her eyes, she extended her opened hands. In less than a minute, a rolled up white rope, candles, and a clear bottle of iridescent flakes all floated above her waist.

"Awesome, how you can teleport stuff to you?"

"You can do it, too, just need to concentrate. What's next?"

"Count from seventeen backwards and hold a piece of your hair over one of the flames. Then take the rope and wrap it around your home, drop candle wax at the north, south, east,

DOLL³

and west ends of the rope, and repeat this walking backwards around the house twice: *Turn around... keep away, keep away, keep away... or face your final fate...* "

Her hands dropped to her side. The candles lit up with the snap of her fingers, and the glass bottle top unscrewed on its own. She picked up the bottle and sprinkled half of the scorpion flakes over each of the lit candles. Bright purple sparks shot up about thirty feet, which reminded me of fireworks.

Lisette plucked a hair from the back of her head, broke it in half, counted from seventeen backwards, and threw it on the waving flames. The candles floated more than seven feet up in the air. She then grabbed the rope and began to unravel it. It was maybe twenty feet, not long enough to go around the perimeter of the house, as the spell called for.

Although I'd seen Lisette practice magic many times, it always made me feel like a little kid watching his first magic show in an audience. Her sophisticated skills made my eyes sparkle and heart skip beats.

"You're going to need a lot more rope." I scratched my head.

"Just watch this." She walked backwards, and the candles followed her. After she reached the rope's limit, she shook it around a few times, and it began to extend itself with each step she took, emitting a slight turquoise glow.

My eyes lit up. "Lisette, that's crazy cool. Hope I can be as good as you, one day."

She smiled and continued to concentrate until the rope

was completely around her house. The candles flew around in opposite directions, dropping wax at the north, south, east, and west points of the rope.

Lisette repeated the words of the spell, and once she stepped outside of the rope next to me, the rope sunk down into the ground and new grass swallowed it up.

My mouth parted. Lisette placed her finger under my chin to lift it up. "Close it before a big, juicy skeeter flies in."

I laughed. "Seriously, that was amazing, Lisette. This will keep uninvited guests out of your house for good?"

"Yep."

"How does the spell know a good guest over a bad guest?" I massaged my jaw with my hand.

"It knows by the person's essence—the spell can read it and prevent the bad from coming too close, to where this rope is now buried. The previous spell didn't possess this prevention."

"Does this rule Sari out as a potential suspect?"

Lisette shook her head. "Yes, if Sari possessed a bad spirit, then before I completed the spell, the house would've forced her out."

"Little creepy. Hey, if it works, then that's all that matters, right?"

"Yes. Thanks for helping, Tomie."

"Welcome, but I didn't do much of anything. Just read the spell out loud to you."

"I wouldn't have been able to do it on my on, plus you

possessed the special spell."

"What about the candles and the bottle?"

She turned around, and they were still floating, so she slapped her hands together and they disappeared.

"Where did they go?"

"In their rightful place, back in my basement."

"I'm going to head in for the night."

"Good night, I'm going to finish up out here." Lisette nodded.

"See you in a few hours."

Walking back inside, I felt safer than before. Maybe it was the spell Lisette just had placed around the house, or maybe it was Sari waiting for me. I opened the door with the swipe of my right hand, and it shut behind me once I stepped inside.

Upon approaching my bedroom, I noticed Sari asleep in my bed with the covers kicked on the floor. Picking them up, I covered her up. She mumbled something I didn't quite understand.

Seizing my cell and charger off the desk, I turned off the lamp next to her. I plugged up my phone under the desk before I sat down in the chair and closed my eyes. Sleep welcomed me.

CHAPTER
FOUR

AFTER A FEW HOURS, I WOKE UP; IT WAS JUST AFTER six in the morning. I heard Sari turn over in bed.

"Come over here. I know it's uncomfortable in that chair." She tapped the mattress with her hand.

I flopped down next to her.

Rubbing my bare arms with her hands, she whispered, "You're freezing. Get under the covers."

With no hesitation, I honored her request.

"Everything go okay, with the spell?"

I nodded. My head rested back on my folded arms against the headboard. I stared down at her, and she lifted her head up and met my eyes.

"What?"

"Nothing," I said.

"Tell me," she commanded.

"I didn't tell you something earlier."

Her body readjusted, and she placed her hands flat over my throbbing heart without taking her eyes off of me.

"Tomie, Opal and her grandmom have bigger plans, don't they?"

There was nothing I could do, but tell her the truth. I'd never been one to keep things from Sari, so no reason to start now. I scooted up higher in the bed. Sari turned over and did the same.

"Is it that bad?" she asked in a shrill voice, blinking her eyes multiple times.

We faced each other. I picked up her hands and squeezed them inside my clammy ones.

"Sari, you're right about Opal and her grandmom. You know about the lies they've planted inside Mr. Fox's mind about us causing Pepper's death," I said.

"Yes."

"Well, they're about to upgrade on a total different level, sooner rather than later."

"Tomie, what are their plans?" Her eyes widened, filling up with tears.

"I want you to know I've learned so much in the little time that Lisette has been training me and reading about my history. Sari, I'm going to protect you to the best of my abilities. You believe me, right?"

"Of course, just tell me." Her pulse rate escalated.

"Mr. Fox, Verlinda Dawn—Opal's grandma—and Opal will be flying and landing in Salem sometime later this morning."

"For what?" She pulled away from me and began to rock back and forth.

"They're planning to meet up with someone very powerful and evil, a Dark Shadow Witch."

"Why?" She started biting around her nail beds, as more tears streamed down her face. I wiped them away gently with the back of my hand.

"Something is needed from this type of witch to help them get revenge against us, including Lisette."

She wrapped her arms around my neck, holding me tight. I could feel her fast heartbeats and warm tears fall against my thin shirt.

Leaning back a little, I looked into her eyes. "Sari, they're planning to bring Pepper Fox back to life."

Sari's eyes bulged.

"What! No... That's not possible because we saw her die on the dance floor at our prom a few months ago." She shook her head.

"You're right. Pepper did, but in the craft world—especially the dark side—the impossible is usually possible."

"It's Opal's fault Pepper died that night. She hated her that much to commit the unthinkable. Now, we have to suffer from her lies, she's buried inside her grandmom's mind. Then, her grandmom did the same with Mr. Fox. None of this is fair," she said in a jerky tone.

Sari rose up, placing her feet on the ground with her back facing me. I massaged her shoulders.

"Oh, Sari, I know."

"Why are they bringing Pepper back?" She clutched one of her arms.

Rubbing the back of my neck with my hand, I said, "Mr. Fox probably just wants his only daughter back, even if it means bringing her back from the dead by a dark spell. Sure, Opal and Verlinda have their own agenda of bringing her back."

"What's our plan?" She turned around to face me and exhaled with her eyes fixed on mine.

"First, to get you back home, and then Lisette and I will talk about what comes after."

"Tomie, I want to stay with you and help."

Smiling, I scooted closer to her. "Gotta get you back home."

We slid down in the bed together and held each other. "Try to get some sleep, Sari."

About a half an hour later, she was asleep. I was still up thinking about everything. I closed my eyes and before I drifted off to sleep, I kissed her lower neck and whispered in her ear, "I love you so much, Sarifena Green." In my mind, I thought hopefully one day it would be Sarifena Dupuy.

CHAPTER
FIVE

BLUEBERRY MUFFINS, BACON, AND COFFEE BATHED the air. My arms were empty. I opened my eyes and tossed the covers off. It was almost eleven in the morning. I heard Sari, Lisette, and Crow's voices in the kitchen. I stood up to make the bed and grabbed my phone.

Sari's sweet scent of strawberries and kiwi, probably from the body wash in the bathroom, lingered on my chest. I wished that could happen every night; I felt so close to her.

Traveling to the bathroom to change into a pair of jeans and a Cyborg T-shirt, I brushed up in the bathroom and made my way into the kitchen. They were all sitting at the table talking. I glanced over to Sabra's spot, and it was vacant.

Lisette looked up. "Good morning, Tomie." She waved me

over to sit. I came behind Sari and massaged her shoulders with my hands. She tilted her head back, and I leaned down to kiss her on her forehead.

"Hey, you," she whispered with a wink.

I sat down next to her.

"Good morning, Crow."

He finished sipping on his cup of coffee and told me the same with a huge smile.

I noticed seven pieces of bacon and two large blueberry muffins left on a square platter in the middle of the table. I looked at them.

"All yours, Tomie," Lisette said.

Pulling the platter in front of me, Sari poured me a large glass of grape juice. Before I consumed my breakfast, I asked, "Any update on Sabra?"

I started chomping on a slice of bacon and followed with a large bite from the moist muffin.

"My tech friend texted me a little bit ago. Sabra is sleeping, and her vitals are stable." Lisette grinned.

"What does the vet think happened to her?" Sari asked, sipping on her juice.

"He thinks that she must've fell down somehow and walked into some glass, which was embedded in her paws. When he examined her, he found only a few specks of glass remaining in her paws."

"I bet she followed that bad guy down to the basement, and

that's where she was injured," I surmised.

"Very possible, Tomie. I'm just so glad that my girl is going to be okay." Crow wrapped his arm around her and pulled her close to him.

"Me too, Lisette," Sari said with a smile, placing her hand on my thigh.

"What's the plan for today?" I wiped my mouth with a napkin. Picking up my glass, I chugged the juice down.

Lisette looked at Sari and then me. "To get Sari home before night fall."

Sari took in a long sigh.

"What is it?" I asked.

"Just not ready to go home yet," she admitted.

"Your parents don't even know you're here with me. They think you're with Luckie."

"It won't hurt anything, if I stay a little longer."

"Sari, it's best if you return home today. I don't want to deal with your dad." I wished she could stay longer, but I knew that wasn't possible, especially with the kind of dad she had.

"I guess you're right, Tomie," Sari said in a dispirited voice, her head bowed down.

Lisette and Crow scooted their chairs from the table. Sari and I gathered up the dishes.

"So, Lisette, how is Sari getting back home?" I asked, handing plates to her near the sink.

She finished washing a plate and then turned around from

the sink to face me. "Tomie, I was thinking teleporting her back will be the best option."

"Really?" Sari asked.

"Yes, Sari, what time are your parents expecting you back home today?"

"By dinner time. I told them that I would be hanging out with Luckie most of Sunday."

"Okay, then we definitely have time to get you back home before then."

"What time should I teleport her back, Lisette?" I asked.

Lisette walked up towards us and said, "Oh, no way, mister. You'll not be the one teleporting her back, especially after what you told me about her dad, Mr. Green."

I paused before I answered.

Sari sniffled. "Lisette makes a good point, Tomie. I don't think it would be a good idea for you to teleport me, even though I would love for you to."

"Yeah, y'all are right. What time will you and Sari be leaving?"

"Around three."

"At least that gives us a little time to spend together." My mouth curved in a partial smile.

Lisette shook her head.

I held my hand out to dry more dishes.

"No, I got this. You and Sari go."

"Thanks, Lisette."

I grabbed Sari's hand. "Let's take a walk."

We headed out back towards the lake.

"Tomie, I'm going to miss you."

There was a slight breeze, but the sun beamed down straight on us.

Once we arrived, I noticed a bench with a tree arching over it, offering some nice shade. With a wave of my hand, the branches leaned in to cover us more like an umbrella. We sat down. She propped her legs up on the bench and leaned back in my arms. The water rolled in and out from the sandy shore. A few airboats passed by.

It was nice just sitting there with her in silence. I knew she didn't want to return home just yet, and I sure didn't want her to go, but it was something she had to do. She turned halfway on her side. "Need you to be honest with me about something."

"Of course, what is it?"

"How will it be the same Pepper that we knew, when they bring her back with that crazy spell?"

"It won't. She's going to need a new body, which is why they're traveling to Salem. Pepper, version two, could be darker than before, when the path of darkness is chosen."

"Tomie, why does Opal hate us so much? What did we do to her?" She sighed.

"We didn't do anything to her. It's just because we didn't support her evil plans in the first place."

41

"So, do you think if we would've went along with her plan, then we wouldn't be in this situation?"

"I doubt it because Opal's very selfish and cunning."

"With your training, do you feel you're ready to face them and whatever else lurks out there?"

Before I answered, I thought about her question for a few minutes. My feet wanted to start tapping. I took a few deep breaths and stilled them.

"Sari, Lisette has taught me quite a bit over these last few weeks. I don't know everything, but who does? The tools I've gained will enable me to fight the best fight I can. There're a few more weeks left before school begins, and I plan to absorb as much knowledge as I can during the rest of my stay here."

"Good magic always wins, right?"

"I sure do hope so." I closed my eyes, and she lifted her body off of mine.

"Hey, you don't think so?" she asked in a fretful tone. The corners of her eyes crinkled.

"Not sure, especially when there is so much darkness and bad magic at play." I turned my head away from her for a quick moment. My mind darted back to why Verlinda and Opal wanted Pepper back, and the only thing I could think of was that they wanted to witness a potentially darker Pepper torment me, at their sick discretion.

"Look at me."

Sari placed her small hands under my chin.

I did. A few more airboats flew by closer to us, and I could feel their spray splash over us lightly. Sari jumped.

"You're right about there being a lot of bad magic out there—I believe in good magic and you."

"Thanks."

"Wow, Tomie, just thinking about everything you've told me about your experiences in Monroe Creek, it's like the town of the supernatural."

I breathed in. "Yeah, you can definitely say that."

"Gosh, this world that we're involved in seems to be way bigger than I ever imagined. I've read a lot of fictional supernatural stories in books and comics, but never thought it would be actually true with you."

"Me either."

"One thing is for sure, my boyfriend is the hottest warlock." She grabbed the collar of my shirt with both of her hands and landed her lips onto mine. We embraced for several minutes.

"Tomie, are you more than just a warlock?"

"What do you mean?" I could feel my fist tightening up.

"Are you *shifter,* too, like Mr. Ray or Crow?"

"Where did that question come from?"

"Just thinking about everything you've shared with me over the last few months, especially your Laveau bloodline."

"I don't think so."

Sari ignited the wheels in my mind to start turning. I wasn't sure if I was a *Gris* Warlock—light and dark. Could I also be more than just a warlock? I thought about that night at the festival, when I'd confronted Garth about Caya, and my eyes had turned a different color, my hands releasing a blue glow. What did that all mean?

With everything that happened that night after the festival— Lisette's house getting broken into, Opal being unbound by the hooded thief, and Sabra being found lifeless—I never had the chance to tell Lisette about my experience, and what it could now mean for me. I planned on telling her soon.

First, Sari needed to get back home. I pulled my phone out of my pocket and noticed it was after almost two, and it was time for us to head back to Lisette's, so she could teleport Sari back to Frost.

Walking back towards the house, I contemplated sharing my experiences with my mom. Sari squeezed my hand. I looked down into her sparkling, brown eyes and shelved that conversation for another time. In front of us, two dragonflies danced a zigzag waltz. They flew above us, and zipped away along the water.

"By the way, have you applied to Falcon Air Force Academy?"

"Not yet. Just so much happening."

"I understand, but you may want to do it pretty soon."

"Yeah, you're right. What about you? Have you applied to Ginger Fashion Project Academy in the U.K.?"

"Tomie, I did right before I came down here, also applied to

NYC Elite Design School, and a few other schools as back ups. I so pray, I get accepted into Ginger's school. Really excited to see what I can dream up."

I saw a glow in Sari I'd never seen before. Studying fashion design was something I knew she wanted, badly. Just the thought of her being in another country made my heart ache.

"You definitely won't need an alternate plan."

We were less than ten minutes away from the house.

"Never know. Ginger Academy is so competitive. Out of five hundred applications, only fifty make it in, and it's extremely expensive with limited scholarships offered." She glanced down.

I stopped and faced her. "Sari, you're going to get in."

"There are other people way more creative than me."

"Believe me, you will. Once that committee reviews your application and portfolio, they'll be blown away with your natural gift. We'll talk when you receive your acceptance letter, Sari."

"By the way, is teleporting scary?"

"Nah, it's like riding a rollercoaster for the first time, but shorter."

"Really? I've never been a big fan." She started twisting her watch around her wrist.

"Just remember to close your eyes, think of something pleasant, and breathe slow."

"Gotcha, I'll just think of you." She grinned, and I did the same. I bent down and kissed her cheek, sliding my hands down her shoulders, all the way to her wrists to distract her.

"Do you think your dad is going to go into cardiac arrest, once he finds out you snuck away to spend time with me?"

"Absolutely. He'll probably force my mom to homeschool me or send me off to boarding school in Australia. Definitely, forbid me to ever see you again."

Sweat ran down my face, and my voice crackled. "Are you serious?"

She laughed, covering her mouth with both hands.

"This is not funny, Sari."

"Oh, I'm sure he'll be totally pissed and will ground me for a bit, especially if he finds out I actually snuck away to be with my bae."

"How would he not know?"

"Luckie knows not to say anything. Plus, by the time I get home via teleportation, it will be around the time I told my dad and mom I would be home, anyhow."

"Hope, it goes that smooth."

"Don't worry. It's going to be fine." Sari chewed on her upper lip for a few seconds.

I really hoped Sari was right. However, deep inside, I had a bad feeling that things wouldn't be. Our time together was dwindling down each minute. I'd been around her for so long, and just the thought of not seeing her every day, after our senior year made my heart feel so heavy.

Her dad probably would be fine with Sari getting accepted into Ginger Academy versus his alma mater, because she would be farther away from me. I believed he was capable of doing anything to separate us; something I don't think Sari wanted to accept.

"Your dad doesn't care for me, especially after what I did to him before we left your house for junior-senior prom."

"Tomie, my dad doesn't hate you."

"Sari, stop it. We both know he does because I'm not who he wants you to be with." I frowned.

"How do you know?"

"I felt it, and he said it in so many words from the last conversation I had with him, when I was texting you that time."

"It doesn't matter because I'm not going to stop seeing you. I'll do what I need to do to make that happen. Anyhow, I'll be out from under his roof in less than thirteen months, give or take. Even if I don't get into design school or college, I'm moving out."

Clicking my tongue, I said, "Girl, you've been thinking about this for a bit."

"Just wish..." Her eyes started watering up.

I faced her and wrapped my arms around her. "Shhh, you don't have to say anything else. We'll deal with it as it comes, okay?" I kissed her on her forehead, and she embraced me tightly. The house was in front of us.

DOLL³

My mind replayed our previous conversation. What if her dad did try to keep us apart somehow? I knew I couldn't force him to change his feelings about me, unless I placed a spell on him, and there was one that stood out, but that would only cover up what I knew wasn't real.

I dismissed that temptation. In order to love Sari, it was inevitable that dealing with her dad was part of the package. I would have to adapt to his hostility towards me because of who I was, an interracial warlock, who he wanted *plucked* out of her life.

CHAPTER
SIX

ASCENDING UP THE STEPS, I OPENED THE DOOR FOR her, and she went in first. The kitchen was empty. I figured Lisette and Crow were in the living room.

"Going to go to the bathroom and gather up my things, Tomie."

Crow was reading messages from his phone.

"Did y'all have a nice visit?" Lisette asked, placing a ballet magazine down on the table in front of her.

"Yes."

"Do you think she's ready?"

"For the most part, but she's nervous, too. I gave her a few tips."

"I'll take care of her, Tomie, probably will place a temporary relaxation spell on her."

"That'll work. Thank you for doing this, Lisette." I bent down to hug her.

"Going to head out and let y'all do what y'all need to do."

"Okay, Crow. See you soon, right?"

"Yep." He winked and rubbed the top of my head with his massive and hairy hand as he sauntered by me.

Lisette followed him out back to his truck.

Sari wandered up the hallway with her bag in her hand.

"Where's Lisette?"

"Outside with Crow. She'll be back soon."

"This year is going to be really different." Her eyes drifted sideways.

"Yes, close your eyes, please."

"Why?"

"Trust me."

She closed her eyes. I placed both of my hands on her shoulders and bent down and whispered, "Relax and just go with it, okay."

Sari nodded.

I spun her around to the right, then to the left one hundred and eighty degrees. My hands waved in a vertical pattern across her body. Within ten seconds, her feet lifted seventeen inches off the ground. Her body wobbled. "Remember, what I told you."

"Okay." Her eyes remained closed.

My eyes shut, and my mind flipped through the spell book to the page I needed, which was a protection spell. I chanted it aloud three times: "Keep her safe from anyone or anything who means her harm day or night, and grant me sight of this evildoer."

Opening my eyes, a swirl of purple-golden smoke appeared and wrapped around her entire body. It flowed into her fingertips and her hair. Each strand stood up and moved around like waves, as if static electricity was running through her hair. I levitated her down, slowly back to the floor.

After capturing a few deep breaths, Sari opened up her eyes. "I didn't think you were going to cast a spell on me. The smoke felt warm and cold at the same time."

"You okay?" I asked.

"Yes."

"Just want to keep you as safe as I can."

Her loose hair swung behind her ears when I blew on it, lightly.

The special necklace Lisette had given me for protection, which I gave to Sari to wear before I traveled here, dropped off from around her neck and fell into my hand.

Lisette entered the room and clapped her hands a few times.

"Good work, Tomie."

"How did you know I was going to perform that spell on Sari?"

She smiled.

"Never mind, you *glimmed* me once again."

I should be used to it by now. Until I figure out how to conceal my feelings better, Lisette will always be able to *glim* me. One day, I would master keeping my feelings hidden.

"Of course. Good decision that you made. That spell will definitely protect Sari for the most part, unless a powerful *supra* breaks it."

"Hope not."

In a sharp tone, Lisette, commanded, "Place your necklace back on you. It always belonged to you in the first place."

"Didn't it provide Sari protection?"

"Very little because it wasn't meant for her. The protection spell was directed at her and will give her way more protection than your necklace."

"Thanks for telling me now about the necklace." I rolled my eyes.

"Tomie, I told you that it was just for you. Just remember when someone says that, it means it's not to be shared. Got it?"

"Yeah," I said in a snapping tone.

"Are you done?" Lisette stood in front of me with her arms on her hips and tapping her right foot.

"Yes."

"I thought so. Now, what made you pursue the spell for her, Tomie?"

"So much has happened over the last few months, especially

here in Monroe Creek. With her returning back to Frost without me, I have no idea what may be waiting for her." I sat down on the arm of the chair. Sari plopped down on my lap.

"Great work. I planned on recommending it, but you beat me to it. Tomie, part of our plan will be for you to wear your necklace at all times, update me about anything strange, and be cautious at all times."

"Understand."

Facing me and staring in my eyes, Lisette said, "They won't fight fair. You must follow the plan."

"Well, Sari, are you ready?"

Sari began to whimper softly. I embraced her. "It's going to be okay. I have less than three weeks or so here left to train with Lisette, and I'll be back in Frost with you."

"Yeah, I know. Just wish you were coming back with me. I understand you need to finish out and all."

Her head dropped for a few seconds and then found my eyes waiting for her.

"Hey, I don't mind leaving now."

"No, you stay and finish up, it's important—I love you, Tomie Dupuy." She kissed me.

"I love you, too, Sarifena Green."

She stepped away from me and stood next to Lisette.

"Tomie, I'll return as soon as I can. Think about the plan."

"Okay."

"Ready, Sari?"

DOLL³

Running her hands through her hair, she said, "Guess so."

Suddenly out of nowhere, a high wind blew through the living room. Magazines flew off the coffee table up in the air and landed on the floor around our feet.

Mr. Ray teleported inside and stood in front of us, sweat dripping from his face. In a quivering voice, he said, "Lisette, Tomie, and Sari, I'm afraid we got a problem."

Beads of sweat gathered inside the creases of my forehead.

CHAPTER
SEVEN

"WHAT MR. RAY?" LISETTE DEMANDED.

"Mr. Fox and Verlinda Dawn are in Salem."

Standing up, she said, "Yes, Tomie and I both knew they were traveling there."

"Do you know who they're meeting up with?" Mr. Ray asked. "Think you should sit back down."

Lisette sat. "Not who, exactly. Only know it's a Dark Shadow Witch."

Sari grabbed my hand—her palm sweaty. I squeezed it and led her to the couch to sit next to Lisette.

In a deep and shuddering tone, he said, "I never thought they would seek this witch out."

"Tell us, Mr. Ray!" Lisette yelled.

DOLL³

There had only been a few times I'd seen Lisette get agitated. I sensed that whoever it was Mr. Fox and Verlinda Dawn were meeting with was really bad, especially for Lisette to demand the name from Mr. Ray like she had.

He turned around slowly to face both of us and mouthed out, "Esmerelda... Sonthiel."

Lisette covered her face with both of her hands and stood. I heard the basement door fly open. A large, jade book flew in the air above our heads and towards Lisette's hands. It landed on top of Lisette's lap. The pages turned by themselves as Lisette waved one finger. Sari and I moved closer to Lisette on the couch. Leaning in to see what Lisette was reading, I noticed how her hands shook under the book.

"Whoa, your coven book. Who's Esmerelda S?" I asked, touching her hands.

Lisette looked up at all of us. "She's indeed a Dark Shadow Witch, according to the Laveau Coven book. Esmerelda is a descendant of the late Ursula Sonthiel."

"Wait, I think I recall reading something about her in the book you gave me, but I just skimmed the page about her, so I don't remember."

"She was a really powerful witch back in the sixteenth century, Tomie."

"Why is she a big deal?"

"Listen, Tomie." Mr. Ray chimed in, as he sat on the opposite side of Lisette.

Scanning us with her glowing eyes, she said, "Ursula was also a soothsayer."

"Like an oracle?" I asked.

"Yes," Mr. Ray said as he stroked his salt and pepper beard with his hand.

"So, this Esmerelda is also one, too?" I asked.

"Yes, the Sonthiel Coven was associated with the Dawn Coven many years ago. Not only is Verlinda in *witch country*, but she's connected with someone who's had a nasty habit to share our deepest secrets, including our weaknesses, with Dupuy Silver Slayers, years ago."

"Why would a witch want to share secrets with someone who's seeking to destroy us and possibly her, too?" My feet started tapping, and I bit my lower lip, tasting salty blood in my mouth. Sari placed her trembling hands on my legs.

"Not sure why. I would imagine it benefits her in some way."

"So, this really changes the game?" I asked.

"It certainly does. Once Verlinda spills her lies to Esmerelda about us, she could make contact with a slayer and send him to Monroe Creek or Frost sooner than I was anticipating," Mr. Ray said.

"A good thing I placed that protection spell on Sari."

In a wobbling tone, Mr. Ray said, "Lisette, there's more."

Sari clutched my upper arm so tight that it went numb.

"What?" Her eyes focused on Mr. Ray.

"I saw them perform the spell using Pepper's remains and another body."

"Tell me what you saw, exactly?" Lisette scooted nearly off the edge of the couch to hear everything he had to share.

"Mr. Ray, how did they not detect your presence there?" I asked, swallowing hard.

"Before I shifted into owl form, I consumed a special concealing potion to make myself temporarily invisible and planted myself on a sturdy elm tree branch, where I had a great view."

"Mr. Ray, please, tell us what you witnessed," Lisette demanded.

He took in a few quick breaths and wrapped his hands around the back of his neck. "I saw Verlinda and Opal write something with a black feather quill pen on small strips of heavy parchment paper. The ink looked like blood. They rolled the papers up and dropped them into the mouth of the new body."

Lisette peeled herself up and walked away from us. She started pacing the floor and mumbling something to herself that I couldn't understand. Sari pulled herself closer to me and whispered in my ear, "Is she okay?"

"They wrote our names down, right, Mr. Ray?" I asked.

He didn't need to answer because I knew by the stern look he had in his eyes and Lisette's reaction.

"What's up with the blood ink?"

"It's a permanent stain of their lies about us and a reminder to the newly awakened one who consumes it. Extremely dark mischief," Lisette said. "Need to go ahead and get Sari back home now, and Tomie, we need to make a trip to Salem tonight."

"Do you want me to get Sari home?" Mr. Ray asked.

"Thank you, but I better get her back. If you wouldn't mind just keeping an eye on her while we're out and until Tomie returns back to Frost, then that would be great," Lisette requested.

"No problem. You got it," Mr. Ray said.

"Okay, Tomie, we'll talk more when I return."

"All right."

"Sari, ready?"

Her upper body was shaking. I hugged her from the side and whispered, "You're going to be fine. Text or call me when you can, okay? Remember what I told you about teleportation."

"Okay, Tomie."

After kissing Sari's hand, I handed her over to Lisette and backed up several steps to give them enough space.

Sari threw a kiss to me in the air. I caught it, placed it over my chest, and then threw her one back. Sari caught it, and placed it over her heart.

"When I count backwards starting at three, we're going to be back near your house. I'll make this teleportation a little slower because this is your first time, okay?" Lisette waved her hand in front of Sari's face to place a short-acting relaxing spell on her.

"Understand."

Sari closed her eyes. Lisette placed Sari's hand inside of hers and stroked it back and forth with the back of her hand and chanted, "Feathers and butterflies float freely with no worries. Imagine yourself as one, right now."

They both levitated about seventeen inches in the air, rotated in a complete circle twice, and vanished.

CHAPTER
EIGHT

M R. RAY SAT DOWN, AND I REMAINED STANDING across from him.

"Verlinda is never going to stop lying," I yelled. My nostrils flared in and out. I thought about what it would feel like to destroy her. "Do we really stand a chance against them, especially with them seeking help from this Dark Shadow Witch, Esmerelda?"

"Tomie, Verlinda is making this way more difficult than I ever dreamed of."

"Mr. Ray, I gotta get out of here for a bit."

"Go. I'll be here when you get back."

There were times I wished I could seek help from a slayer. However, from the stories that I'd been told about slayers,

DOLL³

I would always be perceived as an abomination in the slayer world because I was part-*supra* and associated with their enemies.

I exited through the kitchen and went out the back door. Closing my eyes, I teleported to Lake Beaudin. Using the awaken spell again, in order to communicate with my mom, a shimmering body appeared, floating on top of the water. There was no time to hesitate about what I needed from her.

"Mom, I need your help." I dropped down to my knees into the water.

"Talk to me, Tomie. What's happened?"

"It's just too much. You're not going to believe what Verlinda Dawn has done now."

"Yes, I will, and I'm very familiar with Verlinda from stories my coven told me about her. She possesses a black heart and will do anything in her power to bring destruction to those she views as a threat. If she cannot accomplish it, then she'll seek out someone more powerful and evil than her to complete her goal."

"That's exactly what she's done."

"Is she in Salem, Tomie?"

I gazed up at her. She approached me and stroked my face with her watery hands.

"Yes, how did you know?"

"That's where the Sonthiel Coven resides. She wishes to connect with one of the most powerful covens on the East

Coast. Tomie, the Laveau and Sonthiel Covens were friendly once upon a time, until the Dawn Coven spun lies against Laveau, which caused mistrust to grow. Sonthiel Coven sided with Dawn Coven after that. She's probably meeting with a descendant from the Sonthiel Coven."

"She is. Mom, there's no way that light magic will defeat dark magic, no telling what she conspired with Esmerelda Sonthiel. Verlinda will possess way more power now with her on her side."

"More darkness will definitely be on her side, but there's something that Verlinda doesn't know."

"What?"

"Has Lisette shared the story about the Laveau and Dawn Covens, specifically when Verlinda murdered her coven members and tricked a slayer in murdering someone who looked like her?"

"Yes, she did, but what does that story have to do with now? Esmerelda is going to help her out."

She kneeled down with me in the water and placed her hands on the sides of my face and stared into my eyes. "Esmerelda's great-great grandmom was visiting the Dawn Coven that fatal night. When Verlinda performed her dark spell to murder her coven off one by one, Esmerelda's great-great grandmom was unaware and walked in the vicinity of the spell meant for one of the Dawn sisters, which caused her death. Verlinda knew she needed to do something fast, so she completed an accident spell."

DOLL³

My eyebrows knitted together. "What did she do exactly?"

"Made it seem as if a large, rotting weeping willow tree fell on top of Esmerelda's great-great grandmom. Verlinda figured that she would be severely punished for the crime she committed, and didn't want to face the fury of the Sonthiel Coven. However, she never imagined that the *Upper Witch Council* would order her termination by marking her and contacting a slayer, which is why she tricked them with the spell Lisette told you about."

"Man, she knows how to squirm her way out of stuff. Did Esmerelda's family ever find out anything?"

"Family for the Sonthiel Coven retrieved the body and never knew the truth, not even to this day. They returned back to Salem with no contact among any covens for several years after. Another witch confided in me about it because she witnessed it all. Since Sonthiel Coven cut most covens off, I've held on to this secret until now."

"So, no one ever knew what really happened to Esmerelda's great-great grandmom, not even Esmerelda?" I asked, stunned.

"Right."

My mom placed her hands on the sides of my temples. Her hands felt really warm.

"What are you doing?"

"Giving you a past memory of what happened, so there'll be no doubt, when Esmerelda retrieves the truth from you. I love you, now go." She removed her hands.

"Mom, before I go, can I ask you about a special spell?"

"Of course…"

I asked. She answered and vanished, right after—I teleported back to Lisette's house.

CHAPTER
NINE

"T AKE IT THAT YOU WENT TO TALK TO YOUR MOM again?" Mr. Ray asked.

"Sure did. She told me what really happened to Esmerelda's great-great grandmom."

"Starts with a 'v' and ends with an 'a'?"

"How did you guess?"

"Nothing would surprise me about her involvement in anything, especially if it's related to harming someone for her personal gain."

"Do you really think we have a chance?" I shoved my hands into my pockets and closed my eyes for a minute.

"Tomie, I do. It will not be easy, and someone may even get hurt in the end."

"That's exactly what I'm afraid of."

"All wars from the beginning of time have had casualties, many innocent. We're in a war not only against other *supras*, but also slayers and non-slayers."

Lowering my head, I said, "You know I understand the war between witches and slayers, but not among my own kind. It's senseless."

"From what I've read and witnessed in the craft world, various witch covens were cordial among each other, until the Dawn Coven came into existence. That one coven was born from darkness it seems and has ignited turmoil with other covens, even caused some covens to disband permanently or self-destruct, Tomie."

Raising my head up slowly, I said, "It's like Verlinda was related to Emperor Palpatine."

"That's a new twist of putting it. Maybe something happened to her a long time ago, making her the way she is today."

"Nah, I don't think so. Unless Lisette or someone else tells me what made Verlinda so cold and evil, I'm going to keep believing she was just born soulless."

"Fair enough, Tomie."

Looking down at my cell, I noticed two hours had passed and started thinking about Lisette and Sari. Why was Lisette taking so long? Was everything okay? Did Mr. Green confront Lisette? I thought about teleporting close to Sari's house to just check in, but I rejected that idea.

I didn't want to risk Sari's dad seeing me. I already knew he would blame me for Sari's decision to come here over the weekend. Suddenly, Lisette appeared right in front of us.

She looked calm, but then again Lisette usually did.

"So, how did everything go? Is Sari okay? What took you so long?" My eyes met hers.

"Believe so."

"What do you mean?" My shoulders tightened.

"When I left her, she appeared just fine."

"Was her dad there?"

Mr. Ray watched us like a tennis match.

"No, he wasn't. Her mom was there."

"Did she ask her about anything, or why you were there?"

Shaking her head, she said, "Nope. I didn't allow her to see me. I teleported Sari about a block away from her house just in case, and watched from afar, zooming in when I needed to, of course. Sari plans to try to call you soon."

"Glad her dad was out. I can only imagine how he may have reacted."

"Sari will still have to deal with him, especially if he suspects she wasn't with Luckie."

"Yeah, I know, Lisette. Sure she'll tell me all about it when we do get a chance to talk."

"Tomie, we definitely need to talk to Esmerelda, as soon as possible."

In a lingering gasp, I asked, "We do?"

"Absolutely, I think you may just possess a secret weapon to win her over, maybe."

"You know about my conversation with my mom?"

Mr. Ray grinned.

"I do, and I'm glad she told you. I never knew that about Esmerelda's great-great grandmom."

"Lisette, you did it again." I squinted my eyes.

She smiled and whispered, "Your emotions are everywhere, Tomie Dupuy, as I've told you before. Practice keeping them inside."

"How do I do that?"

"Control your feelings and keep them from channeling outside of you."

Mr. Ray stood up and placed his hand on my shoulder. "It takes practice, Tomie."

"Okay, I'll keep working on that. So, this means we're leaving for Salem, tonight?"

"Yes. I'll need to run into town to check on Sabra. We should be home by Monday or Tuesday night. Pack an overnight bag, Tomie. I'll be back soon."

Lisette teleported into town while Mr. Ray prepared to depart.

"Tomie, I'll be in touch with you soon. I'll be popping in Frost to check on Sari. Your protection spell was a good choice. It should help a lot."

"Thank you for watching over her. Means a lot to me."

"You've matured a lot over the last few months. I'm really proud of you."

"Appreciate that, Mr. Ray."

It was great to hear how Mr. Ray felt about me, but traveling to Salem was something I had not anticipated. Meeting a Dark Shadow Witch wasn't on my to-do list.

Before he opened the front door, Mr. Ray spun around to face me. "It's good you and Lisette are making a trip to Salem to visit with Esmerelda. Once she knows the crime Verlinda committed, she may be more apt to assist you both in some way. I'm not sure what that will mean just yet. Be mindful of her dark presence."

"I hope she doesn't throw us inside her oven." I shivered for a few seconds.

"Oh, Tomie, I don't think you have to worry about that— know I'll be watching out for you."

Mr. Ray thought I was playing about being cooked, but I was serious because Dark Shadow Witches could do anything, the more twisted, the better.

He left. I locked the door behind him and strolled into my room to pack my bag. I sat on my bed to check my cell, nothing yet from Sari.

So much was going on. I rested on my bed and thought about my conversation with my mom, and what this Salem visit with this Esmerelda lady may truly accomplish, if anything. Would she help or deceive us? I wasn't going to trust her, especially after her meeting with Verlinda and Mr. Fox.

It was almost seven. I swung my backpack over my shoulder and returned to the living room to wait on Lisette. My cell phone buzzed. Touching my screen button, I saw a text message from my dad and looked up at Lisette as she appeared in the living room.

"Hey, I see you're all packed. Give me about thirty minutes and I'll be ready," Lisette said.

"Sabra doing okay?" I asked, about to text my dad back.

"Yes. She was moving around and talking to me in her chirp language."

"That's great news." I smiled.

"Thanks for asking."

"Sure thing. Hey, are you really sure about all of this, going to Salem?" I chewed the side of my nail.

"Tomie, it's okay to be scared." She stroked my arm.

Looking over my right and left shoulder, I pointed my finger at my chest. "Who, I'm not." My feet started tapping loudly on the floor.

She looked down at my feet. "Oh, yes you are. That's your biggest giveaway, always has been, since you were a little squirt running around. Look, I'll do my best to save you before Esmerelda throws you inside her oven."

My tapping increased, and I blinked several times. "You're kidding about the oven thing, right?"

DOLL³

Grabbing my hands and snickering, she said. "Stop freaking out. You'll be just fine with me." She headed towards her bedroom. "Be ready in fifteen."

Exhaling out and inhaling in a few times, my footwork let up.

CHAPTER
TEN

I TEXTED MY DAD BACK.

D: **How are you?**

T: **Okay**

D: **How was the festival?**

T: **Lots to tell u face-to-face when I'm home**

D: **Everything okay?**

T: **Yep**

I took in a long, deep breath.

D: **Sure, Tomie?**

T: **Yeah, Dad. Just need to see what our options are** before anything else comes our way

D: **Wait, what do you mean by that?**

T: **Didn't want to worry u like you're doing right now**

D: That's just part of being a parent, Tomie. You'll understand one day, son. I worry about you all the time, more so now.

T: Dad. I'm good. Lisette and I need to go out of town for a few days

D: Where are y'all headed?

T: Salem

D: Oh… there must be someone you and Lisette need to meet.

T: Yes, Mr. Fox and Verlinda are already there, meeting with someone we need to meet with, as well

D: Who would that be?

T: Esmerelda Sonthiel

D: Oh, those Sonthiels are Dark Shadow Witches.

T: How do u know?

D: Your mom told me about them.

T: Since you mentioned Mom, I talked to her again

D: Really? Did she say anything about me?

T: No

D: Understand. When are you both headed out?

T: As soon as Lisette finishes packing

D: Be safe, Tomie. Call or text me when you can. Love you.

T: Luv u, Dad. Mom misses u 2

D: Thanks, son.

Lisette emerged in black leggings and a solid black T-shirt

with purple glitter around her collar. A purple backpack wrapped around her shoulders. I noticed words written on the back of her shirt.

"Ready to teleport to Salem, Tomie?"

"Turn around?"

"Why?"

"Want to read what's on your shirt."

She twirled halfway around and lifted the backpack up. The words on the back of her shirt read, "*Witches Got This.*"

I laughed out loud.

"What's so funny?"

"Nothing. I love your shirt. Think you would make Glinda from the *Wizard of Oz* very proud."

"You think?" She smiled.

I shot two thumbs up.

"Tomie, you're really something. Let's get going." She made her way to middle of the floor and I followed. "Did you give your dad an update?"

"A quick one."

"Is he doing okay?"

"Just worried about us."

"Not surprised. You know how lucky you are to have someone who truly loves and supports you?"

I nodded, sighing, "I know, and I'm grateful to have my dad, you, Mr. Ray, Crow, and of course, Sari in my life."

"Thank you. Ready?"

"Not really."

Grabbing my hand firmly, Lisette and I levitated a few inches off the ground and began to spin around at a faster rate than usual in a complete circle.

"You all right?"

"I think so. This feels different than other teleportations for some reason." My stomach felt like it was being flipped over and over again.

"That's because we're traveling farther than we ever have. Just think of something calming, and that feeling will soon leave."

My thoughts went straight to Sari, and the night we were together talking under the willow tree. Before I could complete my thought, Lisette and I stood on a cobblestone street in front of a butter-yellow wooden building with light grey trim.

"Where are we, Lisette?"

"Martha's Bed and Breakfast."

I could tell whoever owned this building took pride in making sure it kept its classical Georgian Colonial style with a gambrel roof, double-hung windows, flatboards, and wrap around porch. The front door was forest green with eight panels, with smaller panels in the middle.

"Wonder when this was built?"

"I'm thinking around 1813."

"How do you know, Lisette?"

She chuckled. "It's on the bottom of the nameplate, see."

"Oh, yeah. Reading is fundamental."

"Well, let's go in," she said.

"Okay, after you."

We walked up seven steps and wrung the doorbell.

After a few minutes, we heard footsteps approaching the door. An older lady greeted us. Her hair was silky black and brushed up in a loose bun. She wore leopard, oval-shaped glasses. Red and yellow plaid overalls draped over her thin body.

"Greetings, Lisette Laveau."

"Same to you, Martha Proctor."

They hugged.

"Do come in," Martha requested.

We entered the living room.

"Martha, this is Tomie Dupuy," Lisette announced.

"Oh, my, you're very handsome, indeed," she whispered, as she tapped my right shoulder.

"Thank you, Ma'am," I said.

"Please call me Martha."

High beige ceilings, mahogany floors, stairs, and golden wallpaper saturated with black-capped chickadee birds and mayflowers decorated the interior. Two scroll arm, scarlet-checkered print sofas, and round chestnut tables filled the room.

She directed us to our rooms.

"Tomie, once you get settled in, come down and join us for

tea," Lisette said.

"Sure." I nodded. Placing my bag down, I sat on the full bed. The two black and white framed glass paintings caught my attention. I stepped up closer to examine each picture on the wall. The one hanging over a charcoal antique desk was a painting of five teenage girls standing under a huge tree. The curly branches seemed to close around them.

They were dressed in long, dark dresses with aprons and petticoats. The thing that intrigued me the most about this picture was they all wore hooded capes, and their eyes seemed to glow. I noticed an embroidered number five in the middle of their hoods.

As for the second painting, it showed three people being burnt at the stake. The faces were unrecognizable, but the flames were huge and seemed to twirl around the bodies. I climbed on the bed and examined the painting closer and glided my right hand across the glass, which felt really warm.

Jerking my hand back, it hit me: Martha must be a witch, and her last name rang a familiar bell, too. I pulled out my cell phone, looking up her last name and found out more about John Proctor—a former landowner in the Massachusetts Bay Colony during the mid 1700s. Mr. Proctor had been falsely accused and convicted for being a *supra*.

Unfortunately, his hanging took place on August 19, 1692, during the awful Salem Witch trials. Before his death, he had been a very busy dude with three marriages and eighteen children from those unions. I figured that the Martha Proctor downstairs and owner of this bed and breakfast was a descendant of the late John Proctor somehow.

Reflecting back on the family history book that Lisette had first shared with me, I thought about how more than two hundred people were accused of witchcraft during the Salem Witch Trials and twenty were executed.

I also thought about how many out of those twenty were actually witches or warlocks, probably very few. Many families lost their spouses, parents, or children during that heated time. Just thinking about those who lost their lives because of some ridiculous beliefs made my heart pound hard up against my chest.

Women had it really rough back then, I imagined. If they were middle-aged, a little odd, were married with no children, poor, or a confessed witch accused them of being a fellow witch, they may have been suspected of witchcraft and definitely were part of the Salem Witch Trials.

Fast-forwarding to present day, I thought about how the Salem Witch Trials' numbers would look like—definitely way higher. Countless innocent lives would be lost because of someone's narrow and ludicrous beliefs.

"Tomie," Lisette called from downstairs.

I glanced back at the pictures before I left.

CHAPTER
ELEVEN

CLIMBING DOWN THE STAIRS, I NOTICED THE DOOR open. Lisette and Martha sat outside on the porch with a teapot and cookies. A chime made up of a witch on a broomstick and floating jack-o-lanterns hung under one of the beams of the house.

"Please sit," Martha requested.

I did, and she poured me a cup of tea.

"Would you like sugar cubes or honey?"

"Cubes, please."

"How many?"

"Two and thank you."

She dropped the cubes into my cup of tea. I sipped it slowly.

"Lisette, you both are visiting Esmerelda tonight?" Martha

asked.

"No, tomorrow morning when I know that Verlinda and Mr. Fox have cleared the scene—it's too late now, anyhow."

Breathing out, I grabbed two cat-shaped sugar cookies off the saucer. The hairs on the back of my arms stood straight up. It felt like warm cement was being poured down my throat and was hardening fast.

"Martha, how long have you owned this bed and breakfast?" I asked, chewing the cookie and sipping my tea, while thinking about the visit with Esmerelda, in a few hours.

"Oh, it's been passed down from my family for many years. I took over managing this place about thirty years ago."

"It's very lovely, Martha, and the only place I want to stay when I travel up this way, which isn't that often," Lisette shared.

"Thank you so much. You're too kind. Always a joy to see you, Lisette."

"How do you know Martha, Lisette?" I asked, hoping it would confirm my suspicion of who Martha really was, especially from her last name.

"Tomie, you are being very bold tonight," Lisette whispered.

"Just curious," I replied. "Can you blame me? Look where we are?" I threw my hands up in the air.

Martha smiled and sipped on more of her tea. "Oh, Lisette, I don't mind answering his question, or any other questions he may have for me, before you both are on your way."

DOLL³

"Thank you, Martha. I just didn't want you to feel forced to answer," Lisette said.

"No. I'm delighted to have company and questions. There are times when this place is empty. Just me and Miss Gretel." She stooped down to pick up a black cat with one light green eye and the other aqua blue; she placed her in her lap. Miss Gretel purred loudly as Martha stroked her back with her hand.

"Back to your question, Tomie. I've known Lisette's family for years. In fact, the Laveau Coven and Proctor Families have partnered up at different times to assist each other when needed."

"Martha, are you a witch?"

She continued to stroke Ms. Gretel without responding for a few seconds. I glanced over at Lisette, who scrunched up her face.

"Did you notice the two paintings hanging up in your room, Tomie?" Martha asked.

"Yes. The one with the people being burnt at the stake, though, is a little disturbing." My knee started bouncing.

"I agree with you, but that was the reality for those being accused back then. Many non-witches and warlocks lost their lives because of witch hunters wanting to terminate the possibility of someone being a disguised *supra*."

Finishing up the cookie, I asked, "So, Martha, are you or not?"

"Indeed, I am, as are all the women in the other painting in your room. They're my great ancestors. They were forced to conceal their powers in order to remain alive. That was the last painting of them as a group by an unknown artist."

"It's an eye-stopper, both of them. Is Ms. Gretel your familiar?"

She closed her eyes for a short moment. "Yes."

"The late John Proctor, how are you two related?" I leaned in towards her, almost falling out of the wicker chair, and my chewing ceased.

"He was my great-great-great granddad." She opened her eyes. They seemed to glimmer a silver hue.

Squinting my eyes, I said, "I figured he was something like that. Was he really a warlock who died from his accusers?"

"He wasn't a warlock, but my great-great-great grandmother was a witch. She's the one standing in the middle of the painting above your desk in your room. Her name was Blythe Proctor, and she established the Enchanted Proctor Five."

"Enchanted?" My head flinched back.

"Yes, Tomie, they were a very powerful group of witches with extraordinary powers. The witch hunters back then, and later the Dupuy Silver Slayers, surfaced and attempted to wipe them out, or any descendants of the Enchanted Proctor Five."

"Why?"

"Tomie, hunters believed all witches were evil and needed to be exterminated before they became a witch's target."

"That's so far from the truth. There are bad witches, like what I've seen with Verlinda and Opal, but there are also good ones, like Lisette, my mom, you, and others, I'm sure."

"Like you, too, Tomie," Lisette whispered as she leaned over to me and patted me on my shoulder. "Think you've asked Martha enough questions, time for bed. We have an early start in the morning."

"Almost done."

"It's okay. Truly, I don't mind. I haven't had anyone in a long time to be this curious about my history." She smiled.

"Just sad how so many were sought out and killed off. A lot of innocent blood spilled because of fear," I said with a deep sigh, as I stared down at the ground.

Standing up, I walked over to the end of the porch and sat. Ms. Gretel bumped my back with her head. Her tail curled under my arm, and she crawled up into my lap. I stroked her with my hand. She purred a few times.

"Think you made a new friend," Lisette said, chuckling.

Turning half way around, I stared back at her and Martha.

"You think?" I squinted one eye. "Martha, you mentioned that the Enchanted Proctor Five possessed extraordinary powers. What did you mean by that?"

"Well, they could *glim*, time travel, and shapeshift into an array of animals without any special spell or potion."

"What did you just say?" My eyebrows rose and my eyes gleamed.

"Tomie, you heard what Martha said," Lisette scolded.

"Hold up, you referring to time travel like *Time Machine* by H.G. Wells, *Back to the Future,* and *The Girl Who Leapt Through Time?*" My eyes focused only on Martha.

"Yes, which is why hunters sought them out and any of their children."

"They could've killed them or hid with their shifting powers, right?"

"Not if hunters knew of their weaknesses, which we're all vulnerable to— iron and fire. However, the witch-catcher and a witch-killing spell are the most powerful. Only certain covens are aware of that spell," Martha whispered, rocking in her chair.

Lisette's eyes looked watery. I returned back to sit next to her.

"You, okay?" I asked, touching her hand.

"I'll be okay. Just brings up some sad memories about my coven."

Martha pulled out a handkerchief from her pocket and handed it over to Lisette. She wiped her face.

"Please, continue your questions, Tomie. Martha, he needs to know his history."

"How would hunters know that and what's a witch-catcher?"

"Betrayal from another coven or a witch who craved survival and protection. A witch-catcher is an iron collar that has been immersed in a salt bath for a short time with a truth-telling spell placed on it."

She paused for a minute and continued. "The catcher controls a witch and forces them to be obedient. This evil device can eventually strip a witch's powers. The longer a witch wears it, the gadget tightens around his or her neck, and all powers may be lost, or the witch could perish into a pile of dust."

"That's beyond cold." I cringed, replaying a vision of what she just shared. "Bet, I can guess the traitor."

"Sure you can."

"Dawn Coven." I breathed in a few deep breaths.

"Got it. Opal's great-great-great grandmother completed a temporary suspending power spell against them, which allowed the hunters to gather the Enchanted Proctor Five in a holding space. Three were able to escape, but the other two died at the planned stake burnings."

"The Dawn Coven has been poison for a long time," Lisette said.

"Many Proctors changed their names. I kept mine, hoping to encounter an enchanted one, but no luck yet. Not giving up. I know they're out there." Her eyes filled with tears.

Lisette stood up to embrace her.

She sniffled and pulled a yellow handkerchief from her pocket to wipe her nose.

"Please tell me more about the Enchanted Proctor Five's

shapeshifting abilities?" I asked, facing her.

"Oh, witches who can shift are extremely rare, indeed. They all possessed the gift because they were siblings and probably stemmed from the maternal bloodline. I've never met a witch who could shapeshift. However, I heard stories when I was about your age of those who could. Less than five percent of all witches, in the past and present, possessed that spectacular gift."

I whispered, "Is there a sign of some kind to confirm the shapeshifting gift?"

"Yes, Tomie." Her eyes dilated and glossed over.

"What?"

"The primary sign is a glow emanating from the hands."

I took a few deep breaths. "So, is it a certain color?"

"Tomie, why are you so interested in shifting all of a sudden?" Lisette asked, arching her eyebrows and pursing her lips.

"Just curious and all, especially with Mr. Ray's abilities." My right foot started tapping. Lisette looked down.

My attempt to conceal what had happened to me at the festival that night was difficult to do. I felt Lisette trying to *glim* me, but I blocked her out, at least I thought I did.

"Why, Tomie Dupuy, you forgot to tell me something." Lisette placed her hands on top of my hands. Martha touched my shoulders. Ms. Gretel spun in and out between my lower legs with a louder purr.

DOLL³

"Oh my, Tomie, you're a blue-blood, shapeshifter warlock."
They both spouted and stepped back, as if the wind took their breaths away for a minute.

CHAPTER
TWELVE

"UMM, WHAT THE HECK IS A BLUE-BLOOD?"

Lisette looked down at me and so did Martha. They glanced at each other.

I clenched my jaw and clutched my fists.

The wind picked up, and the trees blew back and forth towards the porch. Loose leaves started to swarm on the ground and then up in the air in a wavy, spiral pattern. I knew we weren't doing it. The leaves flew up higher and spelled a message out in front of me, which read: "**Soon you will understand who you truly are…**"

"Tomie, your message is sacred and from a late descendant," Martha said.

I had a strong feeling that it was my mom communicating

with me.

"Let's go inside," she beckoned. Before I entered the house behind them, the leaves fell back to the ground. I closed the door, and Martha locked it with the slight twist of her wrist.

We all sat down in the living room. Martha and Lisette took a seat across from me. My mind wouldn't leave the message. I thought the question I'd pondered several weeks ago was now being answered. Never imagined being a warlock, but now to be a blue-blood shapeshifter?

"Tomie, you're definitely in a different league, being a shapeshifter," Martha uttered.

"Are there different kinds of shifters?" I asked.

Martha's eyes glowed. "Yes. Yellow-bloods can only transform into certain animals for a short time. Green-bloods can turn into more animals, but no shifting into any human forms, including time travel, as I mentioned earlier—this was the category for the Enchanted Proctor Five. Now, blue-bloods are the highest on the witch/warlock hierarchy, and only a few exist."

"Are you serious?"

"Yes, they can become temporarily invisible and shift into any animal or person for short periods of time, no potions needed. The more practiced, then the longer one can remain in the shift-alter state," Martha explained. "One more magical thing about being a blue-blood…"

"What?" I was wide-eyed and barely hanging onto the edge

of the couch.

"Each shifter is granted a unique shift that no other shapeshifter will possess. It only belongs to him or her. Think of how snowflakes look the same from a distance when they fall, but under close examination, each one is unique, which is the same for each blue-blood," Martha said.

"Know that shifting can really drain you. Rest and refueling on liquids, specifically, a special vitamin water, are a priority," Lisette commanded. "You must remember to do those things because if you don't, then your enemy can pray on your vulnerability."

"Lisette, will you teach me the skills to shift?" My eyes fixed on hers.

"Of course. I'll have to do some research because I've never taught anyone. You'll be my first. Mr. Ray will definitely play a big part of this special training for you."

My mind was racing, trying to absorb everything I just heard about my new gift. I figured being a warlock was nice, but now learning that I wasn't an ordinary warlock made me feel more confident facing the inevitable. I still felt shaky in my knees, and my palms were sweaty. Overall, I was feeling like Spiderman, when he first discovered he could climb walls without falling.

"New spells?" I asked.

"No, just practice and plenty of concentration," Martha replied.

DOLL³

"Definitely can do that."

"I've never met a blue-blood, shapeshifting warlock." Martha scanned me from head to toe with her flashing eyes.

"Figured you did, since you've been around a lot of witches."

"When you first stepped over my threshold, I could sense something about you, but I didn't know exactly what it was then."

"Believe me, it's not that big of a deal," I mumbled.

Martha locked her eyes on mine. "Oh, it's really big, Tomie. You possess an advantage that many wished they could have. Your newly discovered gift will serve you well, when it's time."

"How do you know?"

"Just do. You only need to learn how to utilize your gift. Once it knows you're not afraid, it will be simple to call on it when you need it."

My eyes met hers. "Thanks, Miss Martha, for sharing."

"Sure. Oh, look at the time. You both need to get some rest, and so do I—big day tomorrow with Esmerelda Sonthiel."

Lisette nodded.

I bounded upstairs to the bathroom to take a quick shower and brush up.

After I climbed into bed, I set the alarm on my cell, and my eyes drifted back to the family painting of witches. Thinking about everything Martha shared with me about their special powers, I wondered why I was given such a rare gift. I raised my hands above me and rotated them around to examine them. I shook them a few times, thinking that the blue spark would appear, but nothing happened.

When I thought about meeting Esmerelda tomorrow, I began to feel nauseated. Two things were going to happen in the next few hours, either Esmerelda would invite us in and hear us out, or dismiss us with a terrible parting spell.

I knew I possessed information that she would want to know, but her reaction was unknown. Most of all, I prayed that she didn't have an oven in her shop.

Then, my mind drifted to the negative encounter with Garth, and how he had triggered my strange glow that night. Is that what it would take? Someone or something making me upset to unleash this new power? I wasn't sure. I hoped to find out soon. Closing my eyes, I fell to sleep.

CHAPTER
THIRTEEN

A PIERCING RING SOUNDED OFF MY CELL. I REACHED for it on the desk and turned the alarm off. No calls from Sari. I wondered how she was doing; I wasn't worried because I knew Mr. Ray was watching out for her. Plus, she had the protection spell.

I put on some jeans and a Morbius T-shirt and went downstairs. Lisette sat at the kitchen table eating a bagel. I grabbed one off the plate and chugged down a glass of juice.

"What time are you both visiting Esmerelda?"

"We're headed that way now," Lisette said.

"If you feel unsafe, then leave."

"Martha, we'll just have to deal with whatever comes. Communicating with her is our purpose for being here."

"I understand, Lisette. Just be careful. I've met her in passing a few times on the street. Esmerelda has never been one to speak. She's cold, and you can feel her staring into your soul, even from a distance."

"Thank you, Martha."

"Maybe next time you visit Salem, Tomie, it will be more for pleasure. Add the House of Seven Gables and Corwin House—better known as Witch House—to your future list. If you have time after your rendezvous with Esmerelda, then go by Proctor's Ledge."

"What's Proctor's Ledge?" I asked, stuffing the rest of the cinnamon-raisin bagel in my mouth.

Martha sighed. "It's the place where the witches were actually hung."

"People go there?"

"It's one of the hottest spots here for tourists, and many have said that if you place your ear close to the ground, you can actually hear the screams of those who were burnt at the stake. Some claimed to have smelled fresh smoke there also," Martha shared.

"No way, for reals, Lisette?" I asked, my voice juddering.

"I've never actually done it, but I've heard others talk about it and confirm that it's true," Lisette said.

"Believe me, it's true," Martha stressed.

"So, you've actually heard the screams?"

"Yes, Tomie, the late evening and night seems to be the best time to hear them."

"Lisette, that's pretty wicked. Can we go after?"

"Possibly. Our main focus is visiting with Esmerelda at her shop. I do want you to experience a little of Salem while we're here, though. We'll definitely try."

"Do you think she'll really help us out, especially after her visit with Verlinda and Mr. Fox?"

"As far as Esmerelda, Tomie, I'm not sure. It's worth a try. Dark Shadow Witches are extremely unpredictable. If she feels threatened, then she could unleash her dark magic on us," Lisette whispered, snapping her fingers.

Chewing on the bottom of my lip, I asked, "Are you scared, Lisette?"

"Yes, but she'll never know it." The muscle in her jaw twitched. "Tomie, fear is real. Whenever you feel it, you must tell yourself, even if that means repeating it a hundred times in your head that, '*I'm in control of this, and no one will overpower me, ever!*'"

"That's powerful. Not sure if I can, especially in this situation."

"You have to believe and seize it, here." She tapped my heart with her two fingers.

Brushing curls out of my face with my hand, I said, "I'm going to try."

"That's all I can ask. I'll be by your side."

Although it was great to hear Lisette's supportive words, I

still didn't make me feel all warm and secure. For all I knew, we may encounter Esmerelda's chamber of darkness and be stuck there. At least if we didn't return, Mr. Ray and Martha would know why we were never heard from again.

"I do think Esmerelda will assist you two, once you tell her your purpose and whatever other information that could benefit her," Martha said. She stood up.

Lisette looked at me, and I knew exactly what her expression meant. Esmerelda could find the information I possessed interesting, at least I hoped so.

"Ready?"

"Don't have much of a choice, Lisette."

"Just stay near me. I won't let her hurt you."

Could Lisette really guarantee that? I dragged myself behind Lisette.

CHAPTER
FOURTEEN

L EAVING MARTHA'S HOUSE, WE TURNED RIGHT
towards the cobblestone streets, passing various historic
homes. The morning was sunny and a little cool. Tree branches
swayed from left to right. People were out and visiting the
various shops we passed.

"Where's Esmerelda's shop, Lisette?"

"It's not too far from here, maybe thirty minutes."

We hiked up a steep sidewalk and came upon Esmerelda's
Extraordinary Shop. I noticed about seven long amber and
onyx lights swinging back and forth from the ceiling, as I
peered into the semi-clouded horizontal glass window.

No customers were inside. The hours and days of operation
were written on the glass. Lisette placed her hand on a red,

metal doorknob in the shape of a striking rattlesnake head with ebony rhinestone eyes and started turning it. It was locked. She dropped her hand and faced me. Then, I noticed a sign on the upper right window, which read, "Closed."

"Guess we picked the wrong day, huh?"

"We've traveled all this way for this." Lisette pressed her hands against the sides of her temples.

"Maybe this is our sign to just get out of here. Now, we don't have to worry about that hot oven," I whispered and shaky laughter followed.

"We'll just try again tomorrow. Come on, let's go check out some places around town that Martha talked about."

This was our omen, and I didn't understand why Lisette couldn't see it.

Before we turned around, the lock clicked and the door opened up, maybe ten inches wide.

A gruff voice echoed from a distance. "Enter or exit… your choice. You have exactly five seconds before this door locks."

Lisette went to push the door open.

"Wait, is this really worth it?" I pulled her hand back.

"Tomie, yes."

Shoving the door open, she went ahead of me. I paused for a few seconds outside the shop before I followed behind her. She turned and whispered, "Let me do the talking, okay?"

I nodded and closed my eyes for a brief moment.

Once we were both inside, the door slammed closed, and

the two brass locks made a crisp, loud sealing sound. Blood red blinds rolled down.

The swinging lights above our heads froze in mid air and turned off. The veins on my hand pulsated as my jumping eyes swept the room. No one was there. Lisette touched my hand and said in a soft voice, "Be very still and quiet."

"Why?" I stuttered.

"Just do it."

She had that stern look painted on her face, and I obeyed her without further discussion. I glanced around the shop and noticed there wasn't any fun stuff, like T-shirts, candies, or cups. The shelves contained only candles, strange dolls, swirling and colorful liquids in glass bottles, and wooden boxes in different shapes. There were two open areas, one behind the antique cash register and near the back of the store.

All of a sudden, the remaining light disappeared. We stood in the middle of a Dark Shadow Witch's store in total darkness. Lisette grabbed my hand, and squeezed it.

Tomie, remain calm and remember those octopus emotions of yours. She's deep glimming us to read our intent.

I'll be glad when she turns the lights back on.

You'll be fine. She'll figure out soon that we mean her no harm.

"Terminate the telepathic communication now!" Esmerelda roared.

My knees wobbled and my hands jerked at the same time, as my breathing sped up and my eyes twitched.

Candles in the windows and along the shelves lit up one by one and an unidentifiable, smoky snakelike form wrapped around us. I could feel tight constriction around me. My heart sped up, and the hair behind my neck stood on end. I squeezed Lisette's hand tighter. This woman's presence was super freaky. She was talking, but had not shown herself yet. I wasn't sure what her reasons were.

"I've been expecting you two. I know who you both are," Esmerelda bellowed.

My heart jackhammered, as a warm and stinging breath swept across my face.

"Miss Esmerelda, we seek your assistance," Lisette said in a barely audible tone.

"Continue."

"We know that our enemies are plotting to cause us harm."

"Why is this a concern of mine?" she huffed and twirled up higher above us. The bottles on the shelves shook and a couple fell but floated up before hitting the ground and flying back onto the shelves.

"May I please ask you a few questions?"

"Don't waste my time!" she hollered, voice vibrating. The floor trembled under our feet, causing us to stumble backwards.

"A Verlinda Dawn and Mr. Fox paid you a visit recently, correct?"

"What business is that of yours, if they visited me or not?"

she snapped.

"Verlinda has planted lies inside of Mr. Fox's mind and others. We were not involved in what she claims."

"I don't care, and frankly the Laveau Coven has not been associated with Sonthiel Coven for some time now. I have no reason to help you and your companion."

Honestly, her reactions didn't shock me at all. I figured that she would give us resistance. I was ready to bolt up out of there and never look back. In a way, I felt trapped like the last line in that song, "Hotel California."

"You're correct."

"I know, I am. You're wasting my time. Please go!"

The doors unlocked and peeled open with a cracking noise.

"Miss Esmerelda, please, we desperately need your help," Lisette pleaded.

She laughed. "Never thought I would see the day, a Laveau witch beg me. Laveau always thought their coven was so much better, but look at you now. You might as well grovel to me on your weak knees."

"Every coven stands for either light or dark, and it's the coven's prerogative to choose. Just because we follow different paths doesn't mean we can't help each other," Lisette explained.

"What can you do for me? Nothing!"

"Lisette, may I speak?" I asked.

She looked at me and shook her head.

"By all means, let the young warlock share what's weighing heavy on his heart."

The smoky form swirled tighter around my body and then floated in front of me. I could now see the piercing, scarlet eyes darting back and forth, watching every move Lisette and I made. Although it wasn't cold inside, it felt like thirty degrees to me. I could hear my heartbeats ricochet inside my chest and felt paralyzed.

"Come now… talk or leave."

"You had a family member who died a mysterious death many years ago, right?"

Lisette looked at me.

"What did you just say?"

"Your great-great grandmom died, and no one knew what happened to her."

"Continue," she hissed and the glass shook.

"Verlinda placed a twisted spell on her coven and murdered all of her sisters. Your great-great grandmother got in the way. She covered it up well."

The door closed, and the smoky form transformed into a tall human being, wearing a long, white lace dress with a high collar and black stilettoes. Her auburn hair was pinned up with black rhinestone-colored combs—almond colored skin glowed. Esmerelda's eyes seemed to glow like a flame. She stared down at me.

"How do you know of this, young warlock?" She beckoned

DOLL³

us to follow her to the back of the store, where there was a lounge with a table, a plush couch, and a few chairs.

"Sit," she demanded. "Answer my question, now!" The flames in her eyes grew brighter. She remained standing.

"I used the awakening spell to visit my late mom. She's the one who shared with me."

"You know, if this isn't true, I'll gut both of you alive, freeze your body parts, and serve them later, to my pack of Dobermans, right?"

My eyes widened, and my foot began to tap on the floor, as sweat beads ran along my forehead and down the sides of my face.

Esmerelda's curvy, long black nails crawled inside my hair. My legs started shaking. She stared up above me. A black crystal ball about half the size of a bowling ball floated above my head and landed on the table in front of us.

"Now, place your hands on top of it," she commanded.

As I looked over at Lisette, she nodded to me.

Esmerelda placed her hand on top of mine. Her hands felt hot. Closing her eyes, she rocked back and forth.

I felt very light. The blackness inside of the crystal ball faded away. It was clear, and the events my mom spoke about played out like a movie inside of the ball. Esmerelda saw that Verlinda was the one who'd murdered her family member years ago.

Clenching her fists, she stood up. I noticed blood dripping down from her hands and staining her dress. Her sharp nails must've pierced through her skin. Lisette and I looked at each other.

Pacing the floor a few times, Esmerelda swung her entire body around and walked back to where we were and sat. Her eyes transformed to a deep amethyst. "What a mess I've made of myself." She blew on her hands, and the stained area on her dress. The droplets of blood floated up in the air and dematerialized. "This has been buried for far too long."

"Does this mean that you'll help us now, Miss Esmerelda?" Lisette asked.

"Not sure how much help I'll actually be for you both."

"May I ask, if you helped them with the transmigration spell?" Lisette asked.

I noticed Lisette's hands trembled a little; something I'd never seen from her. I placed my hand on her shoulder and looked into her eyes. She stared into mine, until Esmerelda responded.

"I did. In Verlinda and Mr. Fox's case, they told me they would be bringing his daughter back. Lisette, you gave them the bullets. Tomie and Sari murdered Pepper Fox a few months ago because they were extremely jealous of her and desired to get rid of her, so you all used dark magic to accomplish the goal."

"No, Ma'am, that's so far from the truth," Lisette cried out and stood to face Esmerelda eye to eye. "Verlinda is a liar. She's caused so much damage because of her selfish ways."

Leaning back on the couch and crossing her legs, Esmerelda said, "Verlinda also placed a diversion spell on Pepper for her and her granddaughter's benefit."

Lisette's eyes caught mine.

"Miss Esmerelda, we absolutely appreciate your time and information." Lisette paused. "Is there something we can do to reverse the spell on Pepper?"

She stared at us without speaking, and with a half twisted grin, she waved us out.

We made our way from the back of the shop and up to the front. The lights were on and not swinging like when we entered, as I looked up at them. Before I reached to touch the doorknob, Esmerelda said, "Wait. I have something to give to you. It won't stop a spell already completed, but it could help in different ways." She surveyed her shelves with various items outlined in perfect order and floated her body to the top.

Running her long fingernails across the empty wall, a glass drawer popped out. She pulled an onyx box out with mother-of pearl adorning the top, about the size of an average shoebox from the drawer. Floating back down to the ground, she handed it over to Lisette, and the glass drawer disappeared deep into the wall.

"What's this?" Lisette asked.

"See for yourself."

Lisette examined the box.

"What is it?" I leaned in.

"Thank you for telling me the truth about what Verlinda did," Esmerelda said, slanting her flashing eyes.

Lisette noticed four locked clasps on the sides. She lifted each of them up with her eyes, and the lid rose up a few inches. Lifting the lid off, she handed it over to me. I held it in one hand and continued to stare at the box. She pulled out an object wrapped in burlap. Once she uncovered it, she held it up in her hand. It resembled a jagged ivory stick with a wooden handle at the end.

"Well?" I darted my eyes back at forth at the mysterious thing she was holding.

"Miss Esmerelda, is this what I think it is?" Lisette's eyes shimmered into a golden hazel shade for a minute and then back to her natural shade of emerald green.

"Yes."

I was absolutely clueless at what they were referring to. Was it something to help us to fight against Verlinda or possibly a slayer? My phone beeped. I pulled it out of my pocket. It was a text from Sari, but I needed to know what Esmerelda had given Lisette. I slipped my phone back.

Lisette looked into my eyes. "Tomie, this is an extraordinary witch's wand." She waved it in the air, and it glowed a bright turquoise, casting onto the ceiling.

"Okay, what makes it so special?"

"If my memory serves me right, then only one of these wands was created back in the late 1800s by Marie Laveau before her death. How did you obtain this? My family always thought it had either been destroyed or ended up in the wrong hands."

"One of my late descendants secured this wand in New Orleans many years ago, and it has remained in Salem ever since then," Esmerelda replied.

"So?" I prodded. I noticed the glow from the wand penetrated Lisette's hands, arms, and face to the point where she possessed an identical glow.

"This is definitely a very unique wand, indeed. The base is made out of four infused woods—ash, oak, willow, and birch. Each wood possesses individual symbolisms: Ash is *protection*, Oak is *strength* and *invulnerability*, Willow is *intuition*, and Birch is *purification*. This wand is not only used for spells. It can create a circle of invisible protection around the witch or a sacred space," Esmerelda explained.

"Marie wasn't playing around when she constructed that," I blurted.

They both looked at me. Lisette smiled, but Esmerelda didn't.

"Esmerelda, why would you give us this?" Lisette asked.

"It belonged to your family, and you should have it. Like I mentioned earlier, it may provide you assistance against Verlinda, and whatever else you both may encounter when you return back home. You'll know when to use it. Verlinda deserves everything that may fly her way." She thrust her chest out and her piercing eyes beamed towards us.

Why did Verlinda hate us so? It then hit me. Verlinda didn't want Mr. Fox finding out the truth, so she had to try her best to get rid of us, just in case he sided with our story—that's if we could ever get close to him to share.

Lisette wrapped the wand back up and placed it in its cushioned box. I handed her the lid, and she secured it, fastening the clasps back down with one nod. She held the box close to her chest.

"Tomie, it's time to go. Thank you again, Miss Esmerelda." The closed door opened on its own.

She bowed her head. "Not all Dark Shadow Witches walk the evil path to destroy others."

Lisette turned around. "You're right, Esmerelda, and I'll never forget this. Thank you."

The door opened and closed behind us. I looked back and Esmerelda's smoky presence swam around for a few seconds and then absorbed into the wall.

CHAPTER
FIFTEEN

"LISETTE, DID YOU EXPECT ALL OF THAT?"

"No. I figured she would turn us away quickly or worse. Instead, she returned a priceless weapon back to the Laveau family."

"Have you ever used a wand before?"

"This will be my first time. I do believe it will help whenever the time comes, Tomie."

"Glad we have something."

She smiled. "Me too. Do you want to stop by Proctor's Ledge before we head back to Martha's?"

Securing the box under her arm, she said, "Sure."

Pulling out my cell, I noticed it was after five-thirty. We had spent more time at Esmerelda's than I'd expected. We came to a hilly area. One tree with tall and crooked limbs with copper and black leaves stood in the middle of the site. No one else was around, just us.

When I made my way closer under the tree, I felt a cold breeze run across my bare arms. I shivered. I touched the tree trunk, and it felt somewhat warm. Lisette stood near me.

"What are you waiting for? You know you want to do it, ever since Martha mentioned earlier."

I gave her a half grin, squatting down to run the loose dirt in my hand. I pulled a wide rubber band from my pocket and scooped up my heavy, curly hair with both hands, wrapping the band around a few times. Lowering myself down to the ground, I placed my ear as close to it as I could without touching it.

"Are you going to do it, too, Lisette?"

"Oh, no, this is all yours. You have to experience for yourself and believe. If you don't believe the witch trials actually happened, then you'll hear nothing. Be quiet and listen."

Closing my eyes, I lowered my head down a little more. After a couple of minutes, I lifted my head back up and sat on my knees. "Lisette, I don't hear anything."

"Sure? Try again."

I returned to the position and placed my ear as close as possible to the ground, again. After five minutes, I heard shrieking and spine-tingling screams shooting into my ear, including a terrifying vision, which caused me to jump to my feet.

DOLL³

"Tomie, are you okay? Did you hear the screams?"

"Yes, I heard them and also saw something." My heart was beating really fast. "Lisette, I'm ready to go." I jogged away from the tree, turning around a few times to make sure nothing was following us back.

"Slow down, Flash," Lisette shouted. She ran up to me. "Tell me what you heard and saw. I never heard of anyone ever having a vision after doing that."

We were maybe twenty minutes from Martha's place. I saw a bench and we sat down. "Tomie, what was it?" Her eyes zeroed in on me.

"Lisette, it was just horrible... I saw them..."

"What?"

"The executions... I saw all of them. The burning flesh... the heavy sulfur odors stung my nostrils. Unforgettable screams and cries pierced my ears. No one helped any of them. Tight ropes were around their bodies, tying down their arms against their legs. They all were surrounded by logs and endless fires, until they took their last breath." I lowered my face down into the palms of my quivering hands. Lisette patted my back.

"So sorry you saw all of those images."

I lifted up and stared into her eyes. "Lisette, I didn't expect to see all of that. Why didn't someone stop those senseless murders? So many were falsely accused, and even if they were true witches or warlocks, then they didn't deserve that."

"You're right, but that was the mindset then."

"Truly, has much really changed?"

"What do you mean?"

"The 1600s were all about witch-haters accusing a group, and now our own kind are targeting our destruction."

"Tomie, did you ever think that some of those accusers back then were truly witches or warlocks trying to protect themselves from being discovered? They sacrificed many innocent ones in order to conceal their true identities."

I wiped my face with my hands. "Never thought about that until now. You know that makes a lot of sense when you think about it." I guessed every witch had the choice. However, I would choose to face my own consequences versus throwing someone else under the bus.

Lisette nodded. She picked the box up in her hand and stood. "Let's go."

"Will these memories ever leave me?"

"In time. Don't go listening around on those grounds anymore, especially with the experience you had."

"Believe me, I'm not doing anything like that again. Hey, when will I be back in Salem?"

"You just never know."

A black crow rested on a lamppost across from us. It fluttered its wings, staring at us from its cold black eyes.

"Looks like that bird is watching us, Lisette." I pointed.

"You're right. It's trying to read us."

Turning my head towards her, I asked, "What?"

"Somebody's familiar is stalking us, probably Verlinda's. It's time to get out of Salem."

We made it back to Martha's place. She sat in a chair on the porch. "Looks like you two had a full day. Dinner is waiting in the warmer for you both."

"Thank you, Martha," Lisette said. "After we eat, think we're going to head on out."

"Figured you both would. Hope you found out what you needed to."

"We did, and a little more than expected."

Lisette walked to her room to pack up her items. I did the same. My eyes drifted up towards the Enchanted Proctor Five painting. I couldn't resist, so I pulled my phone out to take a picture of it. It was almost eight, and I texted Sari.

T: **Hey**

She didn't respond. I picked up my bag in my hand, flicked the light off with a blink, and pulled the door closed with a wave.

Martha sat down at the table and sipped on a glass of tea with Lisette. "Was Esmerelda helpful?"

"Initially, she wasn't. Once Tomie told her the truth about Verlinda, she opened up and gave us something."

Martha's lips rested on the edge of her glass, and she set it down and asked, "What?" Her eyes sparkled a bit.

"You remember that story about Marie creating a very distinctive wand?"

"Many claimed that it was never made, buried with her, or stolen," Martha said in a low tone.

"Well, the stolen story was right because someone from the Sonthiel Coven did just that, according to Esmerelda's story."

"May I see it?" Martha asked.

"Of course," Lisette said. She scooted from the chair and went over to the couch, where her bag rested and pulled out the box.

Making her way back to the kitchen table, she sat down and opened up the box. She handed it across the table to Martha, where it dropped into her open hands. I sat next to Lisette and watched Martha's reactions.

"It feels so light and warm—I know it's so powerful." She lifted it up, and her eyes scanned it. "I'm so surprised she gave this to you."

"Me too." Lisette clasped her hands together.

"This wand Marie Laveau created, according to the stories I heard from my great grandparents and parents, is one that has never been duplicated. Many witches and warlocks have attempted, but all were unsuccessful. Whatever spell and ingredients she utilized for this is immeasurable to any wand before and after."

"Yes, I recall some of those stories, as well, Martha."

She handed it back to Lisette. "You make sure you keep this in a very safe place because it has been sought out by many and continues to be."

DOLL³

"Definitely will do that," my cousin said.

"Can you imagine if Esmerelda would've given this to Verlinda?" Martha mumbled.

"Oh, I don't even want to. Verlinda's intentions, all awful."

With my mouth full of pie, I said, "Second that one."

Lisette rewrapped the wand up, placed it back in its home, and then inside of her bag.

"Martha, thank you again for allowing us to stay here." Lisette bent down to hug her.

"All my pleasure to have you both. If you ever need a place to stay in Salem, then know my home is open for you both, anytime."

"Same here, Martha," Lisette said.

"Thank you, Miss Martha."

"You're so welcome, Tomie. You learn all you can about your new gift. By the way, did you both get by Proctor's Ledge?"

Lisette and I both looked at each other. "We did," Lisette said.

"Did you learn anything, Tomie?"

"Oh, yeah."

"Not everyone who goes there does," Martha said, rubbing her hands together.

"I guess some don't allow themselves to see," I said.

"Well, Tomie, it's time." Lisette swung her backpack on her shoulder.

"Be safe you two. I'll be thinking of you both. I placed something in Lisette's bag for you both," Martha said.

"You've done more than enough, thank you."

"You're very welcome."

She hugged me and whispered in my ear, "Take care of yourself. Look me up if you're in Salem again."

I took five steps back to stand next to Lisette. We stood in the middle of Martha's living room. Lisette grabbed my hand, and we levitated a few inches off the ground, spinning around a few times.

We closed our eyes, and within several seconds, we were back, standing in Lisette's living room. Everything looked the same as it was before we had left, but I heard something jiggling in the background

CHAPTER
SIXTEEN

LOUD FOOTSTEPS POUNDED ON THE FLOOR FROM THE hallway, approaching closer. Lisette turned around and so did I. Bells jingled back and forth. She looked at me and smiled.

Carrying a kennel on his shoulder, Crow appeared in the living room. Lisette leaped near his chest and peeped inside. Sabra's head bobbed up and down, and she made high chirping noises.

Lisette opened up the cage and lifted her out. Crow removed the kennel from his shoulder. He bent down to kiss Lisette on her forehead and slapped me on my shoulder. We all walked into the kitchen.

When I passed Sabra, she looked into my eyes. I went to pat

her on her head, and she stretched out her tiny paws, as if she was attempting to fist bump my hand.

Crow washed his hands at the sink. He turned off the faucet and tore a paper towel from the stand, resting a hip against the sink. "So, y'all got a lot of things taken care of on your little Salem trip?"

I sat down in a chair, facing him. "You can say that."

"Good. Glad y'all are back."

"Salem was interesting and a nice change, but it's great to be back in good ole' Monroe Creek, pretty much my second home." I clasped my hands behind my neck. "Sure Lisette will give you the full 411 later."

"She's in another world right now," Crow said in a low and deep voice.

Lisette took Sabra out of her cage and cradled her in her arms, leaning against the island.

"I see. So glad Sabra came out okay, after her little accident and all," I said.

"Agreed."

"Thank goodness everything worked out in her favor, Lisette."

"Yes. The vet released her a day early and said she should be back to her normal self in a few weeks," Crow said.

"Great news, Crow." I smiled.

"Well, I'm going to head on out. See you both soon. You have a little more time here before you head back to Frost, right?"

"Yep. Have a good night and tell Caya hello for me when you talk to her again."

"Sure will. Good night." He kissed Lisette on her cheek and patted Sabra, lightly, on her head.

"Thank you for picking her up." Lisette stared into his eyes.

"Anything for my baby." He winked at her.

Crow left, and I locked the back door with a wave of my hand. I jumped in the shower and brushed my teeth. As I went to my bedroom, I noticed Lisette walking back and forth in her bedroom, still cradling Sabra in her arms.

She didn't see me; I smiled as I closed my bedroom door behind me. It was close to midnight, and my eyes were telling me it was sleep time, so I plugged my phone to its charger, set my alarm, and fell onto the bed. My body had been busy over the last few days, and sleep came without any effort.

To my surprise, I woke up the next morning before my alarm sounded. While resting on my back, I picked my phone off the table. I was about to text Sari, but she beat me to it.

S: **Hey. Fell asleep early. Missed your text**

T: **I figured u did. U okay?**

S: **Yes, why?**

T: **Been worrying about u and wondering if your dad ripped you a new 1**

S: **I didn't know he got a work call to be out of town until next week, but my mom knows I was with u**

T: **How did she find out?**

S: I don't know, but somehow she just knew I wasn't at Luckie's like I lied about. I was about to tell her the truth 2

T: That's good u were going to be honest with her. Proud of my girl

S: Whatever

T: So, u got your cell phone privileges restored?

S: Let's just say Mom is allowing me to use my cell until Dad returns

T: Oh… I've always liked your mom

S: She's always liked u 2. We had a really good talk. She gets me, Tomie. Plus, she told me a story about a boy she was in love with when she was our age, and her dad didn't support her either

T: Wow, your mom is really cool

S: Guess u can say that. Hey, how's it been going?

T: A lot has happened, Sari

S: Tell me

T: Way too much to text about. I'll get to tell you more face to face, soon

S: Okay, but give me a clue

T: All right, I'll give you two. Starts with an "s" and horrible murders happened there many, many years ago

S: Umm… Salem???

T: Yes

S: You went to Salem, Massachusetts?

T: Yep. Lisette and I did

DOLL³

S: **Oh, my gosh, u so have to tell me more! You know I did my sophomore history research paper on the Salem Witch Trials**

T: **I don't remember that**

S: **Hey, Mom's calling me. We're going school shopping this morning. I go to work later this evening**

T: **Okay. I gotta get up and get ready. Sabra is back home and doing well**

S: **That's so good to hear. Know Lisette is thrilled. I can only imagine how she thought she could've been gone**

T: **I know. At least some positive things are happening around here**

S: **Always a good thing, especially with all that's happened and what's to come**

T: **I know, right. Hey, how's Phoenixx's dad?**

S: **Last I heard, he was still in the hospital. Should find out more soon**

T: **Cannot wait to see u again**

S: **Same here. Luv u**

T: **Luv u back, girl. Talk soon**

S: **Yes, hopefully even after my dad gets back in town**

I ended the text with a GIF of Scooby Doo barking out, "Hope so, Shaggy." She sent a GIF of pink flower petals falling down and forming a beating heart. Smiling, I placed my phone on the table and rolled out of bed and got dressed.

As soon as I opened up the door, Sabra was laying down

a few feet away from my doorway. She hobbled towards me. I scooped her up. "Hey, there, lady. So good you're home." She nodded her head, as if she knew what I was talking about. Heck, for all I knew, maybe she did. I held her in my arms and paid special attention to her splinted leg. We entered the kitchen.

Lisette was at the stove. I could smell cinnamon, raisins, and caramel. Whatever she was cooking was causing my stomach to start growling. I looked up at the clock on the wall. It was almost ten-thirty.

"Smells good, as always. What you cooking?"

"French toast and turkey sausage. Sit down and get comfortable."

"Can I help you with anything?"

"Oh, no. I'm almost done."

"Sabra, is looking better and better each time I see her."

"Yes, I know." Lisette turned around. "I placed some special healing oil on her last night."

"Looks like it's really working." I put her in her fluffy bed. "Has she eaten?"

"Yes, I fed her earlier, medicated her, and we went on a short walk, too. She'll probably drift off to sleep soon."

I washed my hands at the sink.

Lisette placed a platter of food in the middle of the table.

"I need to teach you as much as I can about your new gift, along with help from Mr. Ray and Crow."

"Sounds like a plan. You know, I didn't even think about Crow. It makes so much sense—they're shifters, too. Caya, as well, but I know she's busy caring for her mom."

"Yes, she has been. I've been meaning to ask you. How did it feel when you experienced the blue glow at the festival?"

I finished chewing. "You know, it came on so fast and vanished. Initially when I noticed, it felt super warm."

"You mentioned Garth triggered the glow from your hands and in your eyes?"

Wiping my mouth with a napkin, I nodded. "Yes."

"That's interesting how this new power of yours is emerging now."

"Why is that?"

"Shapeshifters usually know earlier on about their abilities."

"Guess you can count late bloomer twice in my case."

We both laughed.

"Wander what my unique shift will be?"

"Not sure yet—soon we'll all know, right?"

Slapping my hands together, I rubbed them back and forth. "Sure will. When do we start our training?"

"As soon as Mr. Ray and Crow arrive, which will probably be anytime now. I talked to them both this morning while you were still asleep."

I helped Lisette clear the table and clean up the dishes.

"By the way, Sari texted me."

"How is she and things at home?"

"Her mom knew she was here and is allowing her to use her cell again, while her dad is out of town. Not sure if that will last once he returns."

"Wonder if her mom will share with her hubby?" Lisette finished drying the last plate and handed it to me to place in the open cabinet.

"Hope not. Sari said her mom understood and all. She's always been a fan of mine. Sari's mom knows her husband, Mr. Green, has never cared for me."

"I have a feeling she'll keep that between her and Sari, a mother and daughter bonding thing. Some things are better left unshared."

Shutting the cabinet door behind me, I said, "Hope you're right, because if her dad gets even a little whiff of Sari being with me, then I don't want to imagine how he'll use that to retaliate against me."

"Tomie, seriously, you really think he'll do something?"

"Possibly. He warned me in a past text to stay away from Sari or else."

"That's ridiculous." Lisette's face scrunched up, as she rolled her eyes, placing her right hand on a hip.

"Couldn't agree more with you. He knows about me." I slid against the counter to sit.

"How?"

"Don't know. He knows what I am and about the Pepper Fox incident."

Lisette rested her other hand on her hip, looking up at me. "He's talked to someone?"

"There's a connection between him and Mr. Fox, but I haven't figured that one out just yet."

"Maybe it's work related."

"Don't think Sari's dad and Mr. Fox work in the same field."

Mr. Ray appeared next to me, and I jumped, descending from the counter.

"Dang! You're going to have to give me some kind of warning when you do that. Freaks me out." My hands ran through my curls.

"Sorry, Tomie. I'll try to remember to do something next time to give you a warning." He grinned, massaging his beard with his hand.

"Thank you, Mr. Ray. Good to see you, though."

"Same here. Heard about your Salem experience, especially your new gift."

"I'm psyched to learn how to use my shifting abilities."

"Bet you are. Now, you do understand that you being a warlock and shifter are extremely rare?"

"Yes." I threw up the okay hand sign. "I wondered if I could. Remember on our drive up here for the summer, I asked you about it."

"Of course. I couldn't answer that question for you at the time because I didn't know. I must confess that you're the first warlock-shifter I've ever met face-to-face. I've heard maybe two stories about other witches and warlocks possessing the gift. It's an honor to be able to train you to shift to the best of my capabilities, young Tomie."

"Really, it's no big deal, Mr. Ray."

Lisette came up to me and wrapped her hands around my face. "Oh, but it truly is, Tomie. I cannot even begin to express how unique you are. In a sense, I've always known there was something truly special about you, and now more is being revealed."

Mr. Ray nodded. "Well, I'm ready. Are you, Tomie?"

"Let's do this."

CHAPTER
SEVENTEEN

WE ALL SETTLED IN THE LIVING ROOM.

I thought back to how I wanted nothing to do with becoming a *supra* when I first was confronted with the truth. All I had wanted was to ignore who I was. In fact, I'd hated being someone like this, but I think I had been more afraid of hearing what I was becoming, and how others would perceive me when they found out—a freak.

There was also a time when I'd hated who I was because of what stared back at me when I looked in a mirror. All that self-hatred because of what someone used to think of me, specifically Pepper Fox, during my junior high and early high school years. I wasn't sure when I'd let go of her lies about me, but I just did one day.

I felt so empowered when I peeled back those layers of deceit placed on me by someone else for so long. I just wanted to train harder and learn how to use my new gift.

Lisette snapped her fingers a few times in front of my face. "Earth to Tomie."

"Deep thoughts. Sorry." I shook my head.

"I knew you were somewhere else. You probably didn't hear anything I just said to you."

"Nope, please repeat."

"Okay, pay attention this time." Her eyebrows rose above her sparkly pink and grey eye shadow.

"Mr. Ray was asking me about the glow you experienced. I told him it was the color blue."

"That's correct," I said. "Why?"

"Oh, it tells me that you're a powerful shifter," Mr. Ray said in a gruff and low tone.

"Miss Martha and Lisette mentioned that back in Salem, but I still don't understand what that means."

"Tomie, being a shifter allows you to manipulate yourself out of certain situations, or better yet, conquer them, pending the type of shift."

"Mr. Ray, when did you know you would be a *Mega*?"

"I was pretty much assigned the role, when I was much younger than you."

"Assigned?" A slight frown painted my face.

"Yes, my family comes from a long line of shifters who are

then assigned a specific role. In my case, my dad granted me the *Mega* role to fulfill. He trained me early on and showed me why I was vital in the *supra* world. Transformation was not an easy task to master—something my dad spent much time to teach me."

"Were both you parents, *Megas*?"

"No. My mom was a shifter. My mom taught me the duties of that role."

"That's great you had parents there to coach you." My head drooped.

Mr. Ray placed his hand on my shoulder, "Hey, your dad did the best thing for you."

Looking up at Mr. Ray, I admitted, "He did."

"By accepting who you are, and allowing Lisette and myself to train you."

"Tomie, I'm not here to replace your mom."

"Lisette, I know."

"Mr. Ray and I are both here to help you through your new journey. Anything that we can do to make it easier for you, then we will, Crow too."

"Believe me, I know you all are, and I so appreciate that," I sniffled. "Thank you both."

"You're so welcome," Lisette said.

Mr. Ray nodded.

"Ready to practice?" Mr. Ray asked.

"Sure am. What's first?"

"As with most practices, you're going to need to concentrate," Lisette whispered.

"Okay."

"Close your eyes and count backwards, starting at twenty," Mr. Ray requested.

I followed his instructions. In my mind, I could sense this was not the time to play around with either one. They both meant serious business. I'd read about shifting in books, comics, and saw it in a few horror movies.

My curiosity about the ability had always been something I'd thought about, deeply. Now, I was in the driver seat to soon transform into something, but I was clueless about what the end result would be. Maybe I possessed limitations on what I could actually change into. I figured I would soon have the answers to that question and many others before too long.

"Tomie, you should be close to one by now," Mr. Ray said. "Keep your eyes closed. Tap your side once for yes and twice for no."

I tapped once.

"Okay, we're going to start off small and build up by transforming little things about yourself. Understand?"

I tapped once.

"Change your eye color from green to blue."

"How?"

"Concentrate. Think of what that color means to you. See it in front of you."

DOLL³

After a few tries, the ocean came to me, so I focused on that. I thought about the blue waves rolling in and out on the shoreline. I also thought of Sulley from *Monsters, Inc.* My hands started to feel warm, as if someone had flipped a hand lighter open and flicked it until a flame burst.

"Open your eyes," Mr. Ray commanded in a deep tone.

I opened them and noticed how my hands were glowing an iridescent blue color; I touched my eyelids with the tips of my fingers. They tingled with warmth. Lisette traveled into the guest bathroom; she returned with a hand held mirror. She sat down next to me, holding it in front of my face. "Look."

Staring in the mirror, I noticed how my eyes were a Sulley-deep ocean blue. My hands continued to glow. "Mr. Ray and Lisette, I really didn't think it would work."

"Tomie, you did your first personal shift very well," Lisette complimented.

"Thanks... I don't look bad with blue eyes. What do you think? Keep or ditch them?"

"Either way," Mr. Ray said.

"Honestly, I love your green eyes. They're part of who you are," Lisette shared.

"I get it. So, how do I turn them back to my original color?"

"Un-visualize that color and focus on your original eye color. Then, blink three times," Mr. Ray said.

After following his directions, I picked up the mirror. My eyes were back to their normal color, with a little blue bleeding into the green on my right eye. I blinked one more time, and the blue was completely gone.

"This is lit! Soon, I'll be able to change different things about myself?"

"Yes, you will. Once you've practiced a few times, the transformations will occur faster for you," Mr. Ray explained.

"Okay, so what's next?" I asked.

"Enthusiasm is good, Tomie." Mr. Ray laughed. "Change your hair from curly to straight."

"Really?"

"Absolutely."

For a few minutes, I stared at Lisette's hair. My hands began to glow again, and I reached up to touch a strand of her hair, which started glowing like my hands. Then, I reached up and ran my hands through my semi-tight curls. I shook it out a few times. Lisette's mouth dropped, and Mr. Ray's eyes widened, as if he were in owl form.

"Tomie, you need to see your hair right away," Lisette screamed, handing me the mirror.

I stared into the mirror, and my hair was wavy and straight. "Whoa! Didn't expect that at all." I thought I could rock this Momoa look, not as good as him, of course.

"You're really doing well with this," Mr. Ray said, smiling.

Staring in the mirror, I said, "Thanks. How long will my hair look like this?"

"Concentrate and command it back into existence, Tomie,"

Mr. Ray said.

Closing my eyes, my hands glowed again, and I ran them through my loose, wavy hair seven times. My curls were restored. I could feel the s-shaped strands bounce all through my hands.

"Very impressive," Lisette said.

Drumming my feet against the floor, I asked, "What's next, Mr. Ray?"

Mr. Ray stroked his beard a few times, contemplating my next transformation lesson. These last two were nice—I hadn't been sure if I would be able to pull them off.

If I was capable of making these changes with myself, then what else could I do?

"How do you feel about those two transformations?" Mr. Ray asked, as he stood up and ambled over to the door, turning around.

"Pretty good. Wondering what's next."

"Tomie, I know you're anxious. I don't want to rush through everything, although time is moving fast."

I stood up and shook my hands out, rotating my head to the right and then to the left. I made my way to Mr. Ray. "What are you thinking?"

Lisette remained on the couch, watching our interactions.

"It really will be interesting to find out what your primary shift will be. Every natural shapeshifter possesses his or her dominating shift. For me, I transform into an owl whenever I desire. There are other things I can transform into, but an owl is my principal," Mr. Ray shared.

I leaned against the wall, turning my head to face him. "Never knew you had others."

"Yes."

"Like what else can you shift into?"

"An eagle and hummingbird."

"Seriously, Mr. Ray?" I squealed.

He nodded.

"I wasn't aware of that," Lisette commented. She lifted her legs on the couch and stretched out. "I only thought you could transform into an owl."

"Well, I have some flexibility in my shifting," Mr. Ray replied.

"How do you know what your principle shift will be?" My eyes gaped.

"It will be your total first transformation."

"What can I do to make that happen?"

"Nothing, Tomie. The change will happen all on its own, especially after your recent changes. Sometimes, a special spell can serve as a catalyst to trigger the shift."

"Do all shifters glow?"

"No, only rare ones, like you, Tomie," Lisette said, resting her hand on the side of her face.

"Really?"

"Yes, it's true." Mr. Ray twirled the end of his mustache

with his finger.

"My mom gave me this gift."

"Tomie, what did you just say?" Lisette popped up from the couch.

I smiled. "You heard me the first time."

"What Lisette?" Mr. Ray asked with a frown.

"For him to mention his abilities as a gift is ground-breaking because once upon a time, Tomie wanted nothing to do with becoming a warlock. He perceived it as a *curse*."

"Oh," Mr. Ray said, eyebrows shooting up.

"Yes, Lisette, is right, but all that has changed, especially with what happened at prom, my encounter with my mom, and the festival ordeal."

"Sometimes, it takes certain things to fall into place before we can actually believe. We all have our own pace." Mr. Ray patted me on my shoulder. "Enough for now. We'll start back again soon."

Opening the front door, he faced us. "Glad you both are back, safe and sound. You never know the outcome, when you encounter a Dark Shadow Witch."

"Very true, Mr. Ray," Lisette said.

"I hope that was our last encounter with her." My head fell back, and I took several deep breaths.

"Remember to keep the wand somewhere in a special place where you only know, Lisette," he instructed.

"Already covered." She winked at him.

"I must say I'm really shocked Esmerelda gave that to you. I really thought that wand was destroyed many years ago."

"Think many believe that," Lisette replied.

"I'm sure you're right. Well, I better go. Great work today, Tomie."

"Thanks. I couldn't do any of this without you or Lisette."

He smiled and placed his hands in his pockets. Once the door closed behind him, I locked it with a nod.

"What's next?"

"Rest for now."

"When do you think I'll shift completely for the first time, Lisette?"

"Tough question. It could happen at anytime, even when you're sleeping." Her index finger tapped her right temple.

I sat down on the couch to face her. "That would be strange."

"Really curious when it will happen, Tomie, and what you will transform into, honestly. I was very impressed with you today. For me to change my eye color or hair like you did, I must choose a spell. Consider your new gift a huge luxury that many *supras* would dream to possess."

Glancing down at my watch, I noticed it was past six. My practice with Mr. Ray had lasted longer than I thought. Lisette sat up, stretched, and stood.

"Going to feed Sabra and take her outside for a while."

"Want some company?"

"Sure, that would be nice."

DOLL³

Sabra's head popped up, and she tumbled out of her bed. Hobbling towards Lisette, I almost stooped down to pick her up, but Lisette signaled me not to. Sabra made it to the bowl Lisette placed near her feet. She consumed all her food.

I went to my room to grab my cell and Sabra followed me. I paused a few times, so she could catch up. Lisette was waiting for us in the kitchen. "Ready?"

"Yes."

We walked outside. No floating clouds decorated the open sky, only the sun. Lisette placed Sabra down on the ground. She pointed at the gazebo up ahead, and we made our way towards it. We sat on the steps, watching Sabra play in the grass. A tree arched over us, providing shade.

"This has been one of the most stressful summers I've ever experienced." My hands trembled.

Lisette slanted her head. "I understand, Tomie, so much has been thrown your way in a short amount of time."

She squeezed my hands, but they continued to shake for a few more seconds.

Staring down at the ground, I said, "Don't get me wrong, Lisette, I've learned a lot. Met some amazing people and others I never have to see again, such as Garth and Ash. When I think about everything, there are two things I wish I could change."

"Tell me."

"For one, crushing hard on Pepper in junior high and inviting Opal into my life." I lifted my hands up to cover my face.

"Hey, no need to beat yourself up." Lisette stroked the side of my arm. "We all have regrets. Know that they can either make you stronger or weaker—your choice."

"Yeah." A weighted sigh fell from my lips.

"Look at what you've accomplished."

"Lisette, I want you to know I really appreciate everything you've done for me during my time here with you, especially being so patient with me and never hesitating to teach me things. I'll never forget that."

"Tomie, it was all in you. I just helped you along the way to discover who you are, and what you needed at the time."

"My confidence levels have never been so high. That would have never happened, if it wasn't for you in my life."

She smiled. "Stop it."

"Summer is soon coming to an end. I'll go back to Frost. Sure much awaits me, there."

"Whatever it is, you'll be prepared. Know that I'm here for you."

"Yeah, I know, Lisette. Guess I've gotten so used to you being around and being here."

I knew there would be times Lisette couldn't be with me, and I needed to start preparing myself for that absence. Batman fought many fights alone before and after Robin showed up, and that's what I would have to psych myself up to do, as well. She had shown me how to use my tools against my villains.

"Remember, you won't be alone when it's time to face the

inevitable, whether it occurs in Frost or in Monroe, okay?" Running her hand through my hair, she asked, "Do you still struggle with choosing light or dark magic?"

CHAPTER
EIGHTEEN

HER QUESTION CAUGHT ME BY SURPRISE, AND I thought about it for a minute. "You know, after our encounter with Esmerelda back in Salem, I don't as much."

"Why?"

"Remember when she placed my hand on her crystal ball?"

"Yes."

"Not only did she see the past stuff about Verlinda, but I also saw some of her stuff. Guess I *glimmed* her." My upper body shivered, and I started hiccupping for about two minutes before they went away.

"Tomie, why didn't you say something before now?"

"Lisette, I wanted to tell you—just wasn't the right time, you know? Plus, I almost wet my pants. Kinda figured she knew that I saw." My knees started shaking.

"Hey, I understand. I'm glad we're talking about it now. Thanks for telling me." She patted my shoulder. "What did you *glim* about her?"

"Dark stuff, like using crazy torturing devices and levitating bodies from fresh graves. It didn't give me any fuzzy feelings, you know."

Lisette's closed mouth parted.

"Besides dark magic, Lisette, when I heard those screams and saw those horrid images back at Proctor's Ledge, it made me think about something."

"What?"

"Witches and warlocks can choose light or darkness, but so can humans. Those witches were targeted and murdered for no reason. Humans are just as capable of practicing darkness, even if it's not magic."

"Very true."

Sabra popped her head up for a few seconds, repositioning herself in the grass between Lisette and me.

"With all that I've seen, I've come to the decision to not travel that dark road after all. I wouldn't ever want to be anything like Verlinda or Opal, especially not Esmerelda, a wicked, wicked witch you wouldn't ever want to cross." My muscles tensed up all over my body.

Lisette leaned in, wrapped her arms around me, and hugged me. "So happy to hear that."

"Figured you would be."

She released me.

"Hey, you were going to tell me about your experience with the dark arts, remember, Lisette?"

"Oh, I do. Since you've made your decision, you sure you want to hear about that?" She moaned and rubbed her hands along her shoulders.

I nodded.

Lisette was silent for five minutes before she started.

Closing her eyes half shut, she said, "Shazzia, my best friend, invited me to a house party one Saturday night. It was my sophomore year in high school. The party was pretty wild like, *House Party*, the movie with Kid-n-Play, you've watched, right?"

"You know it. How do you think I got all these incredible dance moves?" I laughed.

"I was having a great time, talking and dancing. Shazzia and I were in the kitchen, including a few others—Ash, Garth's brother being one. She made frozen drinks in a blender and poured the purplish slush in plastic cups. She slid one over to me, but I was hesitant to drink it."

"Okay, I see two things so wrong with this right now—alcohol and Ash."

Staring down at her feet, she said, "I wished I would have seen that, back then. I must confess this was my first time drinking alcohol, Tomie."

DOLL³

"Lisette, I'm not even going to tell you when I had my first drink."

"Believe me, I wish I hadn't made that choice to drink that night. I haven't thought about that night for a while, until recently."

"Don't want to upset you. We can talk about something else, you know?" I placed my hand on hers and gave it a tender squeeze.

"This is important for you to hear. I think it will benefit you in more ways than one. So, getting back to where I was... I took a few sips. It was really sweet, like grape soda. I think I drank half of it before we saw a crowd rush out to the backyard—a fight had broken out. I turned around and placed my drink on top of the refrigerator. We all ran outside to see."

Tightening my eyes, I said, "I'm sure it was Ash, beating on some poor freshman who weighed under a hundred pounds."

"It wasn't. I was surprised, too, because a fight involving him usually included someone he could easily bully. His eyes were focused on me all night. It seemed wherever I went, he was not far behind, just watching me like a pacing vulture after fresh road kill."

Lisette rubbed her left arm up and down with her hand.

"Sounds like stalker trouble." I frowned.

"We all returned to the house, after someone broke the fight up. The DJ turned on a slow jam, and most of the guests danced, while others returned to what they were doing before that all started up. I found my drink where I had left it, and finished it off with about three slices of pizza."

I gripped her hand firmer and quieted to tune into her every word.

"Within a few minutes, I felt very light headed. So, I sat down to rest and closed my eyes. When I opened them, I saw my translucent body sitting on the table in front of me."

"Lisette, it sounds like someone drugged your drink."

"Someone did."

"One guess, Ash?" My heart started beating fast, and my nostrils flared in and out. I clenched my fists to the point where my nails pierced my palms and blood dripped down my leg. After a minute, the bleeding ceased and the markings vanished. "Lisette, you don't have to continue."

She took in a few deep breaths and tilted her head back as tears ran down the side of her face. I wiped her face.

"I told Shazzia I needed to lay down for a bit. She led me upstairs to her bedroom."

"Did she know something was wrong?"

"No. I think she just figured the alcohol in the drink was too much for me, being my first time, and I needed to sleep it off. She slid my sandals off my feet, lifted my legs up in bed, and placed a blanket over me. Before she left out, she told me she would be back soon to check on me, and the door closed behind her."

"Wish she would've stayed with you." I scooted closer over

to her and wrapped my arm around her. She rested her head on my chest.

"Yeah, me too, but I'm sure she figured I would be safe in her room. Anyway, I could barely hear the thudding music from downstairs. My eyes begin to feel heavier and heavier, and I had trouble keeping them both open. A faint light shined from the door. I couldn't make out who entered because my vision was growing fuzzy."

Her tears increased and her body began to shake, so I held her tighter. I whispered, "Hey, you know that I admire you so much. I don't think I could be as strong as you are now, if something like what you're about to share, happened to me." I kissed her lightly on her forehead and rested my chin on top of her head.

"That means so much to me. Thank you." She tapped the side of my face with her hand, burrowing her head deeper into my chest.

"Within seconds, Tomie, I felt the blanket being pulled down off my legs. I tried to lift myself up. Yet, my body felt as if someone had stacked a thousand bricks on top of my chest." Her voice cracked several times.

Tears streamed down my face and my lips trembled. Before they fell down on her, I swiped my face with my free hand.

"Whatever that drug that ass—I mean, Ash—slipped in your drink really affected you in bad way. You couldn't even use your powers?"

Lisette paused for a while before she went on.

"No. It was as if my witching abilities had been shut off. I'm sure it was a side-effect of the drug. Tomie, I tried to open my mouth to scream, yet nothing came out… I felt clammy hands moving up my legs and then under my jean skirt. I tried to kick whoever it was on top of me, but my legs felt so numb that I couldn't even move them. His hot breath smelled like stale anchovies, dried pepperoni, and beer. He covered my mouth with his oily, hot hand."

I held her tighter.

Her heart was beating really fast. She paused again.

"Tomie, he didn't stop, and I couldn't yell out for help. Although I saw a therapist for a while, I still think sometimes… it was my fault. I never should've had alcohol that night."

"Lisette, look at me." She lifted her head up, slowly. "None of it was your fault! Ash took full advantage of you that night, and guys like that are pathetic jerks. I hate it when girls say that because it's the guy's choice, always, to rape someone, which leaves *eternal* scars for her to deal with. She's trapped, while he usually runs free with no freaking consequences!" I yelled, feeling my face heat up.

Lisette sat up and pulled away from me some. Her puffy emerald eyes were smeared with mascara, and she stared deep into mine.

"It's been almost four years since I've talked about this with someone, besides my therapist. You're the first guy I've ever told."

147

Tipping my head to the side and clearing my throat, I said, "Really? Means a lot to me, Lisette. Crow knows nothing about any of this?"

"No. I may share with him one day." She bowed her head back down.

Lifting her chin up with my hand, I said, "Maybe you should give your therapist a call soon."

"I might just do that. It's funny how you think you've worked through something in your teen years, and it takes telling someone about it that you still have a lot more work to do."

"True. Did you report Ash to the police?"

"No, I chose to practice the *dark arts* after what happened to me that night. I figured the law wouldn't have been on my side, and he would've got off. I wanted to make sure he would pay." She squinted.

"Lisette, he had it coming."

Not only did I want to smash Ash like the Hulk, but a part of me also had a brief thought about wanting to hurt him in a bad way, even kill him. If I ever saw him again, then I was going to make sure, he really suffered.

"I craved darkness." She sneered.

"What did you do to him?"

"Shazzia helped me place curse on him. She blamed herself for what happened. She was a descendant of the *romani* people."

"*Romani*? I've never heard of them before."

"Gypsies… who came from India during the Middle Ages. Romani people were powerful *supras*. They possessed phenomenal and mind-blowing powers, such as telekinesis, levitation, astral projection, conjuring, illusion casting, and invoking curses and blessings. After what happened to me, I desired revenge, and she knew it."

"That's wicked!" My eyes locked with hers. "What kind of curse did you both place on Ash?" I leaned in towards her.

"One that can never be undone, regardless of the various uplifting spells someone may try. I met Shazzia at her house a week later, and we completed our dark deed, a transformation and withering curse."

"Are you telling me Ash wasn't born a rougarou?"

"No, he wasn't."

"So, a withering curse, what is that exactly?"

"For him to become impotent, and end up alone without ever finding someone to love, because back then, I thought how could a **beast** ever be capable of that, which gave me the idea about him becoming one. I knew it would become his lifelong burden, and if someone became close to him, Shazzia and I wanted to ensure every person would reject him."

"Man, you definitely gave him something, he can never get rid of." My lips curled upwards. "I think I would've made it worse for him."

"Yes, I loved witnessing or hearing about his torment. My

appetite for darkness increased, and I knew it would consume all of my thoughts and actions. I started feeling something foul growing inside of me. This is when I knew I needed to take a vow not to practice in the darks again."

I paused for a minute before asking her my burning question.

"How did the curse pass down to his brother, Garth?"

"Ash didn't want to be the only one and personally passed on his rougarou curse to Garth, probably by biting or scratching him one night, when he was in rougarou form, which proved his selfishness, even more."

"Heavy stuff you've kept inside of you, Lisette." I hugged her. "Thank you for sharing with me."

"Just wanted you to truly understand that some things can never be reversed, and how you must live with that each day."

"I get it. Ash doesn't bother you anymore, right?"

"No, but I know there's a big part of him that despises me. He moved away from Monroe Creek a few years ago. He still visits his brother and other family on certain occasions."

"That night when Crow and you saved me from Garth and Ash, Crow mentioned something about some kind of council dealing with them. What ended up happening to them?"

She nodded. "I'll let Crow tell you about that. He's coming by soon."

"Okay. Lisette, since you didn't place the curse on Garth, would you ever reverse it for him?"

She puffed out her chest and looked up into the sky. "No.

He's so much like his brother." She wiped her face with the back of her hand.

"Gotcha. Do you think Verlinda helped Garth and Ash with that spell, which withheld my powers at the plantation that night?"

"Doubt it. There are plenty of *supras* around here or in New Orleans they could've contacted easily to help them. What happened to you that night was a personal message from Garth because you befriended Caya."

"Yeah, I figured. Should've listened to you and Mr. Ray that night. Caya and Sari also tried to convince me not to go out there, but I did it anyhow." I lowered my eyebrows and popped my knuckles.

Lisette scooped Sabra up, placed her on her shoulder, and stood, looking out towards the water. "Sometimes, we have to experience things on our own. Next time, I hope that will serve as a reminder for you to make a different decision."

"You're right. Hope I don't run into Garth during the rest of my stay here."

"Tomie, if you do, then I don't think he'll mess with you anytime soon."

"Why do you think that?" I also stood, facing the water.

"Trust me." She smiled and squeezed my hand. "Ready to go inside?"

"Sure."

"Crow should arrive, soon."

CHAPTER
NINETEEN

As we headed back towards the house, I had a thought. "Do you think Phoenixx could be the Dupuy Silver Slayer?"

"I've been waiting for you to ask this question. When I first met him that night at the festival, I wondered the same, especially with the rude comment he made about crystal balls. Something about his aura was a bit off, too."

"Not shocked on that one. Wished I would've known about Opal's devious little plans before Sari and I got involved with her and then brought her to your home."

"There's no way you could've known that, Tomie. Your powers were dormant."

I shrugged.

"Now, since you've opened up that box, I'm not going to rule Phoenixx out just yet as the slayer. I found it interesting how he showed up in Frost the summer before your senior year and will be attending Frost High. Plus, he became friends with Sari awfully quick." Lisette's tone deepened.

"Agree. I think he tried to make a move on her at the festival, too." I wanted to confront him face-to-face, but figured Sari would've thought I was being the bad guy. So, I kept my emotions on the down low.

"Oh, you didn't tell me that." She cocked her head to the side and Sabra did, too.

"I forgot and so much was going on." I tucked my hands in my pockets.

"A lot happened that night, indeed, Tomie. You keep an eye on Phoenixx, and let me know if you notice anything else odd about him. However, don't dismiss the idea that the slayer could already be in Frost and just waiting for a sign to confirm that you're a *supra*."

"Like anyone in the school could be a potential slayer in disguise, Lisette?" My eyes blinked a few times.

"Anyone."

I started wondering who could be the possible slayer suspects. I sorta felt like a detective for a moment. Most slayers I'd read about or been told about had been all males. Could the slayer who was coming for me, be a female? My thoughts went to the new girl, Luckie, who'd befriended Sari, as well, at her job, even though she didn't attend Frost High, but Garrison High, our rival.

"Lisette, could a female be a slayer?" I ran my hand across my chin.

She gave me a puzzled frown. "I've never known of one. It's definitely possible. You're thinking about Sari's new friend, Luckie?"

"Yep."

"Honestly, I didn't pick up anything from her aura. Hers was pretty clean. Keep your eyes open on anyone you encounter giving you a weird vibe, okay?"

"Will do."

Just as we approached the house, Crow's truck pulled up. Lisette and I turned around and waved.

"I'm going to put Sabra down and get the table ready."

I spotted bags in the passenger seat. "Okay,"

"Need a hand?" I met Crow at the passenger's side open window.

"Sure, thanks, Tomie. I had it, though."

I picked up two bags up, and Crow carried a bag and grabbed a bouquet of wildflowers with a pink and green bow wrapped around them from the back seat. "Lisette, will love those."

"Hope so."

"Hey, Crow, can we talk later after dinner?"

"Of course, going to give me a hint?" He lifted his thick

eyebrows and slanted his eyes in my direction.

"Garth and Ash."

He gave me a nod. We walked up the stairs. I opened the door and allowed Crow to walk ahead of me. The table was set with glasses full of ice and a pitcher of lemonade with fresh lemons floating on top.

"Lisette is fast."

"She can be," he said.

We set the bags down in the middle of the table. Crow placed the flowers in front of Lisette's seat.

"How's Caya?"

"Good. She asked about you, Tomie. I'm sure she'll be by when she can."

"Her mom okay?"

"Well, she has good and bad days."

After dinner and my talk with Crow, I planned to text Caya to check on her. Crow and I pulled the warm Styrofoam boxes from the bags and placed them on the tablemats.

"Lisette, dinner is ready," I called out.

"Coming."

Pouring the glasses full of lemonade, I watched Lisette wrap her arms around Crow, and he swung her around twice. "Thank you for the beautiful flowers." She smiled.

He lowered her down. She sat and picked up the bouquet and took in a huge whiff. We all sat down at the table.

"What's the occasion?"

"None. I was thinking of you and saw them at a stand on my way over." He grabbed and kissed the back of her hand.

Lisette stroked the side of his face. I ate everything and half of Lisette's. The pecan pie hit the spot with a tall glass of cold milk.

"Tomie, you're curious about what happened to Garth and Ash?"

Wiping my mouth with a napkin, I balled it up. "Yes, I've been wondering about it."

I stood and picked up the trays, chucking them in the trash. Lisette ran some dishwater and washed the glasses and utensils. Crow scooted back in his chair and stood, walking over to the island. Lisette turned around and looked at Crow. She gave him a slight nod.

"Well, Tomie, they definitely were punished after their little incident with you. The rougarou tribal council recommended for their rougarou powers to be suspended for six months."

"How can the council do that, Crow?" I asked, twisting my mouth to the side.

"The tribal chief works closely with a local coven in town. She'll contact the leader when she needs spell assistance."

"Keep learning something new about this *supra* world all the time."

"Let's just say that Garth and Ash have been pushing their luck with the council for some time by doing things against the rougarou honor code. I think they were fed up with their misdeeds over the last year, and causing intentional harm to someone innocent—you in this case—in rougarou form."

"Council is strict."

"They are, and it's a good thing because without a council, wild or fledgling rougarous wouldn't be good here or anywhere."

"I believe you. I can only imagine if multiple Garths and Ashes existed with no consequences." I picked up my drink to finish it.

"Yes, it would be pretty difficult and place us in the bright spotlight for slayers to hunt us."

"You're telling me that you have to worry about slayers?" My voice halted.

Narrowing his eyes and brushing his eyebrows with his hand, he said, "Absolutely, Tomie. We used to be tracked down all the time, until a council formed to instill rules and punishment for rougarous. Without the council's existence and monitoring of suspicious or bad behaviors, more of our kind would be exterminated. The best way to avoid slayers is to stay hidden."

"Crow, rougarou history sounds similar to witches and warlocks."

"I know." Crow stretched out his muscular and hairy arms up in the air.

Lisette came over and touched Crow's hand.

Rougarous, witches, and warlocks had way more in common

than I'd ever imagined. It all made sense to me now how Lisette was attracted to Crow and vice-versa because of their related history. At first, I didn't understand the connection, since they were both different *supras*.

I think true love had nothing to do with finding the perfect mate more than finding the one person who actually got you, regardless of who or what that person may be. I never planned on falling in love with Sari. My eyes weren't on her, until one day, everything just made sense. Without any help from me, my heart figured it all out.

"Well, Crow, I bet Garth and Ash are furious."

He shrugged. "Possibly, but they both know the rules."

"Tomie, Crow and I are going to take a drive downtown and maybe check out a local zydeco band at Lafayette's. Would you like to join us?"

"Thank you, but I think I'm going to just chill. You two have fun. Tell me about the band."

"Will do, Tomie."

Lisette freshened up, and they left.

The front door was locked already from earlier, so I locked the back door. Grabbing a soda from the fridge, I popped the lid. Sabra watched me and quickly curled up in a ball in her plush bed. Then, she closed her eyes.

Making my way to the bedroom, I picked up my phone. I thought about what Crow said about Caya going back home, so I texted her to check in.

T: **Hey**

I had finished my soda before I finally got a reply.

C: **Hey back. Are u in Monroe Creek?**

T: **Yep. Heard u were at home. How are u? What about your mom?**

C: **I'm fine, and she's okay today. She was sick at her stomach earlier, probably from a new medication, but resting now. Thanks for asking**

T: **Sure. Mind me asking what's wrong with her?**

C: **She has lung cancer**

T: **Wow, Caya, I didn't know. Sorry**

C: **You don't need to be. She's had a good month, actually, compared to others. Crow and Lisette help out a lot. How are Lisette and Sabra? So much happened after the festival**

T: **They're good. Her and Crow are out on a date**

C: **Good for them. They so deserve it**

T: **I agree**

C: **Did Sari make it back home, ok?**

T: **Yes. Wish she wasn't so uncomfortable with u**

C: **Tomie, u and I know that she'll never be Team Caya**

T: **Yeah. Don't see you two ever being a Cher and Dionne**

C: **NOPE!!!!!!!**

T: **Will u be visiting here anytime soon?**

C: **Not sure, with Mom and all**

T: **I get it. Well, if u don't make it back this way, hope u**

keep in touch when u have time

C: **Sure. Tomie, look I gotta go. Thanks for checking on me. Really did enjoy training with u. C u around**

T: **No problem, Caya. Enjoyed 2. Talk later**

Although I was in denial early on about Caya's feelings about me, I sensed she had feelings for me that night, when we went out on Crow's airboat. Even though I knew I wouldn't ever be a Somerhalder heartthrob, a smile danced across my face whenever I thought how I was popular with the ladies.

I almost texted her back to talk about it, but I decided that wasn't a good idea. I just didn't want to say anything to hurt her feelings, as she was dealing with her mom's illness. She knew where my heart lived, but I think Caya's feelings for me didn't want to accept that.

Looking at the time, I saw it was after eight. I decided to take a shower early. As I was returning back to my room, fresh and clean, I heard my phone ringing. Sari's picture flashed on the screen.

"Hey, there, girl."

"What are you doing?"

"Just got out of the shower and was about to call you."

"Really?"

"Yes. What are you up to?"

"Not much. Thinking about and missing you."

"Missing you too."

She sighed. "Ever since you mentioned Salem, I've been

wanting to hear more."

"So much to talk about over the phone, plus it would be safer to share when I see you."

"Guess so…"

"You never know. Better safe than sorry."

"Totally understand, Tomie. What did you do today?"

"Some training with Mr. Ray, and Crow brought over dinner for us. Lisette and Crow just left a bit ago to listen to a band downtown."

"Nice… Have you talked to Caya lately?"

"Seriously, you're going to ask me that question?" I snapped.

"Yeah."

"I really don't want to go there with you, Sari." I sat down on the bed because I knew where she was going with this.

"Why not?"

"You already know. Let's just focus on you, us," I pleaded.

"Nope, I want to know if you've talked to her, Tomie."

"If I tell you, then will you drop it?"

"Probably."

"Okay, I texted her."

"Rewind, you texted her!" she yelled.

"Simmer down, girl, it wasn't a big deal."

"Why would you do that?"

"Sari, she's my friend. I was checking on her. Why are you acting like jealous, mean girl, Regina?"

"I'm not. I just don't know why you need to text her," she

mumbled in a brittle voice.

I could here her pouts pounding against the phone receiver.

"Sari, you okay? This is nothing to cry over, girl. You already know my heart belongs to you."

"Yeah," she whispered in a wobbly tone.

"Listen, I was calling to check on her because her mom is really sick."

"Oh."

"That's an acceptable reason for me communicating with her, now?"

She didn't respond.

"Look, you're going to have to learn to trust me, and I'm going to have to do the same with you. We'll both be leaving each other in a few months, and not just a few hours away, either."

"Tomie, I know. It's just... I know she likes you a lot."

"True, but she won't be the only girl who ever likes me, Sari."

She breathed in deep. "I know that."

"There will be guys who'll like you, too. I'm going to have to learn to deal with that."

"I just know how girls can be, if they're given a chance or misunderstand."

"That may be true. You know where I stand, Sari," I said forcefully.

"I do. Let's talk about something else."

"Sure. How did your school shopping go?"

"Good. Found some great sales."

"You always do. By the way, have you talked to Phoenixx?"

"I did. His dad is getting out of the hospital in a few days."

"Great for him. You do know he has a thing for you, right?"

"Who?"

"Seriously, Sari?"

"You think Phoenixx likes me?"

"Umm, yeah, I surely wasn't referring to his dad."

"He's just friendly." She giggled.

In a stern tone, I said, "Bet he is. Just watch out for him, okay, and all his friendliness."

"I will. Is there something I should be worried about?"

"Don't think so, at least not yet."

"Okay."

"How's Luckie?"

"She's fine." Sari yawned.

"Any plans tomorrow or this weekend?" I ran my fingers through my wet hair.

"Not really, early shift at work in the morning. Dad is returning soon."

"This may be the last time I talk to you until I see you, especially if he grounds you?" I winced.

"Don't think he'll do that because he won't know."

"You and your mom are really cool about all that?"

"Think so. I really never realized how cool she could be,

until recently."

Leaning back, I said, "I know I've said or thought things about how my dad gets on my nerves over the years and all. I take it all back and would give anything to have both of my parents in my life. You're so lucky, Sari, to have both parents. Even though your dad hates me, know that he loves you, and just wants the best for you."

"I hear what you telling me, but I'm not going to let my dad keep us apart, Tomie."

"Just don't want you to ever regret anything."

"Don't worry. My mom and I are going to have a long talk with my dad when he gets back."

"Hope that doesn't make things more tense between the two of you." I exhaled.

"Oh, well. He's going to hear what I need to tell him."

"You need to get some rest." I could hear her yawn under her breath again.

"Probably. Goodnight."

"Night, Sari."

I placed my phone on the table. I waltzed into Lisette's study and downloaded the Falcon Air Academy application from her desktop, which was almost five pages, including an essay. Within three hours, I completed it. Placing it in an envelope, I sealed it and wrote the address out with a black permanent marker.

My mind felt lighter. There were times when I contemplated

not even completing the application because I didn't want to be that far away from Sari. However, spending this summer discovering so much more about myself and the *supra* world, I came to the realization that I couldn't hold her back by trying to follow her.

She needed to go after her own dreams, and so did I. Our relationship would be in a delicate place in a few months, once we graduated from high school. I loved her so much. If letting her fly meant losing her, then I was willing to risk that. I knew my heart would never be the same if I did lose her, but she deserved to discover what she was capable of evolving into.

Sari had always been so amazing at encouraging me to focus and learn all I could from Lisette. Not once did she ever tell me to not go. I knew she needed to pursue her dreams to become the best fashion designer she could be. Maybe I'd get in the academy or not. Whatever happened, I knew there would be something else waiting for me, possibly in Frost or even here, in Monroe Creek.

Turning off the computer and making sure all was in place on Lisette's desk, I reached up to turn off the lamp. I noticed a mirror hanging on the wall above a painting. Distant headlights bounced off the mirror. I figured it was Crow and Lisette, but Crow usually drove around to the back of the house.

Marching over to the window, I pulled the curtain back to look out, squinting to make out the car driving down the dirt

DOLL³

road. Dust clouds encircled it. I rubbed my tired eyes. The bright moon seemed to beam down on the car.

My sight cleared. It wasn't Crow's truck, but an old black Cadillac, which had stopped and parked under a canopy of trees, almost twenty feet from Lisette's house.

The engine revved up a few times before it turned off, and the headlights dimmed until darkness greeted them. The curtain blew closed by itself and a crackly, low voice called out, "Tomie Dupuy. Come out, come out. Let's play truth or dare." That's when I knew—Verlinda Dawn awaited for me outside.

CHAPTER
TWENTY

CLOSING MY THROBBING EYES, I TOOK A FEW DEEPS breaths and teleported to Lisette's front porch without thinking twice. My body floated several inches from the ground. The passenger door opened up on its own and Verlinda slithered out. She wore a long, black cape with bell sleeves and lace.

Wisps of her silver hair blew across her wrinkled face. Her dark eyes were painted heavy with black eyeliner and mascara. A cigarette flew from one of her pockets and landed onto her chapped, orange lips. Barely touching the end of the cigarette with a jagged nail, it lit up.

She started approaching the house. The gravel made loud, clicking sounds as small rocks rolled under her shoes. When she tried to step onto Lisette's grass, the end of her cape caught on fire. Verlinda jumped back and put the fire out with the wave of her hand.

"Tricky, tricky one, Lisette. I must say this protection spell is quite extraordinary. I'm very impressed." She twirled around and levitated herself up several feet in the air with her arms crossed for a short time and then back down.

The spell prevented her from crossing over, even if she wasn't touching the ground itself, so I knew I was safe. Talons raked along the roof above me. An ivory feather with a purple tint fell on top of my hand. I glanced up and saw an owl staring down at me.

Shaking my head, I signaled to Mr. Ray with my hands to let him know I was fine. Mr. Ray focused on her. As I was about to levitate myself down to approach Verlinda face-to-face, I heard footsteps stomping heavily on the floor. The door flew open and Lisette appeared.

"Why didn't you call me, Tomie?" she roared. Her eyes zoned in at Verlinda.

Glancing down at her, I said, "I had it all under control, plus Mr. Ray is here."

"Come down here, now," she demanded.

Slowly, I levitated down to the ground, besides her.

"Tomie, never hesitate to contact me, okay?"

"Got it."

"Please! Can we stop with all the mushy this and that crap?"

Verlinda barked.

"Stay put," Lisette commanded, making her way down the steps towards Verlinda.

I could see Verlinda's braided smile, uncovering her rotten brown teeth. She laughed, pacing around her car.

My urge to disobey her request was about to explode. However, I remained where I was. Lisette had way more experience than me. She knew what she was doing and how to handle twisted Verlinda.

Lisette stepped outside her protective circle, levitating herself up. My foot started tapping, and my palms grew slick.

"Don't you think you need to stay inside your safe zone?" Verlinda snarled.

With a deep leer, she said, "Why are you here on my property, Verlinda?"

Verlinda's lips curled up, and her vicious black eyes shot over to me. "I just wanted to see how Tomie was doing with his training and all. I see you've been teaching him the basics."

"It's none of your business. What's the real reason you're here, Verlinda?"

She levitated back up and then backwards a little. "Like I mentioned earlier to Tomie, let's play a game."

"No time for your silly games," Lisette snapped.

"Have it your way, then." She levitated down next to her car door and started to open it up.

Silence reigned for twenty seconds.

"What game?" Lisette asked.

"One of my favorites, truth or dare."

"Are you serious?"

Verlinda nodded. "You first."

Lisette's mouth twisted in a scowl.

"I don't think you should, Lisette."

"Tomie, it's okay. Let me handle this." She gave me a wink and communicated with me telepathically.

I want to know what she knows. She's after something, Tomie. Plus, I have a question or two to ask her. The trick to this spell is how you answer.

Gotcha.

"Truth or dare?" Verlinda purred and rotated her tongue over her stained teeth.

"Truth."

Floating back up and rotating around Lisette, Verlinda pulled out a hand mirror with matted black fur encasing it. Staring into it, she chanted, "Lies welcome maggots, swamp wasps, and copperheads to torment your home for the next seven days." She spun around three times with the mirror facing Lisette, chanting the spell again. "Be careful, Lisette." She laughed.

Lisette's eyes danced up and down. "Your limited truth binding spell doesn't surprise me one bit, Verlinda. Know that if you lie, then the spell will activate against you, as well. You forgot to cover the mirror when you spoke the spell. Oh, it's too late to reverse it, so ask your two questions."

Verlinda's black eyes rolled. "Did you recently travel to Salem?"

Lisette confessed, "A trip to Salem did take place, Verlinda."

Verlinda nodded. "Your turn."

Lisette asked, "Truth or dare?"

"Truth."

"Were you the one who broke into my home a few nights ago and rescued Opal?"

She stared down at the ground for several seconds. I walked a little closer, so I could hear her response.

"No."

Lisette turned around with a puzzled look on her face. I was shocked because we both knew it had to be her who'd broken in that night, but we were both wrong.

Tomie, she's telling the truth. I glimmed her.

No way.

I'm afraid so.

"My turn, Lisette, truth or dare?"

"I think you know that all will be truths."

Her hideous smile reformed on her face. "Did you find what you were looking for?"

Lisette paused. "Think so."

"What was it?" She flew closer to Lisette.

Lisette put her hands up. "Close enough. I think we're done with this game, and it's time for you to leave, Verlinda."

Verlinda's forehead was painted with crinkles. They both landed on the ground.

She swiped her hand over her car door, and it swung open. Her body whipped around to face Lisette, cape swirling. "I made this trip here to warn you both that neither of you stand a chance once my final plan is fulfilled. I know Esmerelda gave you something. Take this warning. *We won't be defeated*!"

Lisette rested both of her hands on her hips. "Verlinda, whatever you think you have, then by all means, bring it, anytime, day or night. By the way, where are you keeping your precious Opal hidden?"

"Don't you worry about that. Tomie and she will get reacquainted very soon."

She slid down into her car seat, revved the engine a few times, placed it in reverse, and drove off with a trail of dust following her.

We headed toward the house. Lisette nodded at Mr. Ray. He hooted a few times, extended his wings, and flew off into the darkness.

When we entered the living room, Lisette locked the doors behind us. I couldn't bare the silence, so I asked, "What was that all about? Why would she even come here?"

Lisette sat down on the couch, and I sat, facing her. "Tomie, she was hoping to come inside and retrieve something. She wasn't anticipating her inability to do so. I know she's angry. Verlinda knows who broke into my house to rescue Opal."

She scrubbed her hands over her face.

"What do you think she was trying to find out?"

"I have a strong feeling she was fishing about the wand Esmerelda gave me."

"How would she know about that?"

"Believe me, she knows that it exists and would give anything to possess it for her nasty intentions. The one thing that I was thinking about the entire time she was here was…"

"Come on, Lisette, tell me."

"Why Esmerelda gifted me the wand and not her when she was there?"

I knew the wand was safe in the house and in a secret place in Lisette's basement. The special lock-out spell would keep Verlinda out.

"Maybe she just knew Verlinda didn't deserve that kind of magic, especially when she discovered the truth of what she did."

"Possibly. Just strange, Tomie."

My hands trembled. "Do you think she'll return?"

"No. Look, it's late. Get some rest. We'll talk more in a few hours."

I nodded and wandered down the hall to my room.

Crawling into bed, I thought about Verlinda's visit over and over again. I had a feeling she was definitely hoping to get more out of her little surprise visit. Maybe it was about the wand. All I knew was in time everything would become front and center, whether it would be here in Monroe Creek or Frost, like Lisette said earlier.

CHAPTER
TWENTY—ONE

SCRATCHES ON THE BOTTOM OF MY DOOR WOKE ME UP. I looked at my cell phone on the bedside table, and it was almost noon. Placing my hand on the doorknob, I turned it to open it and there was Sabra.

She hopped a few times next to the bed. I picked her up and set her next to my pillow. "What are you up to, lady?" Her cute chirping sounds started. I guessed she was trying to communicate with me that it was time to get up.

"Hey, are you decent?" Lisette asked, standing outside my door.

"Yeah."

She walked in, hooking a hooped earring in her ear. "See she found you."

"Yep."

"Get ready. The post office closes in an hour."

"Oh, yeah, Saturday hours, almost forgot. Be ready in twenty minutes."

"We'll get some lunch downtown." She scooped Sabra out of bed. "I'm going to take her outside for a bit. By the time I return, you should be ready, right?"

"You know it."

The door closed behind her, and I sat up on the bed, texting Sari.

T: **Hey, girl**

She didn't text back after a few minutes, so I took care of my bathroom business. I threw some clothes on and pulled my hair up into a tight bun with a rubber band. Before I walked out of my room, I noticed a reply from Sari.

S: **Hey, u know this is the day that my dad comes home**

T: **Almost forgot. Guess I'll know how all turns out if u don't text me anymore today or the next few weeks**

S: **Lol… not really. Hope it goes okay**

T: **Me 2. Whatever happens, know that we'll see each other soon**

S: **Yeah. What are u doing today?**

T: **Mailing my completed app and who knows**

S: **Very proud of u**

T: **Thanks, girrrrl. Just the waiting game now**

S: **Whatever, you got this!**

T: **We'll see in the next few months**

S: **Okay. Talk more soon, I hope**

T: **Me 2**

Several hearts followed after, and she did the same with a GIF of an animated Wonder Woman and Superman holding hands. Just thinking about her dad's reactions caused me to feel queasy. I picked my phone up, grabbed my envelope, locked the door behind me, and headed out back.

In the passenger's seat, Lisette was waiting and reading a book. I opened the car door and jumped in. "Hey, sorry, it took me a little longer. I was texting Sari."

"No problem. We'll make it to the post office before it closes."

After tossing the envelope in the backseat, I started the ignition. "Hey, what are you reading?"

"*Death's Intern* by DC Gomez."

"Hmm, interesting title. What's it about?"

"I know. Just started reading it. It's an urban fantasy story set in Texarkana. Actually, it's Caya's. She let me borrow it, and she suggested that I read it because it's about someone hunting down the homeless and stealing their souls, which she knew I could relate to on some level. With everything going on, I haven't had time to read it, but I'm making some time."

"Well, let me know when you're done. I may need to check it out and let Sari know. She enjoys reading books like that, too."

DOLL³

"Sure will. I think reading this, planning my wedding, and hearing your updates when you're back in Frost will keep me pretty busy."

"Bet it will. Have you found your wedding dress yet?"

"No, but I have a few ideas."

"I know you're excited."

She smiled.

I drove down the long gravel driveway, made a right onto the main road, and headed towards downtown. The post office was located across from a coffee shop. Once it was my turn, I handed the envelope to the post office clerk.

"All done, Lisette. Where to for lunch?"

"I know a place that fixes the best old-fashioned burgers and milkshakes, any flavor you desire, in town. It's a little mom and pop's diner."

"Sounds good. Tell me how to get there."

With her directing me, I drove us to the spot.

I parked the car and jumped out and went to open up the car door for Lisette.

"Thank you, Tomie. Do you do this for Sari?"

"Of course."

She patted me on my shoulder and whispered, "Good. There are not too many young gentlemen left."

We cruised up to the door. A hostess stood outside.

"May I have your names?" she asked.

Peeping inside, I could see it was a small, busy place with

square wooden tables and blue chairs. All the seats were taken, except one in the far corner. Pictures of celebrities who'd eaten there were spread all over the black and white checkered walls. Four full-screen televisions were posted near the bar. Lisette told the hostess our names.

The hostess returned a few minutes later. We went to step inside; however, she jumped in front of us. Startled, I looked at Lisette.

"Sorry, we're full," the hostess whined and looked away from us.

"Wait, what are you talking about? I see an empty table right over there." I pointed to the far end of the diner.

"Like I told you, we're full," she said, looking back at someone across the restaurant.

As soon as I saw the faux-hawk and braid, I knew exactly why we were being denied entrance to this place. He twisted his body around on the barstool and traveled toward us with a slow shuffle. His hands rested in his back pockets. Lisette noticed him, too.

"Well, well, look who's here, Tomie Dupuy and Lisette Laveau. Want to thank you both for the nice *gift* you gave me and my brother for the next six months."

In a caustic tone, I said, "Look, we're leaving now. We don't want any trouble with you, Garth." I could feel my hands tingling, as I squeezed my fists tight.

"By the way, I wouldn't come back here, because neither of

you would be allowed in. My uncle just purchased this place and new policies are enforced, as of right now. We reserve the right to refuse service to whomever we choose, whenever we want."

The hostess brought out a metal strip about the size of a regular envelope with eccentric symbols printed on it and handed it to Garth. He peeled tape off with his pointy, opaque nails and posted the sign up next to the entrance.

Lisette read it under her breath, "**No Witches or Warlocks Allowed.**"

My hand drifted up to touch the symbols, but Lisette pushed me back. I gave her a bewildered look.

"Wow, Garth, really? You're going to post a sign like that here?" I asked.

"Yep!"

"Tomie, let's get out of here," Lisette demanded.

"Better get out of here, both of you," he growled without showcasing his fangs, because they were temporarily off display.

My eyes fixed on his. He glared back at me and stumbled back two steps. My hands felt really warm, like the last time. I could hear my heart speeding up as I inhaled and exhaled.

"Hey... he's not worth it," Lisette whispered.

"It's not over, Tomie Dupuy! You just wait," Garth howled, clenching his fists.

"Give me the keys," Lisette commanded. "I'm driving."

I tossed her the keys and jumped in the car. Looking back in my side mirror, I could see Garth flailing his arms around and mouthing something I couldn't comprehend.

"You should've let me at him!"

"Absolutely not, Tomie. This is exactly what I'm talking about. You have to learn self-control. What about the next Garth you encounter?"

"I don't know." My eyes focused only on my glowing blue hands.

"Look at me. Yes, you do."

She waved her hands over the steering wheel, and the car drove on its own, while she placed her hand under my chin and turned it towards her.

"Focus and take in some deep breaths."

I obeyed; my glowing hands returned to normal.

"Lisette, I'm sorry. That Garth just knows how to get to me."

"Yeah, I can see that, but that's what he wants you to do. Can you imagine if you hadn't controlled your anger what may have happened in public?"

"It would've probably been bad."

"What else, Tomie?"

"My powers would've been seen by non-*supras*."

"Go on..."

"Trouble for us and making it easier for any of our enemies to detect us."

DOLL³

"Yes, Tomie, you need to practice more self-control whenever someone pushes your buttons. I'm really curious to see what your transformation will be. It wants to be set free. For some reason, the timing is not right for it just yet."

Rubbing my hands on my legs a few times, I said, "Heck, me too. I'm more than ready to see what I can do. What were those weird symbols, anyhow?"

"An old *Greek-Lycan* alphabet."

"Hold on, you're telling me that werewolves had their own alphabet system?"

"Yes, it was a way for them to communicate with each other and to be kept hidden among the non-*supra* world, especially slayers."

"So, that sign Garth put up will keep witches and warlocks out?

"Definitely. The sign is made from iron. Iron keeps our kind—"

"From crossing over."

"Exactly."

"Won't some witches feel bitter and try to go against him?"

"Witches have a enough to be concerned about, and trouble with a rougarou is something they'll avoid."

"Understand. By the way, I won't ever forget what iron feels like."

"I'm sure you won't, especially when you refused to heed the warnings, and you gave Garth the benefit of the doubt at

La Fantasma." She placed her hands back on steering wheel and resumed driving.

CHAPTER
TWENTY—TWO

W E RETURNED BACK TO LISETTE'S. MY MIND KEPT drifting to Garth. I wondered if Caya had been in communication with him, and hoped she had really moved on from him.

Guys like Garth oozed high toxic levels that could leave permanent scars. Caya possessed her share. When I talked to her last, I meant to ask her if her therapy was going okay, but then again, she may not have had time to attend because of her mom.

Figured when I had some down time, I would check on her. With everything she'd been through, she deserved someone who would treat her well, if and when she was ready to pursue a relationship.

Lisette snapped her fingers a few times in front of my frozen eyes. "Hey, you."

"Yeah, I was just thinking about stuff."

"Like what?"

"Garth and Caya. Really hope she doesn't go back to him."

"Me, too, Tomie, but you know that would be Caya's choice, if she did."

"What a stupid decision that would be." I frowned.

"Caya must determine when she wishes to break free from him, and only she can do that."

"Guess so."

I just wanted her to be happy because she deserved it.

"We can just be here to offer her support with no judgments or pressure."

"Lisette, you're so wise."

"You have to allow the people you love to make their own decisions, even if you don't agree. By doing that, they're more willing to listen and see a different perspective." She looked at me with a partial nod.

"Never thought of it that way."

She bumped me. "Plus, Caya is sweet on you, so I would imagine she would hang on anything you had to say."

"Not sure why she feels that way about me. I didn't do anything different."

"You don't have to. She recognizes that you're one of the good guys, especially after being with someone like Garth. The little time you've spent with her has elevated her self-esteem to a level she probably wasn't aware she could reach." Lisette lifted up her hands above her.

"Honestly, all I did was listen to her and tell her some positive stuff that I noticed about her."

"That's all it took, for someone to recognize the uniqueness, and you did just that. Like I told you before, thank you for helping her to find her light."

Shrugging my shoulders, I replied, "No problem—still don't think I did much." I checked my cell.

I didn't see any texts from Sari. I figured her dad must be home by now. The talk should have happened, or maybe it was just beginning. Night came fast. I grabbed some pajamas and hiked the short distance to the bathroom. I showered and washed my hair. Before I left the bathroom, I picked my hair out in the mirror, yawning a few times.

Returning back to my bedroom, I looked at my phone, still no texts from Sari. As I sat down on the side of the bed, my mind drifted back to my encounter with Garth and Verlinda's surprise visit.

I was so lucky to have someone like Lisette in my life to teach me about my powers and to hone in on what I needed to work on even more. Closing my eyes, I took a short catnap.

"Tomie, come on while its hot," Lisette yelled from the kitchen.

"Coming," I said.

I grabbed a bowl of the shrimp and sausage gumbo.

Sitting across from Lisette, I said, "I've been thinking about something."

"What?"

"Truly, what's really the purpose of bringing Pepper back?"

"You tell me, Tomie?"

Leaning the side of my face against my hand, I said, "Opal knows my history with Pepper, and she's bitter I'm with Sari. To watch Pepper carry out her wicked plan, my elimination, would give her the sweetest satisfaction." I blew out deep breaths.

"Think you're probably right. Have you ever heard of this saying: 'The enemy of my enemy is my friend.'"

"Once in a movie, I believe, why?" I reached behind my back to scratch below my neck and continued devouring my food.

"What does that mean in your case with Opal and Verlinda?" Lisette stopped eating and folded her hands under her chin to focus her eyes on me.

"Figuring out a way to convince Pepper to work against them?"

Lisette's pupils grew wide. "Yes, you got it. When Pepper first confronts you, this will be the time to plant your seed against Opal and Verlinda."

Pulling my eyebrows together, I stared into my nearly empty bowl. "You think she'll buy it?"

"At first, no, but you'll give her something to begin questioning. Don't forget to keep your necklace on at all times."

She pointed at her wrist. "My bracelet and your necklace are linked together. It notifies me if you're in trouble, so keep it on mister."

"Didn't know that." I tugged down on my ear.

"Remember also to communicate with me telepathically if you ever find yourself in a jam. I can hear you, no matter what time, got it?"

I nodded.

"Tomie, it's imperative you follow our plan. If you forget one thing, then know you make yourself vulnerable, understand?"

My feet started tapping, as I swept my hand across my forehead to wipe the sweat off. "Yes."

"Really hate it that you cannot have the normal senior year like most kids your age." She reached over to grab my clammy, shaky hands.

"I'll just stick to our plan."

"Let's finish up and get some rest. Still want to travel downtown with me while I look around?"

"Sure." My eyes dropped.

Touching my face with her hand, she said, "Sari will call, soon."

We cleaned up. As I was placing dishes in their proper places, I glanced down at Sabra's bed. She was fast asleep.

"'Night, Lisette."

"Goodnight, Tomie."

Shutting my bedroom door behind me, I picked up my cell—no texts or calls from Sari. It was close to ten-thirty.

I was tempted to text Sari. Placing my phone back on the table, I went to the bathroom to floss and brush up. When I was finished, I pulled out my Louisiana supernatural book and read, until I became sleepy.

A faint beep sounded off around two-thirty. It was a text that had come through around two. I must've not heard it the first few times. Opening one of my eyes, I reached for my phone. Holding it up near my face, I saw it was a text from Sari.

S: **Tomie, I know it's late and you're probably sleeping. Call me. We need 2 talk!!!!!**

Rows of sad emoji crying faces followed.

CHAPTER
TWENTY—THREE

I FUMBLED MY PHONE IN MY QUIVERING HANDS, AND IT fell onto the floor. I reached down to retrieve it and texted her back.

T: Hey, it's me. U still up? What happened?

Staring down at the screen for several seconds until it faded to black, I called her a few times, and it went straight to voicemail. Throwing the covers off me, I jumped up and started pacing the room. I probably did that for more than an hour, checking my phone several times.

I wasn't worried about Verlinda or Opal messing with her because of the protection spell. My thoughts focused more on her father. My heart felt like it was going to pop out of my chest. I stayed up all night.

Around six in the morning, I texted her again and called. No response after several rings, so I called her back and still nothing. As soon as I placed my phone down and sat on the edge of my bed, my phone rang. I grabbed it and hit the answer button.

"Sari! Sari, everything okay?" My voice cracked while my knees bounced.

I heard her crying.

"Talk to me, please."

"Tomie…"

Her voice was low and slower than usual. I knew something was wrong—I waited for her to share.

"Sari…"

"This is really bad," she whimpered.

"I already have an idea of what you're about to say."

"Not everything."

She paused for another minute.

"My dad isn't who I thought he was, Tomie. I'm so sorry, for all of this."

"Sari, it's okay, you have nothing to do with any of this, but what do you mean?"

"Tomie, it's really, really bad. It's so far from being okay."

"What?" My voice cracked again.

Sniffling, she whispered, "He told me that he's the one who texted you that day, as you were driving out of Frost and headed to Lisette's for the summer."

DOLL³

"What! Are you serious?" I almost dropped my phone. I caught it before it hit the floor.

"Yes."

I could hear her voice quivering.

"Sari, I can deal with that. Is there more?" I ran my spare hand through my hair.

"Umm... yeah."

"Tell me."

"My dad is a **monster**... he's awful." Her voice skipped and became muffled because of her loud sobbing.

I wanted to tell her that I'd thought the same thing more than once, but I didn't.

In a deep wail, she said, "Tomie, he's the reason why a slayer is looking for you!"

CHAPTER
TWENTY—FOUR

"THAT MAKES NO SENSE, SARI."

"He's been watching you for awhile, especially after the incident at my house when you were waiting for me to finish getting ready for prom. Plus, he's worked odd jobs for Mr. Fox. Verlinda talked to him that night at the hospital about you, and how you were the culprit of Pepper Fox's accident, when he went in to get his burnt hand examined."

"So, you're telling me that your dad is like a spy for the Dupuy Silver Slayers Corporation?"

"Kind of."

My eyes grew wide and watery. "Sari, I knew your dad didn't care for me, but man, he truly wants me out of your life, permanently?" I clutched my phone tight and swallowed hard.

DOLL³

"He told me that if I break up with you, he would contact the slayer and call off your extermination, and I could attend the school of my choice—all expenses paid by him... I don't care about any of that school stuff, anymore. I just want you to be safe and be with you." She sniffled more.

"Okay, Sari, I understand." I wasn't exactly sure of his complete connection to the slayer world.

"Wait, what do you mean?"

I was silent for a minute. I didn't care about my welfare, but Sari's future mattered. She deserved that opportunity her dad presented to her; a full ride with no money worries later, even if it was a lame bribe to get her away from me.

"Tomie, you there?" she whined.

"Yeah... I'm here," I huffed.

"What are you thinking?" Her crying started again.

"Maybe, we should break up, Sari. I've been thinking about it for a while, now."

"Tomie, what!"

"It's probably for the best."

In the background, I could hear the Terminator, her dad, calling her.

Balling my writing hand up, I punched my headboard.

"What was that noise?"

"Nothing." I frowned and stared down at my bleeding knuckle. I ripped my shirt off and wrapped it.

"Hey, you better go, Sari."

"Are you really breaking up with me because of my dad?" Her crying grew louder.

"Yes."

"Please, I don't want this. Let's just run away from here. We can get married."

There was only one thing I could say to make her believe me.

"It's time we see other people. I didn't want to tell you this, but Sari, I need to let you know something."

"What?" Her crying escalated.

I thought about what I was about to say for a couple of seconds before I blurted it out.

"Tell me what, Tomie?" Her voice crumbled.

"Caya and I kissed... she's coming over later tonight." The lie tasted bitter in my mouth. Tears raced down my cheeks.

"Tomie, you're just making that up. It's not true!"

I could hear the timer on the bomb, ticking inside my chest. "Sorry, girl, it's all true. She even kisses better than you. No telling what might happen tonight."

"Are you serious? I thought you loved me..."

"Look, I gotta go and you do too. It's over. Bye, Sari."

I ended the call.

Uncontrolled tears streamed down my face. I didn't want to break up with Sari. Mr. Green had won, and for a moment, I thought about placing a dark spell on him, but I dismissed the notion because that was Sari's dad.

DOLL³

He'd gotten exactly what he'd been craving, erasing me out of Sari's life. Although it felt like a samurai swordsman pierced me deep in my heart with his katana, this meant he wouldn't try to prevent her from reaching her dreams at her design school of choice, now.

It hurt to be so short and cold to Sari over the phone, especially to lie to her about the one girl, she was most intimidated about. I never intended to break her heart—I just didn't want her to possess a deep regret later on and end up hating me later on. My heart groaned and kicked me against my chest.

Rolling out of bed, I threw on some jeans and a tattered T-shirt. My hand throbbed and looked swollen. I guessed my emotions impacted my healing process. As I was about to leave, my phone beeped. It was a text message from Sari.

S: **Tomie, call me!**

I didn't respond. Right now, I would give anything to teleport to her and hold her in my arms. I left my phone and searched for Lisette.

CHAPTER
TWENTY—FIVE

S HUFFLING INTO THE KITCHEN WITH MY HEAD DOWN, I saw Lisette walk in the back door with Sabra. I flopped down in the kitchen chair and rested my chin on top of my uninjured hand, holding the pulsating one up.

"Oh, boy. You two broke up?"

I mumbled, "Yep."

She sat down next to me. I felt Lisette stroking my upper back. "Tomie, what happened?"

In almost slow motion, I lifted my head and fixed my eyes on Lisette's. "Sari is better off without me in her life."

"Totally disagree!"

"Listen, turns out that Mr. Green was my mystery texter, and the one who communicated with a slayer spy about my powers."

"What!" Lisette stood up, and a chair flew backwards against the wall. Sabra jumped and hopped over to me. I bent down to scoop her up and held her in my lap. The chair shattered.

I gasped.

"Never mind about that, what else? I never would've imagined Sari's dad would've done that. My first guess was—"

"Verlinda."

"Exactly."

Lowering my sore hand down some, I said, "Verlinda did talk to him that night, including someone at the hospital that night when Pepper was taken by ambulance. I'm sure we'll never figure out the mystery person."

"True. Whoever it was has been keeping his ears and eyes wide open for any strange incidents that couldn't be explained."

"Well, that's not even important now."

I wanted to call Sari and take everything back I just lied about. Yet, I knew if I did, then she would self-sabotage her personal dreams for me, and I couldn't live with that. I pounded my head against the table.

"Stop that. Come here." I stood up and placed Sabra in the chair. Bending down to accommodate Lisette, she hugged me.

"Ain't it something how someone can hate you so much, that if they saw an opportunity to make their dreams come true by destroying you, then they would do it without any hesitation."

Stepping back from her, I picked Sabra up and took her to her bed. She looked up at me and blinked her big eyes and feathery eyelashes a few times. A few moments later, she closed her eyes. I ambled back to the table to face Lisette. I wiped my running tears off my face with a napkin.

"It's really unfair. You've never been in any trouble or disrespected Sari or him, Tomie." Lisette grinded her teeth.

"None of that matters. It because of who and what I am. Mr. Green despises my entire existence, ever since I started dating Sari. He wasn't even keen on us being friends back in elementary and junior high. The truth is that in his eyes, I'll never be good enough for Sari. I know Sari is aware of that, but she won't admit it."

"You're going to just let him win? Tomie, your selfless sacrifice makes my heart sing and break at the same time." She closed her eyes.

"What choice do I really have?" My hands brushed over my wet face to wipe my eyes. "Ouch!"

"You'll heal before night. Next time, punch a pillow." She arched her eyebrows up. "Tomie, it would be so simple to cast an undo spell on him, where he would perceive you differently. It's a dark spell, and you know I've told you that I don't delve in that anymore. However, if it means helping you, then I would."

"No, Lisette, I wouldn't want that because I know the promise you made yourself. A spell like that would be just a lie to remind me of what I already know."

"Sure?"

"Yeah."

"How in the world will you get through senior year without Sari?"

Releasing a long sigh, I replied, "It's going to be really hard, not even going to pretend."

"You do know once a slayer has been contacted that he finishes his mission, regardless, right?"

"Figured just as much." My head hung low. "I've known for a while I would face something soon. Mr. Green just sped it all up."

"Tomie, let's get out of here for a bit."

"You go ahead. There's no need for me to go, now."

"Mister, you're getting out of here for a while, come on."

"I'm just not feeling it, Lisette."

"Believe me, I see and hear that. Trust me, this will do you some good."

"Let me go to the bathroom first."

"Okay. I'll be right here, waiting on you."

Strolling to my room, I replayed the conversation I'd had with Sari. My phone buzzed a few times. It was Sari. I wanted to tell her to forget everything I had just said.

I stopped myself from hitting the answer button and just let it go to voicemail. By the time I was ready to go, I'd had five missed calls from her already. I placed it on silent and grabbed my watch off the desk. Looking back at my phone on the bed, I closed the door.

CHAPTER
TWENTY—SIX

CEREAL BARS AND FRUIT WERE IN A RED, WIRE BASKET and some small plastic containers of grape and orange juice sat around it. Lisette was sipping on coffee from her over-sized mug and finishing a banana.

"Aren't you going to eat you something before we head out, Tomie?"

"Nah, not hungry."

Lisette rubbed my upper arm.

"Let's get out of here... Tomie, don't push her away. That's one of the worst things you can do to someone you claim to love. You both have known each other way too long."

We climbed into the car. All I wanted to do was to crawl back under my covers and sleep for days. Then, I thought how that would invite my nightmares of replaying everything in my head. Sari would soon stop calling and not come around me.

Lisette's eyebrows pulled in. "Tomie, you sure you want it like this?"

I couldn't speak.

"Hope you don't regret it. Sometimes, the decisions we make cannot be reversed, once they're made, understand?" Her eyes skipped towards me before turning on the main road.

We arrived at a little antique shop called Miss Jayla's Finders Keepers. The store was a very quaint two-story, golden brick building with a red roof. Green and blue lights hung in the corners as I walked inside, with moderate fluorescent lighting reflecting down the center of the ceiling.

Warm vanilla, cinnamon, and jasmine scents filled the atmosphere. The floors were a dark earth tone. There were maybe a handful of customers browsing the special treasures and holding red canvas bags to place their items in.

Lisette grabbed a bag. She started browsing around the shop herself. I noticed a huge glass case. Before I could reach the area, I heard someone call out my name from behind me.

"Hey, Tomie!"

Turning around, I saw Ranae. She approached me.

Taking in a long breath and guiding my eyes towards the floor, I said, "Hi."

"How have you been? I haven't seen you since the festival

at the talent show. Your performance was great, by the way. Thought we may have tied." She smiled.

"Nope, you had me beat as soon as you started whipping those drums up with your glowing drumsticks."

"Thanks."

"Do you play in a band or something, Ranae?" My eyes weren't focused on her. I thought about what Sari was doing right now.

"No, just me."

"You're really talented."

She blushed. "Whatever. What are you doing here? Hey, you okay?" She touched my arm lightly with her hand.

I took two steps back because Ranae was a Lecteur, sort of like a fortune-teller. She could read your complete past, present, future, with limitations in some cases, merely by touching your hands, arms, or heart. *Glimming* only allowed me to see someone's present and limited future; a deep *glim* allowed more open visions.

"Lisette's idea. Yeah, why you ask?" I looked around to find Lisette climbing up a scarlet, spiral metal staircase.

Ranae touched my hand. It was as if she downloaded the last few days and minutes of my thoughts. "Whoa, never mind. Sorry about you and Sari."

"No, you're not." I left her and planted myself at the center of the glass counter. I thrust my chest out.

"Hey, wait up. Don't be angry. I didn't do it on purpose. I

cannot control it sometimes… You're right, I'm not sorry. I'll save my jumping up and down for later."

Rolling my eyes, I said, "You really should be more careful, Ranae."

"Anyhow, don't be so uptight. By the way, how was your gator night feeding with Caya and her ever-so-lovely boy crew?" She batted her long, sky-blue colored eyelashes, as she leaned her elbow on the glass counter with her chin in the palm of her hand.

"It went just fine."

Her lashes ceased batting. "So, you're telling me that Darth Garth didn't show you his dark side, and try to cut you in half with his red light saber?"

"Nope, he didn't get that close to cut me. Anyhow, can I ask you something?"

"Go for it." She gave me an exaggerated wink.

I rolled my eyes.

"Come on, you know you're a *hottie* with a capital H!"

I fought back laughter. "Ranae, please simmer down."

"Okay, okay, just playing with you. Looks like you need it, after all that's happened with you, anyhow. Go ahead, ask me your question."

"Why are you so concerned about all of that?"

"No big deal, really. Just curious if you saw Garth for what he is." She twirled her rainbow colored ponytail around her hand.

"Let's just say I saw enough."

She took a few steps towards me, and I stumbled back to avoid any more downloads from her touch. Ranae whispered, "I knew what Garth was before you met him, Caya, too. I also know that you're an extraordinary warlock, a really cute one, too. **Be careful, Tomie Dupuy**, you'll soon be face-to-face with the one you've been anticipating for some time now."

I gazed into her eyes. Stepping closer to her, I asked, "Who?"

She looked away from me and started tapping her black nails with red, glittery Minnie Mouse ear tips on the glass.

Laughing under her breath, she mouthed, "You know who?"

I frowned. "Don't have the slightest clue, so tell me."

"The one who's been on the hunt for you, especially after they found out about your birth—the Dupuy Silver Slayer."

Moving in closer, I said, "Ranae, I need for you to be serious with me. Can you do that?" My eyes shimmered.

"Umm, yeah. Love your bedroom eyes." She started stretching her hand up to touch my face.

Leaning my head back a little, I said, "Do you know who the Dupuy Silver Slayer is?"

"I'll have to work my magic and touch you."

At first I was hesitant, but then I started thinking about what this information could mean. I took a few deep breaths and leaned in.

"Okay... Do it."

She placed her warm hands over my heart, closing her eyes.

After a few minutes, her eyes popped wide open, and she backed away from me.

"What did you see? Ranae, tell me." I heard the hook from "Girls Like You" by Maroon 5 playing from her phone in her bag. Stooping down, she pulled out her glittery jade cell.

"Hey, it's my mom. Please watch my bag, need to take this." She found a private place to talk near a wooden column wrapped with blinking white lights.

I studied all the eleven rows in the entire glass case, occasionally glancing towards Ranae—she was still occupied. My palms were sweaty and my heart jerked. I braced myself up against the counter and took in three deep breaths.

A salesman with goatee, oval glasses, and curly hair draped over a purple silk wrap came over to me.

"May I help you?"

"I'm still looking, thanks."

"Sure, take all the time you need. Just let me know if you would like to see something."

Fifteen minutes later, Ranae returned and grabbed her bag. "Get the fifth one from the right. She'll love that one, plus after those twisted lies about you and Caya, you should consider getting her something else. Gotta go, Tomie."

"Wait!" I grabbed her wrist with my trembling hand as she was turning around. "Please, tell me what you saw…" My lips quivered for a brief moment.

"Tomie, it was really a blur. I couldn't identify much." She slipped her hands in her pockets and looked over her shoulder.

"Yet, you saw something, right?"

She nodded. "I did."

"Ranae, what did you see?" I pleaded in a shrill voice, grabbing her by her upper arms and lifting her body five inches off the ground. Some of the customers stared in our direction and whispered. I released her.

"Two," she answered, eyes wide.

Grimacing, I said, "Not following you."

"I saw not just one slayer, but two. They were dressed in dark hooded cloaks. I'm sorry. I never should've read you." Ranae turned away from me.

"No, it's not your fault. I'm glad I ran into you today. This was meant to happen."

"Possibly. Are you going to be okay?" She squeezed my hand.

I looked down, and she dropped it.

"Yeah, I know you gotta go."

"See you around then."

"Hey, can I get your number?"

"Of course, Tomie. Thought you would never ask. Give me your phone?"

"Not on me."

"What? I cannot leave the house without mine. Here, just tell me your number, and I'll add it to my contacts and text you later."

I gave her my number.

"By the way, Tomie?"

"What?"

She whispered, "Stay in on Halloween night."

"Why, Ranae?"

"That's when I saw the hooded capes." She turned around and departed the store. I saw her look back at me from the glass windows.

I stood there thinking how my reality was coming faster than I realized. I needed to talk to Lisette about all of this, but not here.

Focusing my attention on the ring located on the fifth row from the right as Ranae suggested, it seemed to shimmer the brightest. I waved my hand to the same salesman from earlier.

"What would you like to see, young man?"

Pointing to the one I was staring at, he opened up the case. He pulled the chosen ring out of its secured blue, cushiony space.

"Here you go. Just arrived about a month ago. Nice choice."

He handed it to me, and I examined it all around.

"What kind of gemstones are these?" The gemstones formed an X and were outlined with sprinkles of marcasite down the pattern.

"Ruby, coral, sardonyx, and hag stones."

I recognized a few from my past geology class.

Browsing his eyes all around the store, he whispered, "This

ring is really special."

"How?"

"It protects from the evil eye and dark witchcraft."

Squinting my eyes, it made sense why Ranae told me to choose this ring for Sari, but why would the salesman tell me that.

"You're thinking about purchasing this for your girlfriend?"

"We broke up today." I bowed my head.

"Oh, man, I'm sorry to hear that. Think you both may get back together?"

"No idea. I hope to."

"Well, hear me out. If you think there's a slight chance, then get this beauty for her. Believe me when the time is right, you'll score some major points."

Studying his black, starched long-sleeve shirt, I found the salesman's nametag, which read Lazzaro.

"You'll know if and when you need to give it to her."

"How much?"

"Today is your lucky day because we're having an early Pre-Fall Sale, which means fifty percent off everything. Since I've been where you are more than once, I'm going to give you another fifteen percent off, how does that sound?"

"Cool." I flipped the tag over on the bottom of the silver band and determined I could afford it. "I'll take it."

I followed him to the cash register. He placed it in a black box and tied it up with a dark, turquoise bow and grabbed a black bag with the store's name and logo written on both sides. He rung me up; I gave him the exact cash once he shared the total.

"Here you go."

I picked up the bag.

"Hope things work out with your girl."

"Thanks, Lazzaro."

"No problem. Take care." His eyes glistened.

I closed my eyes and opened them, and they did it again. I mouthed, "Are you a…?"

He smiled and nodded, while his red and black Scarlet Witch keychain, slightly levitated above his open palm. I waved with a half smile.

Lisette descended from the stairs, carrying a burgundy garment bag over her left arm. A huge smile painted her entire face, and her emerald eyes sparkled. She sort of skipped over towards me.

"Bet you won't guess what I found?"

"Hmm, I couldn't even imagine. There's been a lot surprises in this store."

She noticed the bag in my hand.

"Don't know if I'll ever give it to her, though. Hey, I need to talk to you about something Ranae shared with me, as soon as possible." My eyes darted back and forth.

"Oh, is she still here?" She looked around.

"No, she's gone."

"Let's go."

"What's inside your bag, Lisette?"

"Saving it as a surprise for when you walk me down the aisle."

We drove to Scooter's Cajun Dinner a few miles away and missed the lunch crowd. Hardly anyone was present. Lisette found us a seat far against the wall and away from the other customers.

"Do you come here often, Lisette?"

"Actually, this is my first time here. The seamstress who helped me was saying really good things about this place." Lisette ordered. I only requested water.

"Tomie, you're going to have to eat soon."

"Maybe later on, not feeling food right now."

"So, spill about your visit with Ranae."

"She read me."

"Really? You let her read you?" Lisette's eyes expanded.

"Yeah."

"I'm surprised a little because I know how you feel about that kind of stuff. When I *glim* you, I know it makes you feel uneasy. I'm trying not to do that as much, though."

"Appreciate that."

Lisette rotated the straw around her drink and took a few sips.

"Her vision was blurry, but she told me what she saw."

"What did she see?" She stopped stirring.

"Slayers."

"Wait, did you just say slayers, like more than one?" Her voice tightened, and she grabbed my hand.

"Yep, Ranae told me that she saw two slayers in hooded cloaks. She couldn't make out any of their features."

"Tomie, that's really rare for two to be on the hunt." Her hand was very warm on top of mine. "I'm wondering why two were assigned. It's really uncommon in the slayer world to send two out. I've only heard of multiple slayers when a large group of *supras* are being hunted down, which hasn't happened in years."

"By the way, Ranae mentioned one other thing."

"What else did she say?" Lisette's eyes squinted, and she repositioned herself a few times in her chair.

"Halloween night, she told me to stay in."

The bill came out along with a to-go box. I reached for the bill, and Lisette snatched it from my hand. The waitress asked, "Can I get you two anything else?"

Lisette handed her credit card to her. The waitress returned the card in a few minutes.

As Lisette signed the receipt and stood up from her chair, I lagged behind her.

"Tomie, Halloween night is huge for supras all over. Strange things can occur. This is one night when dark magic is *extremely* powerful. You need to stay in just like Ranae recommended, mister." She stared me down.

DOLL³

"Yeah, I'm considering it."

"That's shouldn't even be an option to come out of your mouth. Stay in and that's all there is to it! Didn't you just hear what I told you?" She tipped her head at me.

"I can't keep hiding from the inevitable, Lisette, you know that." I clasped my hands together and looked away from her.

"Look at me, I wasn't suggesting that at all."

Facing her, I said, "I have to be ready to fight my own battles."

"You don't have to fight them all alone. Two slayers can really be powerful, even against an experienced *supra*."

Silence filled our space for a few minutes.

"Lisette, you're right. I'll stay in."

Twitching her mouth left and right. "You can be really stubborn, sometimes."

CHAPTER
TWENTY—SEVEN

OPENING THE CAR DOOR, WE STEPPED IN AND drove away. My mind shot straight to Sari. Soon, I would see her in one or more of the last classes we would share together. Avoiding her was only temporary.

However, I also knew while I was here that I needed to soak up everything else Lisette could teach me and just focus on my training. Would that be possible with my mind drifting back to Sari?

Zydeco-like jazz music played in the background. I looked up at the orange, yellow, and blue ribbon sky. We came to a stop, and I noticed a small parade of black-bellied, whistling ducks. One adult and about seven ducklings followed her, swerving around in the water.

DOLL³

My thoughts shifted to my mom. I wish I could just talk to my mom anytime I needed to without limited spell restrictions. So many of my classmates had both of their parents to tell their future problems and dreams to—something I knew I would never have.

I had a pretty awesome dad who finally accepted my dreams and tried his best to protect me from the magic world. I just wished my mom could've been part of all of this, too.

My dad could've easily rejected me because of who I was— he didn't. He loved me, and he'd sacrificed so much for me. He was another reason I had to focus my attentions on my training and the remaining time I had here. I wanted to do my best to protect all who I loved.

"You know we have a few more days before I return to Frost," I said in a low tone.

"I was thinking the same thing."

"Lisette, I know I've told you this before, but I'm really going to miss hanging out with you."

"Going to miss that, too. None of the teary stuff now."

"Really, really appreciate everything that you've done for me." I squeezed her hand.

"You're welcome, and we're not even close to being done, yet."

"Did you ever think you would be teaching me all this magic stuff?"

"No... I always wondered if you would get the *curse*," she

whispered, winking and nudging my upper arm with her elbow a few times.

"Ha, ha, ha… good one."

"You must admit, though, Tomie, when you first found out you were transforming into a warlock, you didn't want to have anything to do with the *curse,* as you defined it. An embroidered "*D*" for denial should've been worn over your chest."

"You're right on all counts, not gonna argue."

"Listen, I get it. That's some major news, finding out things you never knew about your family history, and then coming face-to-face with the fact you would inherit those same *supra* powers, too."

"It was a lot to take in, but I wouldn't have been able to understand and accept who I was becoming if I didn't have you, my dad, Sari, Mr. Ray, and Crow for support, you know."

"Yes, I know."

I sighed and stared out the window.

"Thinking about Sari?"

"You know it."

"In life, you just never know what may happen, Tomie. Look at me. I never imagined staying here in Monroe Creek, practicing as a *supra*, training you, and now marrying Crow next summer."

Tilting my head and staring at her, I said, "Really?"

"Nope, I had plans to study dance in New York with a minor in music." She twirled one hand up in the air in an eccentric and beautiful spiral pattern, as burgundy and gold glitter rained down her arm, forming a miniature ballerina dancing in the air for a moment, before she vanished.

"Wow, Lisette, I never knew that. Which school?"

"Alvin Ailey American Dance Theater."

"What stopped you?" I leaned in closer to her.

"Different things, I guess, but fear was the biggest for me."

"I can't believe you being afraid of anything, Lisette."

"Hey, we all have fears. Remember this, if you really want something, then you have to just take that leap, regardless of the fear trying to hold you back. You have to figure out how to conquer that fear and release it, so you can soar, understand?"

"I get it. Thank you for sharing with me."

"Anytime, Tomie."

After we arrived home, Lisette took care of Sabra, and I went straight to my room. I checked my phone and just as I thought, Sari had called me several times. She had left ten messages, and Ranae had left one text.

I texted Ranae to confirm my number. Sitting down in the desk chair, I pressed play to listen to all of Sari's messages. I could hear her crying and begging me to please call her, as soon as I could. My hand trembled over Sari's picture for a thirty seconds—I found the strength to move it.

CHAPTER
TWENTY—EIGHT

AROUND NINE-THIRTY, I ROLLED OUT OF BED AND got dressed for the day. Sabra was gone from her bed when I entered the kitchen. I saw some pancakes in a platter covered with a plastic wrap. I helped myself to about six of them. "Tomie, we're in the living room. Join us when you're done," Lisette yelled.

"Okay."

I finished my breakfast, cleared the table, and washed my dishes.

"What are you two both up to?"

Sabra rested on her blanket on the couch next to Lisette, who sat on the floor with a teakettle, tin canister, spoons, and white coffee cups with deep saucers.

DOLL³

"Tea time, Lisette?" I laughed.

"Not quite, come sit across from me."

"Are we practicing a special spell?"

She didn't answer. Lisette pushed the cup in front of me with the flick of her index finger. The canister opened up on its own, the spoon levitating up and diving into the jar.

Then, the filled spoon drifted to Lisette, and she dropped dried tea leaves inside the cup. The teakettle floated off the table towards my cup, and it poured warm water over the leaves. The teakettle returned to its original location on the table. A spoon rested on a napkin next to my cup.

"Stir it up well, grab the handle with your left hand, and move it in a circle as fast as you can without spilling any, three times from left to right."

"Lisette, this is a strange way to drink tea," I said and followed her instructions.

"Let it stand for three minutes. Drink it, leaving the tea leaves, and only leave a little liquid at the bottom."

"Why?"

"This is not tea time. I'm teaching you *tasseography*."

"T-a-s-s-e-o—what?" I asked.

"Tea-reading, one of the oldest practices *supras*, including gypsies, used to practice. It's an old art of the magic world. Many don't pursue it anymore, only the older generation. The younger *supras* think it's too old to be of any use. I must tell you it can be very valuable indeed. These readings can tell someone of happenings to come."

"Okay, what do I do next?"

Grinning wide, she said, "I'm happy to hear you're eager to learn, Tomie."

"Of course, Lisette. I know whatever you're teaching me is for my own good."

"Great, turn your cup over and pour out the water slowly into the saucer."

After I poured the water off, I gazed inside my cup. Most of the tea leaves clung to the sides and bottom of the cup. I waited for Lisette's next request.

"Lisette, are you reading my tea leaves because of what Ranae saw in the antique shop?"

"Her vision definitely has something to do with it. I want to focus more on the pattern your leaves made on the side and bottom of your cup."

"Why?"

"The side represents immediate future events, and the bottom symbolizes the distant future."

"What does the rim mean?"

"The present... now, place your cup in front of me," she demanded.

"Has someone read your tea leaves?"

"Yes, I've had them read by Ranae's mom, maybe a year ago. Now, I read my own, but I prefer for someone I really trust to."

"What did your last reading tell you?"

"I would gain two companions, Crow and Sabra."

"It got two things right."

"Tea leaf reading is pretty accurate. Sometimes, you don't know what information it will share, because the readings tell you what you *need* to hear at that time, and not what you hope to hear."

"Oh, so if I wanted to know who was going to win "The Voice," then it wouldn't provide me that information?"

"Exactly, that's something you're hoping to hear. Think of tea leaf reading as a random gift to be given to you."

"How many tea leaf readings have you completed?"

Slanting her head towards her shoulder, she said, "Probably more than five hundred."

I almost knocked the tea in the saucer over with my hand. "Do you charge for them?"

"Depends on who I'm giving the tea leaf reading to. I usually can tell whom I need to charge."

"What's next?"

"Hand me your cup."

I started picking it up with my tottering hand. Sweat flowed down my temples.

"No, please use both hands to hand it over to me."

"Why?"

"Your energy levels will expel from both of your hands."

Grabbing the cup with both hands, I held it up in front of Lisette.

"Drop it."

"I'll break it."

"Trust me."

Once I released the cup, Lisette levitated it up just before it fell on the table. She spun it around slowly with the twist of her hands, to where it remained at her eye level. Tilting it towards her, she studied the contents for few minutes and then the cup floated down, as she lowered her hands.

She looked at me and raised each of her eyebrows a few times. My hands started tapping the table. I leaned over to see what she was looking at. It didn't look like much to me, just mushed up leaves. A few rested on the side of the cup, but the majority clung to the bottom.

"What do you see, Tomie?"

"Just scattered tea leaves in a cup, some in more clustering formations than others."

"Do you see anything familiar in your leaves? Have you ever looked up in the clouds and saw different patterns in the sky?"

"Yeah, but I can't tell you the last time I did, though."

"That's not important. When you did, what kind of things did you see?"

"All kinds of stuff, such as birds, dogs, stars, castles, and angels."

"Exactly, your mind allowed you to see the first thing that made sense, right?"

Shrugging my shoulders, I said, "Guess so."

"Same concept with tea leaf reading. Whatever you see is what you see. Now, there are some standard patterns to look for."

Staring down again in the cup, I attempted to locate any familiar formations—I only saw leaves, as I did before.

"Anything?"

"Nope."

"Open your eyes." Lisette demanded.

"They are open, look," I said, pointing at my eyes.

"Return to your childhood imagination where anything could exist. Relax."

Shutting my eyes for a few minutes, I thought about Lisette's statement and reopened them to examine the contents in the cup again. This time my eyes saw something very different. Lisette tore off a sheet of paper from a tablet on the floor and handed me a pencil.

"Draw what you see."

I placed the pencil down on the blank sheet of paper, drawing what I saw in front of me. Lisette held her hand out, so I picked up my little masterpiece in order to share it with her.

"Well, what did you see?" she asked, as she stood up to stretch her arms and began to pace the living room area in a circle.

"At first, I saw only clustered leaves, and then I opened my eyes wider to see beyond the cluster. I saw the letter, S (twice), the number ten, an owl, and a crooked heart. Did you see the same?"

"Yes."

"What does all of this mean?" I turned my body to face her.

She stopped. "Your reading tells me something is going to happen in the tenth month with sickness or brokenness, possibly being intertwined together. The letter S is probably a name."

In my mind, I thought S must mean Sari, someone was going to become ill, possibly in October—the tenth month— maybe on Halloween, and a crooked heart existed, which was most likely me. I also thought S could mean slayer.

"Good deduction," Lisette said.

I glared at her. "Thank you for *glimming* me."

"Conceal your thoughts better, then," she snapped.

"One day, I will conceal them so good that you're going to ask me, how did you do that?"

Wiggling her eyebrows, she said, "I'll be waiting on that day."

"Seriously, how accurate do you think I am?

"Eighty percent, maybe, being your first interpretation."

"That's it."

"Yep."

"What's your interpretation?"

"S is definitely a name of something, not sure if it's Sari's name or not, maybe. The number ten is probably the tenth

DOLL³

month. Owls can be a symbol of good luck or bad. In this case, I'm leaning towards Mr. Ray. Someone could get sick. Brokenness and heartbreak may be parallel to each other, which most likely is related to your relationship with Sari."

She ceased her pacing and walked back over to the couch to sit down next to Sabra. Sabra rolled over on her back with her eyes closed as Lisette stroked her chest and paws.

"How close does it get to be on target?"

"It can get pretty close, if not one hundred percent. Sometimes, the symbol interpretations may be a little off, like less than ten percent."

"Those are high numbers."

She nodded.

"You did really well to visualize what was in the cup, your mind, and then drawing your interpretation on paper, which was identical to what I saw."

"Thank you for showing me. Have you seen some scary stuff in people's tea leaf readings?"

"Oh, yes."

"Like what?" I placed my arms on top of the table and folded them.

"Lots of heartaches, journeys, and unexpected news."

"You've seen a lot, Lisette."

"Sometimes, more than I wish to see."

"Do you think my reading will come true?" I wrapped my hands around my arms.

"Absolutely! I don't have a good feeling about the 'S' symbol. The more I think about it, Tomie, I doubt it's related to Sari."

Narrowing my eyes, I asked, "You're thinking slayer, right?"

"Yes." She lowered her eyes for a few seconds. Popping her head up and staring into my eyes, she said, "Tomie, just promise me that you'll stay home on Halloween and always stick to the plan we've discussed."

"Okay." I exhaled.

"Tell me, what you would like to practice or learn next?"

"Really? I get to choose."

The tea leaf reading gives me something to look out for. I knew I wanted to learn more about it, but I would save that for another time.

"Think about it and let me know." She carried the teakettle and cups into the kitchen.

I started thinking about what I would like for Lisette to teach me, and the only thing that came to me was discovering what my ultimate shifting power could be. By knowing that, I would be better prepared when I needed to unleash my superpower. I needed for Lisette and Mr. Ray to teach me how to turn whatever it was, on and off.

She reentered the living room with an orange and bowl in her hand. Lisette sat on the couch, and Sabra snuggled her flexible body besides her.

"Any thoughts?" She started peeling the orange.

"Reveal my hidden shifting power to me."

CHAPTER
TWENTY—NINE

LISETTE CEASED HER PEELING. "TOMIE, I'M NOT SURE I can do that. Your power is suppose to be revealed to you naturally."

"If anyone can, then I believe you can. I need to know what I can do in advance, you know?"

"What you're asking is a heavy request."

"Is it impossible?" My eyes glowed.

"No, but—"

Leaning in close to her, "You told me to choose what I wanted to learn, right?" I smiled.

She expelled a long sigh. Sabra stared up at her, and then she looked back at me. "I'm going to need some back-up."

Popping my knuckles, I said, "I don't understand."

"I can't do this on my own. Going to need the *power of three*..."

"Witches?"

"Not a requirement. Powerful *supras* are needed for this."

"Who do you have in mind?"

"Mr. Ray and Crow."

"Lisette, what will actually take place?" I chewed my bottom lip.

"Your hidden energies of your shift will be exposed, if all goes right."

"How?"

"An old ritual that I read about in Marie Laveau's spell book."

"When can we do this?" My eyes gleamed.

"Tonight, there's going to be a full moon, which is perfect for this. I'm going to need a few things from the basement and refrigerator."

"Like what?" I hooted.

"Hold on..." She tore out a sheet of paper and wrote out a list of items.

"I'll contact Mr. Ray and Crow to come by tonight while you're gathering the items. Everything with asterisks will be located to the right, next to my doll glass case."

She handed me the list. I scanned it over a few times, tucked it into my pocket, and jogged towards the basement. The door was already propped open, and the light was on.

DOLL³

Lisette called after me, "There's a grey canvas bag hanging on the hook on the wall next to the glass case. You're going to need it to place all the items inside."

Noticing the bag on the wall, I grabbed it, as I passed the case. Then, I picked up orange, purple, black, and green candles, including a box of crushed, aged cocoons from skipper butterflies and golden beetle dust.

Once I reached the top of the stairs, the light turned off, the door closed shut, and the lock latched all on its own. A floating rug lingered high over my head. I stepped away from the door, and the rug levitated back down slowly on top of the locked door.

With the bag over my left shoulder, I dug out the written list from my pocket to glance at one last time. I opened up the refrigerator and pulled out the vegetable drawer. Pushing away the tomatoes and onions, I saw mini fresh ginger claws. I placed one inside the bag. Lisette was waiting at the table.

I sat the bag in front of her and pulled a chair out to sit across from her. She looked inside the bag. "Looks like you have everything we're going to need."

"Now what?"

"Well, we have to wait until night arrives before we can pursue the unconcealing spell. The moon embodies natural light and truth, which is why this type of spell requires its glow in order to show you what you need to see and know."

Hours ticked away faster that day, unlike any day I'd ever

experienced. Suddenly, it was night, and the moon was full and beamed down from the clear sky. In a way, the moon seemed to spotlight on the land that night. Lisette was preparing outside in the back a few feet from the gazebo.

I heard a knock at the front door. It was Mr. Ray. "Good evening."

"Thank you, Tomie. How are you?"

"Not sure yet, appreciate you being part of this." I balanced myself on the back of my heels.

"Of course. I know you're curious about what you can do. I am, too." He reached his hand up to pat my shoulder. "Where are Lisette and Crow?"

"She's outside getting everything ready, and Crow hasn't made it just yet."

About ten minutes later, Crow drove up in his truck. His windows were rolled all the way down, and I could hear "Boot Scootin' Boogie" by Brooks and Dunn playing from his radio. He jumped out and his gator boots shimmered in the moonlight. Lisette waved him over, and he headed in our direction.

"How's everybody doing?"

"Good," we all replied.

Crow kissed Lisette. "Where you want me?"

She looked at all of us and pointed for Crow to stand in front of her. Mr. Ray stood to her left, and I was in the middle. The candles floated from the bag and made a circular pattern on the ground. Lisette pointed at the wicks with her hand, and each one lit up.

"Tomie, take your shoes and socks off and levitate up above us," Lisette commanded.

I slid my shoes off. Closing my eyes, my feet rose off the ground until I was above them. Lisette grabbed the ginger claw and sliced it with her sharp nail. Then she held it over my feet, letting the juice ooze out. She rubbed the juice all over the top of them.

"That tickles," I said.

"Shhh, concentrate," Lisette commanded.

Three whole cocoons and golden beetle dust floated up into her hands. She slid her hands against each other, crumbling the ingredients. I wondered why she did that, but then I felt a terrible sensation as she spread the dried carcasses on both of my feet.

I felt like I wanted to vomit, so I looked away for a few seconds. When I saw the purple candle floating from the ground and aiming at my feet, my attention focused again and I felt better.

"Why is the candle floating above my feet?"

"Have to seal this part."

"Are you serious?"

I hadn't anticipated dead insects and wax being on my bare skin. My body shivered from top to bottom.

"Yes. Don't you want to know what you can do?"

I cleared my throat. "Of course. Just count to five out loud before you pour it on my feet, okay?"

She grinned. "Big baby, afraid of some harmless candlewax."

"Umm, hot wax."

Crow and Mr. Ray started laughing.

"Five, four, three, two… one."

The wax rolled down my feet, and it felt really warm and wet for about five seconds, and then it was over. The lighted candle floated back to its original position. Lisette stepped away from me and into the circle with Crow and Mr. Ray. They all linked hands.

Lisette tipped her head towards me. Mr. Ray and Crow watched her. I felt myself spin around slowly, like I was on an amusement ride before it picked up crazy momentum. The golden beetle dust swarmed around my entire body and disappeared up into the night air. I gasped and dry heaved for a few seconds. A high wind from the North rolled in. My hair flew up in the breeze, and I could feel my T-shirt billowing around my body.

She started chanting. I tried to hear what she was saying, but the wind was too loud. However, I was able to make out, "Show us, show us… what he'll project. Allow us to see him, and he to see his truth…"

After about two minutes and several rotations later, I raised my hands up, and I noticed they glowed bright blue. The blue shine slithered up my arms, face, and towards my feet. My eyes felt different, brighter. I looked down and could see

Lisette, Mr. Ray, and Crow's thermal body heat images.

"What's happening to me, Lisette?" I felt my body shaking uncontrollably.

"You're transforming!"

"Into what?"

"Not sure yet."

My body spun around faster. Something sharp began to pierce through both of my shoulders. I felt like I was on fire. I hurled myself away from them and ended up falling into the lake, sinking to the bottom. Once my glowing hands touched the sandy floor, the darkness of the water was illuminated. Looking up at the rippling water above me, I could hear voices.

In less than a minute, my entire body shot up, out of the water, and I landed onto the shore. Lisette, Mr. Ray, and Crow were all standing there. They just stared at me with their mouths open, and eyes rounded like saucers.

"Hey, y'all are making me nervous. What is it?"

No one breathed a word.

Turning myself around, I walked over to the water, hoping to capture a reflection of what they were witnessing. The deep, cobalt blue glow grew brighter. I stared down into the water and shook my head. My lips and hands shuddered.

Dipping the palms of my hands into the water, I splashed my face a few times. I shut my eyes tight and whispered to myself, "This cannot be real… It just can't be. None of this…"

I had freakin' wings.

CHAPTER
THIRTY

MR. RAY STOOD BY MY RIGHT SIDE. "TOMIE, IT'S REAL. Your wings are real." He yelped with his eyes glued on me. He placed his hand on the thick blades of iridescent, ebony feathers fluttering up and down. My wingspan was almost thirteen feet wide. I jerked my body around towards him, and he fell backwards.

"Oh, Mr. Ray, I'm sorry."

I offered my hand to help him up.

He dusted himself off with his hands. "It's okay, Tomie. You just have to learn to control them." He grinned and stood a few feet in front of me.

"All I can tell you is that I've never seen a witch or warlock's shapeshifting gift be wings," Lisette breathed, her face stunned.

"Tomie, I must agree with Lisette. This is definitely something very rare in the *supra* world, especially for a warlock to be *chosen* to possess such a magnificent transformation," Mr. Ray whispered, his eyes large.

Crow had not moved and was speechless. He couldn't take his eyes off of my massive wings. I looked at them rise up and down again a few times. I attempted to take flight, but with little success. Mr. Ray and Lisette encouraged me to concentrate.

Without taking her eyes off me, she said, "Imagine, being light as a feather."

I tried that for more than an hour before I was able to take flight. My heart fluttered each time my wings flapped in and out, soaring into the dark sky. I never felt so free as I did now. I wished Sari could've been with me at this moment. After thirty minutes in the air, I headed back down to my audience. I yelled from the sky, "I think I can get used to these." My wings felt strong and soft like cotton when I ran my hands down them.

"Sure you will," Lisette said, examining them from front to back.

"Mr. Ray, why do you think I was chosen to have these?" I landed down next to him.

"Don't know—I have a strong feeling they'll serve you when the time is right."

"Mr. Ray," Lisette said, "Crow and I are going to leave you

two alone." Crow looked back at me, two or three more times.

"Tomie, try to deactivate your wings," Mr. Ray instructed, stroking his beard with one hand.

"Not sure."

"Think of them not being there."

Shutting my eyes, I imagined them disappearing, as if they had never been there before. When I opened my eyes, they remained. Guess I wasn't focusing like I thought.

"That's okay. We'll keep working on it until you finally get it, okay?"

"Sounds good." I concentrated again and again. After my thirteenth time, I was finally able to make one wing vanish and then the other. It tingled a lot, and my shoulders itched bad and felt like they were burning, as if a thousand fire ants were seeking their revenge.

"Focus on releasing your wings again," Mr. Ray requested.

Closing my eyes, I focused on the feel of my wings. After a few tries, they sprang from my back. I pulled my wings in close to my body, as if wrapping myself up in my sleeping bag. They were really warm. Mr. Ray and I practiced a few hours before we decided to return back to the house.

Mr. Ray started whistling.

"Did you know what I could transform into before you were called out here tonight, to help Lisette with the spell?"

Having wings was something that I never imagined. I recalled watching Peter Pan when I was younger. Only Sari knew this, and she swore to never tell anyone, but when we were in the sixth grade, Tinker Bell was always one of my heroes, probably because of all her sass. Tink's magical wings drew me in. Now, I could produce my own.

"No. I had a feeling that it would be something spectacular because of your Laveau bloodline."

"So, I'm really the first that you and Lisette have actually seen with wings?" I stopped where I was.

Mr. Ray swung his body around to face me. "Yes."

"Nah." I could feel my ears becoming warm.

"Tomie, your ears are beet red, by the way." He chuckled.

I reached up to touch them while fanning my wings in slow motion, keeping them close to my side.

"Remember everything that Lisette has been teaching you about self-control. Anger can easily showcase your newly discovered gift if you don't keep it maintained, you know?"

Taking in some quick breaths, I said, "Yeah, I know."

"Always be aware of your surroundings and consider what could happen, if someone saw your wings, who didn't need to see them. Keep your magic and shifting as discreet as you can."

A few months ago, I was just your average teen boy, dodging the bullies of Frost High and growing up in a small Texas town, where nothing exciting ever happened.

Now, here I stood, preparing to confront my enemies in full transformation with wings. I wondered what else could these bad boys do. I figured I would find out, soon enough.

We fist bumped. Before we entered the house, I closed my eyes and concentrated for a while, until my wings retracted.

CHAPTER
THIRTY—ONE

MY REMAINING DAYS IN MONROE CREEK FLEW BY. Lisette and I practiced a few more spells, and Mr. Ray practiced more shapeshifting with me. Sari finally stopped calling and texting me. During my free time, I thought about contacting Sari—I was sure she wouldn't want to talk to me.

Although I had my reasons for not responding to her texts, just seeing them made me feel close to her, even though I knew we weren't. I guess it was that little connection that I thought I would still get. This was my fate, and I needed to accept it.

I texted my dad on Thursday night.

T: **Hey, Dad, I'll be headed back to Frost this Sunday afternoon**

D: **Good to hear from you, son. I was wondering since**

240

school starts that following Monday.

T: Yeah, just wanted to absorb all I could. Lots to update u about when I see u

D: I bet. Been missing you. It'll be good to see you soon. Hey, please tell Lisette and Crow hello for me and thank them both, including Mr. Ray.

T: Will do. See u then, luv ya

D: Love you, too. Be safe.

My phone buzzed early Saturday morning. It was Mr. Ray.

R: Tomie, I'll be by Sunday around one to pick you up, is that okay?

T: Yeah... That's like less than twenty-four hours from now... I'll be ready, though

R: Know it's hard.

T: I'm going to really miss being here

R: Yeah, I know, but just think this is your last year of school.

T: Don't remind me

R: You'll be going off to college in a few months.

T: Something like that... well, I better finish packing

R: Okay. See you then.

Picking up the basket of dirty clothes, I carried them into the laundry room. As I separated the clothes, I reminisced about everything that had happened over the last few months in Frost and Monroe Creek.

My summer with Lisette was coming to an end, and this

would be one I'd never forget. A few tears rolled down my face and hit the metal top of the washing machine. I pulled off a paper towel from the roller and dried my cheeks.

After I completed my two loads, I folded all of them and stacked the clothes on the bed before I placed them in my bag. A faint knock sounded on my door.

"Hey, it's me. Can I come in?"

"Of course. Just packing."

"I see." Lisette sat down at the desk chair with her legs crossed. "Need any help?"

"Thanks, I got it."

My eyes felt as if someone had stacked mini sand bags on top of my eyelids. I felt safest in Monroe Creek with Lisette and wished I could've stayed. I knew I had to leave. Seeing Sari was inevitable. I deserved whatever she dished out to me—my payback wasn't going to be pretty.

"How are you feeling about your transformation and all?"

"Pretty okay, so far. Not sure, when I'll need to use it yet."

"Don't worry about that—it will know."

"I believe you, Lisette."

"Just remember all the self-control stuff we practiced and the plan, okay?"

"Won't forget."

"This house won't be the same when you leave." She lowered her head down to her chest. Her eyes began to water. "I told myself before I came in here, I wasn't going to cry right now."

"Hey, it's okay." I went to her and bent down to hug her.

She pulled away and I stood up.

"Look, I'm going to let you finish up. By the way, Crow will be by in a bit. He wanted me to ask you if you wanted to hang out with him this last afternoon."

After placing my clothes in the bag and zipping it up, I said, "Yeah, I would really like that."

"I'll text him and let him know." She ran her hand down my arm. Then, Lisette closed the door behind her.

Grabbing a few tissues from the table, I wiped my eyes. Unaware of when the Five would be coming for me was something I juggled around my mind more and more, especially with my inevitable homecoming approaching faster than I wanted it to.

I heard Crow's voice in the kitchen, so I packed my last items—my book and Sari's ring in a special compartment. I picked up my phone and slid it in my lower pocket in my black cargo shorts.

Entering the kitchen, I saw Crow and Lisette leaning against the island on opposite sides of each other. They both had drinks. I saw another one next to Crow.

"Hey, Crow." I tossed my hand up in the air to high five him.

"Good to see you, Tomie. I picked up frozen lemonades from Scooter's."

"Thanks."

DOLL³

"Welcome." Crow had a big smile planted on his face.

I dug my spoon in and out of the balanced sweet and tart drink without consuming any.

In a booming tone, Crow said, "Hey, too much glum, let's get out of here, Tomie." Crow whispered in Lisette's ear, "See you later."

"Yep, I see y'all whenever you both get tired of each other." She laughed. "Oh, Sabra gets her splint off today!"

"Nice. She's ready to get that thing off her."

"You both be careful and please stay out of trouble." She smiled.

"We'll try our best," Crow growled, baring his upper fangs.

Making our way to his monster truck, we climbed up inside. It took me a little longer than usual. It felt as if the truck had grown higher than the last time, I rode in it with Sari to the festival several weeks ago.

"Did you do something different to your truck, Crow?"

"You noticed. I added mega wheels."

"That's it." I leaned outside the opened window and noticed the wheels. "Man, if I ever get a truck, then I want tires like these."

"Glad you like them."

"Where are we going?"

"You tell me."

Slumping over in my seat, I said, "Don't matter, really. I'm out, after tomorrow."

"How about Monroe Creek's Zoo?"

"There's a zoo here?" I rose up some in my seat.

"Yes. It's a small one with some great exhibits. I don't go often."

"I'm a huge nature and science guy. Any animal or wildlife activity or shows call my name."

"Didn't know that," Crow said with a smile. His fangs slowly receded back in.

I finished my drink.

He drove about a half an hour before we arrived. The parking lot was crowded. There was a little trolley driving around to pick people up who had to park really far or drop them off.

We landed a close parking spot. I tossed my empty cup in a trashcan and pulled out my wallet to pay for our tickets. Crow shook his head.

"My treat. You're my guest."

"You're a pretty awesome dude."

"Thanks, Tomie. I do my best."

"I'm glad Lisette is marrying someone like you."

He smiled, a slight rosy blush painted on both of his caramel cheeks and nose.

Zoo watching was always an adventure to me. Just to know there were so many endangered species in our world that found a haven in zoos like this one was priceless. Now, I could truly relate to these animals about what it was like to be hunted and also caged.

DOLL³

Once we finished a two-hour tour and the parrot feeding, we purchased drinks and decided to rest on a metal bench. Crow asked, "Were you really surprised with your shapeshift transformation?"

"Yes, I wasn't expecting what I saw, or what I could do."

He nodded. "In all honesty, Tomie, I've never witnessed a warlock transform into what you did. I mean, I've seen or heard of witches transforming into cats, rabbits, wolves, and spiders."

This *supra* world was much bigger than I really knew. What else existed here or anywhere? I started thinking about all the cheesy horror movies I used to watch when I was younger and still did. Could some of those stories be real?

I decided to just keep my mind open to anything, because I was sure this wouldn't be the last time I found out something that sounded too ridiculous to be true, but in reality it was.

"Crow, I really hope that I'll be able to stand my ground with my enemies when the time comes." My feet started tapping against the pavement, and my left eye twitched a couple of times.

"To be a strong *supra*, you have to believe in yourself and all of your capabilities. Once you doubt, that leaves room for your enemy to take full advantage of you and use your weaknesses against you. Know that you're stronger and smarter than your foe at all times. Your ultimate strength doesn't come from your powers, which are really nice, but here and here." He tapped the side of his temple and chest.

"Never thought of it like that before, Crow, thanks."

His heartfelt advice hit me, and my feet tapping stopped.

"Of course."

"When you first transformed into a rougarou, were you scared? Have you ever regretted it?"

"It happened for me when I was much younger than you. My granddad and dad prepared me, though. They told me what to expect. The pain that came with it was just part of what I knew I had to embrace from my family tradition. I was born to be an alpha. It's an honor to carry the symbol of my family's tribe. So, I've never regretted my gift."

What Crow had just described to me was powerful and passionate at the same time. I needed this time we were spending together. To bond with another male *supra* was comforting. Talking to my dad was great, but to actually know what it was like to be a *supra* was something I knew he would never understand fully.

"Crow, I've been wanting to ask you something really personal and serious since the day I found out what you were."

"Okay, shoot." He leaned back.

"Have you…" I paused.

"Don't be shy now." He laughed and slammed his Hulk-like hand down on his massive thigh.

"Well, I've been wondering if you've ever… killed someone as a rougarou?"

He leaned in closer to me and looked around to see if anyone was listening. Most of the crowd had left. The food truck guy across from us and a groundskeeper were the only ones around.

"You sure you really want to know?" His eyes locked on mine.

I nodded. "Yes." My eyes grew brighter.

He tapped his fingers on the back of the bench. Loud, clicking sounds rang from his growing nails. I rubbed my arms.

"Tomie, I've never wanted to harm someone or another *supra*, unless he or she was a threat to me or someone I cared about, and I'll leave it at that." He stood and walked over to the trashcan to throw his cup away. "Ready to get out of here?"

"Yeah, sure," I mumbled, standing up and jamming my hands under my armpits.

As we reached Crow's truck, his response to my question kept replaying in my mind. I was almost tempted to ask him how many *supras* he had slaughtered.

I decided not to pursue it. There were probably one or more reasons why Crow didn't wish to share those details about his life, which I respected.

"Wow, it's almost seven," Crow announced. "Didn't know it was that late, sorry for keeping you out. Sure you have stuff you'd rather be doing."

"No, it was really nice to spend time with you. I'm going to miss our talks like this."

"Hey, you're not far away, plus you can call or text me anytime, although I'd rather talk to you face-to-face, any day. Don't forget to let me know if you need me, okay? I know you'll have a lot to contend with, soon."

"You know whatever comes my way, Crow, I believe I'm ready. I owe most of that to Lisette and Mr. Ray."

"She's one of kind. I know she's been teaching you well. Mr. Ray, too."

We got up in the truck. Crow turned on the radio to a nice Cajun-jazz station.

"Tomie, how's Sari?"

"Well, let's just say I'll know more when I get back to Frost."

He looked at me, and his nails returned back to normal size. "I'll let that rest."

"Thank, appreciate it."

"No problem."

Once we arrived back at Lisette's, I opened the door and jumped down. I noticed the curtains were all drawn, including the blinds, and it was still daylight. Lisette usually didn't close everything up until later on. Something wasn't quite right. Yet, I didn't know exactly what it was.

Crow looked at me. "Going to check things out with you." He sniffed the air, and his claws started to emerge.

I was glad he sensed it, too.

"Want to make sure Lisette is okay." He swung the door up

DOLL³

and jumped down from the truck and shut the door quietly. "I'll stay behind you, just in case." Waving his hand, he motioned for me to go first.

Clambering up the steps, we both looked all around and behind us. No one and nothing were in sight. I placed my hand on the doorknob. It opened on its own. My breathing increased and my hands wobbled.

Stepping into the kitchen, nothing seemed to be out of place. The rest of the house was dark. "Lisette!" I yelled out. No response. My heartbeats shot into overdrive.

CHAPTER
THIRTY—TWO

CROW POINTED TOWARDS THE LIVING ROOM. I crept down the long hallway, trying to see in the dimness. As I was about to turn to Crow, I saw movement near the front door. I could feel my warm hands. Before the glow shot down to my palms, the lights flicked on, and I heard several voices shout, "Surprise!"

Looking around, Lisette, Ranae, Mr. Ray, and Ranae's mom were all standing in the center of the room. Caya detached herself from the door. A chocolate cake with yellow icing drizzled on all sides, rested on the table, along with paper plates, forks, waters, and a rainbow of drinks inside an ice-filled barrel.

I was speechless, until Caya stood next to me and bumped

the side of my arm with her elbow. "So, you really had no idea?"

"About this?

"Yeah."

"Not even a hint. Lisette, you know you didn't need to do anything for me."

She came up next to me. "I know I didn't. I wanted to send you off in a special way. After all, you deserve this. Now, cut the cake, please. We've been waiting for over an hour. Crow kept you longer than I thought he would."

"Hold on." I stepped up to Crow. He stood against the wall.

Showcasing my pearly whites, I asked, "Hey, you knew about this all along, didn't you, the whispering exchange between you and Lisette? That's why you took me to the zoo?"

He laughed. "Yep, Sherlock Dupuy. Lisette talked about it a few weeks ago."

"You know how to keep secrets."

"I certainly do. Go enjoy." He patted me on my back and I stumbled.

Rejoining the small circle, I picked up the knife and sliced the cake in several pieces for everyone.

"Thanks, Tomie," Ranae whispered with a wink.

"No, thank you." Caya said with a sigh.

"Please, Caya," Ranae barked.

"What's your problem?" Caya tightened her face and narrowed her eyes.

Ranae took a big bite of cake and rolled her eyes. "Tomie's been knowing about your silly crush on him."

"Why are you being like that?" Caya asked with a frown.

"Don't know what you're referring to." Ranae sashayed in front of her and out the door.

"Maybe I should go." Caya stared down at the floor.

"No, I haven't had time to catch up with you. Plus, I'm out of here tomorrow, so please stay. Let me talk to Ranae, all right?" I grabbed two cold waters.

"Okay."

I went outside and sat down next to Ranae—far enough away where she couldn't brush against me and give me one of her "oops, I'm bad," readings.

"Here." I sat my bottle between us.

She took it, unscrewed the top, and took a long drink.

"Thanks."

"Welcome."

"You want me to make nice with Caya, right?" She turned her head sideways.

"What's up with your hissing back there?"

"Oh, I don't know. Maybe it's because I know you're really cute, and she does, too, or she tends to play the victim way too much for me." She pressed her lips together and gripped the water bottle tight, spilling some on the ground.

"What do you think you actually know about her?"

"Enough," she snapped.

DOLL³

"Caya has a lot going on in her life."

Scooting a few inches toward me, she asked "Like what?"

I moved away from her. "That's not for me to share. If you really want to know her, then talk to her—no reading without consent." I raised my eyebrows.

"Whatever, Tomie." She leaned back on her elbows and tossed her head back, staring at me.

"Look, you're a very—"

"Yes, Tomie."

"We will never be… The same goes with Caya."

She quickly jerked her body around. "Really? So, Caya doesn't stand a chance with you, either?"

"Nope. We're just friends and that's it."

"Why, Tomie Dupuy, I must confess you're rare in more ways than one. Good for you." She stood, facing me. "Guess I can settle for just being your friend," she whispered. "Shake on it?"

"You know, we can do a virtual shake."

"Okay."

We held our hands out without touching.

"Come on back in."

Music was playing. As soon as I opened the door, "Ain't My Type of Hype" by Full Force from *House Party* was playing. Lisette waved me over to her. Everyone else just ate cake and watched us from the couch.

"What?" I asked with my hands raised in the air.

"Dance with me."

"You can't keep up!"

"Please. Is that a dare, Tomie?"

"Maybe."

Lisette surprised me with her dance moves, which were similar to the choreography from the movie during the iconic dance scene at the party with Kid-n-Play.

"No fair because you've watched the movie how many times now?"

"Probably fifteen."

"There you go."

I looked over my shoulder and noticed Ranae talking to Caya. After a couple of songs with Lisette, I headed straight to sit down, which was perfect timing because a slow song came on.

"Crow, your turn," I said.

"Just waiting, patiently."

"Go, she's waiting for you, man."

"Thanks."

He walked over to her and she held out her hand. Crow wrapped his hand around hers, held it up, and kissed it twice. Then, he pulled her in and swung her around.

I reflected back on last year's prom with Sari and our special dance under the huge tree surrounded by fireflies, I'd summoned around us at the festival. I had a pretty good idea what Crow and Lisette were thinking because I'd been there. I wasn't sure if I would ever get a chance to hold her close to my body, to feel all of her, and breathe her in.

Something cold hit my chest, and then I heard my name, "Hey... hey, snap out of it, Romeo," Ranae giggled.

"What's this?" I looked down and noticed ice chips on my legs. I stood up. "Real mature, Ranae." I picked them up and tossed them into an empty cup and threw it in the trash.

Caya and her just laughed.

"You needed some cooling off," Ranae said with a half wink.

"Glad to see you both getting along better."

"Yeah," Caya said. "Hey, you and Sari doing okay?"

My head dropped down for a few seconds, and I looked away from her.

"You know, I've got to get up early for work, so I'll see you around, Caya," Ranae said. "Goodnight all."

"Leaving so soon, Ranae?" Lisette asked.

"See you around. Text me, Caya, maybe we can hang out together soon, just like we used to."

"I would really like that," Caya said with a faint smile.

Ranae hugged her and turned around.

Her mom gave Lisette a hug and approached me.

"Well, Tomie, I didn't get a chance to spend a lot of time with you. Ranae thinks you're amazing. She talks about you all the time."

"Bet she does." I grinned.

Ranae winked at me.

"Have a safe trip back home and be safe. Definitely take heed to Ranae's vision." She gave me a side hug and left.

"Caya, I'll be back soon."

"Sure, Tomie." She brushed her hair back.

Escorting Ranae out, I closed the door behind me with a slight blink.

Her mom was checking her cell phone in the car.

"Thanks for hanging out with us."

"Of course, you know, anytime I can stalk you, Tomie, I will." She guffawed at the expression on my face. "Just kidding."

"No, you weren't," I replied, massaging my wrist.

"Well, maybe just a little."

"Hey, watch out for Caya while I'm gone."

"Will do my best. When will you be back in town again?" Before I could respond, she blurted out, "For Lisette's wedding. I saw when I took your last reading. By the way, you're going to rock your duck tails tux on Lisette's big day."

I leaned in a little closer to her. "You saw that?"

"Sure did." She snapped both of her fingers together.

Rubbing my hands together, I asked, "Did you see anything else?"

"Oh, you mean, was Sari with you or around?"

"Yes, did you?"

My heart started racing.

"Sorry, I just saw you and Lisette. Wow, her dress is amazing."

"Ranae, you're something else. You keep just enough from someone, don't you?"

"Listen, I only see what I see. Do me a favor?"

"What?"

"Like I told you before, avoid going out on Halloween."

"Yeah, I remember. Still think I could take care of myself, Ranae." My green eyes glowed.

"Just do it," she commanded, biting her nails.

Looking away from her, I said, "Let up already. You can stop worrying because I won't have any reason to leave, anyhow." I pressed my lips tight.

"Don't get me wrong, I love your Iron Man confidence." She played with her hair and blinked her eyes three times in a row really fast, staring into my eyes. "Hold on."

She ran down the steps and opened up the back door of the car. A green paper bag was swaying in her hand as she stood in front of me. "Here you go."

"What's this, Ranae?"

"Nothing much, just something to remember me by." She handed me the bag by its black handles. I made sure to avoid her neon pink and golden glittered fingertips, although she was wiggling them all around the place.

Slanting my eyes, I asked, "How could anyone not?"

"Tomie, that's rude, especially after I've given you a gift for your parting."

"Sorry."

"I accept. Now, open it, already. Gotta go soon." She bounced up and down.

Pulling the taped bag apart, I pushed some black tissue paper back and grabbed a clear plastic ornament ball with various items on the inside, hanging from a seven-inch purple ribbon.

"Thank you—what is it?"

"What? You don't know what this is?" Her mouth dropped open.

"Nope." I spun it around a few times with my index finger.

"It's a witch ball."

"Okay, why do I need it? I'm a warlock."

"Whoa, you must have skipped that section in your spell books and all."

"I skimmed a lot of stuff."

"Tomie, what a shame that you missed the section on this wonderful device."

"What does it do?"

I squinted and inspected it closely.

"Primarily, it protects you from evil *supras*, spells, and negativity. You're supposed to hang it in the east window of your home. Many hang them in any window or outside in a garden."

"How is this supposed to protect me?" I lifted it up to my nose. "It smells sweet and spicy."

Her beaming face caught me. "The magic is what's inside—

don't let looks deceive you, my sweet friend." She winked twice. "Pay attention now: *shredded cinnamon* for happiness/comfort, *sage* for long life, *cloves* to attract good luck, *bay leaves* for protection, *jasmine* to attract sweet dreams, *anise* to ward off the evil eye, and a wad of *yarn* at the bottom to capture the bad stuff." She rested a hand on her swaying hips.

"So, I just hang it up, and it's going to do all of that?"

"Yes."

"Did you make this?"

"Sure did. After I read you, I knew I had to do something. So, I did my research, and my mom helped me some."

Ranae's gift made me really think how I needed to pay attention to everything.

"Very thoughtful, Ranae, thank you." I went to hug her and quickly rethought my plan.

She turned her right cheek and leaned a little closer to me.

"Well, can't expect a girl like me to wait around for what I know you should do." She grinned.

"Seriously?"

"Hey, can't blame me for trying. Knew you wouldn't."

"I have a really good feeling that you're going to meet someone soon, who's going to be perfect for you."

"Dang it, you just *glimmed* me, didn't you?"

"Yes." I laughed.

"Without my permission."

"I did. You shouldn't have anything to say about that."

"Guess I'll let it slide this time because of the awesome 411 you just fed me, plus, you owe me a dance at the wedding, Tomie."

"Only, if it's a fast dance."

"Ha! Fair enough, you're smart."

"That's what they tell me."

"Tomie, take it easy. Hang the ball up and celebrate Halloween at your house, only!"

I smiled at her, as she walked away.

She waved to me from inside of the car. Her mom waved, as well. Once I returned back inside the house, I noticed that Mr. Ray, Lisette, and Crow were gone. Caya sat on the couch, watching television.

"Hey, I'll be right back."

"No problem." A closed-lip smile followed.

Lisette, Mr. Ray, and Crow were all sitting around the table talking. I stood next to Lisette. "All okay?"

"We were just talking about everything," Lisette replied. "What's in the bag?"

"Ranae gave me a witch ball."

"Can I see?" she asked.

"Sure." I handed it to her.

"Now, I haven't seen one of these in a few years. I didn't know they were still popular." Lisette analyzed all the contents inside, sniffing it.

"Ranae thought it would be good for me to have one,

especially after her vision."

"Yes, I understand. That was really sweet of her, Tomie."

"Tell me about it." I tucked my hands behind my neck.

"Tomie, you're a natural girl magnet," Crow said. "Man, it's your hair and height, I'm telling you." He chortled. "You're turning really red."

"Whatever. I'm going to spend some time with Caya, okay? Mr. Ray, I haven't forgotten about you."

"No worries. We have the trip back and then some. I'm about to head out myself to get some rest for the trip tomorrow. I'll be by in the early afternoon like we already talked about. Have a goodnight everyone. I'll see myself out."

"Sounds good, Mr. Ray."

I returned to the living room. "Sorry for the delay."

"It's fine. I know you need to share your goodbyes with everyone."

"What were you asking me before, Caya?"

"How are you and Sari doing?"

In my mind, I thought about lying to her. I already told one lie to Sari, so I decided to tell her the limited truth.

"We're taking a break for awhile."

"Oh..."

Facing her, I said, "Look, it's not what you may be thinking."

"Tomie, I'm not assuming anything. We all have our reasons to do what we need to do. I made the decision to break it off with Garth because now I know, with my therapist's help, that he wasn't good for me. In fact, he was toxic, and a big part of my low self-esteem."

"Proud of you." I touched the top of her hand.

"Just for the first time, I realized how damaged I was. Now, I understand Caya needs to figure out who she lost, like my therapist has been working with me to rediscover. I want you to know that you really helped me a lot, especially to start paying attention to see what was really in front of me."

"I wanted you to know you deserved way better."

"Thank you. Seriously, I hope you and Sari work things out, when you go home."

"Taking it slow, Caya." My eyes focused away from her for a few seconds.

"No plans for me to jump in a new relationship anytime soon. This year, I'm just going to focus on my senior year and help my mom out."

"By the way, how's your mom doing?"

"A little better. She had a doctor's appointment two weeks ago, and the doctor started her on a new medication regimen to help her pain. So far, it seems to be working. Tomie, I want you to know that it was really good to meet you this summer. I'm going to really miss you."

"I'll miss you, too, Caya. Text me anytime."

"Definitely—I want be the Ranae-Stalker, type. You do the same. Before I become a leaky faucet, I'm going to get out of here, okay, Tomie?"

"Good to know."

We both laughed.

Before she opened her car door, we hugged. She slid into the driver's seat and started her ignition with a slight nod.

"You know, Monroe Creek won't be the same without you."

Smiling, I said, "Thanks."

She handed me a small gift bag.

"What's this?"

"Just a little something for your trip back."

Opening it up, I smelled sweet aromas. Fruity and chocolate candies, in clear wrappers, were inside, along with a few chewy lollipops, too. A CD was buried at the bottom. I lifted it up. It was titled, "Tomie," in large colorful letters with glitter.

"Thanks, Caya. I didn't get you or Ranae anything. Honestly, I didn't think I would see either of you before I left."

"Never expected you to get me anything. Anyhow, you gave me the best gift that anyone can give someone… I know the CD is old school, but my mom gave me the idea. Most of the songs are upbeat, except a few sappy ones on there."

"Best gift?" I asked.

"*Kindness* and *real* friendship. Take care of you and be careful out there. Let me know if you need my help in any way."

"Appreciate it, you do the same, Caya."

"Maybe, I'll see you at the wedding."

"Oh, you will."

She backed her car up and drove off.

CHAPTER
THIRTY—THREE

WHEN I CAME INTO THE HOUSE, I NOTICED CROW and Lisette sitting in the kitchen table with coffee mugs.

"Everyone gone?" Lisette asked, taking a long sip from her Wonder Woman mug.

"Yes."

"Hope you enjoyed the surprise."

"Sure did, thank you."

Crow stood and gave me a hug. This time I could actually breathe.

"Take care, Tomie. Call anytime, and we'll see you at your graduation."

I looked over to Sabra. Her cast was gone.

"What did the vet say?"

"She's good. Her walk will be a little wobbly, but she should improve, day by day."

"That's really wonderful news, Lisette."

"Yes, I know. My girl is totally back." Her eyes twinkled.

I bid them both good night. After taking a shower, I checked all the drawers and closet. My bag was full and ready.

The next morning arrived. I woke up and headed directly to the bathroom to shower. I made waffles, turkey bacon, and freshly squeezed orange juice. All the dishes were washed and dried. Sabra trotted up next to me. I lowered a slice of bacon down, next to my leg. She grabbed it, hopped, and chirped to herself back to her bed.

I heard Lisette. "Hmm, what smells so good this morning?"

"Made us breakfast, voila!"

"Thank you, Tomie. Everything looks so delicious. I really do appreciate you taking time to fix all of this."

"My pleasure. It's just a little something to tell you how much I appreciate all you've done for me this summer and beyond."

"It's all because I love you."

"Dig in."

It was nice to know how much I meant to her. I knew I would always be welcome to her home.

The clock on the wall read after eleven-thirty. Mr. Ray would be driving up soon. When he arrived out front, he honked his horn twice. I gathered up my bags and swung them on my shoulders.

Lisette walked me outside, Sabra wrapped around her neck. She handed me two paper sack lunch bags and a plastic square container full of leftover cake. I had a strong sense of déjà vu. This was exactly how I'd first met Sabra.

"What's inside the bags?"

"Sandwiches, chips, apples."

"Thanks."

"No problem, now give me a hug. I know you gotta get out of here."

I bent down to her height, embracing her. Sabra lifted her head and made chirping noises. I patted her, she closed her eyes, and opened them up to stare at me; she licked my hand. I could feel her sharp fangs graze against my thumb. My heart started pacing. She resumed her snuggling position.

Lisette whispered, "Don't ever think twice about contacting me, whether it's night or day. Remember the plan—have to keep drilling it in your head. Be careful, and pay attention to everyone around you. Keep that necklace on."

Shuffling my feet back and forth, I smiled.

"Talk to Sari, when you can."

I knew that regaining her trust wouldn't be easy. Leaving Lisette caused my heart to feel all tangled up. In a way, I just wanted to tell Mr. Ray to go without me, and tell my dad I wasn't returning, but I knew I was only avoiding Frost.

Opening the back door, I placed my bags in the back and the sack lunches down in the seat. Then, I stepped into Mr. Ray's truck. He placed his car in gear, and we waved at Lisette. She waved back. My tears wanted to burst, but I kept them locked away.

CHAPTER
THIRTY—FOUR

M R. RAY WAS QUIET FOR THE FIRST HOUR OF OUR trip.

I couldn't stand it any longer. "Mr. Ray, why you so quiet?"

"Just focused on driving and thinking about everything that's happened when we first met up, 'til now."

"Did my transformation shock you that night, Mr. Ray?"

He flashed a wry grin. "Well, I didn't expect it."

"Me either," I confessed.

I reached behind the seat to pull my shades out of a side pocket from my bag.

"Your gift knows when you will need it to emerge." He looked over at me. "Hope I'm there to experience or at least to hear about it."

I nodded and turned on the radio to a station Mr. Ray would approve of and dozed off. More than three hours passed, and we had stopped at a Valero. Mr. Ray was pumping gas. I opened the door, stepped out to stretch, and darted straight to the bathroom.

When I returned, Mr. Ray had moved the truck from the gas pump and parked on the side out of traffic under a tree. He sat in the driver's seat, eating. I noticed the two lunch bags sitting in the middle of us with cold water bottles inside cup holders. "Tasty sandwich Lisette made."

"She's an awesome cook." I grabbed my unopened bag and pulled out two sandwiches and the bag of chips. "Why didn't you wake me up?" I swallowed. "You let me sleep most of the way."

"Tomie, you needed it. Hey, why did you want to return home so close to your first day of school?"

"I wanted to spend as much time as I could with Lisette before leaving Monroe Creek."

"And?"

Dragging my words, I said, "Didn't want to run into Sari. At least in school, I know where she'll be, and I can avoid her, if necessary. She doesn't want to be around me, anyhow."

"Okay, wait. I'm really confused. Did I miss something? You two broke up?"

I grabbed the Macintosh apple from the bag, taking a huge bite. "Something like that," I muttered around the fruit.

"Thought you two were working things out?"

"Her dad is the one who made contact with someone who told the Dupuy Silver Slayer Committee about me."

"Sari's dad did that?" Mr. Ray almost aspirated on his food.

"You okay?" I looked over at him.

"Fine, just wasn't expecting that." He coughed a few times and sipped some water.

I finished off the apple and chunked the core in the bag with the other trash.

"How in the world did he make contact with someone who knew about slayers?" Mr. Ray's jaw dropped and his pupils dilated.

"It was at the hospital that night of Pepper's accident. He told a doctor or nurse what I did to cause his burn on his hand, plus Verlinda talked to him."

"Oh, now that makes sense. You just never know who's involved in the hidden slayer world. Whoever he talked to used the information he supplied to bait him in."

"Why are *supras* so hated by slayers and non-slayers, Mr. Ray?" I stared out the side of my window and rested my hand against my face.

"There are many reasons, I'm sure. One of the main reasons why we're so hated is because we instill fear, due to possessing something that they don't, which intimidates them. Therefore, their one goal is to hunt and exterminate us—or help the exterminators out."

"We didn't choose to be a *supra*—it chose us. Not all of us are bad."

"This I know, but hate doesn't discriminate between the good or bad *supras*, Tomie."

"Exactly, just like it doesn't for how I look on the outside, Mr. Ray." I opened up the water bottle and drank it down slow. "What time do you think we'll make it to Frost?"

Mr. Ray pulled out his silver pocket watch with an owl imprint on the cover. "We have probably about thirty or so more miles. Should be back home before dinner time, if we don't stop anymore. Have you talked to your dad?"

"Texted him recently. He's been busy with a lot of truck jobs all over."

"Bet he has. I know he'll be happy to see you soon."

"I'll be happy to see him, too."

Grabbing the candy from my bag, I offered some to Mr. Ray. He took a lollipop.

"Thanks. Who gave you the bag of candy?" he asked, unwrapping the sucker and placing the car in drive.

"Caya."

"Really?" He smiled with the candy twirling from the side of his mouth.

"What does that mean?"

In a low tone, he said, "Nothing."

"Ranae made me a witch ball for protection."

"My, my, my..."

DOLL³

"C'mon, Mr. Ray." My cheeks felt warm.

"Hey, I'm not the one blushing with multiple suitors." He laughed out loud, as he removed the candy from his mouth.

"Whatever."

"Call it as I see it, Romeo."

"I'm praying my Juliet will welcome Romeo back and allow me to climb up her balcony to serenade her."

"Why wouldn't she?"

Scratching my head and running my hands over my face, I admitted, "I lied to her about something she may not forgive me for, but I had to," I said in a croaky voice.

"No need to tell me more—you'll have your work cut out for you. She probably won't give you time of the day, at first—don't fret. Sometimes, it takes constant persistence to win a young lady's heart back."

"I'm going to do all I can."

"Good. By the way, witch balls, if made correctly, really do work. I had one years ago made by a good friend."

I shook my head. "I plan to hang it near my window in my room."

Clicking his teeth, he said, "Perfect location."

We passed the time talking about Salem and my tea leaf reading, until I saw the "Welcome to Frost" sign. My mind sailed to Sari. "Hey, Mr. Ray, before you drop me off at home, can you do me a tiny favor?"

"Sure, what?"

"Drive by Sari's house."

"You want to talk to her, now?"

"Not exactly."

"Young people these days, goodness." He shook his head.

Before we reached Sari's house, I noticed the back of her hair and some guy sitting on the front end of a red Camaro. I slid down low in my seat.

Squishing his eyebrows together, he said, "What in the world are you doing, Tomie?"

"Just drive, not too fast, Mr. Ray, please. I want to see if I'm right about who this guy is."

"You got it."

Mr. Ray drove just slow enough for me to catch the guy's face. He turned towards me, a huge smirk planted on his face, throwing his hand up at me to give me a half salute. I rose up and looked back.

CHAPTER
THIRTY—FIVE

I T WAS PHOENIXX. SARI SAW ME, AND THE MOST terrifying glare protruded from her face. It made me want to crawl under a bed; I could feel jagged daggers screwing inside my back. I knew Phoenixx had a thing for Sari, especially after his little stunt at the talent show during the festival—he was loving this.

My hands started heating up, and the blue glow appeared. I glanced down and started breathing in and out, slowly, thinking about what Lisette had taught me. The glow gradually faded.

"Good job, Tomie. Lisette told me how she was teaching you how to control that."

"She did, in ways I've never imagined. I'm seeing it's effective."

"Is that Sari's new beau?"

"What?" I jerked my head towards him.

"Calm down there, cowboy. It's obvious your feelings are very strong for her. You may need to talk to her sooner than you planned on."

"You're probably right. It's just her dad and all."

"That's the thing about loving someone. You never know what will come with that person."

"No kidding. Well, he doesn't have a problem with Phoenixx hanging out with her. Why is that?" I clenched my fists.

"I don't know." He sighed and rolled the end of his mustache between his fingers.

"Mr. Ray, I thought maybe he was the slayer. Now, I don't think he is."

"Why?"

"Just have that feeling, I guess."

"Watch him, still. Pay attention to everyone, because slayers can be very sneaky and disguise their appearance."

Mr. Ray arrived at my house. I unloaded everything from his truck. He attempted to help me, but I told him, "Thanks, Mr. Ray, I got it. Keep the cake."

"You sure?"

"Yes."

"Guess I won't see you on my bus this year, being a big senior and all."

"Maybe if I have car trouble, again." I laughed.

DOLL³

He chuckled. "I recall you riding my bus last year, because of your car issues, which ignited my warning to you about Opal."

I closed my eyes. "Don't remind me. I should've listened to you."

"Hey, all was supposed to happen as it did. Look how much you've achieved." He patted me on my shoulder. "Wanted to tell you that I'm thinking about retiring this year."

"Really?"

"Yes. You'll be leaving next fall and all. I don't have any commitments here."

"Frost High won't be the same without you."

"Believe me, they'll be fine."

"Thank you again for driving me and all you've done, Mr. Ray."

"My pleasure. I'll be around."

We hugged.

He jumped back into his truck. As I approached my door, I turned around and threw my hand up to wave at him. Driving off, he honked his horn twice. Before I reached the door, Dad opened it up and embraced me.

"So good to see you, son. Hand me your bags." He placed them down on the floor next to the couch.

The door closed behind me.

Smoked barbecue chicken, corn on the cob, green beans, and mashed potatoes dressed the kitchen table. The house was just as I left it. There was so much I wanted to share with Dad, and I knew that I would start tonight at dinner.

"Everything smells great."

"I hope you enjoy."

"Sure I will, thanks, Dad."

"Missed you, son."

"Same here."

"Sit."

"Be back in five." I picked up my bags from the ground and walked to my bedroom to set them down. Then, I went into my bathroom to wash up. As I was rinsing my face a few times, I thought about Phoenixx being at Sari's house. Taking several deep breaths in and out, I grabbed a towel to dry my face and hands off.

Peeping down the hall, I saw Dad pouring drinks in glasses. I hung the towel on the bar to dry and left. Pulling my chair out, I sat down. Dad followed and held out his hand. I grabbed it, and he said grace.

"Help yourself."

"How has work been?"

"Busy. I'm off the next seven days and on again for seven."

"I know you're happy."

"Yes, I'll get some time with you, not much because school begins tomorrow. Are you excited about your senior year?"

My fork vibrated against my plate, tossing my food from one side to the other, as I thought about when Opal, Verlinda, or Pepper would show up.

Dad gave me that look. He wiped his mouth with a cloth napkin and folded it on his lap. He pushed his plate to the side and propped his arms on the table, clasping his hands together. "Son, what's wrong?"

Taking a few sips of the cold, sweet lemon tea, I set my glass down in front of my plate. "So much happened over the summer, Dad, I don't know where to begin."

"Just start with what's heaviest on your heart, Tomie."

I wanted to tell him about my feelings about the unknown slayers, but I didn't want him to worry.

"Sari and I broke it off. I guess you can say I broke it off more than she did."

"Why?"

"Her dad."

I told him everything that had transpired with her father. He was silent for several minutes before he stood up from the table and made his way over to the kitchen sink.

"Tomie, I've always been cordial to Mr. Green in public and all. I never would've thought he would do something this low, especially to you. That's just wrong. Now, it's caused a huge problem with your relationship with Sari. I'm so sorry, son." His head hung low.

"You have nothing to apologize for."

"It makes me feel awful, how this is impacting you. I know you told me before you didn't want me to talk to him—maybe

I really should, Tomie."

"Oh, no, Dad. Seriously, that would make things so much worse," I pleaded as my feet started tapping under the table.

"You really think so?"

"It would. So, promise me that you won't go confronting him about anything. Don't get me wrong, I really appreciate you wanting to make things better."

Dad shook his head and turned around to start washing the dishes.

"Promise me," I repeated, biting my lower lip and wiping sweat from my forehead with my hand.

"Won't say anything, scout's honor." He threw up the three-finger salute.

I cleared the table and placed leftovers in plastic containers. I filled him in about the rest of the summer, including my Salem visit and my shifting gift.

Dad listened in, as if he was watching an action movie. The expressions on his face were almost comical.

"Boy, you had a summer." He rubbed the back of his neck with both hands.

"Sure did."

"I've always wondered if you possessed something extraordinary. Never figured it would be what you just shared with me."

"Did Mom ever tell you any stories about witches or warlocks possessing a gift like mine?"

"Tomie, I can't recall any specifics... I know the worst is not behind you yet. I strongly believe the training Lisette and Mr. Ray provided will benefit you."

"Yep, I agree." I dried the last plate and handed it to dad to place in the cabinet.

"I know you're tired. Why don't you get a shower?"

"It can wait. Let's watch that western show you like to watch."

"Really? I know you don't like my shows." His hand flew towards his chest.

"Hey, I never gave them a chance. No time better than the present, right? That's what they say."

Two hours passed, and it was a little after seven-thirty. I stood up to stretch. "Wasn't half bad. Dad, thanks for dinner and listening."

"You're welcome, that's what I'm here for, son."

"Feels good to be home."

"Good to have you back. I spent a lot of lonely nights here when I wasn't on the road, and of course, on the road is way lonelier."

"Will your truck routes change back to more local now?"

"Yes, they'll resume back soon. I just took more out of state jobs because you were gone all summer, and took a few extra jobs for co-workers, who needed some time off. Try to help out where I can."

"That's something you do very well." I smiled.

"Means a lot to hear that from you. I was thinking…" He stood, turned the television off, and placed the remote on the table. We started down the hallway, and he flicked on the light.

"What's that?"

"You being gone was lonely, indeed. When you leave for the academy… It's going to be really different, Tomie."

"I haven't been accepted yet. For all I know, I may be attending Frost Junior College."

"Never just settle. That's not your dream, son. I have no doubt that you'll be accepted."

"Lisette said the same thing. Anyhow, Dad, I'll be home for the holidays and some summers." Honestly, it would all depend if I survived my encounter with you-know-who.

"When you start making friends, joining clubs and different things, the way you spend your time is going to change more than you realize."

"I'll make time."

"Tomie, I know you won't do it on purpose. Your life is about to evolve once you graduate, and I'm going to have to learn to accept that, even though I wish that I didn't." He placed his hand on my shoulders and stared into my eyes.

"Let's just worry about that later. I have this time with you, right now. Well, get some rest. I'll see you in the morning."

He hugged me tight.

"Goodnight, Dad. Love you."

DOLL³

"Love you, too, Tomie." He went down the hall towards his room.

Before I showered, I unfastened the necklace and placed it on the bathroom counter. I flicked the light on in my bedroom and noticed my bag was unzipped. I heard something tapping against my window. I assessed my room and saw the witch ball hanging up. The ribbon was tied around the lock.

I saw a text on my phone from Lisette.

L: Hey, there. Glad you made it back safely. I took the liberty to hang up your very thoughtful gift from Ranae. Remember what I told you. Talk soon.

T: **Thanks Lisette. 'Night**

I wanted to text Sari, after seeing her today and still feeling those knives in my back, I wasn't looking forward to seeing her tomorrow. It was after ten.

Pulling my *Aliens* comforter and sheets back, I crawled into bed and attempted to close my eyes. After thirty minutes, I was still up. The witch ball bounced up against the window a few times, and I turned over, throwing the pillow on top of my head. It was almost after midnight before I finally drifted off to sleep.

Then, I heard something scratching, so I turned over towards my window. Opening my eyes wider, I saw something, but I wasn't sure what it was. I tumbled out of bed. Grabbing my cell phone off the table to turn on the flashlight, I pointed it toward the window.

The witch ball twirled to the left and right. Several skeleton-like handprints were all over my window. They lifted up like stickers off a page and disappeared.

Peering out the window, I saw three people running in dark cloaks into the night. Faint light from flashlights seemed to bounce into the darkness with them, and then they were gone.

The ball ceased its movements. My hands floundered to pull my curtains closed; I returned to bed, as my heart galloped inside my chest. Although Ranae liked playing games with me, her gift was already paying off.

I texted Lisette; I couldn't stop thinking about what just happened.

T: **Hey, u still up? Sorry 2 bother u but something just happened with my witch ball**

She responded in less than two minutes.

L: **What?**

T: **That thing starting banging loud against the window**

L: **It was warning and protecting you from something bad. Did it give you a sign of some kind?**

T: **If u mean showing me creepy handprints on my window and watching three cloaked people run from my house, then I guess it gave me a big sign**

L: **Tomie, someone evil was trying to place a spell on you tonight, probably Opal or Verlinda. Thank goodness you have that. Are you still wearing the necklace I gave you?**

T: **Not wearing it at the moment**

L: **Put that on, right now! It will protect you outside the house. Wearing it at all times is part of the plan, okay?**

Getting out of bed, I retrieved the necklace from the bathroom and fastened it around my neck. As soon as it touched my chest, I felt really warm. A bright, golden glow reflected off my chest.

T: **Done. Man, it's really warm and glowing bright tonight**

L: **Good. Recall, it's syncs me to you, if you're ever in trouble and cannot communicate with me directly or telepathically, then I would know. Don't take it off anymore, got it!**

T: **Yep. Do you think I need to do a protection spell around my house, like I helped you with at yours?**

L: **Nope, the witch ball that Ranae created for you will detour any darkness trying to harm you in your home, including your dad because he's within your environment. Ranae put a lot of thought in her special gift to you.**

Lisette followed with a laughing emoji.

T: **Funny. Please thank her again when you see her. I appreciate her help**

L: **I will. I think I'm going to ask her to make me one.**

T: **U should**

L: **Listen, time for you to go to bed. Keep me posted about anything strange, that's part of our plan.**

T: **Will do. 'Night. Thanks, Lisette**

L: **Anytime, goodnight.**

I closed my fluctuating eyes to try to sleep several times—failed each time. All I could think about was Opal and Verlinda's next move and what was coming my way next. I tossed and turned, most of the night.

My piercing alarm sounded from my phone. I didn't hit the snooze button, as usual. I rolled out of bed slowly and pulled on a wrinkled black T-shirt and jeans. Brushing up in the bathroom, I looked in the mirror—red eyes screeched at me. Searching for some Visine in my bathroom drawer, I leaned my head back and dropped two drops in each eye. I shook my head without picking my curls out.

Tossing my backpack over my shoulder, I straggled to the kitchen and poured a bowl of cereal, spilling some milk on the counter. I wiped it up with a wet dishrag from the sink and slid my backpack on the chair arm. Dad walked in the backdoor with a rolled up newspaper in his hand.

"Good morning. I was about to make you some pancakes and bacon."

"Maybe another time. I kinda want to get to school a little early today."

"Sure you do—how much sleep did you get?"

Lifting a spoonful to my mouth with my shaky hand, I said, "Very little."

"Son, you all right?" He placed his paper down on the table.

"Yeah. Just not sure what will happen when I see Sari."

287

"Just be yourself. Maybe you two will get to talk."

"Not counting on it." I wiped my eyes with my hand and ate half the cereal.

"What are your plans for today?" I asked.

"Running a few errands in town—Tomie, you never leave cereal in your bowl. Did something happen last night?"

Pausing for over a minute, I confessed, "Unknown intruders were at my window. My witch ball kept them out. I talked to Lisette about it. Don't worry because no one can harm us here."

"Thanks, son, for sharing. I knew you were worried about something. You just try to focus on school as best as you can. Anything I can do to help, Tomie, then let me know."

Twirling my necklace between my fingers, "Dad that means a lot—there are just things I'll have to face soon on my own."

"Know you're not alone. I understand I possess no special powers, but think back to how Spiderman never expected humans to help and protect him in that train scene. Sometimes, it's the little things that count just as much as the bigger ones, if not more." He stood, bent down, and hugged me.

"I get it, Dad. Thanks." I sniffled.

He patted my back. "Love you."

Picking up my bowl, I started towards the kitchen sink to wash it.

"Don't worry about that. I'll clean it up later. Go ahead and get to school," Dad called to me.

"Thanks." I grabbed my backpack from the chair. "See you this afternoon."

"Hope your day gets a little better."

Waving my hand at him, I left the house, going to my car. I started the engine, placed it in gear, and drove to Frost High. It was almost seventy degrees already.

I found a close parking spot at school. Pulling my backpack from the seat and stepping out of the car, I saw Sari getting out of Phoenixx's car. He spied me watching. Sari dropped something on the ground, so he bent down to assist her.

All I wanted to do was to jump back in my car and drive off. Instead, I slid my keys back into my pocket and lowered my head for a couple of seconds.

As they were stooped down to the ground, her hair fell towards her face. He handed her phone to her and brushed back the strands, tucking them behind her right ear. He looked over at me with a twisted smirk. They stood up and entered the cafeteria doors.

Heat invaded my body. In a way, I felt like I was on fire. I closed my eyes and counted backwards, slowly starting at twenty. At ten, I could feel my body cooling and returning back to normal. *Calm down, Tomie—breathe.*

Taking in several deep breaths, I opened up my eyes and chose the side door of the school building. It was burning me to confront her and Mr. Sly Fox, but honestly I had no right, especially after what I had told her. She was justified to move on with her life, even if it meant I could never be part of it again.

I pulled out my phone to download my class schedule, traveling to the library to retrieve my books and placed my earbuds in. From my playlist, I chose "I Don't Want To" by Toni Braxton. The book pick-up line wasn't bad this year because there were more volunteers. There were a few electives I swapped out for something different. I wasn't sure what classes I would be sharing with Sari.

When I entered the hallway, I saw them walking in the middle of the noisy crowd towards me—not Sari and Phoenixx—worse, the three *Vipers* with a new replacement— Opal Dawn.

CHAPTER
THIRTY—SIX

OPAL'S FIERY EYES LOCKED ON MINE. SHE WHIPPED back her long, black hair, sporting fuchsia and turquoise tips. A cut-off black lace blouse barely draped her mid-drift. The blue bra underneath seemed to shimmer. Her boots made a clicking sound every step she took closer to me.

Turning around to punch the number pad on my locker, I watched as Opal leaned against the locker next to mine and propped her leg up. My skin crawled, and I felt my stomach doing multiple somersaults. She popped her gum a few times and blew a huge, green bubble out. Inhaling it back in her mouth without a trace of gum web, she tilted her head towards me. "How was your summer?"

I unzipped my backpack, pulled the door open, stacked

most of the books in an upright position, and kept the books I needed for my next three classes. Mollie Darling and Cecilee Hawkins, Viper Two and Viper Three, mimicked Opal's positions.

It was interesting to watch Mollie assume the second place role again, especially after she thought that she would be promoted to first place, once Pepper was removed from the competition. Opal appeared to be the new Viper in charge.

From what I remembered, Mollie hated her skin and dabbled in various skin-bleaching products to resemble her idols on those girly magazine covers. She was very strong-willed and vocal. Mollie knew her place when Pepper once ruled Frost High. As for Cecilee, she was an automatic follower and would do anything Pepper had asked her to do, which made Pepper's control much easier.

The two biggest differences between Mollie and Cecilee were that Mollie's family didn't have money and Cecilee's family did. Pepper had considered Mollie one of her charity projects who she could mold to her satisfaction.

Although Pepper had detested being around Cecilee's plump appearance, she tolerated her because of her family's financial connections and her older brother's celebrity status on a popular television series, which would benefit her family, as well.

"Didn't you hear my question?"

"Opal, I heard you." I slammed my locker door and stared

down at her, pressing the button on my phone to stop my music.

"Well." She continued to pop her gum. Cecilee and Mollie just stood there watching, until Mollie decided to speak.

"You know, Pepper's back."

"Mollie, you need to keep your loose mouth shut," Opal shouted and extended her hand out and whacked her across her face.

I shook my head.

Rolling her eyes and rubbing the side of her face with her jeweled up hand, Mollie said, "Ouch! Why did you do that? What's the big freaking deal, anyhow? He probably knows." She rummaged through her Coach purse.

The bell rung and everyone in the hall scurried to their classes.

"Just stop talking," Opal barked, attempting to adjust her tight skirt.

Repositioning my backpack and placing it on my shoulder, I began to walk away from the back and forth hissing. Before I was ten feet away, I heard Opal speak.

She stood in the middle of the hallway and shouted, "Did you sleep well last night?"

Jerking my body completely around, "What did you say?"

The hallway was nearly empty.

Opal's eyes shifted and transformed to solid black with a yellow glow encircling them.

"You heard me, so don't pretend!"

Mollie and Cecilee stepped away from her, and Cecilee staggered behind Mollie.

"Figured it was you last night, Opal." I pulled my earbuds out, one by one.

I stepped toward her.

She looked at me, crossing her arms over her puffed out chest. "Your time is running short, Tomie Dupuy."

"Hey, you name the time and place." My eyes shimmered a golden bronze.

Opal placed her finger on my chest and began to poke me. "You'll know—oh, tell your girl to watch her back. Accidents happen all the time," she whispered in a gravelly voice. Her vacant eyes throbbed.

"Stop touching me, Opal." I commanded.

Flipping her hair back and smacking her gum, "You're not going to do anything, especially here." Her voice cracked.

"I'm really not in the mood." I squeezed my eyes shut.

She dug her finger deeper into my chest like a corkscrew. A burning sensation swept over my face and chest. Counting backwards starting at ten, I opened up my eyes, but her finger remained in the irritating position. I looked over my shoulders and scanned the hallway in back of me. No one was present, even Mollie and Cecilee had vanished.

Lifting my hands up, I peeled her finger off my chest and levitated her five feet off the ground. I began to chant a spell,

"One, two, three…" Before I could finish, I felt my necklace becoming extremely warm, and it let off a bright orange glow. Lisette's voice followed.

Tomie, what are you doing?

About to shut her down for a little while.

Not there, too risky. You need to bring her down because someone is approaching, fast.

So sick of her and all her little threats.

Listen to me, Tomie, do it now. You have less than fifteen seconds.

I placed her down on the ground.

Ms. Gobblestein flew around the corner in her black and white checkered wool suit. She clapped her hands together and stood between us.

"Mr. Dupuy and Ms. Dawn, why are you two not in class?" she demanded. "Speak up!"

"Ms. Gobblestein, we were just headed that way," I offered.

Opal backed away from me and mouthed, "See you around, loser."

I wanted to mouth back something to her. Yet, Ms. Gobblestein's piercing eyes remained on me.

"You'll both be written up for being tardy. Now, go." She waved her hands in the air.

Fresh mothballs and warm black licorice lingered, as Ms. Gobblestein started walking away from me.

I had made it only a few feet from her before she called

out my name and reapproached me, "Mr. Dupuy, hand them over."

Huffing loud, I met her eyes and dropped my earbuds in her open hand.

Raising one of her crooked, hairy eyebrows, "You know the rules—no more huffing, by the way, young man."

"Yes, Ma'am." I headed to advanced physics.

I wanted to turn around and go after Opal. Instead, I listened to Lisette and entered Mrs. Longoria's class. She turned around from writing on her white board and stared at me for a few seconds, pushing her sparkly, red and white polka-dot eyeglasses onto her nose, before she permitted me to sit down. I planned to keep an eye on Opal and the Vipers, with an even closer eye on Sari.

Reaching in my backpack for my book, notebook, and pen, I thought about Mollie's comment about Pepper. She was close and under Opal's twisted influence. I planned to plant a seed of doubt in her mind, when I came face-to-face with her, as Lisette had instructed.

Lunch time arrived and I entered the cafeteria fifteen minutes later. I hadn't seen Sari again since earlier this morning—once I had my tray in one hand, I spotted her sitting across the table with Phoenixx and some other students. They were laughing.

Phoenixx dipped his spoon in the plastic cup of pudding, and he held it in front of Sari's mouth to feed her. He saw me.

I grabbed the turkey sandwich from my tray, tossed it in

the trash, and exited out the back. A tree hung over a wooden bench. I sat down and replayed the scene over and over in my mind.

"Aww, poor Tomie's heart is breaking, piece by piece," someone said from behind the tree in a husky voice.

I turned around. "Who's there?" I sensed it was Pepper.

"That's not important at the moment. Looks like your relationship with Sari is fading away."

"You don't know anything about us," I growled.

"I don't need to know much because I saw what I needed to from here. See you around." A low laugh followed.

Standing up, I started towards the back of the tree.

"Stay where you are!"

"Pepper, wait."

She didn't respond for thirty seconds.

In a penetrating voice, she wailed, "What? I don't have all day, freak!"

Narrowing my eyes and rotating my hand over the warm bark, I said, "Why is Opal in control, and why did she *really* bring you back from the dead?"

Pepper exhaled. "What are you talking about?"

"Looks like Mollie and Cecilee are bowing down to her now. She's the new Queen Bee of Frost High. Someone had to take your place, after all. Plus, how would it look if others knew of your return."

"Whatever, Tomie…" She swallowed hard and ran off.

DOLL³

The conversation ended.

I could only spot floating ebony silk layers around a body; she never turned around where I could see what the new Pepper looked like.

Lisette communicated with me telepathically.

Tomie, I did a live glim and saw your interactions with Opal and Pepper. Understand that was not the time or place to challenge Opal. Always be careful of your surroundings. Never know who could be watching.

You're right. How did I do with Pepper?

Very impressed. I do think you gave her something to contemplate.

Hope so, Lisette.

As long as you're wearing your necklace, I can live glim anytime when it senses trouble, so keep that baby on!

Will do.

Hey, how are you? I know things aren't good with you and Sari, still.

Think my heart will be broken forever.

No… You gotta reach out to her even, if she rejects you over and over again. Don't give up on her.

Maybe.

Going to go, remember to control your anger.

Will keep working on it, Lisette.

Talk soon.

CHAPTER
THIRTY—SEVEN

TRAVELING INTO THE MAIN BUILDING BACK TO MY locker, I went to retrieve a book I forgot for Honors Calculus II. Loud heel clicks seemed to vibrate up against the metal lockers behind me as I was punching in the code to open my locker.

My first day kept getting worse—a second visit from Ms. Gobblestein, what were the odds? It didn't matter because my life was really sucking big time.

"Mr. Dupuy, may I have a moment?"

I grabbed the five-pound book, closed my locker, and cradled the book in my arms.

"What's up now, Ms. Gobblestein?"

She cleared her voice a few times. "Excuse me."

DOLL³

Her right foot started tapping with arms crossed. The oval glasses slid halfway down on her nose. "Come to the principal's office right now, young man," she commanded. "I didn't address something with you earlier."

Traveling down the long hall next to her, she examined me from head to toe. When we arrived at the office door, I said, "Please, after you, Ms. Gobblestein." She arched her eyebrows, and they looked like they were stuck for a few seconds before they slowly fell again.

Ms. Gobblestein dug in her right pocket and pulled out thicker eyeglasses with a loose hanging chain. "Turn to your side."

I followed her request

"Now, turn to face me."

Her eyes scanned my entire face, and it felt like she had zoned onto the mustache area, which I had decided not to shave. I could hear the alarms going off, and see the red swirling lights in my mind.

"Have a seat, Mr. Dupuy." She sat at her desk.

I sat down in the old plastic chair that squeaked every time I moved in it.

As she was writing something down on her yellow pad, I glanced behind me and saw both Mollie and Cecilee giggling, as they passed by the glass window.

"Here."

A yellow leave slip was handed over to me. I took it from her wrinkled hand, littered with scattered brown moles with some hairs that played peek-a-boo.

She demanded in a deep tone, "Go and get your hair cut three inches and shave immediately before you return back to school tomorrow. If not, then you'll be suspended for two days, and it will be unexcused, due to your noncompliant behavior with Frost High's grooming policies. Two unexcused absences may detain a student from attending extracurricular events, including graduation."

Clenching my fists and breathing in hard, I thought about my encounter with Opal and her outfit. Shaking my head, I folded the paper up and stuffed it in my pocket.

"Simmer down, Mr. Dupuy." She peeled her eyeglasses off.

"Ms. Gobblestein, I'll take care of this, after school." I stood up.

"I hope so. Mr. Dupuy, may I ask you a question?"

"Sure, Ms. Gobblestein."

"Out of all the years that I've known you, why have you pushed the rules so much?"

"Don't think I've pushed that many."

She slid her glasses back on, tapping her pen against the desk.

"Maybe a few," I admitted. "Don't know, guess I like to bend the rules sometimes."

"Rules are made for a reason, Mr. Dupuy. If we had no rules, then our world would be in *perpetual chaos*. I'm keeping my eye on you, until you cross the finish line at graduation."

"Yes, Ma'am. I will try to do better." I nodded.

"Please do. I don't want to see you in this office again."

"May I ask you a question, Ms. Gobblestein?"

Running her tongue over her teeth, she said, "If you must, Mr. Dupuy, proceed." She folded her hands together and placed in front of her.

"Sometimes, I feel like you've targeted me the most over the years and no one else, and I know there are some serious rule breakers roaming the Frost hallways."

"Sorry you feel that way. I don't just target you. When I do, I'm doing it to instill discipline inside of you because it's vital. Don't be concerned about the other rule breakers here—I'll discipline each, accordingly. By the way, Opal Dawn is next on my hot list."

I almost tripped over something on the floor and took in a few deep breaths.

"Ms. Gobblestein, how did you know I was thinking about her?"

"Mr. Dupuy, I know more than you'll ever *realize*. We're done here and you're excused."

She strolled behind me to close her office door.

Opal came my direction, shooting both her index fingers at me. She trotted to Ms. Gobblestein's office.

I finished the rest of the day without running into Sari and Phoenixx, and then I drove to the barbershop.

CHAPTER
THIRTY—EIGHT

SMOKY, GRILLED BURGERS IGNITED THE AIR AS SOON as I stepped out of the car. I noticed the back gate was open. My stomach was growling. I placed my backpack in my room and shaved.

I whispered to my witch ball, "Thanks for the protection last night." It swung slightly to the left, froze for about ten seconds, and then swung to the right, as I stood on the side of my doorframe. Kinda felt it understood what I was saying.

Dad was outside in an apron with #1 Dad painted on the back in different areas. It was a Christmas gift that I'd made for him in the third grade. Most of the paint had faded off. "Wow, I can't believe you kept that all this time."

He flipped the burger patties. "Hey, there, son. Of course,

it's my favorite. Even when it starts falling apart, I plan to keep it."

"Need any help?"

"Think I got it."

Dad kept his head down and placed the cooked patties on a plate. "Come on, let's eat."

He pushed the sizzling patties closer to me, eyes on the food.

Before Dad grabbed it, he looked up at me, jerking his head back, "Whoa what happened to your hair and mustache?"

"Ms. Gobblestein enforcing those school policies again. You know how she is about rules."

"That I do, son. Turn around. You sure you're okay about taking that much off?"

"Just told the barber to do whatever. Don't think this is going to be a good year for me, anyhow." I pushed a pickle and onion back and forth with a plastic fork.

Dad chewed a bite of his burger and took a sip of his soda. "Tomie, did something happen at school today?"

A long sigh escaped me. "I think I made a big mistake. I should've listened to Lisette."

"Son, what kind of mistake? You know you can tell me anything and whatever it is, I'm here to help you through it." His hand reached out to mine.

"Dad, it's not like that... I mean, it's serious for me, but nothing for you to be getting worked up over." I had a good feeling where Dad's mind was going.

"Thank goodness. You had me pretty nervous. Regardless, I would help you, no matter what."

"Means a lot to me, thanks." I lifted my head up. "Actually, it's all related to Sari and when I told her that it would be best for us to cool it for a while because of all the stuff with her dad. Plus, I lied to her. When all of it happened, I never returned any of her calls or texts. I've lost her to someone else, Dad."

He pulled his chair closer to mine and just wrapped his arms around me. I hugged him back and stayed there.

"Listen to me. It's going to all work out, son. May I ask what was the lie?"

"I told her that Caya and I hooked up."

"Oh." His eyes expanded. Dad scratched his head. "Lies can ruin a relationship—sometimes the relationship can be rebuilt. However, it takes work and the other person to give the one who lied another chance."

"You really believe that?" I lifted my head up and rested it on his shoulder.

"I think it's possible, especially if the other person truly cares for that person. Who's this guy, anyhow?"

"His name is Phoenixx, and she met him at work over the summer. He came up to Lisette's for the festival with another friend to drive Sari. He's well off and not bad looking, I guess. Actually, if BTS held auditions for an extra member, then he wouldn't have to try out. They would choose him, just like Sari has, and she has every right." I sniffled.

DOLL³

"Hold on. Why do you think Sari has chosen him?"

"I saw him at her house when Mr. Ray and I went by on our way home. Sari looked really happy before she saw me. Today at lunch, they were sitting together, and they looked like we used to."

"You and Sari have known each other for a long time. Just few months ago, you discovered you had romantic feelings for her, although she's always had special feelings for you—that cannot be erased."

"Dad, I really don't think any of that matters now."

"Oh, that's were you are wrong. All of it matters. That's the funny thing about true love. It just doesn't stop, as if you were turning off a dripping faucet. Real love endures all things and is eternal. Believe me, Sari hasn't stopped loving you. Sure, she's very angry and disappointed in you. I'll never stop loving Alexxa, your mom."

Picking up a napkin, I wiped my eyes and nose. "You think so?"

"Most definitely. This Phoenixx guy, well, he's just her temporary distraction. It happened way too fast. You did a good job making her upset, so she's paying you back in one of the oldest ways."

"What?"

"The jealously card."

"Hold on, so, Dad, you're telling me that she's just pretending to like Phoenixx to make me jealous?"

"Possibly." He tipped his head to the side.

"I should call and talk to her right now."

"Totally up to you, son."

"You know, I'm going to think about it some more."

"Whenever you decide to reach out to her and she's receptive, then prepare yourself for a good chewing out, though."

"Thanks, Dad." I hugged him again.

I told him all about my encounters with both Opal and Pepper.

We cleaned up the outside and kitchen. Afterwards, I pulled out my book, *The Bluest Eye*, by Toni Morrison for Advance Literature IV, which would serve as a dual credit for college.

I read over half of this extremely powerful book in less than two hours. I found my *supra* identity and Sari's dad feelings about me relating to this book on more levels than one, which I didn't anticipate.

Other books awaited me in our library, so I knew I wouldn't be lonely for too long, especially with no communication from Sari. There were so many times I wanted to stop and talk to her in the hallways each week, but Phoenixx seemed to always be around.

One day, I noticed Sari trying to open up her locker. She failed twice. I *glimmed* her, discovering she had an argument with her Dad earlier. I flicked my wrist once, and her locker door flung open slowly on its own. Sari eyed me; I waved at her. She ignored me as she grabbed her book out, shut the locker door, and barreled away.

We shared two classes, but no interactions occurred, even if we were assigned for small group assignments. She always requested to be in another group, especially if I was in hers. I couldn't take it any longer, so I texted and called her after a few weeks. She didn't respond. I tried again, several more times. Nothing.

There were friends I could've hung out with, but I chose to exclude myself. Therefore, my social circle diminished every day, so my studies became my new identity.

CHAPTER
THIRTY—NINE

NAVY BLUE AND GOLD STREAMERS SWUNG DOWN from the ceiling beams on each hall. Before the pep rally, cheerleaders demanded everyone to clear one hallway outside the gym. I sat down on a window ledge while my backpack dangled from my hand.

Mollie, the captain, and a few other cheerleaders performed several cartwheels and backflips down the hall. They jumped up in the air and shook their glittery pom poms, shouting nauseating cheers and rotating tiny bells adorned on their bracelets and ankles.

Homecoming was one of the biggest nights at Frost High, even bigger than prom. Frost's Polar Bears were playing against our rival, the Garrison Pirates. They'd beaten Frost ten years in row. I had a feeling this would be their eleventh victory. Whispers about the dance circulated in the school. I knew that I wouldn't be attending the dance this year.

From a distance, I watched Phoenixx hanging on Sari's locker door. I was sure they would attend the game and the dance together. Sari turned her body half way around and glanced in my direction. I shot my hand up to wave at her.

Before I lowered my hand, she pulled Phoenixx by the collar of his shirt with both hands and kissed him. Then, she looked back at me, wiping the side of her mouth with her finger.

Dropping my bag from my hand, I lowered my head. Slumped over, I stood up and started towards my last class, 3-D art, dragging my bag behind me. Before I touched the door handle, I completed a U-turn and traveled down to the band room. I figured it would be empty with the game tonight.

Upon opening the heavy metal door, only chairs and instruments greeted me. I found an empty space with a small propped up window that was a few feet above my head. I slid down the cold wall, extended my legs out, and pulled out a Dr. Strange comic. My eyes scanned the pages, and my mind replayed the kiss, over and over again.

Strong cigarette odor floated down, encircling me. I dragged a chair over and stepped on it. I was about to close the window until I heard familiar voices. Staring down, I saw Opal and Cecilee smoking their c-sticks and blowing twirls of white smoke out of their mouths. I lowered my head just enough, where they couldn't see me, but I could watch them and hear their conversation.

"Don't mess up tonight, at the dance, Cecilee," Opal commanded and took in two short puffs, blowing out from her nostrils.

Cecilee yelped in a quivering voice, "I won't. I'll bring her to where we talked about."

Blowing a cloud of smoke in Cecilee's face, Opal said, "See you around eight. Let's go." She squished the cigarette into the brick wall. They picked up their packs and left.

Stepping off the chair and shoving my book inside my bag, I knew who they were referring to. I pulled my phone out and texted Sari.

T: **Sari, I know you're still mad. Don't go to the dance. Opal & her Vipers are plotting something against u!!**

I waited for a few minutes. She didn't answer, so I dialed her number. I called her probably five times and left the same messages about avoiding the dance, but heard nothing back from her.

Grabbing my stuff, I dashed by her locker area. She wasn't there. I then ran out to the parking lot and saw her driving off. Phoenixx was following her in his car. I jumped into my vehicle and sped off.

They were headed to her house by the roads they took. Five red lights caught me. When I arrived there, Sari was showing him her phone. She noticed me and hurried into the house.

Phoenixx stayed behind, leaned up against his Camaro, with his arms crossed and chin up in the air.

Slamming my car door, I sprinted towards her front door. Phoenixx jumped in my path with his arms stretched out. "Hold on, man. She doesn't want to talk to you. When will you get it? You need to back up and leave."

"Move, now!" I glanced down at him and felt my body heating up fast.

He grabbed my arm and extracted it back quickly. "Dang, what's wrong with you! You're burning up." His bright, raspberry palm trembled.

I closed my eyes and counted backwards from ten to bring myself down and prevent my blue glow from appearing. Phoenixx fell back a step as I went to knock on her front door.

"She's not going to believe you. I saw your cray-cray messages. Just stop lying to her, already. Just let her be happy and get over you. You're so pathetic." He shook his head.

"You don't know what's going on, so shut up," I yelled.

Beating my closed fist against the door, I hollered, "Sari, please talk to me. Don't go to the dance tonight."

My hand was throbbing. Mrs. Green slowly opened the door. "Tomie, Phoenixx is right. Sari doesn't want to see you, ever again. I'm so sorry, please go home." She closed the door. My heart dropped out and broke in so many pieces that I couldn't even locate them all.

I saw Mr. Green staring out the window, drinking from a

coffee mug with a fat, ugly smirk pasted on his face. I turned around and walked back to my car.

"Sari doesn't want or need you anymore. She's my girl now, and I'll take care of her."

Looking at Phoenixx, I clenched my hands. I wanted to give him something that he would never forget, instead, I drove off. I pulled over twice to think about everything.

Although I knew Sari wanted nothing to do with me, I was going to the dance tonight, even if it meant getting my feelings bulldozed, over again. I refused to allow Opal and her venomous squad to harm her.

Before I lowered my head down on my steering wheel, my phone beeped. I thought Sari was giving me a chance. When I turned the phone over, it wasn't her, but a text from Lisette.

L: **Hey, I saw and heard everything. Sorry, Tomie.**

T: **It's useless. She hates me**

L: **No, she doesn't. She's very angry and hurt.**

T: **Yeah**

L: **Listen, you can be there at the dance, but not.**

T: **What?**

L: **You remember how Mr. Ray used a concealing potion to make himself invisible for a short time, when he spied in on Esmerelda, Verlinda, and Mr. Fox in Salem?**

T: **Yes, I could use a concealing potion?**

L: **You don't need to. With your special shifting abilities, you can become invisible for a bit. Just remember what we** practiced with Mr. Ray.

T: **How long is a bit?**

L: **Maybe fifteen minutes.**

T: **Umm, is it or isn't it?**

L: **Depends on your anxiety and anger levels. If you don't keep them managed, then your time could be much shorter.**

T: **Great**

L: **Keep that necklace on. Regardless if you can maintain your invisibility five minutes or fifteen minutes, I'll be close by.**

T: **Sounds good. I'm going to head home to practice**

L: **Good. I'll be tuning in.**

I flew by my dad in the living room.

"Hey, what's the hurry? Everything okay?"

Stopping in the hall, I turned around. "Dad, something is going down tonight at the Homecoming dance."

Dad approached me. "Opal and her friends?" He frowned.

Running my hand across my forehead, "Yes, they plan to do something to Sari. I tried to warn her by text, calling, and going by her house. She keeps shutting me down and out."

"Son, I wish she would hear you out." He rested his hand on my shoulder. "What's your plan?"

"To attend the dance, sorta." I rounded my shoulders.

"What do you mean by that?"

"I'm going to be invisible."

"Really?" His fingers slid from his parted lips.

"Yep, I practiced some transformations back in Monroe with Mr. Ray and Lisette. Lisette believes I can do it, so I'm going to practice for a bit before I head out."

"Can I help?"

"Dad, I would appreciate that. Need someone to be my eyes, to see if it's working or not."

It was almost five-thirty. Dad closed the blinds in the living room and kitchen. I sat down on the couch, and he sat across from me. "Okay, let me know if you notice anything."

He nodded. "Got it."

Closing my eyes, I replayed all my practice sessions and read some pages from my inner spell book about invisibility. I thought about a glass of water and its clarity. I attempted to imagine myself as that same glass. I ran through this sequence more than twenty times, and I was still sitting there with no change.

"Keep going, Tomie. I know you can do this. Think about how Captain America held a helicopter down with his bare arms—you got this. You must believe that you can do this. Just think, Sari needs you. She just doesn't know it, yet." He tapped the back of my hands.

Exhaling several times, I thought about my entire body being clear to the point where no one could see me. My heartbeats decreased, and I began to feel very light, almost as if I was floating in the air.

DOLL³

"Tomie, Tomie! You did it. I cannot see you." My dad was reaching for me with both of his extended hands.

Reopening my eyes, I couldn't see my arms, hands, or legs. I was invisible. The first few attempts, I remained out of sight for about two minutes. Each time I reappeared and returned to my invisibility, my minutes increased. I never made it to fifteen, only eleven. My dad's mouth dropped each time.

Tomie, wow, I'm so impressed.

Thanks, Lisette. I wouldn't have even thought about this until you mentioned it. You and my dad gave me encouragement.

What time does the dance start?

At eight, but nothing jumps off until the football players and cheerleaders arrive, which will probably be after ten.

When do you plan to leave?

Maybe in the next hour or so, it's almost nine-thirty. The game should be ending soon.

Okay, I want to see what you can do. If I see you need me, then I'll know. Stay focused, Tomie.

Going to do my best…

"Be careful, Tomie. If you need me, then call me."

"Thanks, Dad. Lisette will be close by."

"Oh, you definitely don't need me." He looked down to the ground.

"Hey, yes, I do. I wouldn't have accomplished this without you. So, I'll call you, if I need you."

We hugged, and I drove to the school gym.

The music was loud.

I didn't see Sari or Phoenixx, yet. I figured they were still at the game. I planted myself in a deep, dark corner near the punch bowl, where I watched people enter. Most of the girls were weighed down with mums and a ton of trinkets and sparkly ribbons.

Opal or Mollie weren't in sight. I scanned the room for a new face, Pepper—she wasn't there, either.

When half of the football team and cheerleaders came in with no noises or hooting out loud, they confirmed my prediction earlier about losing again to Garrison.

Sari and Phoenixx came in together. They weren't holding hands. Sari was looking all around. I hoped she was looking for me, but I knew I was a fool to even think that. She was wearing a strapless, cream jumpsuit with an oversized black and gold belt wrapped around her waist.

Mollie came up behind her in the punch line. "Look at you, trying to fit in. That piece of trash you're wearing was maybe three seasons ago. I admire the poor, attempting to look like the rich."

"I paid for this, unlike someone who makes shoplifting her top extracurricular activity," Sari popped off with a smile.

"Whatever! I'm not a thief," Mollie screamed and stomped off.

Sari smiled bigger. She picked up her cup with cherry colored punch. She was holding it with one hand and started sipping it. Cecilee came from behind her and bumped her hard, spilling most of the punch in Sari's chest area and mid-section.

"Why are you so clumsy?" Sari cried out.

"I'm so sorry. There's some stain remover spray in the girl's locker room. Let me show you." She smiled, showing all of her teeth.

"Oh, I'm good."

"Please, I insist, let me help you before a stain sets, such a cute outfit." Cecilee started pulling Sari by her arm, zipping her through the dance floor.

I had a feeling that this was my cue. I crept around the back corner, and no one was around. Concentrating like earlier, I succeeded after three tries. I swept through the crowd. A few heads turned, and I could hear someone whisper, "Did you just feel something brush against you?"

They were headed towards the girl's bathroom. Cecilee pushed the door open wide and scooped up the bottle from a shelf. I floated in and perched myself on a counter, a few sinks down from them.

"This isn't necessary, Cecilee." Sari raised her arms up as Cecilee sprayed the remover and dabbed damp paper towels on her mid-section. Before she could reach her top, Sari jerked the towel from her hand. "I got it, thanks."

Cecilee backed up, her huge eyes bulging out like Puss in Boots. "I'm sorry, Sari."

"Seriously, it's no big deal. It'll wash out." Sari's head was lowered, soaking up some of the juice with the towel, not paying attention to Cecilee's body language. "Back in Black" by AC/DC echoed from the gym's speakers.

Within ten seconds, three metal bathroom doors swung open and Opal, Mollie, and Pepper stomped out. Sari slowly turned her trembling body around and mumbled, "I should've listened."

Opal started to approach her. Pepper looked really pale. She was dressed in tight, ripped black jeans, a cut-off shirt with hanging fringes, and candy apple red high heels, yelled out, "I got this." She bumped Opal against her shoulder and rolled her eyes. "Give me the burlap bag and rope!" She held her hand out and snapped her fingers. "Come on, I want to get this over with, so I can go to the dance before it's over."

Opal tossed it over to her, and Pepper's hand missed the catch. "Pick them up, Mollie," Pepper demanded. Her eyes fixed on Opal.

Mollie headed over to Pepper to pick the supplies up, but before she could, Opal whispered something in her ear, and Mollie retreated next to Cecilee.

Pepper's eyes lit up and blazed toward Opal. "So, you calling the shots now?" She puffed her chest out.

"What does it look like?" Opal circled around her. "You just better stay in your place before you go back in your box."

Snatching the bag and rope off the floor, Pepper threw them

319

towards Opal's chest. She whispered to Sari, "Yeah, you were right, you should've listened." Pepper left, shoving the door against the wall. A loud bang followed.

Opal approached Sari, but her feet were cemented to the ground before she was ten inches within her personal space. Opal couldn't touch her. The protection spell was working. I smiled. I could feel my body tingling all over. My invisibility was getting ready to wear off.

"Someone must really care about you to place such a spell on you. You're lucky, tonight. You won't always be." She spat towards Sari's face.

The spit froze before it could touch her and dropped to the floor and shattered in Opal's direction.

"Mollie and Cecille, come on!"

Cecilee grabbed the stuff off the floor and scampered behind them.

Sari jumped as I reappeared in my natural form.

"Can we talk, please," I begged, sliding down from the counter.

Tears ran down her cheeks. She stared in the mirror. I went to wipe her face, and she pulled away from me. She yanked her purse off the counter and stormed out.

Standing there, Lisette teleported next to me and placed her hand on my shoulder. "Hey, Tomie."

I hugged her.

"It's going to be okay. Just give her a little more time. How was it, being invisible?" Her eyes shimmered.

"Pretty unreal. Sari was safe without me because of her spell, just wanted to be sure."

"I know. You just wanted to be close to her in some way. I can stay, if you need me to."

"Oh, no. Dad's home. You get back home. We'll talk again."

Lisette nodded. "By the way, your seed is growing, regarding Pepper and Opal. I felt and saw it."

"Truly, a nice advantage to hear and watch their interactions."

As soon as I checked the time on my watch, she was gone.

CHAPTER
FORTY

HALLOWEEN NIGHT TUMBLED IN WITH A HEAVY shower of auburn, yellow, mocha, and faded lime leaves throughout Frost. A light afternoon rain followed for about two hours, and the temperature tiptoed in at forty-two degrees. After six, a mini horde of trick-o-treaters carried their bags and were dressed up in all types of costumes, ranging from Black Panther to Jedi-Rudolph, which made me look twice.

I watched them parade up and down the neighborhood. Dad had an emergency truck run yesterday that he had to complete, and would return early next week.

It had been over sixty days since I'd talked or texted Sari. My days had been so different without talking to her. I decided to marathon the *Halloween* series.

Before I showered, I took the necklace off and placed it on the bathroom counter. After showering, I fixed a mega bowl of buttery popcorn on the stovetop. I added a few drops of hot sauce on top. Sprawled out on the couch, I started the movie with a few handfuls of popcorn.

My phone beeped a few times. I dove for it and almost spilled the popcorn bowl on the table, but I froze the bowl before it hit the floor and levitated it back to the table. It was a group message from Lisette and Ranae. I sighed and paused the movie. Several pumpkin, ghost, zombie, and vampire emojis followed.

L: **We're headed to a Halloween costume party at Crow's place. Join us.**

T: **Nah**

L: **Come on! Think it will get your mind off of things for a little bit.**

T: **No thanks**

R: **You're not going anywhere tonight, right?**

T: **Nope, just Michael Meyers, Laurie Strode, Dr. Loomis & me**

L: **You must be watching Halloween. Love that series! Hey, I'll come there.**

T: **No, no… Y'all go and have fun. Hey, what are y'all dressed as?**

R: **I'm Elvira with fangs**

L: The Bride of Frankenstein in a steam-punk costume.

T: Bet y'all look awesome

R: We look pretty good

T: Is Crow Frankenstein?

L: No, I begged him to go as him, but he decided to dress as Blade.

T: Oh, y'all have to take a group pic and send it to me. Know he looks badass! Tell him hello for me

R: Umm, what about us?

T: You both are, 2!!

L: Okay, we're about to head out. You text, call, or communicate with me telepathically, if something comes up anytime tonight, okay?

T: Will do

L: Promise me, Tomie!

T: Promise

R: C u around.

T: Hey, will Caya be there with y'all tonight?

L: Yes

T: Who is she dressed as?

R: I think she's going as a mash-up, Jedi-Squirrel Girl

T: Wow, y'all came up with some awesome costumes

R: Thanks

T: Don't forget pics and tell her hello for me

L: Sure, all okay, Tomie?

T: Yeah, pretty quiet so far. Just a few trick-o-treaters

R: **Night is still young, so don't assume or underestimate darkness, ever! Just stay in… Oh, have u and Sari patched things up yet?**

T: **Not talking about that with u, Ranae**

R: **Nope, u haven't**

She sent a GIF of a young girl skating backwards with a sign that read: "I may just still have a chance…" Then she followed with two balloons popping with this floating message: "Just Kidding!"

T: **No, you're not!**

R: **U got that right. Hey, if u know what u want, then u keep after it**

She followed with several winking emojis.

L: **Enough, you two. Talk soon. Remember what I told you.**

T: **I will.**

R: **STAY IN!! OK!!!**

T: **Roger that, Elvira…**

I tossed my phone on the opposite end of the couch and pressed play to continue the movie, thinking about Ranae's silly texts. I smiled. In a way, I needed that. A few more trick-o-treaters stopped by. I decided to turn the porch lights off after an hour, so I could finish the movie without constant interruptions.

With more than half of the popcorn bowl gone, it was time to start the sequel, so I paused the television because cheese dip was calling me. I put the dip in the microwave.

As soon as the microwave bell rang, the doorbell did, too. I looked up at the clock on the wall, and it was almost eleven. It was probably some desperate older kid trying to get more candy or play some crazy prank, so I continued getting the dip ready.

The doorbell rang again. My eyebrows shot up. I grabbed a paper towel and wet half of it to dab my eyes from the spices wafting from the dip.

I was halfway to the living room when the doorbell rang a third time. It was time to play a fun game with whoever this was. I pulled out my Nosferatu the Vampyre mask that I'd purchased two years ago from the hallway closet. Sliding it on, I crept slowly to the door, looking out the peephole. A white Murano SUV was parked in front of my mailbox.

It was Luckie dressed in a Rydell High School cheerleader costume, pacing back and forth. Peeling the mask off and unlocking the door, I opened it only a few inches and looked around in all directions. Something was off with her being on my front porch, especially on this night. A black envelope waved inside her hand.

"What are you doing here, Luckie?" I continued to scan the outside area and the street.

"Tomie, sorry it's so late. Sari wanted me to deliver this to you." She shoved the envelope towards me. "Here."

"Hold up, why would Sari give you this and not come in

person herself?" My eyes focused on her.

"Look, I don't know."

"Where is she?"

"We separated about an hour ago at a Halloween dance. I just know she took off with Phoenixx. Before she did, she gave me this in the bathroom and told me to get it to you."

I held it up to examine it closer. Nothing was written on the front or back. It was sealed.

"That's all I know, Tomie. Hope you two figure things out. Gotta go." She turned around.

"Thanks."

She popped her hand up in the air and ran off.

As she started her car up, I shut my door and locked it behind me. I looked out the peephole again. My heart was thumping hard while I stared down at the envelope; my hands started to tremble.

Was this a joke? Why would Sari write me a letter now? She'd never been a letter writer. Anyone could start, right? I wrote her my first, earlier this summer. Maybe I was just reading too much into it. This could be her way to communicate with me.

Tearing the top edge off slowly, I pulled it out. It was a pink sheet of paper with a written message. I fell back against the door and slid down after I read it.

I pulled myself up, making my way to the bedroom and changing into black cargo pants and a Candyman T-shirt. As I inserted my feet into my tennis shoes and tied them, I saw the letter in my mind and read it again.

Tomie, I'm ready to talk, now. I'll explain everything when I see you. I've never stopped loving you. It's been way too long, my Tomie Dupuy. Meet me at The Bristol House on 2345 Union Road.

P.S. Hope you can forgive me for ignoring you in the hallway that day, not returning any of your calls and messages, and the Homecoming drama.

Love, Sari

I stared down at the letter for more than fifteen minutes. It was definitely Sari's handwriting, and the letter smelled just like her fruity and sweet scent. I stepped into my room to grab my wallet off my desk. I heard the ball slightly tapping my window.

The closer I approached the threshold of my room, the ball swung at a faster pace like a pendulum. I thought about my ball acting up before, Ranae's vision, and the recent conversation tonight with her and Lisette. I knew it was a huge risk to leave my house.

For all I knew, Opal and company could be waiting for me. This was a gamble I was willing to take. I needed to talk to Sari—it had been way too long—this was my chance to maybe, make things right.

Scooping up my keys and phone, I locked the back and front door. I drove about ten miles to Union Road. On my way there, I thought how Lisette would be upset with me, after I made the promise to her about not going out tonight.

On the flip side, I hoped she would understand my desperation of taking a risk like this. Who hadn't taken risks, right? Anyhow, I hoped Lisette would never need to find out about this, so I prayed that I wouldn't experience any tricks tonight.

Bristol House was a pretty shabby mansion. Regardless, kids usually went out there every Halloween to throw parties, never my Halloween choice.

When I arrived, there were several cars parked in front. I didn't see Sari's car, but I noticed Phoenixx's red Camaro. So, Luckie was probably being truthful about her leaving with Phoenixx. "Party Up" by DMX played so loud from the house, my car windows shook. I traveled down the curvy sidewalk and started to ring the glowing doorbell. The door was open already.

Some guy with a Freddy Krueger costume pulled the door back and beckoned for me to enter, holding a huge candy bowl. The place was crowded. People were dancing, bobbing for apples, and playing pin the tale on the longhorn.

My only purpose was to find Sari. I asked a few people about her, and they told me they hadn't seen her. I dug into my pocket for my phone and started texting Sari, leaning up against a wall downstairs.

Florencio Sanchez approached me before I hit send. He was dressed as Light Yagami from *Death Note*. Although he was a junior, I'd known him for years.

We used to hang out more in junior high. We just drifted apart, especially after he became a high school basketball all-star and joined several extracurricular clubs. I enjoyed watching sports only; I was lousy on any court and field. Thank goodness for my brains.

Flo, his nickname, was earned because he came in first place at the state spelling bee in the seventh grade, and then tenth place in the Scripps National Spelling Bee.

"Hey, Tomie, what's up, bruh?" he asked, tossing a red apple up in the air.

"Not much, Flo." I kept glancing back and forth down the hall.

"You look thirsty."

"Flo, I don't want anything to drink."

"Guey, I'm not talking about drinking, but tú chica, tell me I'm wrong." He winked and bumped the side of my arm.

I gave a slight grin. "Nah, you're not wrong."

"Knew it… Heard you were trying to find her. I saw her go upstairs about fifteen minutes ago with some guy. I haven't seen her since. She's looking muy caliente tonight in her tight, black leather pants and red heels—giving Sandy some serious competition. You better find her before someone else does, you feel me." He winked.

Heat filled my hands. I folded them behind my back, so Flo wouldn't notice. I took several deep breaths. The outfit that he described must've been Sari's costume. Maybe she was going as the sexy Sandy from the movie, *Grease*, since Luckie was dressed as one of the cheerleaders, at least that's what I hoped.

"Hey, you straight?" Flo asked.

"Yep, I'm good." *Relax...relax...* My temperature dropped back to normal. I pulled one of my hands slowly from behind my back. There was no glow.

"Let me show you," Flo said.

He walked me down the hallway and then pointed up the stairwell.

"Is this your first time partying at Bristol's?"

"Yeah."

"Well, it's the best Halloween event in Frost."

"Looks like it." I kept looking up the stairwell.

"You got it from here?"

"Thanks, Flo."

We fist bumped.

"See you around, Tomie. Go get your girl!"

I nodded, and he worked his way through the crowd.

Sprinting up the squeaking wooden stairs, people were talking loud and laughing. Thick smoke and the smell of alcohol filled the air. I started coughing, so I pulled my shirt halfway over my mouth and nose.

"Awesome costume," some stumbling guy mumbled before he tripped and fell. His car keys fell out onto the floor.

I reached down to help him up and snatched his keys.

"Hey, are you a ninja guy?" he slurred.

"Guess I'm whoever you think I am. Take it easy on the drinks, man."

Another guy came to his rescue. "Ryver, where you been, bro?"

"Everywhere!" he shouted and threw his hands up in the air.

"Hey, is this your friend?" I asked the guy.

"Yeah."

"Are you sober?"

"Yes, why?" he asked.

I *glimmed* him, and he was being honest.

"Look at him."

He did.

"These are Ryver's keys, get him home safely, okay?" I dropped the keys inside of his hand.

"Come on." The guy placed his arm around his friend's shoulder and brought him downstairs.

Every opened door I walked by, I peeped in to see if Sari was there. No luck. Then, I saw the attic stairs pulled down. On each of the thirteen steps, I noticed a white sticky note attached, one word written on each one.

Stooping down, I picked one up. Before my foot touched

the first step, someone pulled me by my arm. I turned around. "Mr. Ray." My eyes bulged out. "What are you doing here?"

"Think I could ask you the same question. I just flew in." He quickly read the first three sticky notes. "Tomie, this doesn't look good."

Gripping his wrist, I said, "Mr. Ray, I appreciate your opinion and concern, but I need to talk to Sari."

"How do you know for sure it's her?" He squinted his eyes.

"I don't." My heart flip-flopped.

"Then, that's a sign not to continue."

"Not necessarily."

In a booming voice, he said, "Tomie, come on. You really think a girl like Sari would want to meet you in a place like this. On top of that, in a dark attic?" He frowned.

"Mr. Ray, you're probably right. If I don't see for myself, then I'll never know. Please step aside."

He did, and his chin fell hard towards his chest.

I started going up the stairs and picking up all the notes, which read:

You are really warm. So happy you came here tonight, Tomie. Find me...

I crumbled up the notes and tossed them down. I heard footsteps behind me. "Mr. Ray," I gasped.

"Go ahead, I'm not going to leave you alone."

We stepped up into the dark attic.

"Sari, are you up here?" I shouted.

DOLL³

Mr. Ray looked at me, and I did the same.

"Tomie, let's go," he begged, grabbing me by the arm.

"Okay, maybe you're right. Let's get out of here." Just as I said that, I saw Sari standing next to a window.

Releasing some deep breaths and wiping my face, I peeled away from his grasp. She fluttered her eyelashes. I crossed the room.

Looking back, Mr. Ray mouthed, "Be careful."

Sari embraced me. For a minute, everything felt right. Once she pressed her lips against mine, I jerked back because her lips tasted like bitter chocolate—my mouth began to grow numb.

"You're not Sari!" I yelled and stumbled backwards. My hand reached up to my neck, and the necklace Lisette had commanded me to wear at all times wasn't there. It was resting on my bathroom counter. I went to grab my cell. Someone yanked it from me and rubbed something wet on my hands. In seconds, they felt paralyzed.

Mr. Ray ran over to me, and someone threw some kind of liquid spray on him, which froze him like a statue.

"Of course, I'm not," fake Sari purred.

CHAPTER
FORTY—ONE

A CREEPY AND TWISTED SMILE FORMED ON HER painted red lips. Her body transformed right before my eyes, and Opal Dawn stood in front of me. She had used an impostor spell. I squeezed my eyes shut for a few seconds. What a mess I had not only placed myself in, but also Mr. Ray. He didn't ask to be part of my stupidity.

"What was on your lips?" My legs began to buckle.

Stepping back from her, I felt some kind of heavy, steel net being thrown over me. I tried to teleport and communicate telepathically with Lisette, but I couldn't do either one.

In a raspy voice, Opal said, "*Bad Magic* gloss. Comes in many flavors, chose the chocolate one for you."

All my powers deactivated, and I dropped to my knees. My

DOLL³

bare skin started burning, and I collapsed face down to the ground.

Finally, my eyes opened, after ten minutes. My sight was blurry. I knew I wasn't in the attic anymore because this room was larger and emptier. My eyesight was returning, slowly.

I tried to lift my arms, but they felt like double-filled cement bags. I looked down and saw my wrists were chained to the table I had been placed on. I had a good idea who was involved and knew I would find out very soon.

Within thirty minutes, my vision returned. I searched for Mr. Ray and saw him with his frozen hands stretched out several feet from me. A still spell must've been used on him. If I could get out of this mess, then I knew how to reverse it. It felt like someone hit me with several bats all over my body, and my skin tingled all over. A door opened, and I heard several footsteps advancing in my direction.

Attempting to lift my head up, I couldn't make out who was approaching me because dimness filled the room. When they got closer, I saw Mr. Fox dressed as the Punisher. Verlinda needed no costume because she looked like an evil witch all year long.

Opal, Mollie, and Cecilee were all dressed in Santa Clause strapless dresses with hats and tall black boots. They were all silent, their eyes locked on the door in front of them. After a while, more footsteps tapped against the cement floor.

"How did I get here?"

"A teleportation spell, silly," Opal said, adjusting bracelets on her arm.

"Why am I here?"

"You'll find out soon enough, Tomie," Verlinda whispered, as she slithered herself around the table and ran her boney fingers around my face. She stepped away.

Mr. Fox, Verlinda, and the Vipers divided up to allow the other guests to enter into the room. I couldn't make out their faces. Their outfits made me shiver all over. They were dressed in maroon short cloaks, oversized hoods covering their heads. Dark gloves covered their hands and upper arms. Ranae's vision was so on point.

My entire body shivered as my mouth went dry. I brought all of this on myself. The warning signs were clear, the first being the letter that Luckie dropped off, but I denied all of them. Now, I had to face my fatal mistake.

Their shoes squeaked, louder and louder as they got closer to me. Once they did, they turned around backwards and uncovered their heads in slow motion.

"What do y'all want from me?"

"Tomie, we're here to exterminate you and every other *supra*, as well, unless they serve the Dupuy Silver Slayers."

"What? Serve—"

"Why of course," they both whispered in unison. "There's an array of benefits. We already knew you wouldn't submit."

"You're both right on that. Never would I want to be part of such a hateful group. You've killed innocents for no reason."

Laughter circulated the air. "You really believe that. What my ancestors did back then had to be. If it had not, then this world would be filled with darkness. *Supras* are an abomination. We must wipe the world clean, and spilling *supra* blood is the solution," one of the girls dressed in a cloak said in a low tone.

"Are you both serious? Do you hear what you're saying? Not every *supra* is bad. Even if they were, who are you to judge them? What did we ever do to you?"

"Exist!" Mr. Fox fired out with a spray of spit.

They both turned around and stood there in front of me, their faces fully exposed. My mouth dropped twice. I was speechless. All these years, I had not one clue these two were slayers, who would one day want to hurt my loved ones and me.

There I was, thinking the slayer was the new kid who'd come to town or someone much older who didn't live in Frost. I never would've imagined that my slayers would be two kids I'd taken classes with since elementary, served food to at Pizza Beat, and sided with a few times in debate class.

"Star and Shine, the Colby twins, is this a freaking joke?" My eyes widened.

"No," Star shouted.

"Out of everyone who could've been a suspect, I've never thought it would be you two."

"Exactly. We stay hidden until someone contacts us about spotting a possible *supra*. Then, we watch and wait," Star explained.

"For what?"

"The perfect time to catch our prey, hold it, and then annihilate it," Shine said, stroking her black hair with one of her hands.

I just shook my head.

Mr. Fox and company were all laughing and watching me squirm.

"You deserve everything they're going to do to you," Mr. Fox popped off, invisible, mini torpedoes flew out of his watery eyes.

"Mr. Fox, look, I'm sorry I didn't say something at the hospital about what I knew about Pepper that night, but Sari, Lisette, and I had nothing to do with her death. She was murdered that night, by Opal."

"Tomie, I know you did it," Mr. Fox snarled.

"You're wrong, Mr. Fox. It was all Opal. She even stole a spell she wasn't supposed to possess from a special book. We were only planning something to scare Pepper, but Opal took it much further. She hated your Pepper. She wanted to be her. She even looks like—look at her!" I slanted my head towards Opal.

Deep redness washed over his face. "How dare you!" He stormed out.

DOLL³

Opal and Verlinda watched him. They whispered back and forth to each other.

"Tomie, are you ready to meet your fate?" Star asked.

All of my powers were unplugged, which I was sure Verlinda played a big part in with a possible blocking spell. I wished I had not answered the door because I wouldn't be here now. Forgetting the special necklace Lisette gave me, which she drilled in my head over and over again to wear, made me feel beyond worthless—if only I had not been an idiot in haste. I wouldn't have jeopardized Mr. Ray's life.

"Tomie, don't look for anyone, especially your *Mega* to swoop in and save you. My grandmom made sure of that," Opal grunted as she approached me.

Verlinda shooed Mollie and Cecilee out the door, then they stood over me. Opal ran her cold hands over my face. My entire body recoiled, and I tried to turn my head away from her; she squeezed my chin tight with her hand and lowered her face closer to my lips.

"Too bad, we could've made the perfect power couple, like Bey and Jay," she whispered against my mouth. "You could've grown to love me, just as much as what's her face."

"Never!"

I felt like gagging. My eyes rolled back, and I slammed my head back against the cold table.

"Whatever. It doesn't matter anymore. You're so gullible, and your end is approaching. Think before you jump to someone's request. I knew Sari was your kryptonite, and I so wanted to have her here next to you, but Lisette or you placed some kind of stupid protection spell on her. No worries. There are always ways around any spell."

She pressed her cold lips against mine.

"Are you done?" Star asked.

"What did you ask me?" Opal questioned, gnashing her teeth with crimson coloring her face.

"We need to finish what we started. No time for games now."

"Listen up, Star, you should be thanking us, my grandmom and me, for everything we've done to make this happen, especially making it easier for you, two weak slayers."

Verlinda paced in front of me and beckoned Opal to her.

"Opal, we didn't need your dark witchery help at all. Yes, you both helped us confirm Tomie's powers, but we could've done it ourselves, sweetheart," Shine said, flipping her hair back. "Now, if you'll excuse us, we'll finish up here. You and your granny can go." She pointed towards the door.

They stared at them and slammed the doors behind them.

Star picked up an oxygen mask to place over my face. I noticed a long plastic tube running along a pole and above me and down. It was connected to some kind of black tank.

"What's in the tank?" I asked in a broken up tone.

"A permanent gift for you," Shine bellowed with a crooked smile.

"Enough with the riddles, already. I can hardly move. You can at least tell me how you're going to torture me." A pool of sweat beads on my forehead floated down the sides of my warm face.

Shine's eyes narrowed in thought. "Star, I think we should tell him."

"If you want to Shine, then go ahead."

"It's sarin mixed with iron powder."

"You're going to turn my own nervous system against me, and the iron powder will speed it up, in my case." I started panting and sweating more. I wanted to scream. I knew no one would hear me. It was useless, and my time was running out.

"Yes, Tomie. This is our purpose and your destiny." Star dropped her eyes to the floor.

"It doesn't have to be."

Shine snatched the mask from Star's hand and started lowering it down on my face. Star headed towards the tank.

"Do you both really think Opal and Verlinda are done with you two? They may have helped you with me. Just know that they're going to come after you both," I yelled.

They looked at each other.

"Believe me, they're on our agenda next, once we're done with you. They've served their time for us, and the timer is ticking fast. We're not afraid of them," Shine shared in a smoky voice.

In a brittle voice, I said, "You should be scared of them." I closed my eyes tight and thought about everyone I loved. Once I took a few breaths of this gas mixture, my expiration date would be confirmed. I never thought I would know, when I would die.

Counting backwards starting at twenty, I figured I might make it to ten before I took my last breath. How would my dad cope after the news was shared with him? Would they go after Sari next? Her protection spell would shield her from a lot, but not from all magic. Mr. Ray would be next on Star and Shine's list—then Lisette and Crow would follow.

I placed others and myself in a careless situation where I couldn't save myself, let alone warn my loved ones. Shine secured the plastic mask around my head. Star placed her hand on the tank knob and before she could turn it towards the red gauge, a loud crash shook the room.

Glass shattered from the windows, and long shards shot towards Star and Shine. They ducked with their arms, covering their faces. Both Verlinda and Opal were sitting inside the bare window frame with their arms crossed. High winds blew their hair up in the air. Twisted smiles decorated their faces. A bitter coldness ran over my face and down my arms.

Star and Shine stood up. Galloping towards them, they completed three round-offs until they stood in front of the witches.

Opal hopped off first and then Verlinda followed.

"Did you think we would leave so easily, Shine?" Opal asked, pushing Shine in her chest.

"Why can't you and your granny understand that we don't need your services anymore?" Star pointed her finger in Opal's face and shoved her.

Opal stumbled back a few steps.

"Get out of my way," Opal commanded her.

"What are you going to do if I don't," she replied with a large grin.

Star stepped closer to Shine.

Verlinda walked around them in a circular pattern, keeping her eyes on Opal.

Star uncovered a chain belt wrapped around her waist. She unbuckled it and tapped a button. The belt unraveled into a whip. "I only planned on terminating one *supra* tonight. Looks like, we'll be increasing our numbers."

"What's that?" Opal asked, frowning and pointing at the object in Star's hand.

"Oh, just a little something to keep you and your granny out of our way until we can get to you."

Verlinda stopped pacing and tilted her head towards Opal. Verlinda flipped her wrist and slid Opal over a few inches on the smooth floor, as Star shot out the metal whip at her. However, she didn't move her fast enough because the end of it burned the side of Opal's hand and ripped out a chunk of her skin. I could see smoke twirling up in the air, and a strong charcoal-like odor followed.

Opal hollered, "What is that thing?" Tears ran down her cheeks.

"A whip braided with iron razors," Verlinda whispered as she stepped back. "I haven't seen one of those since I was a young girl. It's an old weapon that hunters used a lot on witches, especially to torture us."

Shine clapped and said in a snappy tone, "Great history lesson, but we don't have time for this." The whip retracted back to Star.

Verlinda circled around them again and laughed.

Star and Shine braced their backs against each other, while Star's eyes stayed on Opal and Shine fixed hers on Verlinda. Shine pulled out a small pouch from the inside of her cloak. Then, she slipped on circular spike rings on her thumb, index, and middle fingers.

"My, my, ladies. I'm very impressed with your trainer. Your weapons are extraordinary. The *kakute*. Let me guess, the metal is iron and the inward one on your middle finger possesses some kind of poison on its tip, most likely a rooster blood and mistletoe concoction?" Verlinda asked in a thundering tone. Veins popped out of her neck, and red eyes darted back and forth between the slayers.

Shine nodded and started approaching her, and Star did the same to Opal. Before they could take three steps, it was as if their feet were stuck to the ground. They tried to move, but were unsuccessful each time.

"What's happening?" Shine asked with a frown pasted on her face.

Verlinda's laugh grew deeper, her smile sinister. "Stay put, stay put, you little varmints." She waved her hands in a circle around them. Their weapons dropped, flew up, and stuck above the ceiling.

"You placed a trapping spell on us, you crazy witch," Shine yelled, clenching her trembling fists.

Verlinda twirled around and flung her arms backwards. Opal watched, and Verlinda slid her against a wall, as she grabbed her injured wrist with her hand.

The twins soared high into the air like tumbling weeds and slammed against the wall a few feet behind them. There bodies rolled down, and they fell over like cotton-stuffed, motionless dolls.

Verlinda pulled Opal up by her collar and came over to me.

"Tomie, we're not done with you. See you when we're ready to dispose of you and your meddling cousin," Verlinda growled. They teleported all the weapons and tank, then themselves, out of there.

My cuffs unfastened. I rose up off the table and peeled the mask off my face, still feeling a little light headed. I made my way to Mr. Ray. I closed my eyes and touched the statue and chanted, "Undo this work and return as you once were." After a minute, the stone crumbled and Mr. Ray appeared.

"You okay?" I hugged him.

"Believe so, feel a little stiff." He ran his hands over of his body, brushing off the dust. "Are you okay, Tomie?"

"Yes, look, you need to fly out of here."

He nodded. "We'll catch up another time." He squeezed my arm and shifted into a snow-white owl—mocha, amber, and navy blue painted the ends of his massive wings. His big light green eyes blinked at me before he took flight out the open window.

I ran over to the twins. I stooped down to feel their pulses. They each had one and were breathing. After searching the room for a few minutes, I found my cell under some loose rags and dialed 911.

Shine woke up before the EMT guys busted in and she whispered, " Is Star okay and why are you helping us?"

"Yes, and like I told you, we're not all the same."

Her eyes shut.

Ambulance and police sirens penetrated the walls. The EMTs arrived first inside of Bristol's basement and transported the girls out on stretchers. A few Frost police officers arrived right behind them, including Office Webber.

"Why Mr. Tomie Dupuy, we meet again. I shouldn't be surprised, especially after our last run in at your school. It seems like when there's trouble, here you are. What happened?" He pulled a pen and pad out of his heavily starched pocket.

I thought about telling him everything. Then, I paused to

rearrange my thoughts. Although I wanted to expose Verlinda and Opal, I would be placing all *supras* and myself in danger, if I went that route. How did I know if Officer Webber or someone on the police force had a connection to the slayer world?

While rubbing my wrists, I said, "A Halloween prank went bad, Officer Webber. Some kids from Garrison."

"What did they look like?" He squinted his eyes and stepped up closer to me.

"You know, they were all wearing costumes, and I was blindfolded for most of it, so I don't know."

He twisted his mouth back and forth while bouncing his head up and down, tapping his pen against the brim of his white cowboy hat. "Really? You expect me to believe this poppycock?"

"Sir, I wish I could tell you more."

He snorted. Leaning in towards me, he whispered and pointed his pen at my chest. "Tomie Dupuy, one day I'm going to catch you. There's something strange about you, boy. Just can't put my finger on it yet, but I promise you, I will…"

"Am I free to go?" I asked, pulling my head back and peering into his twitching eyes.

An EMT tapped him on his shoulder. "What, now, dadgummit!"

"Need to check him over," the EMT guy pleaded with a slight jump.

"Go ahead. I have no further business with you at this time, but if something comes up after I interview the Colby twins, then know I'll find you, so stay put." He threw his hands up in the air and moseyed over to his fellow officers near the broken windows, looking back at me.

The EMT checked my vitals and approved me to go home and rest.

As I followed one of the EMTS out, I saw Sari in the crowd, and she yelled out my name.

"Tomie!"

She ran up to me with tears in her eyes. "Are you okay? All kinds of rumors are floating around that something bad happened down here with all the noises and someone called 911."

I imagined caressing her hands and arms. Then picking her up and holding her while pressing my lips against hers, making my confession in her ear. She would tell me how she forgave me and would kiss me more. I snapped out of it. There was no way it would be that easy, but my fantasy did feel nice. She had not been this close to me in so long.

"Sari, I'm okay. Thanks for asking." My eyes froze on her. "How did you know I was here?"

"I bumped into Flo, and he told me you were looking for me earlier. He asked me why I had changed my outfit. I told him that I didn't, and then I knew Opal must've be involved, somehow," she said in a low tone.

"Can we talk, Sari?"

She was silent for a while.

"Listen, I'm glad to know that you're okay. I'm not sure, if I want to be around you just yet."

"I get it." My head detruded while my shoulders hunched over, and I made my way through the crowd to climb the stairs.

Before I reached my car door, I heard Sari call, "Hey, when did you start giving up so easily?"

Turning around, I saw her standing in front of me. "After everything, I cannot blame you, Sari." I started towards her to open the passenger door for her.

"I got it."

We drove off.

It was almost five-thirty in the morning.

"What time do you have to be home?"

"No time. My parents are out of town."

CHAPTER
FORTY—TWO

A S I WAS DRIVING, I THOUGHT ABOUT COMMUNICATING with Lisette to tell her everything that had happened, but I decided to wait. I figured that she would be enraged with me, and I finally had this chance to talk things out with Sari, no tricks this round, so I took it.

We drove out to Caroline's Leap, which was a huge cliff overlooking the lake. I left music playing in the car and parked several feet from the edge, where we could still see the water.

Her arms were crossed as she stared out the window. My fingers tapped the steering wheel. I reached out to touch her hand, and she ripped it away. Shutting my eyes, I lowered my head on my headrest.

For the oddest reason, our song played next, "With You,"

by Chris Brown. I glanced to see if she was listening. She wouldn't even look my way once during the entire song.

"Sari."

She didn't respond for a long time.

"Why?" she asked, sniffling and wiping her face with the inside of her shirt.

Turning my head towards her, I said in a wavering voice, "I wanted to call you back so bad."

"I called you so many times. You didn't text me back once, Tomie." Tears streamed down her face.

"So sorry. Wish I could rewind everything. I didn't care if your dad called off the slayer or not. What did matter to me was your future. You dad is giving you a full-ride to wherever with no strings, now or later. I was willing to make that sacrifice of losing you then. After I made that decision, I hated what I told you to convince you it was over because none of it was true."

Sari uncrossed her arms and faced me. She scrunched up her face and raised her eyebrows. "What did you just say?"

Pulling myself up and gazing into her eyes with tears filling mine, I confessed, "The Caya stuff—I never kissed or hooked up with her."

"Are you serious?" Her eyebrows lowered.

"Yes."

"Tomie, do you know what you put me through? I mean, I've been crying every night since our last conversation. I decided not to participate in any extracurricular activities this year because of you. My mom had to take me to the doctor before school started, and now I'm taking an anti-depressant."

I went to touch her arm. She jerked it away from me, again.

"No, this isn't going to be easy for you." She frowned, covering her hands with her face.

"Sari, I'm willing to do whatever it takes to make it up to you." I tilted my head up and closed my eyes tight.

"Can you take me home now?" She lifted her head up and wiped her face with her hands. "Look, I'm glad you're okay."

"Hey, you sure you're ready to go?"

She nodded.

"Please know I'm so sorry for everything. If you never want to see me again, then I'm going to have to live with that for the rest of my life." I started the car up.

Only the radio played with no conversation between us, as I drove her home. Once I put the car in park in front of her house, she placed her hand on the door handle. I began to open my door, so I could open her door for her.

"No. I got it," she said without looking at me.

"Sari, know I never stopped loving you, and I never will. You'll always be in my heart, even when I die." I beat my chest with my closed fist.

Turning her head around, she stared at me for a few seconds with her red and puffy eyes. "Tomie, I cannot make any promises to you right now, but you can call me later, if you want."

My eyes widened. "Don't worry, I will."

She stepped out. I watched her until she got in the house. I missed her throwing a kiss at me, catching it with my hand, placing it over my heart, and then shooting one back to her. Sari didn't step back outside to do that. I waited more than twenty minutes, and the door remained closed.

My actions brought all this on me. She had every right to feel how she was feeling about me. At least, she was giving me a chance by allowing me to call her later. I wanted my friend back.

I didn't know where that would place us. The thing about forgiveness that I read somewhere was that it doesn't happen over night. It takes time, sometimes years, and plenty of patience. Thinking back on everything, I now knew I shouldn't have lied to Sari about Caya. That one lie may have destroyed my relationship with Sari. I drove away.

Before returning home, I decided to get breakfast at a coffee shop not far from the hospital. I wanted to check on both Star and Shine, specifically I wanted to ask them what they planned to tell Officer Webber. I asked the receptionist at the hospital counter their room numbers. Upon lumbering into their room, I noticed an older man sitting in a recliner near the window.

"We didn't expect to see you here," Star said, as she scooted herself up in the hospital bed with tubes dancing from her arms.

In a tremulous voice, I admitted, "Me either. Sure once you two get rested, round two, right? I won't be tricked again. I was so dumb to fall for all of it."

"Tomie, the letter thing and getting you to Bristol's House was all Opal's idea. We planned to come to your house. Our assignment was to kill you," Shine said flatly, staring at me with her dead eyes.

"I'll be waiting. Just wanted to see how you both were doing for my benefit."

"Well, our heads and bodies are really sore. The doctor admitted us because he wanted to make sure we didn't suffer a concussion or have any internal bleeding. We're getting a few more tests this morning," Shine shared.

My eyes widened. "You told the doctor everything?"

"No. We told him that we got in a fight with some strangers at a party."

"Oh—I shared something similar with Office Webber. I told him that some kids from Garrison played a bad prank on us that got out of hand, and they jetted out before the cops showed up."

"Quick on your feet, Tomie Dupuy. You didn't want him to suspect anything unusual, especially what you are," the old man hummed as he stood up.

"Excuse me, I didn't catch your name, sir."

"Mr. Hashimoto."

"He's our granddad," Star said.

"What did you mean by that?"

He lowered his eyes at me and kept his arms close, remaining silent.

"Now, Granddad, don't be that way," Shine begged. "*Sutekina koto.*"

A puzzled look appeared on my face.

"Shine asked him to be nice in Japanese," Star said, brushing her hair behind her ears and bowing her head. "Granddad is very stubborn," she muttered.

"Thank you for stopping by," Shine said.

"Stop it, Shine," Mr. Hashimoto scolded her, slapping his hands together.

"He could've left us to die there! Instead, he helped us, Granddad," Star stressed.

"Please go," he ordered and turned his back to me.

"I'm going, sir, but you don't have to be rude," I snapped and started heading out the door.

"Young warlock, do you know who I am?" he asked in a deep voice.

My hand slid from the door handle, and I turned around. "What did you just say?"

"I know your tricky kind. Too bad my granddaughters didn't succeed. This was their third test, and they failed miserably. Guess I'll have to finish you off and then your family." He pulled out three glistening metal throwing stars from a bag behind his chair.

My hands lit up a deep blue. My hair and body levitated off the ground.

He glared at me, biting his top lip with his teeth and squeezing his weapons tightly in his hand. I noticed droplets of blood fall and splatter on the white, slick floor below him.

"Just stop it!" Shine shouted. "I'm so tired of all of this. I never wanted to become a slayer. That's what you wanted, Granddad."

"What, Granddaughter?" Mr. Hashimoto asked, dropping his hand down and turning to face her.

I concentrated on my self-control lessons, disengaging my glow and lowering myself back down to the floor.

Shine started crying. Her granddad moved closer to her and embraced her in his arms. Star stretched out her hand to grab Shine's hanging hand off the bed next to her.

"Granddad, I don't want to do this anymore, either," Star said. "Not all witches are evil like you've drilled in our heads during our training with you in Osaka since we were five years old."

My mouth dropped.

"Tomie, excuse us," Shine sighed.

I shook my head and stepped out the room. Medical staff dodged in out of the circular nurse's station.

While they talked, I leaned up against a wall with my hands tucked in my pockets and communicated with Lisette. It was almost nine in the morning.

DOLL³

Hey, are you busy?

No, everything okay?

I think so.

What do you mean?

Can you meet me at my house in about an hour?

Sure. Tomie, did something happen last night?

Yeah, a lot then and now.

I can come right now.

No, no— I need to finish something up first. Trust me, I'm okay. See you then.

Okay, I'm going to hold you to that.

Talk more soon, Lisette.

I texted Mr. Ray to meet at my house, too.

The door opened up after fifteen minutes and I reentered.

"Tomie, Granddad is the captain of the Dupuy Silver Slayers. I explained to him that it's time for slayers to start thinking about reassessing our interactions with dark and light witches," Star said.

My feet started tapping really loud. I dropped my hands deep into my pockets, as my eyes grew wider. "What are you actually saying?" They all cast their eyes down at my feet and my tapping slowly came to a standstill.

"Granddad will consider contacting the *Upper Witch Council* soon to begin this process, especially a new protocol for dark witches only. After our incident with you, I realized who needs to become the focus for future slayers. Sorry for trying to kill you." She smiled.

"Never imagined this, a slayer's perspective changing about *supras* and vice-versa. I still will have to wait to see if this really happens," I said, taking in a deep breath. I *glimmed* them, and they were being honest.

"Understand that nothing is promised yet, young one," Mr. Hashimoto said, returning his weapons back in a purple velvet drawstring bag.

"Well, I better get out of here. I'll be seeing you two around."

"That you will," Shine said. "Hey, before you go, Star and I want to give you something."

"Like what?" My eyes blinked.

"Granddad will follow you out," Star said with a cough. "Don't worry about Officer Webber. Our stories will match yours."

"Thanks, I think." I rolled my neck around.

I allowed him to walk in front of me out the door and stayed a few feet behind him, just in case he wished to continue our earlier confrontation.

He opened the trunk of his silver Lexus ES with a click of a button on his San Antonio Spurs keychain. I stood behind him. He lifted out a 12x18 black box and held it up in his hands.

"What's this?" I asked with a pause.

He placed it in my hands.

"Huh?"

DOLL³

"Open it," he demanded, tapping his leather loafers against the pavement.

Lifting the lid off, I noticed two large collars with heavy chains. I went to pick up one to examine it closer because I wasn't sure if they were what I thought.

He slapped my hands. "Don't touch. Iron will burn and make you very, very weak."

Once he said iron, I didn't need to hear the rest—I knew from experience. "These are witch catchers, right?"

"Yes, they bind and control witches, while also tormenting them. Good weapon, especially for Verlinda and Opal to use on them. How did you know this weapon, young warlock?" He narrowed his eyes and looked up into my eyes.

"A new friend from Salem told me about these. I appreciate this, Mr. Hashimoto. Tell Star and Shine the same. I need to run," I said and bowed towards him, taking a few steps backwards. I kept my eyes on him until I found my car.

He laughed quietly under his breath, placing one hand behind his lower back

I placed the box in my back seat and drove home to meet Lisette and Mr. Ray.

CHAPTER
FORTY—THREE

WHEN I PARKED IN MY DRIVEWAY, I SAW LISETTE and Mr. Ray sitting on the front step. I took in a few deep breaths; I figured he had updated her about everything. Retrieving the box from the back, I carried it in both hands. The temperature seemed to be dropping.

"Hey, sorry for running a little late."

"Unbelievable, Tomie!" she snapped, arms crossed.

We all went inside.

"Where's your dad? Does he know?" She sat on the couch. Her eyes locked on mine.

"On a truck run and no."

I slid some magazines and remote control over on the coffee table in order to sit the box down. Lisette tossed the top off with the flick of her index finger.

Firing off in a brassy voice, she said, "Witch catchers." Her eyes flickered. "Only slayers keep these. Why do you have them?"

"Simmer down, let me explain everything," I fanned her with my hands.

"Let him explain, Lisette," Mr. Ray begged. "I told her some, not everything, Tomie."

"After we talked last night before you and Ranae headed to Crow's party, Luckie stopped by with a letter from Sari to meet her at a Halloween party."

Her pupils flared. Lisette stood up and started pacing with her hands on her hips. "What did I tell you?"

"I know, I know, just hear me out okay, before you give me the lecture." Creases appeared on my forehead.

"Opal tricked me with an impostor spell, pretending to be Sari. Verlinda, Mr. Fox, the other Vipers, and the slayers were all present. I was tied down on a table. Opal and Verlinda didn't like how the slayers told them to get lost."

"Tomie, you didn't wear your necklace?"

"Please, let me finish."

She continued to pace faster, watching me. Mr. Ray scooted closer to me.

"Verlinda placed a trapping spell on the slayers and ended up hurting them, but they're in the hospital and okay. The slayers want out. They asked their granddad, Mr. Hashimoto, who's the leader of the Dupuy Silver Slayers to meet with the *Upper Witch Council* to discuss a refocus on dark witches only."

Lisette sat down next to me. "Wait, first of all, who are the slayers?"

"The Colby twins in my class."

"What!" Lisette shouted, shaking her head.

"I had the same feelings."

"Why are slayers wanting to play nice with us now?" Her eyes squinted, and she tapped the side of her face with her fingers. "I don't trust them."

"Me either, Lisette." Mr. Ray pressed his finger against his nose.

"Lisette and Mr. Ray, I thought the same, but they're being truthful. I know." My chin flopped down.

Tipping her head to the side, she asked, "You *glimmed* them?"

Looking up at both of them, I said, "Yes."

"Just don't know, Tomie, this bad blood between witches and slayers has been going on for so long."

"True. Sometimes, it takes the right situation and person to initiate a change."

"Okay, enough about that. Time will definitely show what it needs to. Look, you're really going to need to be way more careful and stick to the plan, which is?" Her eyes blinked several times.

DOLL³

"To wear my necklace at all times, contact you or Mr. Ray when something doesn't seem right, and stay put until I hear back from one of you," I said, dragging each word out and looking up at the ceiling. "Oh, and no more parties for me."

"Tomie, this is really serious and like your second time being powerless! They could've killed you." She started tearing up.

"Will follow plan, sorry—what about those?" I asked, staring down at the box.

"Hmm, I'll take them back with me for now."

"Okay." I exhaled.

"Hey, I don't mean to sound so harsh, but things are getting scarier. Has Opal or Verlinda made contact with you since the incident?"

"No."

"Did they say anything else to you?"

"Something about they have a different plan when the time is right."

"Figured. They're waiting on something. You need me to stay until your dad returns?" She grabbed my hand.

"Lisette, I'll be close by," Mr. Ray said.

I retrieved my necklace from the counter and put it on. "Look."

"Good, keep it on. Wear it in and out of water because you forget to put it back on." She pointed at my necklace and reached up to hug me. "I'm going to go. I'm working on some wedding stuff with Caya and Ranae."

"Tell them hello for me."

"Will do. How are things between you and Sari, any break through yet?"

"A little. We talked after the Halloween incident. I plan to call her later tonight."

"Good. I have a feeling that she's going to forgive you, just give her time and space, as she needs it." She bent down to pick up the box.

"By the way, Lisette, my tea leaf reading you gave me was right."

Bouncing on the end of her toes, she said, "School me, Tomie."

"Well, the two S's turned out to be the slayers, Star and Shine, targeting me. Ten definitely stood for Halloween, and the crooked heart symbolized me for being a liar and breaking Sari's heart. The owl was Mr. Ray showing up to convince me to rethink my decision, which we all know how that turned out."

She clapped both of her hands. "Excellent interpretation, Tomie. You nailed it! I think I may request a tea leaf reading from you in the immediate future."

"Really?" I squealed out.

She nodded. "Yes—see you soon."

She teleported out. Mr. Ray stayed around for a few hours before he left.

Picking up my phone, I dialed Sari's number. It rang

about seven times and went straight to voicemail, and I left a message. After I finished up some reading and flipped through channels for a few hours, my phone buzzed.

"Hello."

"Hey, it's me."

"So good to hear your voice, Sari. How was your day?"

"Okay, I guess." She took in a long sigh.

"Did you ever hear back from the Ginger Academy in Europe?"

"Yeah, I got in, but decided to study at a design school in New York where I received a full scholarship, including room and board with a small monthly stipend, as long as I maintain a 3.5 GPA. Now, my dad can't tell me where to go to school or hold paying for my education over my head. I'm in control."

"Oh, wow. I respect that. Just thought Ginger Academy was your fashion school of choice?"

Her voice broke up. "Things change, just like us. What about you, did you get in?"

"I did. Just received my acceptance letter a day before Halloween." I so wanted to share with Sari that same day. Yet, she wasn't responding to any my calls or texts, so I stuffed it in my drawer to share with my dad, upon his return from his truck run.

"Told you."

"That you did… you always knew."

She paused. "Thanks for suggesting we wait, a few months

back," she said.

"No problem."

"I would've so regretted giving myself to someone I thought I could trust." She sighed again and tapped her nails against her phone.

"Sari, whatever I need to do to make this up to you, I'm all in."

"Hey, I gotta go."

"Sure. Hope you sleep well."

"Think it will be one of my better nights in a while."

"Hope so."

She ended the call.

Feeling a little more hopeful than before, I planned on giving her all the space and time she needed, as my dad and Lisette suggested.

Our conversations increased a few more minutes each day through Thanksgiving and the spring. We didn't talk every night on the phone, mostly at school.

I asked her out on a few dates, and she shot me down each time, until after the twentieth time asking her, she accepted my invitation to senior prom. Although we weren't a hundred percent yet, I could live with being at a steady sixty.

CHAPTER
FORTY—FOUR

O PAL AND HER VIPERS MADE A FEW MORE FAILED attempts to disrupt my senior year. Graduation and Lisette's wedding were approaching like Secretariat crossing a finish line. Before I knew it, graduation day was here.

Star and Shine were awarded valedictorian and salutatorian honors, respectively; I was third runner up. Things were still going well with Sari and me. Her dad would never be Team Tomie, and I think I really freaked him out when he saw me several months ago, after Halloween at the mall.

I really think he expected me to be gone. Now, he knew there wasn't much he could do to hurt me or keep Sari from me, since the slayers hadn't. There were days I wanted to confront him, but I chose not to.

Standing in front of the mirror and near a packed brown box, I admired my midnight blue gown. I tried to place my cap on my head. My hair had grown out. I decided to tie it up in a bun, so the cap would fit easier.

Dad walked in. "Look at you, son. Your mom would've been so proud of you on this special day. I'm very proud of you."

"Thanks, Dad." We embraced. He sat down on the side of my bed, repositioning his tie a few times.

"You've grown up so fast. I remember when I first taught you how to ride your bike without training wheels, how to shave, cook macaroni, change a tire, drive a car, how to treat a young lady, and now there's nothing left for me to teach you." He started tearing up.

Placing my arm around his shoulder, I said, "Hey, there, Dad, I'll always not know something, so I'm going to need you to keep teaching me."

"You will?" He sniffled and wiped his wet eyes with his hands. I handed him a few tissues from the box on my dresser.

"When the time is right and I get married and start a family a little later, when my wife and I are both ready, then I'm going to need you to show me all the daddy ropes."

He started laughing and the tears stopped.

"Thank you, son."

I grabbed my phone and the blue and gold tassel off my desk. I took my cap off. I was sure Sari would hook me up with the special trick to keep it on.

Dad grabbed the keys off the table. He turned off the television. "Any parties tonight?"

"Sure they will be, but Sari and I planned on just hanging out at the house, after dinner, if that's okay. We plan to watch a few of our favorite movies."

"Now, I didn't expect that."

"Why not?"

"Parties are the hot ticket for you kids."

"Yeah, we'll we're just getting back on track. There'll be plenty of that in the next few years. I just want to enjoy the time I have with her. She's going to be busy this summer with stuff, and I will, too, before we both head off to our schools."

"True. I'm so proud of you and the young man you're becoming."

I smiled.

Dad opened the front door, and my jaw dropped.

"You okay, son?" He reached up to rub my shoulders.

"I think so. What's that in the driveway?"

"Your graduation gift."

Lisette and Crow were leaning up against a black Ram 1500. The truck shimmered from the sunrays and the tires sparkled. I ran over. I examined the interior from the outside, and I opened the door to check the inside out. The grey seats were plush. Dad stood next to me and dropped the key fob in my hand.

Jumping in, I ran my hands over the steering wheel and dashboard. I revved her up with the touch of the button to check out the display and sound system. I started bobbing my head and tapping the wheel like it was drums.

"Wait, you can't afford this, Dad. I really do appreciate it. You should take it back." My head drooped.

"Oh, Tomie. It's fine. I've been saving for a while, and with all the extra overtime, we're more than okay. You're going up north soon. It gets cold up there, lots of snow and ice. A reliable car is a must. Don't worry. I didn't do this all on my own." He smiled and glanced towards Lisette and Crow.

They laughed. I stepped out to hug them all.

"Thank y'all so much. Appreciate you both coming to my graduation."

"Of course," Lisette said. "We wouldn't miss your important day."

"Wanna take her for a quick spin?" Dad asked, patting the side of the door.

"Later for sure."

"Hey, Tomie, check it out closer," Crow whispered, pointing at the tires.

I looked down and spun around with a huge grin. "Baby mega tires, for reals?"

"Yep, thought you riding around with big mega tires up there may intimidate them, just a little bit." He smiled with a deep chuckle.

DOLL³

Admiring my truck for a few minutes, Lisette asked, "Tomie, have you heard anything else from any of them?"

"Nope."

"They're planning. I can feel it." She rubbed her hands up and down her arms. "Keep watch."

I gave her a slow head nod.

"By the way, how are you and Sari doing?"

"Let's just say, I'll be bringing a date."

"Wonderful, Tomie. Hey, I'll need your measurements for your tuxedo. Text me soon."

"I sure will later tonight, after things settle down."

"Okay, we'll follow y'all."

Dad drove me to the back of the school's gymnasium and I got out. I saw Opal, Mollie, and Cecille ahead of me. Opal stopped and turned around and whispered, "We're coming for you, Tomie Dupuy." She whipped her hair around and skipped off in her black snakeskin heels with her Vipers.

"Can't wait!" I shouted after her.

I found Sari inside.

Bending down, I was about to give her a kiss, until I saw Ms. Gobblestein seated across from our path. All I could see in a flashing neon sign above her head was, "You can sit out from graduation, if you violate the conduct code," look on her face. So, I stood upright and asked Sari about my minor cap situation. Even after thirty minutes, Ms. Gobblestein kept her eyes locked on us. I didn't think she blinked once.

"How do I remedy this?" I pointed at it.

"Sit down." She took about six bobby pins from her purse and worked her magic.

"Thanks, Sari."

"No, problem." She smiled and swiped her strawberry and coconut lotion smelling hand, softly down my cheek.

Thoughts about Verlinda, Opal, and Pepper's devious plan played in my mind constantly, even on this special day. It was nice to have a short break with Sari by my side.

When my name was called to collect my diploma on stage, I smiled for the cameras, especially Dad and Lisette's. I saw all the families huddled together in the bleachers. I knew I would've felt different, if my mom could've been here.

After graduation, Phoenixx strutted over to us with Luckie a few feet behind him.

"Congrats, guys!"

"Thanks."

Leaning in close to me with a lopsided grin, he said, "I just wanted to come over here and make sure there are no hard feelings between us, Tomie, right? Sari just wanted to make you a little jealous."

"We're good, Phoenixx." I watched him move around like loose spaghetti. His feelings for Sari didn't matter because I had my girl back. It was his time to drool, and he knew it.

"See you both later at Trish's party?"

"No, we're staying in, especially after Tomie's Halloween

incident," Sari said, grabbing my hand.

I looked down because this was the first time in a while she'd initiated contact. My heart sped up, and a huge smile curled up my lips.

"Understood, but if you get tired of staying in, then come on out. It's going to probably be an all-nighter."

Mr. and Mrs. Green approached us next. I prepared myself for anything that could be uttered out of her dad's mouth. He went to hug Sari. She stepped back and glanced away from him. Her mom hugged me.

"Congratulations, Tomie," Mrs. Green said, flashing a large smile.

I stared and waited for Mr. Green to say something to me, cracking my knuckles.

Mr. Green remained quiet with a crooked frown on his face.

"Stop being like that, Charlie. Remember, you promised," Mrs. Green begged.

"Nothing new for him, Mrs. Green, pardon me," I said, eyeballing Mr. Green.

I noticed Lisette and how she was about to say something, but Mrs. Kulverhouse, my lit teacher, approached us. Dad followed close behind. I noticed Lisette's eyes change colors. She moved her lips in silence, and she scratched the top of her hand. Then, she pointed at Mr. Green.

"Mr. Dupuy, I just wanted to tell you how it was a pleasure to have Tomie in my class this year. He excelled on different levels. His class presentations, specifically the fall one, were simply outstanding. What a wonderful young man who's definitely going places."

Mr. Green began to squirm a lot in his suit, as Mrs. Kulverhouse continued giving me praises.

"Sari is very fortunate to have someone so respectful and passionate about women's rights in her life—lucky young lady. Congratulations, Tomie and Sari. Take care. Let me know how your first year goes, Tomie. Have a beautiful night everyone," Mrs. Kulverhouse said and departed.

"See you at home, Sari," Mr. Green said. He started scratching his head and face.

"I won't be home until later."

"Where will you be, young lady?" he demanded.

Sari's eyes spun over at me.

"Midnight is your curfew," he shouted as his face turned red. He bent down to lift up his pants as his nails raked up down his leg.

"No, it's actually two. I extended it because it's a special night, and Sari will be turning eighteen next month," Mrs. Green replied. "Enjoy honey, be safe, and think smart, always." She winked and hugged both of us. "Tomie, don't worry about Mr. Green. Have a nice time," she whispered in my ear.

"Thanks, Mrs. Green."

"Nice to see you again, Mr. Dupuy." She reached out to

shake my father's hand.

"Likewise. Wish I could say the same about your husband."

"Understood. Take care, Mr. Dupuy."

Mr. Green practically ran out, tugging at his clothes.

Lisette was giggling. I slid over, next to her. "Did you do something to Mr. Green?"

"Me?" Her eyes glistened.

"Tell me," I begged.

"Just a little something to keep him occupied for a little while."

"Placed an itching spell on him. It should wear off in a week or so. Sari's life will be less frantic now."

I high-fived her and smiled.

On our way out to celebrate at Mackie's Bistro, Opal bumped my side and said in a low tone, "Soon." She flew off on her invisible broomstick down the hall. I just shook my head.

"I'll see you both next weekend, right?" Lisette asked.

"Yes! We're so excited," Sari said for the both of us.

"Wish you could make it, Mr. Dupuy," Crow said.

"Me too. Have a mandatory run to make. Please take plenty of pictures for me, okay? I know it's going to be beautiful."

CHAPTER
FORTY—FIVE

ORGANIZING MY ROOM AND DOING SOME LIGHT packing for the academy kept me busy most of that week, especially the nights I hung out with Sari when she wasn't working. My mind focused a lot on what Opal and Verlinda's next move would be, especially after Opal's little comments at graduation.

Sari wasn't a huge fan of teleporting. So, Lisette emailed Sari and I two airline tickets a few days before. She figured it would be a lot easier to fly for less than two hours for a short turn around trip versus more than four hours on the road. Lisette would be getting married on Saturday night at seven in her backyard, hopefully.

Friday morning arrived. I woke up and got dressed. I packed

my bag. Looking around the room, I made sure I didn't forget something.

Before I stepped over the threshold of my bedroom door, the witch ball swung high to the right and then to the left, from the corner of my eye. I turned around. It froze for about fifteen seconds, spun around several rotations, flew off, and landed right in front of my feet.

Stooping down, I picked it up and placed it in my bag. I wouldn't ignore a warning from it again, and contacting Lisette next was on my agenda.

Dad was waiting outside in his work truck. "Got everything?"

Opening the door and stepping in, I said, "Think so." I placed my bag on the floor behind my seat.

Dad handed me a sealed card with Lisette and Crow's name written on front.

"What's this?"

"Lisette's gift from both of us."

"Is it what I think it is?"

"Yes, the money that she wouldn't take before and a little extra."

I pressed down on it, and it wasn't light.

"How much?"

"Don't worry about that, son. It will help them out, however they wish to use it. They were extremely generous to help me with your graduation gift to the point, where I won't have a monthly bill, so this is the least I can do."

I didn't respond for a few seconds.

"Wow, Dad. I didn't know that. They'll so appreciate it."

"No problem, I'm so grateful to both of them. I wish them many, many years of health and happiness."

"I'll sure tell them both."

"Okay. Let's get you off to the airport. Oh, do we need to pick Sari up?"

"No, her mom is dropping her off."

I pulled my cell from my side pocket and started texting Lisette while Dad drove to the airport, which was about thirty minutes away.

T: **Hey, something weird just happened with my witch ball in my room**

L: **What?**

T: **It did the craziest thing**

L: **Share**

T: **It rotated, froze, flipped off, and rolled to my feet**

L: **Where are you?**

T: **Headed to the airport. I packed my ball 2**

L: **Good.**

Dad stopped at a red light. I heard a piercing squawking sound close by. I looked around and noticed a crow perched above a lamppost.

T: **Lisette, you remember that bird we saw back in Salem?**

L: **Yes**

T: **Well, I'm not sure if it's the same one, but it looks** similar

L: **Tomie, it's Verlinda's familiar and the witch ball movement and rolling over to you means... It's a harbinger.**

T: **Wait, is it what I think?**

L: **Yes! They're coming...**

There was need to guess who Lisette was referring to—Verlinda, Opal, and Pepper. I didn't text her back right away. The inevitable door of fate had finally opened up, and I knew we would be face-to-face with all of them soon on Monroe Creek soil.

In a way, I always felt this encounter would end up in Monroe and not in Frost. Maybe it was because of all the rich supernatural history that was buried and breathed there.

Although I felt prepared, uncertainty lingered inside me. Would we be able to defeat them? Did they possess special spells or weapons?

L: **Are you almost at the airport?**

T: **About ten minutes away**

L: **How are you feeling?**

T: **Little queasy, but I'll be okay**

L: **Can feel it. Glad you're wearing your necklace. Tomie, we got this!**

T: **I believe u...**

I grabbed my necklace and could feel the warmth inside my hands.

L: **Let's concentrate on you and Sari getting here safely.**

Don't think they'll show up at the airport, but if they do, then you teleport out of there with Sari, okay? Maybe you should just teleport now.

T: No. We'll be fine. I agree with u about them not making a big scene at the airport, and they want us all together, anyhow

L: Tomie, this is really SERIOUS!! Promise me, if they happen to show up there, then you'll teleport out with Sari?

T: Promise

L: Good. Contact me if you need me. I'll be picking y'all up.

T: Okay, see u soon, Lisette

L: Be careful.

Dad arrived at the airport. Mrs. Green's car was ahead of us at the drop-off point with flashing blinkers. I got out of the truck and grabbed my bag, and then I walked over to him and gave him a firm hug.

"Son, what's going on?"

I looked at him.

"What's wrong?" He stepped closer to me.

"Our fight will happen really soon with Opal, Verlinda, and Pepper."

"How do you know?"

"I received a sign, and Lisette explained it to me."

"Tomie, I can call a buddy to see if he can make this run for me and travel with you."

"No, Dad. I just want you to know how much I love you, if something happens to me."

"I know Lisette will not let anything happen to you, plus your gift is going to get you through it all. Believe that, son." He grabbed me and pulled me into an embrace.

Pulling back slowly, I said, "Thanks, Dad, love you." I picked up my bag.

"Love you. Beat them all!" He shot both of his arms up in the air.

I gave him a shaky thumbs-up sign as I walked backwards a few steps before turning around.

Sari and I entered into the airport together. "I'm so excited to attend Lisette and Crow's wedding with you."

"Me too." I gave her a forced smile.

"Something wrong, Tomie?"

"Company will be arriving soon." We obtained our boarding passes from the kiosk and headed towards our gate.

Sari's hands quivered as I handed her the pass. "Here, Tomie?"

"No, but probably sometime today or tonight in Monroe Creek." I grasped her hand in mine.

"Are you serious?"

"Wish I wasn't."

Her teeth began to chatter.

"Tomie, I wish none of this was happening right now," Sari said, her voice wobbly, she started tearing up.

"Hey, girl, I'm not going to let anything happen to you, I promise. Trust me, right?" Lifting her chin up with my hand, I gazed into her brown eyes and kissed her on her lips softly.

"Yes." She gave me a partial smile with a slight nod.

When we arrived at our gate, I noticed a group was beginning to board, and then I saw a familiar face staring back at me in a seat near the check-in.

"Mr. Ray, what are you doing here?"

"Accompanying you and Sari to the wedding, of course."

"You know something, don't you?"

He nodded as our group number was called to board and stood up behind me. We each handed our boarding passes to the attendant and walked down the curved hall towards the plane. Sari requested the window seat, and I chose the aisle seat.

Mr. Ray said, "I saw Verlinda's familiar in a dream last night and again in person early this morning, when I took the trash out. I knew she was preparing for something major, and I needed to be near you."

"That witch ball also was acting freaky. Lisette explained everything to me. I packed it in my bag."

"Good you packed it."

Lisette was waiting for us once we disembarked off the airplane and into the lobby. She hugged each of us, and we traveled to her car to load up. "Was your flight uneventful?" she asked. It was around two-thirty in the afternoon.

"Yes, thankfully," I said.

"Sari, I'm happy that you're here. Just wish it was under better circumstances," Lisette sighed. "Mr. Ray, I'm glad that you're here with us, too. I take it, you're aware of everything?"

"Yes."

"They may arrive tonight. Tomie, I want you to stay near Sari inside the house and don't leave her by herself, okay? Crow, Mr. Ray, and I will be in the forefront. Got it?" Lisette said. Her eyes appeared to shimmer in the rearview mirror.

"Yes," I said.

"Tomie, I really need for you to follow through," Lisette stressed.

"Promise."

"Crow is already at the house, and Caya may be in later tonight. She's doing some things for her mom, so she may not arrive until tomorrow."

I looked over at Sari. With everything that had happened, I knew she would never be besties with Caya, but she was able to tolerate her name better than before, which was a major accomplishment for her. I slid my hand over to hers and wrapped my pinky finger around hers.

"We all knew this time would arrive, and now it's here." Lisette looked at all of us with her intense eyes.

Once we arrived at the house, she parked in the back, as she always did. Crow's truck was parked under a tall tree. I noticed how there were lights strung all up in the trees, around the gazebo, and the house.

I wanted to tell Lisette how nice her decorations were, but I was too focused on what was to come with Opal, Verlinda, and Pepper. Sari and I stepped out of the car with our bags.

"Our wedding may be delayed, indefinitely. I apologize ahead of time for you all traveling into this mess," Lisette shared in a faint tone.

"None of this is your fault."

"I agree, Tomie," Mr. Ray said.

Crow greeted us all, and we entered inside the house. He didn't laugh or smile, which was unlike him. Securing all the doors, I also noticed Lisette looking outside the windows in the kitchen and living room. "Tomie, please show Sari to her room."

"If it's okay, I think I'm going to stay in Tomie's room," Sari said.

Mr. Ray decided to camp in the living room. I didn't think there would be much sleep going on for most of us. After tonight, I wasn't sure who would still be left here. Keeping all the ones I cared for safe was my only priority, even if that meant me dying tonight.

CHAPTER
FORTY — SIX

A FULL, BLOOD-MOON USHERED NIGHTFALL INTO Monroe Creek. The stars seemed to exhibit a low glow that night, as well. Sparse, swirling clouds with a glowing yellow tint drifted in the sky.

High winds blew in from the east and west. Large raindrops began to smash against all the windows, along with white, violet, and yellow lightning bolts zigzagging around Lisette's house. The building shook.

In a steel voice, Lisette said, "You both stay here."

She flung the front door open, going outside. Crow and Mr. Ray followed her. Sari and I watched from the doorway as water flew inside. I shut the door. We went to look out the window.

The rain stopped, but then grey ash flakes poured down. Once the flakes dropped down on Lisette, Crow, and Mr. Ray's bodies, they transformed into large, red-eyed, hairy worms with razor-like teeth. Lisette, Crow, and Mr. Ray pulled them off, threw them onto the ground, and stomped down on them. They made shrieking cries and evaporated into the air. Thunderous howls saturated the winds.

I didn't see anyone else outside, not even on Lisette's long, gravel driveway. They returned back into the house.

"Lisette, are y'all okay?" I mumbled, as sweat ran down the sides of my face, and my heart banged loud against my chest.

"Yes."

"What about those nasty worm bites?" Sari asked, trembling against me. I wrapped my arm around her.

"I can hear your heart racing," Sari whispered, as she rubbed her hand a few times over my chest.

My hand pushed her fallen hair out of her face.

"They weren't real," Lisette said.

"Wait, but we saw them." Sari blinked her eyes multiple times.

"I know. We did, too. That was an illusion spell. See." She extended her arms out, and they were clear of bites. "A spell like that is used to try and distract you from something. Verlinda is really trying to break my lock-out spell around the house."

"What now?" I asked.

DOLL³

"All we can do is wait. What just happened is only the beginning. They have something much bigger planned. I think they just wanted to see how we would react, or if she could actually enter into my protective realm."

We waited for hours. Lisette headed towards the kitchen and made some tea and coffee for all of us. It was after eleven-thirty. Sari had drifted off to sleep on the couch. She looked so uncomfortable crunched up. I carried her to the room and placed her in bed.

Checking my bag for my witch ball, I placed it on the bedside table. She reached her hands up and mumbled, "Don't go," and closed her eyes with hands falling down next to her.

"I'll be in the next room. Rest." I kissed her forehead, pulled a blanket over her, and left the door cracked behind me.

I returned to the living room.

"Lisette, what do you think they're waiting for?" I asked.

"Not sure, but I'm really wondering myself." She paced the floor until Crow convinced her to come and sit down. She rested her head on his huge shoulder.

"Where's Sari?" she asked. She scanned the room.

"She's been asleep in my room since you made tea. I have my witch ball with her."

Jumping up, Lisette demanded, "How long has she been alone?"

"Maybe five minutes."

In a raspy voice, her eyes swelling, Lisette asked, "What

time is it, Crow?"

"Midnight, why? What's wrong with you?" He blinked a few times.

Mr. Ray's zigzagging eyes watched Lisette.

"It's the witching hour. Go, check on Sari, quickly, Tomie!" she shouted and bolted behind me.

Running down the hallway, I pushed the bedroom door wide open so hard, it came off its hinges. The blanket was on the floor, and the bed was disheveled. I noticed scratch marks from fingernails on the wooden headboard, as if Sari was dragged out of bed.

The window was open, the screen was on the ground below, and the white curtains billowed high in the air around us. Something wet was on them. It looked like blood, and a message was written on one: *You and Tomie come alone, or Sari will be no more.*

How had Verlinda and Opal managed to scoop Sari up from underneath our noses? I could feel my heart beat in triple time, and my glow spotted my arms and hands.

"Tomie, calm down. We're going to need you to save all of this for when the time is right. Remember what we practiced, okay?"

My head dropped down. "I thought the witch ball would protect her."

"It would've, if it was gifted to Sari, but it was created for you and your surroundings."

I just didn't think this would happen. This was all my fault, and I was going to do everything in my power to fix it, no matter what. I shook my head, bringing my breathing under control. Within a few minutes, my heartbeats were normal again, and my glow was gone. "Lisette, what did you mean about the witching hour?"

"It's a very special hour for witches to utilize their magic, and it's also the time when certain spells can be at their *weakest* point, which is what Verlinda and Opal focused on."

Pacing the floor, my head hung lower.

"Leaving Sari alone, even for a few minutes, allowed them to practice their dark and twisted magic to cast a silence/transfer spell on her. One, I didn't expect. They knew they couldn't enter into my home, but they could remove her from here during this delicate time, even with the protection spell you had placed on her."

"They did that so we would come to them, right?" I asked, breathing hard through my flaring nostrils.

"Exactly. They want to meet us on their grounds. I don't like it one bit, but we're going to have to go."

"Where?"

"La Fantasma."

"Why there?"

"It's the place where *darkness* lives. A lot of bad things are buried around there, including wandering spirits."

I walked over and sat on the bed, cradling my head in my

hands. "Sari would still be safe, if I hadn't left her!"

Lisette sat beside me. "We knew they were wanting to lure us out. They just went another direction. I hoped they would've left her alone, but Opal knows how much Sari means to you."

Mr. Ray and Crow entered the room.

"They took her," Mr. Ray said with a heavy sigh.

"Yes," Lisette moaned.

Crow snarled and his fangs crawled out. "Let's go get her! I'll go pull the truck up."

Lisette looked at him. "Crow, you and Mr. Ray must stay behind, only Tomie and I can go. If one or both of you go, then they could kill Sari."

"No, no, Lisette, I must go to protect Tomie!" Mr. Ray yelled.

"I don't want you to go alone, Lisette," Crow growled in a deep voice.

I was ready to face Verlinda, Opal, and Pepper. I needed Sari to be safe and defeating them, even if that meant blood on my hands, would be the only solution. My heart tumbled hard and my breathing increased.

"Listen, I'll be okay. Tomie is in good hands with me—you both know that."

Mr. Ray took a deep breath. "I understand. At least let me be close. They'll never know I'm there."

"I'm so sorry, Mr. Ray. Yes, they would. I don't want to give them one little reason to hurt, Sari, okay? We need to go now.

DOLL³

No time to waste."

"We'll be here waiting on you both," Crow said, pounding a hole in the wall with his fist, as a lone tear drifted down his jawline.

He hugged Lisette, and he did the same to me. I coughed a few times from the intense pressure of his oversized arms.

"Tomie, listen, when we get there, let me talk to Verlinda to see if I can figure out what she really wants."

Leaning in closer to her, I whispered, "Are you taking the wand?"

"I plan to teleport it at the right time. I don't want to have it on me just yet, in case one of them figures it out. Now, your special gift will definitely come in handy. When the time is right, I want you to really concentrate and allow it to take over, okay?"

"Got it."

"Tomie, we're going to get through this together. Now, if something goes wrong, you teleport the wand to you, okay?"

"Lisette, nothing is going to happen to you." I frowned.

She placed her hand up on my shoulder. "I'm counting on that, but you never know."

Turning around to face Crow, she whispered, "I love you." She grabbed my hand and squeezed it tight. "Ready, Tomie?"

All kinds of thoughts flew in and out of my mind. I heard what she was asking me, but I felt so heavy and speechless. It took me a few seconds to respond.

"Yes," I gasped.

Her emerald eyes faded into a fiery, hazel glow.

In less than thirty seconds, we were levitating down on the front porch of La Fantasma, and before we planted our feet down, a cloud of white powder was blown into our faces. We both collapsed onto the cold porch floor.

CHAPTER
FORTY—SEVEN

Furry hands with claws tied my hands behind my back. My vision was blurry and I felt drowsy. However, I could make out three wavy bodies in front of me. Attempting to turn my head to the right, I saw Lisette with her head lowered down to her chest in the same position as I was.

I faded out again for a couple of minutes, and then I woke up. My eyes widened, finally clear. Staring down at my legs, I could see that Lisette and I were both bound on a long, wooden stake, with an iron chain wrapped around our bodies. A small, oval wooden stool held our bare feet up. Several logs were placed in a circular, upward fashion near our feet.

All that I could think about was the disgusting vision and odors I'd experienced at Proctor's Ledge, when I was in

Salem—burning hair and flesh, something that would never leave my memories. I knew they wanted me to feel what the poor accused went through. Was this our end? My pulse accelerated.

Ash and Garth in full rougarou form galloped around with a lit torch held up high in their claws. They snarled and hissed every time they got close to us. Lisette was still unconscious. My arms, legs, and chest felt frozen. I couldn't move anything except my eyes.

I attempted to communicate with her telepathically, but she didn't respond. As far as my powers, I couldn't use them due to whatever was in the powder they'd sprayed and the iron chains.

In front of me, I saw Verlinda and Opal talking to someone I couldn't identify. Sari was to my left, and she was in the same position as Lisette and I. She was also still asleep.

Opal levitated to me.

"Poor, poor, Tomie Dupuy... I bet you never imagined this."

"Look, Opal, release Lisette and Sari. You can just take me!" I demanded, staring into her cold eyes.

"Aww, look at this, he wants to be *Boy Wonder*, too sweet."

She ran her black painted nails over my lips.

"Opal, what did we ever do to you?"

"Silly boy, you don't know, and to think that you were runner up for salutatorian for our graduating class."

DOLL³

"Stop with the games and just tell me. It's not like I'm getting out of this." My face contorted.

"How right you are! Let's just say, it's time for the Laveau line to end and for Dawn Coven to resurrect fully, and rule without any interference from you or your meddling cousin. There are changes we're making for other covens around the world. First, we must destroy your Laveau Coven, starting with its two most powerful *supras*."

"You really think your plan is going to work?"

Opal may have had a plan; however, I also had a plan with a few surprises that she and her company wouldn't be anticipating.

"Of course, look around you before you all meet your fates."

A slender figure with a midnight blue cloak and hood draped over her head walked out. Opal levitated her up, and the interior of her hood resembled a dark abyss until she peeled it back. Long, tight black curls with silver highlights hung down her shoulders.

"Hello, there, Tomie. Bet you didn't think you would see me again."

Hardening my eyes, I said, "It was just a matter of time. Why do they have you here, Pepper?"

"To do the honors, of course." Her eyes darted away.

"You mean to set each of us on fire?"

"No, just you, old school style, at the stake. You all ruined my prom and murdered me on the dance floor, so..."

"Pepper, Opal filled your head with her lies!"

Swinging around to face Opal, Pepper shouted, "Opal, is there any truth to the freak's accusations?" Her slanting eyes bounced in my direction.

"No. Why would you believe somebody like Tomie?" she asked in a breathy tone, her nostrils flaring. She clenched her fists, and her eyes turned firebrick red.

"Well, he's always been honest since I've known him in junior high."

Verlinda paced slowly and kept her eyes glued on us.

"Pepper, what did Opal tell you, exactly?" I asked.

"Sari, Lisette, and you placed a horrible, dark spell on me."

"Ask yourself this one question, Pepper? Why would all three of us want to kill you? Remember Opal's diary you found back in junior high and all those awful things she wrote about you? Go back, way back. Think about all of those salty entries."

"Shut up, Tomie. Just shut up!" Opal yelled, landing on the ground and bringing Pepper down, as well.

"Opal, I've always known you wanted to be me. Look at you. You're still not close. I may not look like I used to, but I'll never be a loser like you," Pepper said in a bitter voice. "For the record, Opal, I had a feeling you were associated in some way with my demise, especially after your little stunt with Sari and my girls."

"Whatever!" Opal shouted and turned away from her.

DOLL³

"Give me those torches, you foul-smelling hyenas!" Ash and Garth both growled at her. She jerked the torches away from them and threw one to Verlinda, who caught them without looking up.

"Grandmom, let's end this, now!" Opal shouted.

Opal lit up the wood in a slow-moving flame under Lisette; Verlinda followed and set the wood on fire under Sari.

Verlinda handed the other torch to Pepper. "Do it!" Opal shouted. "Burn Tomie!" Opal's black eyes grew larger as red veins throbbed underneath.

I could feel the heat from the Lisette and Sari's waving flames. Sweat flowed from my face and all over my quivering body. My guilt weighed heavy on me because now Sari and Lisette's lives were in trouble because of me, once again.

Pepper paused. She stared Opal and Verlinda down.

"After everything we did to bring you back, you're not going to listen to me," Opal hissed.

"Everything is really true, right Opal?"

"What?" Opal huffed.

"You know what," Pepper said, rolling her eyes.

"Listen, sometimes stuff just happens."

Tomie, can you hear me?

I can. I wasn't sure if you were going to wake up. Think it's time to put that wand to good use, don't you?

Yes... Tomie, I agree. Our powers are dead right now because of these iron chains, but the wand is all powerful. I almost have

398

*my hands free. I'm getting pretty warm. Try to hold Pepper off a
little more, I'm almost free, okay?*

Got it.

"Pepper, you know that I had a thing for you a long time
ago, right?"

"Yeah, most of the guys at Frost did too," she said, eyes
searching my face.

"I wouldn't have ever done something to hurt you
permanently," I pleaded with her.

Pepper delayed her response. "Tomie, I know. Maybe
I deserved what happened to me at prom because of all the
mean stuff I did to others for so long, especially tormenting
you and Opal, while urging others to join in. I never wanted
to be brought back. Initially, I craved revenge upon my return,
but after reviewing my entire life and listening to you, I don't
want anything else to do with hurting someone, again. This is
one do-over I wish to cancel."

Pepper dropped the torch and walked behind me, in attempt
to unwrap the iron chains. Opal retrieved it and threw it on
my wood stack. Ash and Garth jumped up on the roof of the
mansion and howled, piercing my eardrums. They perched
themselves there to watch.

"We should've never resurrected you with that spell. You
didn't deserve life again then and you don't now. I'm glad I
changed the spell, I stole from Lisette."

"Thanks for your confession, Opal. I needed to know for

sure. Tomie was right all along. You and your grandmom surely didn't bring me back for the sake of my dad's happiness."

Grinding her teeth, Opal said, "Pepper Fox, you're right because you made my life miserable, and yes, I hated you so much I was willing to do whatever I needed to do to get rid of you. I also plan on destroying you for good, including your dad, after I finish up with these three."

Pepper went to push Opal, but Opal froze her, but not like what happened to Mr. Ray months ago. Pepper could move her eyes back and forth, just nothing else.

"Stay put. I'll take care of you in a bit." She flung her hair back.

I saw the flames around Sari flare higher.

"Lisette!" I yelled.

She broke free from her bondage and levitated above me with the glistening turquoise wand in her hand.

Opal and Verlinda looked up.

Lisette pointed her wand towards them and wrapped a rope made of small spheres with spiky thorns around their bodies and hands to hold them.

Within seconds, Lisette swooped down to face me, pointing the wand at me and dousing the flames. The chains dropped from my body. She levitated me up, as I watched the flames engulf Sari. I saw her squirming all around and her piercing screams penetrated my entire body.

I dropped and snatched her down off the stake.

"Tomie, I'm so sorry," Lisette screamed, as tears streamed down her face.

"No!" I roared. "No, no!" Blue sparks flew from my body in all directions.

Sari's skin looked like warm candlewax, and her eyes were slightly open. She uttered a faint moan. I placed my ear down to listen to her heart, and the beats were sluggish. "You can't leave me!"

"Tomie, I thought I could save her in time," Lisette cried, lowering herself down to the ground.

"Why didn't you save her first, Lisette!" Tears ran down my face.

I bared all of my teeth, clenched my fists, and slammed them down, causing the grass to ripple and the ground to tremor. Lisette stumbled and caught herself before she fell. My pulse escalated as I stood.

My eyes glowed and shimmered, deep blue rays shooting out. I locked onto Garth and Ash on the roof. I raised my hand and lifted the roof up, causing them to slide off. They bolted into the dark woods leaving screeching howls, lingering behind them.

"I'm so sorry—so sorry," Lisette screamed.

Bending down, I felt my heartbeats racing faster and faster. I lifted Sari in my arms. The blue glow consumed all of my body, eyes, and hair. Levitating high above Lisette, my wings fully emerged. I surrounded Sari's entire body with them.

We rose higher into the dark sky, rotating rapidly, close to the moon. My wings began to glow a darker blue, taking on a golden hue. They felt warm. More sparks flew everywhere for several seconds.

Lowering myself back down to the ground, I unwrapped Sari from my wings. Her body was completely healed—no burns. I could feel the pulse beating in her neck. My wings retracted. I laid her down on the ground and waited until she opened her eyes.

"Tomie, what happened?" Sari moaned.

Verlinda and Opal remained trapped in Lisette's lasso.

"We'll talk about all that later."

She attempted to wrap her arms around my neck, but they flopped down near her side.

Lisette ran up to us both.

"Tomie, I'm speechless."

"Yeah, me too... Sari, I'm going to teleport you back by yourself to Lisette's, so you can rest, okay?"

She nodded slowly. Her eyelids closed. I placed a forgetting and sleep spell on her. "Rest, rest, rest now. When you awaken, all will be forgotten of this night," I whispered, sweeping my hand over her face, three times, counter clockwise, while teleporting her back to the house.

Mr. Ray, can you hear me?

Of course, Tomie.

I know you've been doing a live glim, so you're up to speed.

Yes, and I am...

Sari's returning back in a few seconds. Please keep watch on her. She's really weak.

No problem. Crow and I are on guard.

Thank you.

Do you need me?

No, we got to finish this cleanup.

After I finished the conversation with Mr. Ray, I felt very lightheaded and exhausted. I heard Verlinda's slithering tone, "I never thought I would see the Laveau wand and a blue-blood supra in action. Lisette, I knew you possessed it that night I came here."

"Well, you just never know about us Laveaus, Verlinda Dawn," Lisette bellowed, extending her open palm out and waving her wand over it. In less than a minute, she handed me a bottle of milky brown water.

"What's this?" I sniffed it and pulled it away from my nose.

"Drink up."

"This?" My eyes widened.

"Absolutely, Mister. Need your strength to build back up fast after your presentation, which was extraordinary to witness, by the way." She stroked my arm.

"Bottoms up." I drank it all down in one gulp. It tasted super tart with a lingering aftertaste like warm Pepto-Bismol mixed with sardines, but worse. "Nasty stuff." I stuck my tongue out and scrunched my eyes closed for a few seconds.

"Well, it will do the trick in a few minutes."

Then Lisette waved her wand, levitating them off the ground.

"By the way, Verlinda, since you're all tied up with nowhere to go, tell me this."

"Tell you what, Lisette?" Verlinda asked in a raucous voice.

"Who broke into my house that night and released Opal from her glass prison?"

"None of your business," Verlinda hissed and glared at us.

"This won't hold us for long," Opal barked.

Smiling, I said, "You know what, Lisette, I think I have something that will help her answer your question and quiet Opal down. Remember the box?"

"Oh, I do." Lisette laughed.

"What are you two talking about?" Verlinda asked, scanning her black eyes over us.

"You'll find out very soon," I said.

I teleported the witch catchers from Lisette's. They floated in front of me.

"Please, please, we'll cooperate," Verlinda pleaded with tears in her eyes.

"What's wrong with you, Granny?" Opal asked.

"Stupid girl, you're so clueless. Those are a witch's nightmare."

Waving my hands in a circular pattern, the witch catchers swung towards their throbbing necks, unclasped themselves, and molded onto them, while the clasp clinked in a locking position. The chains rested in front of them. They dropped to the ground. The thorny rope crumbled into ashes below their feet.

"Now, Verlinda, please answer Lisette's question," I requested with my arms crossed.

Lisette patted my arm and mouthed, "Excellent job, Tomie."

"Cage Fox did it. He knew that bringing Pepper back wasn't going to happen unless I had my Opal back first. That's all he ever talked about. I got so sick of hearing about his sickening story of his only child. I propositioned him for a very nice lump sum to pay off my mortgage, Esmerelda's fees, Opal's college of her choice, and a comfy retirement for me."

"Our names were given to Cage in place of Opal's, so he would fund your projects, even though Opal was responsible for Pepper's death, right?" Lisette asked.

"Yep, you're figuring it all out," Verlinda sighed.

"You used the triple spell, deception/concealing/suspension, so I couldn't identify him?"

"Bingo!" Verlinda cackled. "I needed a non-supra to enter inside your home with my familiar acting as my eyes and Cage as my hands. They got my Opal from under your wicked grasp. I waited outside. I knew y'all were at the festival and later tied up with my nincompoop nephews."

Immediately, my eyes focused on Lisette.

DOLL³

Massaging my chin with my hand, I asked, "Wait, you mean Ash and Garth?" My hand fell to my side.

A deep sigh flew from Verlinda's wrinkled lips. "Unfortunately, yes. They've never been successful with much as you have witnessed, but I adore them. I never wanted anyone, especially the Laveau Coven, to discover my kinship to them, so I placed a hidden spell over them before they were born."

I stepped closer to her. "Is this why you did all of this to us?"

"Something like that. I've always despised the Laveau Coven, but this is more personal because of the torment Lisette issued my sweet Ash. He was young back then. We waited and wanted to destroy you and your companions, when the time was perfect because you destroyed his life. He can't keep a girlfriend." Her mouth twisted several times.

In a deep voice, I yelled, "You do know, what he did to Lisette?"

Averting her black eyes from me, she cast a cold stare on Lisette. "She shouldn't have been such a tease."

Pulling me back by the end of my shirt as I leaped forward, Lisette said, "Tomie, everything makes sense, now."

Out the corner of my eye, I saw Ash lunge towards Lisette with his outstretched claws. Whipping around, I yanked Lisette out of the way, and she fell on top of me. I reached my free hand up to freeze Ash in mid air. Garth stood behind a tree and started backing up.

Rolling Lisette over, I jumped up. I waved my hand to levitate Garth towards me. Garth dangled in the air upside down, whimpering. Lisette waved her wand on the ground, and a huge divided cage appeared in front of us. I threw them both inside and locked it.

I closed my eyes and waved my hands all around their temporary home and chanted, "Keep them in this transformation until sunrise. Allow Ash to feel a pain mightier than a thousand stinging yellowjackets—give him a constant reminder, now."

"Please don't hurt them," Verlinda begged, tears climbing down her face.

Ash and Garth paced back and forth, snarling for a few seconds before the spell kicked in. They went to grab the bars, but they cried out and yanked their burning claws back from the silver and garlic laced bars. Ash jumped every time he moved in his tight area; his floor was made up of electric currents, which were activated by movement.

Shivering Garth crawled in his corner and buried his head between his hairy legs. Lisette looked at me and whispered, "Thank you, Tomie." I levitated them inside the mansion and silenced their howls, until Crow could retrieve them for the tribal council to determine their fates.

Verlinda yelped, "What are you going to do to us?"

CHAPTER
FORTY—EIGHT

BEFORE LISETTE COULD ANSWER, AN IRIDESCENT tornado waved in and out between us. We both fell down. The hairs on my arms rose. Both Esmerelda and Ms. Gobblestein appeared in front of us in the flesh.

"Umm, Ms. Gobblestein, what are you doing here?" My heart froze and my mouth fell open.

"Mr. Tomie Dupuy, you only know me as Ms. Gobblestein at Frost High, but that's my late spouse's name, not my birth name, which is Proctor."

"Hold up. Ms. Gobblestein, you're a Proctor, like the witch family?" Trying to wrap my mind around this revelation, I ran both hands through my hair. Could she be one of the…?

She nodded and straightened her black and purple glittery

witch hat on her head. "Yes, Mr. Dupuy, I'm one of the Enchanted Proctor Five descendants and president of the *Upper Witch Council.*"

My mouth dropped again. Lisette placed her index finger under my chin. "You should close it, just in case a night skeeter flies in there." She smiled. "They're worse than the daytime ones."

I closed my mouth. "Lisette, did you know?"

"No, this is all new to me, as well, Tomie."

"How did you know to come here tonight, Ms. Gobblestein?"

"Esmerelda and Mr. Hashimoto gave me a full update, especially after I sensed dark magic with the transmigration spell that Verlinda and Opal requested her assistance for."

Lisette's emerald eyes glowed bright. "What will happen to Opal and Verlinda?

Ms. Gobblestein chuckled. "They'll be taken away tonight, a bounding spell will be placed on both of them, and they'll soon face trial by the council and about ten covens, including the Sonthiel Coven. Let's just say that the Dawn Coven will probably be stripped of all their powers, forever."

"Pepper really surprised me, tonight."

"I'm already aware, Tomie. Pepper's situation is unique, and the council and I will determine her fate, including her father's, Mr. Fox. Don't worry about him believing you were the culprits of her murder."

With her jade cloak flying high behind her, Esmerelda

stood next to me and in a guttural voice said, "I'll take care of his memories. Whose idea was it to use witch catchers against them?" She pointed towards Verlinda and Opal with a dark glare. They were both shaking on their knees and crying.

I slowly raised my hand up.

"Good choice. I'm going to take those," Esmerelda whispered, as deep purple with red highlights dispersed from her pupils.

Goosebumps wrapped around both of my arms. "Keep them." I stepped closer to Lisette.

The witch catchers detached from their necks and zoomed over our heads, swinging in mid air next to Esmerelda.

Ms. Gobblestein cleared her throat. "Excuse me, Mr. Dupuy?"

Stepping out of her way, I said, "Never expected any of this, Ms. Gobblestein."

Nodding and waving her hand around all three of them, seven times in the directions of north, south, east, and west, three dolls in their exact images dropped in Ms. Gobblestein's hand.

Then, she untied one glistening orange and one dull coffee bag with stripes off the side of her puffy black skirt, and opened them. She slid Pepper in the orange one; Verlinda and Opal were placed in the other. She tied them tightly around her belt.

"Well, looks like my job is finished here. Great work, Lisette and Tomie. You both continue to shine in our *supra* world. Thank you both. Let me know if you ever need my assistance."

She winked at me and tapped the brim of her sparkly hat twice with her black cat and green owl ring. I noticed a plum, cursive number five tattoo etched on her inner wrist. Ms. Gobblestein vanished. Esmerelda nodded and followed right behind her. That was when it hit me. I remembered Ms. Gobblestein's owl brooch she used to wear all the time. I never imagined the connection would be this.

Young Tomie, I've always known about your family history. Just needed for you to embrace your gifts. Now, do well in flight school. Come visit me after you graduate. I think I may have a special assignment for you. Oh, the conversation has started with Mr. Hashimoto about a possible truce in the future.

"Lisette, did you hear what Ms. Gobblestein shared?" My chest tightened.

"Certainly did."

Rolling my neck to the left, I said, "What do you think she's talking about, regarding a future secret job?"

"I'm not sure. I have a feeling that it will be something worth your while. It's the highest honor to be recognized and called upon by the *Upper Witch Council*. Let's get out of here. Don't think I want to see this place, ever again. We gotta get some rest before tomorrow night. It's my big day!"

"I know. What time is it?"

Lisette looked at her watch. "After four in the morning."

DOLL³

We teleported back. She updated Crow on everything. He planned to take care of Ash and Garth on his way out in the next hour. He was busy repairing the wall section from earlier. I also updated Mr. Ray.

Although I knew Ms. Gobblestein took care of Verlinda and Opal, I decided to pull a cot out of Lisette's closet and sleep in the same room with Sari. I wanted to sleep right next to her and hold her close, but I wasn't going to push my luck. After that experience with Verlinda and her family, I wanted to ensure Sari's safety.

CHAPTER
FORTY—NINE

LISETTE'S BIG DAY ARRIVED. I COULD HEAR PEOPLE talking outside the door. I raised my head up and noticed Sari was still sleeping. She had a huge smile on her face. It felt so good to have her back in my life. I looked at the time on my watch—almost five in the afternoon. I jumped up. Only two hours before I would be walking Lisette down the aisle.

I crept out of the room and jumped in the shower. I saw Lisette walking around with huge rollers all over her head in a hot pink terry cloth robe with splattered purple stars. "Hey, why'd you let me sleep so long?"

"Mister, you needed it, especially after that amazing magic you performed last night. Your energy was still low. There's some food in the microwave."

After waking Sari up, she stared into my eyes. Then, she scanned the clock on the bedside table. "Tomie, why did you let me sleep so long? I got to do my hair, nails, and shower." She rolled out of bed and ran out of the room with her make-up bag.

"You were worn out," I yelled, as she slammed the bathroom door.

Smiling, I thought to myself how she didn't remember anything, which was my goal. When I walked into my room, my tuxedo with a wing collar and long tails hung on the closet door. Shiny gator boots were in front of the chair. I knew this was Crow's addition. I noticed the hot pink bowtie on the side. There was a folded aqua note on the nightstand.

Tomie, hope you like. You forgot to text me your measurements, so I guessed. Thank you so much. It means the world to me. No matter where you go, I'm here if you need me. This is your second home anytime. Love always, Lisette.

I folded it up and placed it in a special zipper compartment in my bag. I got dressed and left my coat off. Sitting down on the bed, I reflected back on everything since junior high, up until now. I never thought I would be connected to the supernatural world. So much had happened to me this last summer. What awaited me in the next few months or years? I had no idea—just was going to do the best I could and enjoy my life.

Light tapping sounded on my door. "Can I come in?"

"Yeah… Wow, girl, look at you."

Sari's hair was curled and pinned up with butterfly purple hairpins. She held a white bag in her left hand.

A grey, off-the shoulder dress with a lacey purple bodice hit above her knees. She twirled around, and the bow in the back was the same purple lace in the shape of a butterfly. Glittery purple heels with a strap decorated her petite feet. I took a few deep breaths.

"I thought you couldn't outdo your prom dress."

"Really, you like it?"

"Sari, I love it, and you look simply beautiful in it. Come here."

Holding my arms out, I embraced her. She kissed me on the left and right side, close to my mouth. Then, she landed a super slow one in the center. Her lipstick tasted like root beer and cherry Starbursts.

I really missed her incredible kisses.

"Yum. I always know your sweet kisses."

She stared down at me. "You better know."

"Hey, what's going through that mind of yours?"

"Just you, Tomie Dupuy… thinking how much I'm in love with you."

Leaning back, I asked, "Girl, you love me?"

"Stop it, you know it." She pressed her soft hands on the sides of my face. I could smell jasmine and strawberry all over her.

"Gotta ask you something. It's been bugging me for a while now." I rubbed my hands together.

"What?"

"Who's the better kisser? Phoenixx or me?"

Without one blink, she said, "He's not even close."

I hugged her tighter and whispered, "Sarifena Green, I'm going to love you always, no matter what. I *breathe* you in every time I wake up or see you."

"Tomie, I love you, too. Always will. By the way, what happened last night? Did Opal, Verlinda, or Pepper ever show up?"

Arching my eyebrows up, I asked, "You don't remember, anything?"

She gazed deep into my eyes. "Nope, just falling asleep and you carrying me to your room."

"Let's just say, we'll never have to be bothered with them again."

"You're not going to tell me, are you?" She squinted.

"No, Sari."

The spell that I placed on her was solid; however, I didn't want to risk it by divulging anything of what happened to her because it could traumatize her. I did that once, already. So I used distraction.

"What's in the bag?"

"Lisette's gift, want to see, Tomie?"

"Sure, if it's okay."

"Yeah." She pulled out something wrapped in pink tissue paper, holding it up.

"That's what I think it is, right?"

"A veil."

I picked it up out of her hand and unwrapped it. It was about twelve inches long with a butterfly shaped back in white and hot pink lace. The lace in the front probably would rest just above Lisette's lips. I noticed mini-rhinestone butterflies under the corners, where it would fit her eye area.

"Sari, she's going to love this. Where did you get it?"

"I made it a few months ago, including my outfit."

"See, this is what that European design school is going to be missing. Talent, talent!"

"Thanks, Tomie. I really hope she likes it."

"Oh, she's gonna love it. What time is it?"

"Quarter to seven."

"You better go find your seat out there and give that to Lisette." Removing a red bag from a drawer, I asked, "Would you mind carrying this to the reception with you?"

She shook it up. "Sure, what's in it? Feels really light."

"A thank you gift I ordered online a few weeks ago for Ranae and Caya. I'll give you a signal later when to share it."

"Okay, that's really thoughtful of you." She kissed me on my cheek. "See you soon." She ran out, shutting the door.

I grabbed my jacket, dropping Sari's ring inside an inner pocket, and buttoned it up. I picked my curly hair out again, sprayed some cologne on, and spun around to look at myself in the mirror. My coattails flew up in the air.

Let's do this, Lisette.

I'm outside your door.

Stepping up to my door, I opened it.

Lisette's make-up shimmered with every turn she made. Glitter danced up and down her bare arms. A strapless, fishtail champagne dress hugged her curves. Hot pink and golden sequins in the shape of tiny butterflies dazzled the lower portion of her dress. Sari's veil was perfect. Her pinned up hot pink and golden curls cascaded over her shoulders and bounced above her neckline.

"Okay, are you going to say something, Tomie?"

My mouth had trouble moving.

"Lisette... Whoa, you're gorgeous!"

"Stop it!"

"Honestly, you're the most beautiful bride I've ever seen."

"Aww, thank you so much. Ready?"

"Yes."

I extended my arm out, and she locked her arm inside. She lifted up the back of her gown, holding her small bouquet of white and pink orchids, her favorite flower, in her right hand, wrapped with sparkly black ribbons.

"Oh, let me." I waved my hand and thought of a floating spell, so she wouldn't have to worry about the back of her dress touching the ground all night.

"Tomie, thank you so much."

"This is part one of your gift. You have one more from me and a last one from my dad and me."

"You walking me down the aisle is the best gift, I could ever ask for." She squeezed my arm.

"Just enjoy. This is your very special day and you deserve it."

The door was already open. I walked in front of her to help her down the steps. "Lady" by Kenny Rogers started playing.

White and hot pink lights lit our path, and all the lights in the swaying trees guided us easily to Crow, who stood on the steps of the gazebo, which was also decorated with glowing lights.

The guests were all standing in front of white chairs dressed in white and pink bows. I saw Sari in the second row, standing next to Caya and Ranae. They all waved with triple winks from Ranae.

I took some deep breaths in.

"Tomie, what in the world are you going to do when you go off to school," Lisette whispered, squeezing my arm tighter.

"What do you mean?"

"All the girls are going to be *chasing* you."

"Umm, Lisette, let's focus."

"Okay, you know it's true. You're blushing."

I guided her up the stairs. Crow's tuxedo was exactly like mine, with the exception of a pink and black tie. I waited for the pastor to give me the verbal cue before I handed Lisette's hand over to Crow. He had a huge smile reflecting off his face. Giving me a thumbs-up, he pointed down at my gators. I grinned.

Making my way back down, I noticed her matron of honor dressed in a hot pink, strapless dress with a long black sash tied in a bow on the side. Lisette mouthed to me, "That's Shazzia." Lisette handed her bouquet over to her. Smiling at her, I went down to find my seat up front.

Crow and Lisette shared their personal vows. He grabbed both her hands.

"Lisette, I believe I fell in love with you when I first met you ten years ago. I've always known you were my best friend, but I dreamed for you to be my wife one day, when you were ready. I promise to love and support you always. You're my life, and I give all of myself to you, only."

"Crow, it did take me a while before I accepted your deep commitment. You've never stopped loving me, even though I attempted to push you away, many times. Thank you."

She paused for a minute, staring into his eyes. Her eyes twinkled and transformed from forest green to light brown and back.

"I also know that you've tried to save me a few times. You know that a girl like me doesn't need to be rescued. Yet, it's a great feeling to know that my *Superman* was always waiting there to swoop down, if I gave him that signal. I promise to love and support you always. You're also my life, and I give all of myself to you, only."

Lisette then recited *To Be in Love* by Gwendolyn Brooks. Crow started crying and embraced Lisette for a short moment.

The pastor asked, "Rings?"

While still holding Crow's hands, Lisette turned around and whistled. I heard bells ringing. Tiny feet ran down the steps of the house and down the trail we had just taken. It was Sabra. She was dressed in a fluffy, hot pink and white collar. Sabra ran up the stairs towards Lisette.

Lisette picked her up and untied shimmering turquoise rings from a black bow attached to her collar. Then, she placed Sabra down. Sabra ran back down the steps and towards me. I picked her up, and she rested in my lap. Crow placed the ring on Lisette's finger and vice-versa.

"Now, I pronounce you husband and wife... Crow Durant, you may now kiss Lisette Laveau Durant," the pastor said.

Lisette tilted her head, and Crow cupped his hands around her face, placing his lips onto hers.

Closing my eyes, I chanted a spell to myself. As they started down the stairs, large, pink orchid petals and snow began to fall down over them and the guests for a few minutes. They smiled and clapped.

Lisette looked at me.

Tomie, are you doing this?

Yep... Mom helped me with this weather spell when I talked to her last.

DOLL³

I winked.

It was summer time in Texas with no hint of odd weather. Thank goodness this was a wedding made up of mostly *supras*, minus Sari. Lisette and Crow walked down hand and hand towards the tent. All the guests followed. I found Sari and grabbed her hand, while Sabra rested on my shoulder.

Sabra had a plush bed in the back of the wedding party's table, next to Lisette and Crow. Her eyes shimmered a bright, golden tangerine with turquoise specks as I placed her inside her bed. Squeezing my eyes shut and opening them, I whispered, "Sabra, are you Lisette's familiar?" She nodded. I backed up. What other surprises would unfold tonight? I looked back, and she just watched all the people.

Their wedding song, "Could I Have This Dance," by Anne Murray began to play. They took center stage and started dancing. Midway through the song, Crow motioned with his hands for everyone to join in.

I led Sari out onto the floor and pulled her close to me. Bending down some for her, she stood on her tiptoes to wrap her arms around me. Her head rested on the side of my chest. When I looked up, I noticed the tent was open. Every star shined brightly onto the floor.

This was the moment to give her the ring. I pulled it out and slid it on her right index finger. I kissed the back of her hand. She slid her hand down my racing heart. Her eyes sparkled.

"Tomie Dupuy, I love it." She kissed me. "It's a promise ring?"

"No, your graduation gift. Plus, it will protect you." I smiled.

She wrapped her arms tight around my neck. I held her tighter around her waist. The only thing that mattered was my right now with Sari. She was safe. The threat was terminated. If it were meant for us to end up together, then I would allow that day to arrive on its own.

After about five slow songs and three fast ones, I saw Ranae approaching from the corner of my eye. "Hey, Sari, okay if I have this dance with Tomie?" Ranae asked. "He did promise me a dance."

"Sure." She walked back to sit down next to Caya.

Ranae brushed her hands against mine. I stepped back. "Hey, no funny readings."

"Okay, keeping my hands right here. So, I heard my witch ball came in handy."

"Thank you, Ranae, it sure did."

"Welcome. Told you to stay in for Halloween."

"Yeah, I know, but it all worked out."

"Guess it did. Got your girl back, you even saved her, and now you both will be headed in different directions in the fall."

"Yes, I know you just read me, by the way. We plan to keep in touch as much as we can."

"Sure you both will, if you ever get lonely, then you know where I am."

"Don't think so, Ranae."

"Thanks for the dance. Hope you hang up the witch ball in your new dorm room."

"That's the first thing I'm doing. Hey, would you do me a favor?"

"Of course." She started reaching up towards my chest.

"Not that. Would you make Sari one?"

She stood there with her hand on one hip while looking up in the sky, "For you, I guess, only because she's your girl, at least for now. I'll work on it this week and mail it to you with her name on it, but only she can open it, got it?"

"Thanks, Ranae." I bent down to hug her lightly. "Left you and Caya a gift in that red bag on the table."

I waved my hand at Sari and pointed towards the bag. She held it up.

"What's in the bag?" She grinned.

"Maroon 5 concert tickets."

"I love that band, Tomie! Thank you." Ranae jumped up.

"That I know. Hey, you've done a lot for me. Want you and Caya to have a good time together."

"See you around, Tomie," she purred with double winks and exited the dance floor.

Caya came up. "May I have this dance with you, Tomie?"

Looking across the room, I noticed Sari nod her head with a smile.

"Of course."

"I heard about everything earlier from Mr. Ray and Crow. I'm glad all worked out. Sorry, I couldn't get away. Bet it was super scary dealing with Verlinda, Opal, and Pepper."

"It was, but all is good now. Don't worry about that. I understand why you couldn't be there. Your mom doing okay?"

"She is. Thanks for asking. Good you and Sari are doing better."

"Yeah, I'm really happy about that."

"Have you had any problems with Garth?"

"Nope. Crow told me that the tribal council will be meeting with him and Ash soon about the other night. Don't think it's going to be good."

Smiling, I said, "I bet... Promise, you'll stay in touch, Caya."

"Will do. I'm going to take some classes online in the fall while helping Mom at home. If she does well, then I may enroll for the spring semester at our local college."

"I think that's a good plan. Keep me posted. Talk to Ranae about the gift I got for you both."

"Hope to see you for the holidays." She leaned in to hug me and kissed me on my cheek. "I'll talk to her. See you around, Tomie." Caya turned around and headed towards Lisette and Crow's table.

Sari returned. "Hey, there. You're *Mr. Popular*."

"Nah." I smiled and grabbed her by her waist to pull her

against my chest.

"I get it. My boyfriend just got it!" She locked her arms around my waist. I kissed her on her forehead. We danced for a while until Lisette walked up to me.

She tapped Sari on the shoulder. "Okay if I catch this dance with Tomie?"

"Sure."

Before I knew it, I heard the beat before the hook started on Lisette's song of choice, "Level Up" by Ciara. "Sure you can keep up in those heels?"

"Umm, what heels?" She pointed down at her feet.

Lisette was wearing sparkling Wonder Woman tennis shoes with silk, scarlet bows.

Once the dance was over, I whispered in her ear, "Just cannot tell you enough how grateful I am for everything, Lisette. I couldn't have faced them alone."

"Everything was my pleasure, Tomie. Told you I would be there. Promise me that you'll keep me posted about your air academy adventures, and you'll visit us sometimes."

"I can do that and visit more than that. You and Crow are welcome to visit me, too."

"We want you to focus on your studies."

"You two won't bother me."

"I appreciate it, but when you have time, you just visit us anytime. Don't forget to wear your necklace at all times, okay?"

"Okay, don't forget to open up the card on the gift table that Dad and I gave you. Remember it's a gift, and you cannot return it, deal?"

"Tomie..." She gave me that look with the raised eyebrows and both hands on the hips.

"No exceptions."

"Okay, I plan to open gifts in the morning before we fly out tomorrow night to Fiji. By the way, I loved the temporary snow and orchid petals."

"Figured you would. You know, I thought tonight wasn't going to happen, especially after earlier... Lisette, do you think the Dupuy Silver Slayers and *Upper Witch Council* will really work together to form a truce?"

"I thought the same. Thank goodness for all those surprises. Let's just say I'll have to wait to see what unfolds in the coming months about the slayers. Hey, does Sari have a clue about you know what?"

"Nope, and I'm going to keep it that way."

"One more dance before I hand you back to Sari?"

"Most definitely. Let me go get us something to drink. Back in a few."

Mr. Ray nodded at me from afar. Even though I felt more than confident to protect myself in the future with everything that Lisette had taught me, it was just a good feeling to know that my *Mega* would be close, especially after my near death experience and battling dark witches. I hope I didn't have to face that terror anytime soon.

Spying the tables, I noticed Sari chatting it up with the girls and laughing while showing off her ring. They all had full punch glasses.

I grinned and felt warm inside, making my way over to the punch. A freckled teen girl with long, multi-colored braids was preparing drinks.

"Two, please."

She handed the glasses to me.

"Thanks. You from around here?"

"Nope, a little town in south Texas."

"I'm from Texas, too. What brings you here?"

"Helping my aunt over the summer with her catering business."

"Oh. Enjoying the night?"

"Actually, no."

"Why?"

"Really hate my life. Sorry, I tend to over share, sometimes."

"No problem." I deep *glimmed* her and saw something I never anticipated. Lisette was right about there being so much more to the *supra* world.

"What's your name?"

"Oxee. My mom gave me a really weird name, and I hate it, so I use that for short." She frowned, staring down and stirring the punch around with the spoon inside the glass bowl.

"Oxeejen."

"How did you know?" She looked up at me.

"Lucky guess, maybe."

"Possibly." Her eyes squinted.

"Oxee, know that one day really soon your life is going to **change**, and you're going to really like it. Just be patient."

"Doubt it, but I appreciate your sympathy." She twisted her plastic bracelets around her arm.

Sari threw me a kiss, I caught it in the air, and placed it over my heart. I did the same to her, and she covered her heart. Then, she danced towards me. She shouted, swinging her hips side to side, "Por favor, baila conmigo," as a "Hips Don't Lie" remix and "Baliando" mash-up blared from the speakers.

Carrying the two glasses in my hands, I headed towards Sari. I glanced back at Oxee, and my eyes glowed an intense blue, as I mouthed to her, "*Trust me…*"

THE END

MI
QUINCEAÑERA LOCA

IF I TOLD YOU WHAT HAPPENED TO ME ON MY quinceañera, then you probably would just laugh and tell me I needed to stop making up stories like that.

Well, I probably would've laughed at you, too, if you told me what I'm about to share with you. My story could possibly save more lives in the future.

Let's start one day before my big day. Now, I didn't want a big, fancy quinceañera like my older sister, Veronica, had almost thirteen years ago.

Little did I know, I didn't get to make a huge decision like that because my hard-driven mama, Santana Gonzalez, who was the district attorney in our town of Flores Grandes, Texas, wouldn't take "no" for an answer.

My mama couldn't wait to drive me to Amalia's Dresses the eve before my big celebration for one more fitting. I pleaded with her a year ago to choose a simple dress, but she told me, "Mí hija, no worrying about that. Money is no object. This is a special gift that your papa and me want to do for you. We've been saving up for this since you were a surprise jellybean in my tum-tum." She grabbed my cheeks with both of her hands and kissed me on both.

"Oh, Mama…" I looked around to see if anyone was watching, and I noticed the young sales girl at the counter; she looked around fourteen, like me. She was reading a fashion magazine and popping her gum. Mama walked to the back with the seamstress.

I plodded to the counter and whispered to her, "Did you see anything?"

She lowered the magazine slowly until only her light blue eyes were visible. "Talking to me?"

"Umm, yeah, not talking to the mannequins. Of course, I'm talking to you."

"No, I didn't just see your mama grab your rosy cheeks, squeeze them, and then plant two wet kisses on both. Nope, I sure didn't see that." She began to giggle, and the magazine hid her eyes again.

"You did see! Please don't tell anyone."

"Take a look around here. Who would I tell? Oh, I know, the mannequins, right?"

I smiled. "Hey, my name is Consepcion Gonzalez. I attend De Leon Prep Academy."

Bobbing her head up and down, she said, "Oh, you attend the snobby school. You look the part."

"So untrue."

"Really?"

"Well, maybe some are, but I'm not."

"Consepcion, right? Yes, I bet outside of here with your besties that you wouldn't even be talking to me, like you are now."

"Not necessarily," I protested, arching my eyebrows.

"Come on, would you, if some of your friends were here and shopping around?"

"Depends."

"On what... Oh, I know, if they didn't see you talking to me. Am I right?"

"Consepcion!" my mama yelled out. "Come here, time to try on your dress for the final fitting."

"Well, you better go."

"Hey, what's your name, anyhow?"

"Rosa and I attend the non-snobby school, Marshall Heights High."

"I know that school. We played y'all a few weeks ago, and you guys beat us, like seventy-six to seven."

"Yeah, our football team is pretty awesome, basketball not so much."

We both laughed.

"Consepcion, I'm counting to ten backwards. Diez, nueve,

DOLL³

ocho…"

"Look, you better go," Rosa said.

"Mama, I'm coming. Give me ten minutes, por favor."

"Okay, the stopwatch is starting, mí hija."

"Let me see your phone."

Rosa handed it to me, and I added my phone number.

As I was handing her phone back to her, I noticed a stack of weird rocks next to her juice box.

"What are those?" I stretched out my hand to touch them.

Before I could, Rose slapped my hand away. "Hey, no toques!"

I rubbed my stinging hand. "You could've just told me not to touch in the first place, chica. What are they, though?"

"You wouldn't believe it, if I told you."

"Try me."

She looked to her right and then her left. "Piedras mágicas," she whispered.

"What?" I yelled.

"See, I told you so."

I laughed. "Sorry. How are they magic?"

"They tell me things."

"Like what, Rosa?"

"Whatever the stones want to tell… they tell."

"Wanna try." My eyes remained on the colorful stones.

"Sure about that?"

"Yes."

Rosa pushed the stack of pink, green, and yellow stones in front of me with her hand. "Pick them up and shake them up in your hands. Count backwards, starting at siete, then drop them in front of me."

I did exactly as she instructed.

"Okay, now what?"

"We must wait and be quiet." She placed her finger up against her lips.

"For what?"

"A sign." We waited for more than five minutes and nothing.

"You know, I gotta go. I think you need to get new stones, Rosa."

When I started heading towards the fitting room, Rosa screamed out my name, "Consepcion, look."

"Rosa, it was nice chatting with you and playing with your rocks, but I really have to go."

"No, look!" She pointed up in the air.

I swung around and noticed the stones twirling all above Rosa's head. They were glowing on the ceiling in a wavy pattern.

"Rosa, what are the stones telling you?"

She paused.

"*Peligro, Consepcion!*"

(To Be Continued... Mini-series)

MISTIES
CHAPTER ONE

OXEEJEN (OXEE) TURTLE DIDN'T HAVE A CLUE THAT planning to attend the Homecoming bonfire with her misfit friends would be the catalyst to welcome her into a new world that she'd only dreamt about, watched on television, or read about in her comic books.

Losing the stubborn twenty pounds she'd been trying to shed since she was in eighth grade or becoming a member of all the extracurricular clubs her freshman year in high school, none of that mattered. She would always be seen as a geek by the ones who would reject her.

Each day after school, Oxee would waddle as slow as she could home, with her head bowed. Tears usually trailed behind her. She was the target of cruel jokes by a lot of the students. Some of her teachers wouldn't discipline the bullies and allowed Oxee to be the constant target, so they didn't have to wear their personal bullseye shirts.

Her parents didn't speak to her about school stuff, so they either worked later hours or avoided her. Whenever they did sit down to have dinner together, the subject that circulated the most was never about her.

Oxee had been hospitalized a few times over the last two years for her depression and anxiety. In a way, she liked the hospital environment better than home because it allowed her an outlet and someone who would actually listen to her.

Tonight was homecoming, and Oxee told her only three friends— Za'Mya, Tobee, and Cypress –she would meet them at the bonfire. She left her house and took the shortcut to the school, which was along an abandoned railroad track in the back of her house.

As Oxee hiked along the metal tracks, she felt a brisk wind blow all around her; the loose gravel caused her tennis shoes to make crunching sounds, like popcorn being eaten with each step she took.

An empty train car was about thirteen feet from her. Red and black striped legs swung back and forth. Smoke twirled out and danced in the air before evaporating.

She got closer and noticed by the curvature of the body that it was a lady reclining back, but she couldn't see her face hidden in darkness.

"What are you doing here, miss?"

"I've been waiting for you."

"What? Why?"

The mystery lady rose up a little more. "To give you something, Oxee."

"How do you know my name?" Oxee stumbled back and fell onto a sharp rock. She lifted her hand up and noticed it was bleeding.

The lady straightened more and sniffed the air. "I know a lot. You smell like ripe bananas and milk chocolate—so sweet and delicate you are, little precious one."

Oxee wiped the blood on her stretchy black jeans.

"Stop that! You're wasting it!"

"Huh?"

"Your delectable, rich blood."

"Lady, sorry to have bothered you. I got to go." Her hands trembled, and her heart thumped faster than it ever had, as if it was to pop out of her chest.

"So soon?"

"Yeah."

Standing up and dusting herself off, Oxee looked down.

When she glanced up, the lady was standing right in front of her and salivating.

Oxee started running from her, but the lady vanished and appeared in a bluish-black mist form, crawling all around her.

"You'll never out run me, so please stop."

She did and fell to the ground with her legs pulled in close to her chest, rocking back and forth.

DOLL³

"I'm nobody!" She covered her head with her arms.

"Oh, my sweet, yes you are. I want to give you something that no one could ever, take away from you."

"What?" Tears shot down her cheeks as she stared up at the lady.

"Don't cry, darling. I know you're so tired of all the humiliation, being placed last, someone telling you that you'll never be good enough, or that you're detestable to look at. Are you ready, Oxeejen Turtle, to receive it?"

She said nothing for over a few minutes, and then she whispered, "Yes."

The lady swooped down to Oxee's exposed, throbbing jugular vein and penetrated it with her long, shimmering, curved fangs.

TO BE CONTINUED...
(ANTICIPATED RELEASE DATE SPRING 2020)

PLAYLIST
SONGS THAT INSPIRED
DOLL 3: THE HUNTING

"Smooth Criminal": Alien Ant Farm

"Nothing's Gonna Change My Love For You": George Benson

"Take My Breath Away": Jessica Simpson

"I Think We're Alone Now": Tiffany

"We Don't Have To Take Our Clothes Off": Jermaine Stewart

"Let's Wait Awhile": Janet Jackson

"Treat Her Like A Lady": Temptations

"I Like It": DeBarge

"Ho Hey": Lumineers

"Beautiful": Camila Cabello & Bazzi

"A Million Ways": Will Downing

"Let's Fall In Love": Dinah Washington

"My Boo": Ghost Town DJs

"You Are Not Alone": Michael Jackson

"On the Darkside": John Cafferty & The Beaver Brown Band

"Livin' on the Edge": Aerosmith

"Issues": Julia Michaels

"'Til It Happens To You": Lady Gaga

"High On You": Survivor

"They Don't Care About Us": Michael Jackson

"They Can't See": Michael Tyler

"My Life Would Suck Without You": Kelly Clarkson

"Milkshake": Kelis

"Let It Flow": Toni Braxton

"Never Ever": Ciara & Young Jeezy

"All Cried Out": Lisa Lisa & Cult Jam

"She's Out of My Life": Michael Jackson

"Holding Out For A Hero": Bonnie Tyler

"Never Can Say Goodbye": The Jackson 5

"Single": Ne-Yo and New Kids on the Block

"Try Again": Aaliyah

"Seven Whole Days": Toni Braxton

"Wait": Maroon 5

"I'll Be Loving You": New Kids on the Block

"My Heart": Toni Braxton

"Gone": NSYNC

"Emotion": Destiny's Child

"Try a Little Tenderness": Otis Redding

"Scream": Janet Jackson & Michael Jackson

"Hotel California": Al B. Sure

"Long As I Live": Toni Braxton

"Damaged": Danity Kane

"Nothing Compares 2 U": Prince

"Meeting in the Ladies Room": Klymaxx

"Back In Black": AC/DC

"Cry Pretty": Carrie Underwood

"Back Stabbers": The O'Jays

"I Bet": Ciara

"Party Up": DMX

"Ain't My Type of Hype": Full Force

"Kitchen": Mary J. Blige

"Not My Kind Of Girl": New Edition

"Living It Up": Ja Rule & Case

"Control": Janet Jackson

"Take It Back": Toni Braxton & Babyface

"Girls Like You": Maroon 5

"Work It": Missy Elliott

"Can You Feel It": The Jackson 5

"Werewolves of London": Warren Zevon

"Lose Yourself": Eminem

"Cell Block Tango": Chicago (musical)

"You Got It All": The Jets

"Close To You": Carpenters

"Alright": Janet Jackson

"The Second Time Around": Shalamar

"Boot Scootin' Boogie": Brooks & Dunn

"Meant To Be": Bebe Rexha & Florida Georgia Line

"Forever And Ever, Amen": Randy Travis

"The Way You Look Tonight": Frank Sinatra

"She's More": Andy Griggs

"Off The Wall": Michael Jackson

"Lady": Kenny Rogers

"The Wedding Song": Kenny G

"Could I Have This Dance": Anne Murray

"Love Has Finally Come At Last": Bobby Womack & Patti LaBelle

"Level Up": Ciara

"Hips Don't Lie": Shakira & Wyclef Jean

"Baliando": Enrique Inglesias, Descemer Bueno, & Gente De Zona

"With You": Chris Brown

ABOUT
THE AUTHOR

MIRACLE AUSTIN works in the social work arena by day and in the writer's world at night and on the weekends. She's a YA/NA cross-genre, hybrid author; adults also enjoy reading her works. Miracle has been writing since junior high, and *Drive* by The Cars is one of her biggest inspirations to write.

Writing free-verse poems/mini-stories and short stories inspired her to write longer works. *Doll* is her debut YA Paranormal novel with diverse themes intertwined; it won **second** place in the Young Adult category in the 2016 **Purple Dragonfly** Awards. Paranormal, horror, and suspense are her favorite genres, but she's not limited to them.

Miracle enjoys attending diverse book festivals and comic conventions; she has been honored to participate as a panelist on several. She hopes to present at many more teen book events and conduct school visits in the future. Texas is her home with her little family. Miracle looks forward to hearing from her awesome readers who already know her and new ones, too.

P.S. Miracle is a Marvel/DC/Horror/ComicCon FanGirl and T-shirt collector! Wonder Woman, Blade, Squirrel Girl, Captain America, Kevin Wendell Crumb, Freddy Krueger, and Michael Myers are a few of her faves.

Find Miracle online at:

WWW.MIRACLEAUSTIN.COM

Email: shadesoffiction@miracleaustin.com

Twitter: MiracleAustin7

Instagram: @MiracleAustin7

Facebook: Miracle Austin Author

HELPFUL
RESOURCES

If you and/or a friend ever need someone to talk to, then please consider:

National Domestic Violence Hotline
1-800-799-SAFE (7233)

Rape, Abuse, and Incest National Network (RAINN)
1-800-656-HOPE (4673)

National Suicide Prevention Lifeline
1-800-273-8255

ALSO BY
MIRACLE AUSTIN

Coming Soon: *Misties*

Doll

Doll 2: The Revealing

Boundless

www.ingramcontent.com/pod-product-compliance
Lightning Source LLC
Chambersburg PA
CBHW020459260626
47156CB00006B/1786